No Turning Back

No Turning Back

Book One in The Kathleen Turner Series

Tiffany Snow

Published by Amazon Publishing
P.O. Box 400818 Las Vegas, NV 89140
ISBN-13: 978-1-611-09961-4
ISBN-10: 1-6110-9961-7

This book is dedicated to Tim,
my husband and best friend.

CHAPTER ONE

Planting your face in someone's lap usually isn't considered the best way to begin a new job. Well, maybe some jobs, but not this job. I was a runner at the prestigious Indianapolis law firm of Gage, Kirk, and Trent, a position that occupied a rung right above mailgirl but below copyboy. Unfortunately, that position currently had me facedown in the lap of the aforementioned Kirk of said prestigious law firm.

Blane Kirk was a partner and second-in-charge at the firm. In his early to midthirties, he was a rich, blue-blooded type with the looks to match—tall, with dirty-blond hair, gray-green eyes, and perfectly even, perfectly white teeth. A small dimple appeared when he smiled. That dimple was nowhere in evidence at this particular moment.

I remembered with vivid clarity the phone call I'd had with Clarice, Blane's secretary, not ten minutes ago.

"Can you please get the Kimmerson file off my desk and take it to Blane?" she asked. "I'm trapped in traffic and he texted me that he needed it right away."

"Sure, no problem."

I did as she requested, retrieved the file, and took it to the conference room on the third floor.

When I walked into the room, everyone immediately turned to look. My hands got sweaty and my face flushed at being the center of attention. There were about a dozen people there, all men, of course. If that wasn't bad enough, Blane was the farthest away from the door, at the far end of the conference table. I headed straight for him, the sound of my heels muffled on the carpet, and everyone returned to their discussions, which my entrance had interrupted. I breathed a sigh of relief. Unfortunately, that relief was premature.

I was about two feet from Blane when my heel caught on the carpet. The papers I had in my hand went flying and I landed face-first in Blane's lap, like an overeager dog sniffing hello.

His hands gripped my shoulders like a vise as he tried to pry me off. In my scramble to right myself, my hand landed somewhere it shouldn't and Blane grunted.

"Oops." The word was desperately inadequate for the situation, but it fell out of my mouth anyway.

My eyes flew up in a panic to meet his and I saw his jaw clench and his gray-green eyes flash. Could this possibly get any worse?

I winced as his hands tightened on me. He was a strong guy and he quickly picked me up and removed me from his lap, standing and setting me back on my feet. I didn't dare look up to see what expression was on his face, as I could imagine it just fine, thank you very much.

"So sorry," I gasped out weakly, like a suffocating fish. Dropping abruptly to my knees like a marionette with its strings cut, I began crawling around on the floor, gathering the mess.

The room was absolutely quiet. It had happened so quickly I think everyone had been stunned into silence. Then I heard the sound of muffled laughter, quickly covered up by coughing and the clearing of throats. Papers shuffled above me as I scooted around under the table, avoiding the men's shoes and frantically grabbing sheets, heedless of how crumpled they were becoming as I shoved them into a pile.

I climbed clumsily to my feet, thrusting the papers, now a disordered and crumpled mess, at Blane. Mumbling another "sorry," I beat a hasty retreat, watching the floor carefully as I escaped the room.

As the door swung shut behind me, I heard one of the men say, "Now they're literally throwing themselves at you, Blane. What will they think of next?" This was followed by laughter. I squeezed my eyes shut in dismay as the door closed.

What a horrific ending to how excited I'd been at the prospect of being face-to-face with Blane Kirk for the first time since I'd started working at the firm. I'd been in silent awe of him since the first moment I'd laid eyes on him.

Lori, one of the paralegals, had showed me around on my first day at the firm. She was introducing me to a few of the other paralegals gathered around the coffee station, all female, when Blane walked by.

"God, I love to watch him move," one of them sighed.

My eyes followed him down the hall and I silently agreed with her.

"Well, look your fill, because that's all you're going to be getting," another one shot back, to a round of laughs and sighs.

"Who was that?" I asked Lori, watching him disappear into the elevator.

"That was Blane Kirk," Lori said. "He's one of the partners and a real big shot in this town. Rich, smart, and absolutely divine."

"And doesn't he know it," another girl said.

"Maybe when he runs out of rich socialites to date, we'll get a shot," one of them offered.

"Right," said Lori with a snort. "He doesn't date girls at work. Everyone knows that."

It seemed that quite a majority of the women were enamored to some degree with Blane Kirk. But who could blame them? After all, what wasn't to like? Blane was clever and well-educated, successful and ambitious, with a face that made women weak in the knees and a body that made their mouths water.

A man like him intimidated mere mortals like me, so I avoided him, admiring from afar, and had never spoken to him until today. Ironic that the first words out of my mouth had to be an apology. I groaned quietly in embarrassment, wanting to bang my head on the solid oak-paneled door at my back.

Hurrying back to my cube, I huddled with my head in my hands, wallowing temporarily in my misery. My phone rang and I saw it was Clarice calling from upstairs. She and I had gotten to know each other since I'd been at the firm and had hit it off right away, even though she was several years older than me.

"Hey, Clarice," I greeted her with false gaiety.

"Morning, Kathleen," she replied. "Thanks so much for helping me out. Did you find the files and take them to Blane for me?"

Yes, I certainly had.

"Um . . . yeah, I guess," I said weakly.

"What's the matter?" she asked. "Did everything go all right?"

"Uh, well," I hesitated. "I kind of tripped and . . . landed . . . on Blane. In a rather . . . unfortunate position."

She gasped, then I heard a snort of laughter.

"So not funny, Clarice," I warned her.

She tried to quell her giggles. "I know, I know! It's just the image . . . of you—"

Her thought was cut off by laughter and I waited in sour silence for her to finish.

"The look on his face had to have been priceless," she finally sputtered.

"I tried not to notice," I said dryly. Although I was still embarrassed, I could see the humor in it, and a huff of my own laughter escaped.

I may have been able to laugh with Clarice, but that didn't mean I wanted to be within ten feet of Blane Kirk at any point in the foreseeable future.

To my horror, later that morning I saw him heading down the hallway to Diane's office. Diane Greene was the formidable office manager and my direct boss. Had Blane come to fire me?

I listened intently from my cube as he gave her instructions on something he wanted and files he needed her to prepare, hoping beyond hope he wouldn't tell her what had happened. My heart sank when he asked, "Who's the new girl?"

"You mean the new runner?" Diane asked. "Her name is Kathleen."

That's me—Kathleen Turner. And no, I'm not *that* Kathleen Turner. Consider it a family joke. My dad's name was Ted Turner, my grandma was Tina Turner. My parents were just carrying on the tradition when I came along.

"Why?" Diane continued. "Is there a problem?"

I held my breath. It had only been a month, but no matter how nice I was to Diane, I couldn't get on her good side. Somehow I didn't think it would take much for her to fire me, and I needed this job.

"You could say that," he replied, and I winced at the irritation in his voice. "Where is she?"

Oh God. I panicked when I heard Diane tell him where my cube was. This could not be happening to me. What was I supposed to say? What if he thought I'd done that on purpose? I'd have to get a new job because I'd be too mortified to work here any longer.

Tossing aside my pride—that ship had sailed—as well as the thought that perhaps I might be acting more like a twelve-year-old rather than a mature twenty-four, I dove underneath my desk, and not a moment too soon. I saw Blane's shoes as he stepped into my cube. I held my breath, waiting. I noticed he wore really nice leather shoes—were those Gucci? Whatever. They were big. A thought flashed through my mind about something I'd once heard, that the size of a man's feet was in direct proportion to the size of his—

6

I cut that thought off, squeezing my eyes shut in mortification. That was not an appropriate thought to be having about a partner in the firm, no matter how attractive he was. When I opened my eyes, I saw he had finally turned and walked away. I heaved a sigh of relief before climbing out.

Over the next several months, I stayed true to my word—I didn't let Blane Kirk lay eyes on me more than a handful of times. My job seemed secure and I breathed more easily.

Today as I got ready for work, I was grateful it was Friday. I worked two jobs to help make ends meet, tending bar several nights a week. Not really what I'd envisioned for myself at this point in my life, but I'd much rather be doing this than a lot of other minimum-wage jobs.

I didn't have to work tonight, but I did last night and had not gotten to bed until after one. Those nights always made it hard to get up for my day job, where I got to do all the jobs no one else wanted to do. Need to file documents at the courthouse? Have the runner do it. Want coffee from Starbucks for the staff meeting? Send the runner. Carl in accounting needs a lift into the office because he totaled his car again? Kathleen can pick him up.

I grabbed my coffee and headed out the door. I lived on the top floor of my two-story apartment building. It wasn't in the greatest part of town, but I hadn't had any problems. It was a gorgeous October morning, the sun shining brightly with a chill in the air. I was glad I'd added a jacket before leaving. I jogged down the stairs, running into my neighbor on the way.

"Morning, Sheila," I said, smiling at her.

Sheila often came home in the early morning hours. She was about my age, but her life was drastically different.

Sheila worked as a high-priced call girl. Her plan was to work until she had enough money to put herself through medical school and then quit.

When I first moved here six months ago, she'd offered to hook me up. I'd tried to conceal my shock (my small-town upbringing had never been more apparent) and politely declined. I couldn't imagine that kind of lifestyle, no matter how much money was involved. It seemed to work for Sheila though. She was several inches taller than me and had long, straight brown hair. Being pretty and well-spoken, she could pull off a sophisticated look very well.

"Hey, Kathleen," she said. "Off to work?" I nodded. I was running late, but paused for a moment.

"Another day and all that," I said. "You doing all right?" I worried about her. I couldn't accept that her occupation was safe, no matter what she said about the clientele being upper-class.

"Oh yeah," she said, smiling tiredly. "I've got a customer now who's real into me. He's been a repeat five times now."

From what she had told me before, I knew that was good, since repeat customers for her were money in the bank.

"That's great," I said. I would have asked who he was but she'd mentioned once before that her clients demanded confidentiality. "Is he nice?" I asked instead.

"He's all right, I guess," she said, leaning back against the stair railing as she talked. "Not sure what he does for a living, but I think he's loaded." She hesitated for a moment before adding, "I just hope Mark doesn't get all weird about it."

Mark was her boyfriend. It was a relationship I couldn't really figure out, but it seemed to work for them. Mark was a pretty decent guy and didn't say very much about Sheila's profession. I'd met him a few times and they seemed very into each other. He was one of those quiet, geeky types that I never would have guessed Sheila would go for. I suppose the old saying that "opposites attract" really was true.

"I thought he didn't mind . . . you know," I said, waving my hand vaguely. I wasn't really sure how to put into words "didn't mind you having sex with random men for money" without offending her. She was very adamant about being a "high-priced call girl" and not a hooker.

"He didn't, but he's been acting weird lately," she said, chewing on her lower lip.

"Weird how?" I asked.

She shook her head. "I don't know. Just . . . distracted maybe? Like he's with me, but not all there. I don't know if it's me or us or something else." Sighing, she added, "I'm probably just being paranoid."

"He really cares about you," I reassured her. "Maybe he's just preoccupied with work or something."

"Yeah," she said, not seeming convinced. "I guess so." She seemed to shake herself out of her reverie. "Hey, I'm making you late, aren't I?"

I glanced at my watch and grimaced. "Sorry, you're right, I'd better go. Dragon Diane will be watching to see if I'm on time, I'm sure."

Sheila laughed. She knew I disliked Diane and that the feeling was mutual. "Well, get going then, Kathleen," Sheila said, giving me a squeeze on the arm and smiling ruefully. "I'll catch you later. Thanks for listening."

"You bet," I said, giving her a quick hug before hurrying to my car. I drove a ten-year-old blue Honda Accord that ran like a top, thank God. I couldn't afford a car payment. I felt slightly envious of how much money Sheila made—she'd told me once—but knew I couldn't live that life. I made a mental note to stop by tonight when I got off work and see how she was doing.

Traffic wasn't bad and I made it to the firm in just over half an hour. I lived close to downtown Indianapolis, but the firm was in the much-nicer northern part of Indy, full of brick office buildings, trees, and wide expanses of green lawns.

Pulling into the parking lot, I noticed who else but Blane Kirk leaving the building. Crap. I was already late, but I waited in my car anyway so he wouldn't see me. I carefully sipped my hot coffee and watched in my rearview mirror as he walked across the lot. He was dressed for court today, wearing a dark suit and tie and carrying an expensive leather briefcase.

I wondered if I'd ever be able to look him in the eye again. The Incident (as I'd taken to calling it) still made my cheeks burn whenever I thought about it. Not that there was much cause for me to interact with Blane anyway—since he was a partner and I was just the runner. He'd never tried to find me again after that one disastrous morning, though I still wondered what would have happened if I hadn't hid under my desk.

"Fired me, most likely," I muttered to myself.

Rumor had it Blane had ambitions for political office, and it was obvious that he was a natural. Blane was charismatic and charming. When he walked into a room, people noticed, their eyes drawn to him, the very air around him seeming to crackle with electricity. His face never gave away his thoughts, even when he'd flash his killer smile, the kind that sprang from nowhere and turned any female within sight into quivering mush. It seemed I was the only one who noticed that his smile never touched his eyes.

Blane finally disappeared around the corner of the building to the partners' reserved parking spots. I gave it just another minute or two to make sure he'd gone before I got out of my car and headed inside.

I heaved an inward sigh as I stopped by Diane's desk for any morning deliveries. This was the part of the day I hated the most. Diane took her job as office manager very seriously, had absolutely zero sense of humor, and was a singularly unattractive woman. Her harsh demeanor only emphasized her sourpuss face, which she never wore a stitch of makeup on. We maintained a stiffly polite relationship.

This morning Diane wasn't at her desk when I stopped by and for that I was grateful. The stack of deliveries was waiting for me on the corner of her desk, so I grabbed them and headed for the sixth floor. I also had to stop by the three partners' offices to see if their secretaries had anything for me.

The fifth floor was occupied by Blane Kirk and Derrick Trent, another partner in the firm, and their secretaries. The sixth and top floor was where the oldest partner and founder of the firm, William Gage, had his office.

When I got to the fifth floor, I stopped to see Clarice. Blane's door was closed and the lights were out. He had a corner office with windows on two walls and it was gorgeously furnished in rich mahogany. Clarice's desk was a smaller version of his, positioned outside his office, with the luxury of a large work area.

"Hey, Clarice," I said, and she looked up from her computer, smiling when she saw who it was. Clarice was only thirty but dressed much older than that, I guess because it suited her profession as a legal secretary. Her dark hair was pulled back into a bun and she always wore sensible shoes. When she smiled, it softened her whole face and made her appear younger and more carefree.

"Hey, yourself," she said. "On your way out?"

I nodded. "I have a stack for the courthouse and some other firms around town today."

Glancing around to make sure we were alone, she leaned forward, grinning as she spoke in a low voice. "Do you want to hear the latest?"

I moved closer. "Of course," I said eagerly.

Clarice and I had a running joke about the women Blane dated, betting each other on how long each would last and if the latest one would make a scene or go quietly when he ended it. There had been some memorable scenes from the more dramatic ones. Clarice liked Blane well enough—he was always polite and cordial to her. He just wasn't really "our" kind of people here in the Midwest—a little too snobbish, way too rich, and a tad condescending.

Clarice had told me yesterday that Blane had asked her to send the requisite farewell flowers to his latest flavor of the month. Some took the news well and some . . . didn't. This latest girl—her name was Kandi-with-an-i—had seemed the dramatic type, and I'd bet Clarice five bucks she wouldn't go quietly.

"Okay," Clarice started, as anxious to impart the juicy gossip as I was to hear it. "So the story is she got the flowers yesterday and went nuts. Showed up at his house and waited for him to get home. Then she proceeded to scream and curse at him while standing on his front porch. And"—now her grin widened—"that wasn't even the best part."

I was practically holding my breath in anticipation. "What was the best part?"

"She posted on her Facebook page that he has a tiny dick."

I gasped, clapping a hand over my mouth.

"I know!" Clarice said with a mischievous grin. "As if anyone's going to believe her."

"No kidding," I breathed.

Our eyes met and we both laughed. Blane's appeal was a universal constant. He was over six feet of male perfection. The idea that he'd not be . . . well-endowed . . . was ludicrous. I remembered what I'd thought when I'd been in close proximity to his sizable shoes while hiding under my desk, and I felt my face flush.

"How did you hear about it?" I asked, pushing aside thoughts I had no business thinking about Blane Kirk.

"Debbie downstairs heard it from her husband, who works with Ryan Dunstan, who's dating Gillian Tate, who's Facebook friends with Kandi," Clarice explained. "It's a small world, my friend."

"She's either really stupid or really vindictive," I said.

Clarice chuckled. "Knowing the kind of women Blane dates, probably both."

"Where is he today?" I asked.

"In court," she answered. "An embezzlement case."

"All right, well, gotta go. Thanks for the gossip. Catch you later, Clarice."

Clarice gave me a finger wave and I headed to the elevator and back out to my car. It was warming up now and I rolled the window down, letting in the autumn breeze as I drove. I dropped off the packages for the law firms first before I headed to the courthouse.

I managed to find a spot on the street to park—miracle of miracles—and hustled inside.

"Kathleen! How's it going on this fine day?" This was from Hank, one of the security guards at the courthouse. Hank was a tall, imposing black man with a teddy-bear disposition. Why he became a security guard was beyond me. He was no more likely to tackle a bad guy than he would be to dropkick a puppy.

"It's going good, Hank," I said, stepping through the metal detector. "You?"

"Better now that you're here," he said with a grin. Hank was an incorrigible flirt.

"I bet you say that to all the girls," I teased. It was almost impossible not to be in a good mood around Hank. He was always so cheerful.

"Just the pretty ones," he retorted and I laughed. Grabbing my purse and my stack of files off the table where it had been searched, I headed down the hall.

The hallway was quiet and my steps echoed slightly as I walked. I was passing the various courtroom doors when suddenly one flew open, startling me. A man rushed out, furtively looking both ways in the nearly empty hallway before spotting me standing only feet away. He was wearing a suit but looked very bedraggled, like he'd slept in it or something, it was so wrinkled.

His eyes lit on me and he rushed toward me so fast I didn't have time to react. In a moment he'd pulled my arm behind my back, my files dropping to the floor in a messy heap. I gasped in pain and shock as he pulled upward on my arm. Then he abruptly released my arm only to put a knife to my throat.

At that moment, the courtroom door burst open again and a crowd of people came rushing out. They froze when they saw the tableau before them. I heard someone scream down the hallway. The man behind me pulled me closer to him, and my hands came up to his arm, trying to hold the knife away from my throat. He was several inches taller than me and stronger, dragging me with him as he backed up to the wall.

Security guards rushed around the corner, guns drawn.

"Stay back!" the man holding me yelled. "Everybody stay back! Or I'll kill her!"

Adrenaline and fear were pumping through my system and I could feel my heart pounding. The cold edge of the knife was pressed against my throat as he held me in a vise-like grip. The security guards glanced at each other, clearly uncertain what to do. Behind them the crowd stood silently watching.

"I want to get out of here," the man yelled, desperation evident in his voice. "I'm not going to jail! Let me out of here or she dies!" As if to emphasize his point, he pressed the knife harder against me and I felt the blade nick me slightly.

The pain from the wound served to clarify my jumbled thoughts. My father had taught me many things before he died, and being a victim had not been one of them. I took a deep breath.

In a sudden sharp movement, I grabbed the arm holding the knife with both my hands as I thrust my head backward away from the knife. Yanking down on his arm with all my strength, I twisted my body, moving under his arm and away from him. My new leverage shoved the knife back toward him, and a split second later, he collapsed, the knife embedded in his side.

I took a few steps before I started shaking and slowly slid to the floor, my legs no longer able to hold me. Shouting and movement were all around me now as the security guards surrounded the man and paramedics were called. I was having trouble breathing and spots danced in front of my eyes. While I'd known how to get away from such an attack in theory, until today I'd never needed to use that training. The reality of what had just happened was starting to seep in and I felt tears welling in my eyes as I struggled to catch my breath.

"Put your head between your knees."

I heard the words but couldn't respond. The dots got bigger and my breathing shallower and more rapid. I felt someone pressing on my head, pushing it down insistently. When my head was between my knees, they stopped pushing but held me there. After a few moments, my breathing calmed and the spots disappeared. I tried to sit up and the hand moved away. Glancing upward, I saw a man standing there looking at me, a concerned expression on his face.

I nearly stopped breathing again. I didn't know if I should swoon or cower in fear. Towering over me stood a black-clad male with dark, wavy hair and piercing blue eyes.

His brows were also dark and arched sharply, giving his face a slightly malevolent or mischievous look, it was hard to say which. A chiseled jaw and lips that would have made an artist weep completed the picture. I realized my mouth was hanging open and I wondered if I needed to put my head between my knees again.

Dropping down to a crouch so he was at my level, he spoke to me, looking carefully in my eyes. "Are you all right?"

I couldn't speak so I just nodded. Surely this had to be a figment of my imagination. Men like this didn't give me the time of day.

"You're bleeding," he said, reaching out and touching my neck. His fingers came away with blood on them.

"Just a scratch," I managed. His lips curved ever so slightly. I was mesmerized.

"Nice move," he said. "What you did to get away," he clarified at my questioning look.

"Thanks," I said. "Will he be okay?" I asked, jerking my head toward the man now surrounded by security and EMTs.

"Yeah," the stranger said. "The wound isn't deep and the medics got here quickly enough."

I closed my eyes in relief. Even if he had tried to kill me, the knife hitting him had been more accidental than planned.

When I opened my eyes, the man in black was gone. Dismayed, I looked around, but with the crowd of people, I didn't see him anywhere. I scrambled to my feet.

"Kathleen!" Hank was barreling toward me. "Holy shit! Are you okay?"

I reassured Hank, who was completely distraught that the man had managed to get in the building with a knife.

Not that it was entirely his fault—it seemed the metal detector had been on the fritz earlier this morning. Surreptitiously, I kept watching for the stranger, but never saw him. I sighed. He could have been a figment of my imagination, for all I knew.

It was hours later before I was able to get back to the firm. The paramedics had wanted to check me out, the knife wound requiring only a bandage, thank God. Then there were police reports to fill out and a statement to make. It was now after six and the sun was setting.

Wind gusting through my car windows had blown my hair to pieces and I tried to comb it with my fingers, wishing I had a ponytail holder with me. My hair was long and strawberry blonde—and one of my best features, in my opinion. Not that I had a lot of great features. I was probably short but I preferred "vertically challenged." Ten pounds that I could never seem to lose made me a little too curvy, and I had one of those voices that was too high and too soft for anyone to really take me seriously.

I thought I'd stop by Clarice's desk before I headed home. She might still be around and I dearly needed just to chat for a few minutes. No one else was around when I reached her, tucked away by Blane's office in the corner. Clarice was typing at her computer, her eyes on the paper clipped to the side of her monitor as her fingers flew over the keyboard.

"Hey," I said quietly.

She jumped, startled at the interruption. When she saw who it was, she leapt to her feet.

"Kathleen!" she exclaimed, throwing her arms around me in a tight hug. "I heard what happened. Thank goodness you're okay!"

I hugged her back just as tightly. "Thanks, Clarice," I said. "I'm all right."

After a moment, she released me. "I can't believe that happened," she said, resuming her seat. I sank down in the matching chair opposite her.

"Yeah," I said. "Pretty crazy." I didn't really want to talk about it. The cops had talked me all out. "How was your day?"

"Not as exciting as yours," she said with a snort. "Just trying to get this file typed up for delivery to a client tonight. Blane faxed it to me last minute." She glanced at her watch and sighed. "Jack and I were supposed to have dinner tonight. I guess I'll call him and cancel." Clarice was divorced with two kids. She had been dating Jack for several months now. He taught science at a local high school and, from the way she talked about him, seemed to be a really nice guy.

There were at least a dozen or more papers stacked on her desk that she had yet to transcribe. It was getting late and nearly everyone else had left to enjoy their weekend.

"Want me to do it for you?" I asked. "I don't have any more runs and no plans tonight."

She looked hopefully at me. "Really?"

I nodded.

"But I don't want to impose," she dithered. "Especially after all you've been through today. I should probably just cancel."

"C'mon, Clarice," I urged her, "it's not a big deal. I'm fine and I have nothing better to do. You go on."

I really didn't mind. I liked doing things for people. And it wasn't as if I had anything to go home to except an empty apartment and the harrowing memories of today. That thought depressed me, so I shoved it to the back of my mind and smiled brightly at Clarice.

"Go out and have fun," I said, "I'll take care of this."

She still looked uncertain, but after glancing at her watch again, she gave in. Grabbing her purse from a drawer, she said, "Thanks so much, Kathleen. Just leave it on Blane's desk when you're through."

Giving me a quick hug, she headed for the elevators and I sat down at her desk. Taking a look at where she'd left off, I started typing.

Typing had been one of the most useful classes I'd ever taken in high school and I was good at it, averaging around seventy-five words per minute. It was so quiet the only sounds I could hear were my fingers tapping the keys and the solemn ticking of the big grandfather clock that stood in the alcove by the elevators. It was relaxing, especially after the events of today, and I felt myself sort of drop into a zone.

This particular document was about a case the firm had taken awhile back defending a local union that serviced voting machines. During the last election, there had been reported cases of fraud, and the accusers had singled out the union as the perpetrators. It made for interesting reading even if quite a bit of it was legalese.

I wasn't surprised at the famous names involved in the case—all people I recognized as being well known in Indianapolis. Blane's career was high-profile in this city. While his social life made the lifestyle pages of the newspaper, his exploits as a lawyer often made the front page. Defense attorneys and trial lawyers had a reputation for being morally questionable and more showmen than men of substance, and I wasn't sure where Blane fell in the mix, though no one questioned his ambition and drive.

"What are you doing?"

The words came from behind me and I let out a piercing shriek, so surprised was I by the interruption. I jumped up and whirled around, accidentally overturning the chair as I did so.

Blane was standing there looking as startled as I was. "Jesus!" he said, shoving a hand through his perfect hair. "What the hell was that for?"

"You scared me!" I said, embarrassment making me snappish. "You shouldn't sneak up on people."

"I didn't sneak," he replied matter-of-factly. "And you didn't answer me. What are you doing?"

Still unnerved, I didn't consider my words before they fell out of my mouth. "I'm typing, obviously," I said, heavy on the smart-ass.

His eyes narrowed at that and I swallowed nervously, dropping my eyes to keep from having to meet his. It belatedly occurred to me that he was one of the owners and if I pissed him off, he might not be as lenient this time in whether or not to fire me.

Blane wasn't dressed in his normal business attire but much more casually, in jeans that hugged his lean hips. Catching myself gazing at his crotch, I abruptly remembered his ex-girlfriend's Facebook post and flushed. I jerked my eyes upward and saw he had on a black long-sleeved henley with the sleeves pushed up his arms to just below his elbows. He had very nice, muscular forearms. Why was I staring at his forearms? Desperate for a safe place to look, I dropped my eyes to his shoes. His very nice, very expensive, very large shoes.

I cleared my throat and answered again, making my voice as pleasant as possible. "Clarice had plans, so I offered to help finish this for her." I glanced up at him, but his expression was unreadable.

"Don't you have plans for tonight, too?" he asked.

I shook my head, feeling my cheeks heat even more as I inwardly cursed my fair skin. Nervously, I looked back down at the papers. I was nearly done. Just needed to finish up, save, and print. When Blane didn't say anything else, I turned away, righting my chair and resuming my seat before typing again.

The skin on the back of my neck seemed to prickle as he silently watched me. Finally, he moved past me into his office and I released the breath I'd been holding. Looking over what I had typed, I grimaced. I had to correct numerous typing errors. In my own defense, I never did well when someone was watching over my shoulder.

I finished up the document and printed it before gathering up my things to leave. Glancing into Blane's office, I saw him working at his computer. Clarice had said to leave the document on his desk, so there was no avoiding talking to him.

Cautiously, I tapped on his office door. He glanced up from his computer and I hurried inside.

"Clarice said to leave these for you," I said, handing him the file.

"Thank you," he replied, returning his attention to his monitor.

I hesitated for a moment, but there didn't seem to be anything else I should say and he wasn't paying attention to me anyway, so I just headed for the elevator.

The night had gotten colder and I shivered as I unlocked my car and slid behind the wheel. I tossed my things on the passenger seat and shoved the key in the ignition. I turned the key and . . . nothing happened. I tried again. Same result. Two more times. Two more nothings.

My head dropped to the steering wheel and I groaned. It felt as if this day was never going to end. I would have dug out my cell phone, but I had one of those pay-as-you-go plans, which was currently out of minutes.

I sighed in defeat. I was going to have to go back inside and call a tow truck. Which cost money. Really didn't want to do that. And if I did go inside, that meant I'd have to see Blane again. Really, really didn't want to do that. I banged my forehead lightly against the steering wheel.

A tap at the window made me jerk upright and I stifled another shriek. Blane was standing outside my car. I couldn't roll the window down without the car being on, so I opened the door partway.

"Yeah?" I said, less than gracious at the interruption to my crap of a day.

"Car trouble?" he asked, jerking his head slightly toward my engine. The cold seemed to have no effect on him even as I started shivering again, the wind blowing my hair as I sat in the car.

"Guess so," I said miserably. I wondered if I could ask to borrow his cell phone so I didn't have to go all the way back inside, but then I figured he'd probably think I was an idiot for not having one of my own. I really didn't want to tell him about the pay-as-you-go thing. I doubted he would even know what that was.

"Need a lift?"

I instinctively recoiled from that. Blane made me a nervous wreck. I no longer entertained romanticized notions of him—disdainful as I was of his callous approach to relationships and women—but he was a formidable, intelligent, and way too good-looking man. I'd no doubt do or say something idiotic out of sheer nerves. I shook my head.

"No, thanks," I replied. "I'll just call a tow truck or something."

"It's late and it's cold," Blane persisted firmly. "Let me take you home."

I still hesitated, wishing vile things on my car for choosing this night to give out on me.

"Come on," he said firmly, pulling the door open the rest of the way and grasping my upper arm. "I have to run an errand first, but I should be able to get you home before a tow truck would show up here."

I didn't see how I could refuse at this point without it seeming ridiculous, so I grabbed my things and got out of the car, locking it before shutting the door. Blane still had a hand on my arm as we walked to his car. This was the closest I had ever been to him while standing (I tried to ignore the memory of kneeling in front of him), and he was quite tall. The top of my head only came to his shoulder.

Blane led me to a car parked close to the building in one of the reserved spaces. I gasped when I saw it. He drove a black Jaguar with tinted windows. It suited him.

He opened the passenger door for me and waited until I'd gotten settled inside before shutting it. The leather seat was richly decadent to someone used to vinyl and I inhaled deeply. The car smelled of leather and Blane's cologne. Yum.

Blane climbed in the driver's side and I shivered again, though I didn't know if it was from the cold air or from how close he was to me in the confines of the car.

"Cold?" he asked, and I nodded wordlessly.

The engine purred to life and he pushed the button for the heater. Pulling out of the lot, he headed south on Meridian toward the center of the city.

There was something very masculine about a man driving a car like this one and I savored the experience of being in a beautiful, powerful car with an equally beautiful and powerful man. Blane might be a shameless womanizer, but I tried not to focus on that at the moment. We did not converse and I watched out my windows as the houses lining the street flashed by, their lights muted.

After a while, Blane broke the silence. "Kathleen." He said my name slowly, as if testing it out. "What's your last name, Kathleen?"

I hesitated in telling him. People always teased me about my name. "Turner," I finally mumbled, and waited for the jokes to begin. To my surprise, he didn't immediately respond. I turned back to the window.

"Do you go by Kathy?" he asked, and I was forced to turn and look at him again.

"No." I hated nicknames.

"Katie?"

Even worse. "No."

"You prefer Kathleen," he stated rather than asked.

"Yes."

At another one-word response from me, his mouth curved sardonically. "You seem to be a woman of few words," he said, glancing at me.

I hesitated. He was making me feel idiotic. "Sometimes," I finally said stiffly.

He must have realized I was uncomfortable, because he switched tactics.

"We didn't get off to a great start, Kathleen," he said, and I felt the color leave my face. Please tell me he was not going to bring up that disastrous meeting where I planted my face in his crotch.

"Why don't you tell me where you're from?"

I let out a sigh of relief. He wanted to know my life story? Well, this should be a short conversation. "I'm from Rushville, Indiana," I answered, "a small town east of here. I moved here six, seven months ago."

"And what did you do in Rushville?" he asked, looking my way again.

His eyes did funny things to my insides when he was focused so intently on me like that. I thought he was just making idle conversation, but it seemed like he was actually interested in what I was going to say. I harshly reminded myself that he was very good at making people think that.

"Not much," I said vaguely. "Tended bar. Took care of my mom."

"Took care of your mom?" he repeated, questioning.

"She had cancer," I said. It didn't hurt as much now when I said it. I felt a twinge inside and a brief wave of grief that I was able to shake off.

"Did she . . . ?" He left the rest of the sentence unsaid as I nodded.

"Two years ago now," I answered his unasked question.

He paused. "I'm sorry," he said quietly.

I didn't say anything to that and resumed my study of the scenery passing by the window. I didn't want him being nice to me and changing the preconceived notions I had. It would be too easy to become infatuated with a man like him, and also decidedly unwise, considering the female debris left in his wake.

"And the rest of your family?" he asked.

I turned back toward him, wondering why he was asking so many questions. Then I remembered; that was his job. Knowledge was power, or so *Schoolhouse Rock!* had always taught me.

"My dad was a cop," I replied. "He was killed in the line of duty when I was fifteen."

Blane didn't say anything to that and, thankfully, stopped with the questions.

A few minutes later, we pulled up to the front of a building in a seedy part of town. It was headquarters for the union the firm was representing. Blane parked and opened the door. Before he got out, he turned to me.

"I'd say you could wait inside the car, but it's not the best area," he said.

"It's not a problem," I replied, getting out of the car. I shoved my hands into the pockets of my coat to protect them from the cold. Blane headed for the building and I followed a step or two behind.

The lobby of the building was deserted and I followed Blane down the hallway. He seemed to know where he was going. Pausing outside of a door, he rapped sharply on it. A muffled voice said to come in, and Blane pushed the door open.

We entered a nice office, nicer than I would have expected from the outside of the building, where two men were sitting on opposite sides of a desk, smoking cigars. The man behind the desk stood when Blane came in, a wide smile creasing his face. He was older, I'd say in his late fifties, with a receding hairline and expanding waistline. He exuded "used car salesman" and I took an instant dislike to him.

"Blane!" he exclaimed in a voice that was roughened by years of cigars. I detected an underlying Italian accent by way of Brooklyn. "Fantastic that you could get here tonight." His eyes lit on me and I saw a gleam come into them. "Who is your lovely friend?" he asked.

Blane turned to me. "This is Kathleen," he said. "She works for me. Kathleen, this is Frank Santini."

I pasted a fake smile on my face and stepped forward to shake Frank's hand. His name was familiar but I couldn't place it. Frank removed the cigar from his mouth briefly, took my hand in his, and pressed his wet lips to it. Eww. I tried to conceal my grimace of distaste.

"It's a pleasure, Kathleen," Frank said, still holding my hand.

I nodded and kept smiling as I slid my hand out of his grip and sidled backward a bit so I was behind Blane. Frank gave me the creeps. I glanced at the other man, still sitting in the overstuffed leather chair watching us. He took another drag of the cigar as his eyes met mine, and he didn't smile.

"I brought the file with the affidavit summary you requested," Blane said, handing the file in his hand to Frank. "I'm not sure why it was so urgent that you had to have it this evening." His statement hung in the air, the question unasked but there nonetheless.

"I spoke with Bill about it," Frank said, shrugging off Blane's question as he rounded the desk, tossing the envelope onto its surface. I assumed he was referring to William Gage, the senior partner of the firm, though I'd never heard anyone refer to the older man as "Bill." He didn't seem to be the type of person who would go by that; it was always "William" or "Mr. Gage."

"We'd like a quick word with you," the man in the chair said. "Alone, if you wouldn't mind." He shot a pointed look in my direction. He was about the same age as Frank and could have been his brother, their physical similarities were so pronounced. But while Frank was friendly, perhaps overly so, this man was decidedly not.

"Jimmy can take her outside," he said, motioning to the door. I turned my head and saw a third man in the room, who had escaped my notice. He was standing in the shadows and now stepped forward into the dim light cast by the lamp on the desk. I felt my eyes widen and I instinctively stepped closer to Blane.

Jimmy was tall and thin, gaunt even. The hollowness under his pronounced cheekbones emphasized the darkness of his eyes and brows. His lips were thin and I could see a faint scar that ranged from the tip of his eyebrow down the side of his face. His appearance wasn't the worst of it. Jimmy reeked of menace and his eyes were cold, hard chips of granite.

He stepped toward me and I looked at Blane, my eyes wide. Blane's face was grim but he gave me a curt nod. I took that as a signal that I didn't have a choice in the matter.

Swallowing heavily and despite my trepidation, I preceded Jimmy out the door and into the hallway. I heard the door shut firmly behind me.

There was nowhere to go but forward, so I walked, feeling Jimmy close behind me. The hairs on the back of my neck stood up as he silently followed me out to the lobby. There were a few chairs and a couch scattered around, so I sank into a chair. Jimmy eyed me for a moment, then sat in the chair next to me.

He stared at me and I could feel my hands get sweaty and my heart rate increase. Jimmy was making me extremely uncomfortable. I glanced at him a couple of times out of the corner of my eye as I fidgeted. My nervousness made me want to babble. Maybe if I got him to talk, he wouldn't seem so intimidating.

"So," I said a little too brightly, "what do you do here?"

He stared at me, unblinking. "I take care of problems," he finally said, his accent much thicker than Frank's.

Okay, well, that wasn't much to go on. "What kind of problems?" I asked.

He smiled and it sent a chill down my spine. "People problems," he answered.

I decided I didn't need to know any more about Jimmy. I smiled weakly at him and looked around nervously for a magazine or something.

"You're not going to be a problem, are you?" he asked and I jerked my head around to face him. The way he was looking at me made my stomach turn to knots.

I shook my head, unable to say anything.

"Good," he said, "because I'd hate to have to mess up that pretty face."

Okay, now I was getting seriously freaked out. I could think of nothing to say to this and I prayed Blane would come out so we could leave.

"Knock it off, Jimmy," I heard and turned to see Blane standing a few feet away.

I heaved a sigh of relief. It was the first time I had ever been glad to see him. Compared to Jimmy, my fear of Blane seemed ridiculous. I jumped to my feet as Blane strode toward us. Jimmy stood as well and didn't move as Blane approached. Jimmy was several inches shorter than Blane.

"You got a problem, Kirk?" Jimmy asked snidely. I noticed he was now playing with a switchblade that he must've pulled out of a pocket, but he'd done it so fast, I hadn't seen him.

Blane's fingers wrapped around my upper arm as he tugged me behind him. "Stay away from her, Jimmy," he gritted out, low and threatening.

They stared each other down for a minute. I watched, barely breathing. Finally, Jimmy smirked. "Watch your back, Kirk," he said. He flipped the knife open and shut, and then it disappeared. Whether it had gone in a pocket or up his sleeve, I couldn't tell. Jimmy backed off, heading back the way we'd come.

Blane hustled me toward the door, passing several offices along the way, which were all darkened. We were halfway to his car, me struggling to keep up with his long strides, when his tight grip on my arm became too much.

Wincing, I said "You're hurting me." His hold immediately loosened and he slowed his steps.

"Sorry," he said tersely, glancing behind us at the now-ominous building. We reached his car and he had me inside and himself behind the steering wheel in seconds.

I was still frightened, not only from the encounter with Jimmy, but from Blane's reaction as well. "Who was that guy?" I managed to ask as Blane drove us out of the lot.

His jaw tightened before he answered. "He's called Jimmy Quicksilver. His real name is James Lafaso."

I was afraid to ask but couldn't help myself. "Why is he called Jimmy Quicksilver?"

"Because he's good with knives," Blane answered, his eyes on the road.

I knew what Blane meant without him having to elaborate and remembered Jimmy saying how he'd hate to mess up my face. I felt queasy and this news did nothing to ease my mind. Shakily, I lifted a hand to rub my forehead, wondering how my relatively dull and mundane life had suddenly become like a James Bond movie in the space of a little over twelve hours.

"You all right?" Blane asked and his eyes were concerned as he glanced at me.

"Um . . . yeah," I said hesitantly. "I guess so." What was I supposed to say?

Blane stopped the car and I looked around. I had completely forgotten to tell him where I lived and hadn't been paying attention to where he'd been driving. We were parked near a restaurant downtown that I'd never been to, mainly because I couldn't afford it, but also because it was the kind of place you didn't go by yourself.

"Why are we here?" I asked as Blane turned off the car.

He looked at me and I had to catch my breath again, he was so close. His green eyes studied my face, dropping briefly to my lips.

"I thought you might be hungry," he said finally, his eyes meeting mine again. "And I could use a drink."

He stepped out of the car, leaving me with my jaw hanging open. Before I could recover from my surprise, he was at my door, holding it open for me.

As he took my elbow to go inside the restaurant, I wondered if this day could get any stranger.

CHAPTER TWO

The restaurant was quiet and dimly lit. There was a large circular bar in the middle with a few tables scattered around. Blane steered me to a corner table with two barstools. Pulling a stool out, he stood politely by, waiting for me to sit.

I grimaced. Stools hated me and I hated stools. My feet always dangled, which made me feel like a six-year-old at the kids' table. Refusing to look at Blane, I gamely hopped up on the seat and wondered how I was going to scoot it closer to the table since my feet didn't reach the floor. Blane must have read my mind, because he gave me a push. I mumbled a thanks and thought I saw a hint of a smile before he turned to seat himself across from me.

A waiter materialized at our table. "Good evening, Mr. Kirk," he said to Blane. "What can I get you this evening?"

Apparently, Blane was a regular. "Hello, Greg," he said. "I'll have a Dewar's and water, on the rocks. And the lady would like . . ." He looked expectantly at me.

"I'd like a manhattan, please," I said. A flicker of surprise crossed Blane's face. He'd no doubt assumed I'd order a fruity girlie drink.

"Right away, sir," Greg said and vanished as quickly as he had arrived. We sat in silence for a few moments, Blane sitting back on his stool studying me while I studied the room.

Greg was back with our drinks within minutes, setting them carefully on cocktail napkins. "Would you care to order dinner, sir?" he asked Blane.

"Give us a few minutes," Blane replied.

"Of course, sir." Greg disappeared again.

I took a sip of my drink and sighed. The cool liquid warmed in my stomach and I felt my nerves ease ever so slightly. I could still feel the weight of Blane's stare and it irritated me. I cut my eyes to his.

"Why do you keep staring at me?" I asked tersely.

His lips curved slightly. "My apologies," he said. "I suppose I was just waiting for you to go into hysterics."

My brow furrowed. "Why would I go into hysterics?"

"It's been my experience that hysterics would be the typical female reaction," he answered with a shrug.

"Well, I'm not your typical female," I said sourly, thinking of all the tall blondes he had probably brought here.

His smile widened. "I can see that."

"Why would Jimmy feel it necessary to threaten me?" I asked and, as I'd hoped, his smug grin faded.

"It wasn't anything personal," Blane dismissed with a flick of his hand. "It was just Jimmy being Jimmy. He's not happy unless everyone in the room is terrified of him." I thought Jimmy probably didn't have to work real hard to accomplish that.

"Who were those men anyway?" They'd certainly creeped me out, Frank with his fake friendliness and the other guy who'd just sat there stiff and unsmiling.

"Frank and Richie Santini. They're brothers and they run that local union we're defending against election fraud."

That was why Frank's name had seemed familiar. I remembered now. The papers always hinted at dodgy business when he was involved, though he'd yet to actually be caught doing anything illegal. He was well known in the city and I'd recently seen an article of him out palling around with the current mayor.

Greg returned while I was mulling this over and I realized I hadn't even looked at the menu. He was waiting for me to order as I fumbled with the booklet, belatedly realizing with dismay that I didn't know what half the items were.

"Um." I hesitated, skimming the menu for a dish I knew. "Do you have any soup?" I asked hopefully. Soup was good. Soup was universal. Every place had soup.

"Of course," Greg said. "Our chef's soup of the day is celery-root soup with bacon and green apple."

Okay, not what I had been expecting, but it had bacon, how bad could it be?

"I'll take that," I said, handing him the menu.

Greg and I looked expectantly at Blane. That smile was tugging the corners of his mouth again and I tried to ignore the fluttery feeling it gave me in the pit of my stomach.

"I'll have the strip, medium-rare," Blane ordered.

Well. That sounded good. Crap. I should've ordered that instead. Except I wasn't a hundred percent sure he was buying. He probably was but, just in case, it would be really embarrassing to be stuck with a check I couldn't pay. I didn't have a lot of cash on me and I used my one credit card for emergencies only.

"You sure all you want is soup?" Blane asked me.

At my nod, Greg left again.

"You've had a busy day," Blane said. "In one day you've had someone holding you hostage, and someone else threatening you."

I blanched. I hadn't realized he'd found out about the incident at the courthouse.

Reaching across the table, he tugged slightly at the open collar to my shirt, exposing the bandage at the base of my neck. I was so surprised, I didn't immediately react. His eyes were on mine, then moved down. I jerked backward.

"Excuse me," I said, my voice frosty. I didn't like where this was going. Was this the reason he'd brought me here? Did he think I was going to demand workers' comp or something over what had happened today?

"Where did you learn to get away like that?" Blane asked, taking another sip of his drink and completely ignoring my reaction. He leaned toward me, folding his arms on the table.

"My father," I said, sitting back slightly. His gray-green eyes were focused intently on me and I had to look away. Blane made me nervous, my fascination with him notwithstanding. The energy that always seemed to float around him was nearly palpable. My surreptitious observance of him over the past few months had shown me that he was intense in everything he did. Now, apparently, I was his focus. I fidgeted under his steady gaze, taking another swallow of my manhattan.

"What else did he teach you?" he asked.

I thought for a moment, then decided to be truthful, no matter if I came across as oddly different from Blane's usual companions.

"The fine art of making a proper whiskey drink, as any good Irishman knows. How to shoot, and more importantly, how to hit what I'm shooting. Not to trust what people say, but only what they do."

I had been hoping to set Blane as off-balance as I was, but his face gave nothing away. He took a sip of his drink, so I took the opportunity to pose a question of my own.

"How did you find out about today?" I asked.

"I was there," Blane answered, setting his glass back down on the table. "He was my client. On trial for embezzlement. Couldn't handle the pressure. I had no idea he'd do something like that, though, I swear."

My lips pressed together. In all the commotion, I hadn't seen him in the crowd, but obviously he had been there, and this dinner was about me possibly holding the firm accountable. I felt a weight in the pit of my stomach. I hadn't realized that I'd been hoping, just a tiny bit, that it might have been something else. I downed the rest of my manhattan. Blane's eyes narrowed as he watched me.

Greg arrived with our food and I was grateful for the diversion, though my little bowl of soup looked pretty paltry next to the slab of beef he set before Blane. I looked longingly at his plate, then back at my soup, which was a pretty light green. It reminded me of the color of Blane's eyes, which just made me cranky.

I picked up a spoon and dug in, hoping the bacon would make it taste better than it had sounded, and was pleasantly surprised. It was pretty good. I hadn't realized until I started eating how hungry I was since I had skipped lunch. I finished the soup too quickly. Probably not the most ladylike thing to do, wolfing down my food, but I knew this wasn't about Blane being interested in me, so I didn't care.

When I finished, I realized Greg had brought me another manhattan. I was still hungry, but the soup had taken the edge off. I took a deep swallow of my drink, eyeing Blane's steak as he ate.

Greg appeared again, taking my bowl. "Would you like anything else?" he asked me. I shook my head and Greg went away.

"Why did you come to Indianapolis?" Blane asked.

I didn't really want to talk more about personal stuff with Blane, but didn't want to be outwardly rude. I cleared my throat, buying some time. "Just needed a change," I finally said vaguely. No need for Blane to know my life history or how I'd wanted to be a lawyer someday. It would sound too much like "Gee, I wanna be like you when I grow up!"

"So how's the embezzlement guy?" I asked, taking another sip of my drink.

Blane finished off his steak and pressed the snowy linen napkin to his mouth before answering. "He's going to be all right," he finally said. "We'll press for a psychiatric evaluation once he's recovered."

"The insanity defense," I said. "A bit cliché, really." I might have been able to appreciate it more had I not been the target of choice to prove how crazy he was.

"Not something I would have encouraged him to do," Blane said carefully.

I decided to just get it out in the open. Playing games wasn't really my thing. I much preferred honesty.

"I'm not going to sue the firm," I said, letting him know I was on to him. The stress of the day and the alcohol was getting to me. He was right, this hadn't really been my typical day. I couldn't wait to get home, take a nice hot shower, and climb into bed.

"I didn't think you were," he said, and I just looked at him, disbelief etched on my face. Did he think I was an idiot as well as a hick?

"C'mon," I said with an unladylike snort, "like I don't know what this is about."

He leaned forward, his eyes narrowing again. I felt another flutter in my stomach and nervously swallowed some more bourbon.

"I'm glad you're not going to sue the firm," he said quietly, "and we're grateful for your loyalty. We'd like to offer you compensation for what you had to endure today."

I blinked slowly. "Are you trying to pay me off?" I said bluntly.

"Of course not," he said. "It's what I just said. Compensation for hardship endured under our employment."

They *were* paying me off. "How much?" I asked, angry now.

I thought I saw the slightest glint of disappointment in Blane's eyes. He leaned back on his stool.

"Five thousand," he said, watching me carefully. My eyes widened slightly. Holy crap. That was a lot of money.

"Five thousand?" I repeated, my voice squeaky.

"Or ten," he said with a shrug, "if you feel that would be more appropriate."

Ten thousand dollars. That would go a long way toward paying off the debt I was in from my mom's medical bills. I got lost for a minute in imagining how freeing that would be. I could quit my other job and maybe find a nicer place to live. Go back to school even. Then I shook myself. It wasn't going to happen. There was no way I was going to take money from them. It just felt wrong to take that much money, regardless of the fact that it was to buy my silence and cooperation. Blane buying dinner was one thing; taking ten thousand dollars from him was quite another.

I shook my head. "Forget it," I said regretfully. "I don't want your money."

Now I'd surprised him. "What do you mean, you don't want the money?" he asked, looking quizzically at me.

"I don't want it," I repeated, more forcefully this time. I didn't want him or the firm to have that much power over me. I wasn't naive enough to think that kind of money didn't come with strings attached. But I didn't say that.

Greg came by then with the check and I watched with relief as Blane tossed some money down on the table and stood. I felt like I had to be on my guard with everything I said and it was wearing on me. Blane held out a hand to assist me down from the stool and I reluctantly took it. The last thing I wanted to do was touch him, but falling on the floor also held little appeal. I was anxious to return our relationship to a distant employer-employee one. A very distant one.

His hand was large, warm, and surprisingly rough for a man who worked a white-collar job. My hand was swallowed in his. When I reached the floor, he took hold of my elbow. He led me to the car, where once again he held the door open for me until I'd climbed inside. I couldn't fault his mother for his manners.

"Where to?" he asked, once he'd started the car.

I gave him my address and he headed that way. The bourbon had relaxed me and I settled back and closed my tired eyes. The seat was warm under my thighs and I smiled a little. Heated leather seats.

The next thing I knew, a warm hand was touching my face. I slowly opened my eyes and blinked blearily. Blane's face was very close to mine and it was his hand that was cupping my cheek. Coming awake quickly now, I jerked upright. Blane dropped his hand, but he didn't move away. I looked outside. We were in the parking lot of my apartment building.

"Sorry I fell asleep," I said, somewhat breathless. "Thanks for the ride." I opened the door and saw him get out as well.

"I'll walk you," he said.

I grimaced. It's not that I was embarrassed about where I lived, exactly, but it certainly wasn't one of the nicer places around. I really didn't need any other reminders tonight of the complete disparity between Blane and me.

I climbed the stairs, my senses overly heightened. I could hear the soft sound of Blane's jacket moving as he walked, and I fancied I could feel his presence behind me as well. We reached my door and I turned to find him glancing around curiously. I noticed Sheila's lights were off and I thought she must be out.

Grabbing my keys from my purse, I unlocked my door and turned to face Blane again.

"Do you live alone?" he asked, looking over my head behind me into the darkened apartment.

"Yes," I answered. I fiddled nervously with my keys. Surely he wasn't waiting to be invited in?

"What are you going to do about your car?" he asked. He made no move to try and come in as I stood awkwardly in the doorway.

"I guess I'll call a tow truck," I said. At times like these, I really missed my hometown. There I had at least known neighbors and friends who could help with things like car trouble.

"Do you have any family here?" he asked, and I shook my head.

"Boyfriend?"

I shook my head again.

Blane was quiet then and he moved a bit closer. I had to tip my head back to look at him. I was still fiddling with my keys, which were making a jangling noise. Blane's hand closed over mine, stilling my fingers. My heart started beating faster.

His hand came up to touch my hair, tracing a long lock before gently wrapping its wavy length around a finger. I didn't move.

"I'll take care of it," he said softly.

I didn't know what he was talking about and I felt like I couldn't breathe. His chest was inches away from me and his eyes intently gazed into mine. I couldn't look away from him.

"Take care of what?" I finally managed to say, my voice much breathier than I would have liked. My eyes drifted unwillingly to his mouth.

The corners of his perfectly carved lips tipped upward. "Your car," he said, and I jerked my eyes back up to his. "I'll take care of your car."

Oh. Okay. Of course I knew that had been what he meant. "You don't have to do that," I protested.

His finger tugged my hair lightly. "It would be my pleasure," he said, his lips still curved in a smile that was part friendly, part wicked. I unconsciously licked my lips. His gaze dropped to my mouth before returning to my eyes.

"I'll need these," he said, gently removing the keys from my hand. "Good night, Kathleen." He released my hair and stepped away.

My vocal cords were no longer functioning properly, so I didn't get a chance to say anything before he was gone.

Shakily closing and locking the door, I flipped on the light switch. The lamp next to my mother's old couch turned on and I sank down into the familiar cushions, trying to catch my breath. No wonder he had women falling all over him. Being near him and experiencing his full attention was enough to make me forget all the reasons for staying far away.

I rubbed the back of my neck. I could feel a headache coming on. Heaving myself to my feet, I headed back to my bedroom. Too tired to take a shower, I just brushed my teeth, changed into a T-shirt to sleep in, and fell into bed.

A pounding at the door woke me. Glancing at the clock on my bedside table, I saw that it was after ten in the morning. Grabbing a pair of knit shorts, I pulled them on and hurried to the door. I looked through the peephole and saw a man standing there with a clipboard. He had on a pair of navy overalls with his name stitched on them. Larry, it proclaimed in red letters.

I opened the door. Larry's eyes widened when he saw me. I self-consciously smoothed my rat's-nest hair.

"Yes?" I asked.

"Are you"—he checked his clipboard—"Kathleen Turner?" He looked back up at me dubiously.

I cleared my throat and gave up on my hair. "Yes, I am," I confirmed.

"Well, your car is done," he said, shoving the clipboard at me. "It's down in the lot. I locked it for you."

I took the clipboard and tried to look beyond him at the lot. "What was wrong with it?" I asked, scrawling my name on the sheet.

"Needed a new battery," he said, taking the clipboard and handing me my keys that Blane had taken the night before.

"How much do I owe you?"

He shook his head. "Already been taken care of," he said. "Have a nice day."

He left and I closed the door. Well. I guess Blane had been as good as his word. He had taken care of it. I breathed a sigh of relief. Most women probably would rather have received flowers or jewelry—I was grateful to have a new battery for my car.

Since it was Saturday, I didn't have to work until this evening, when I had to go in for my shift at The Drop. It was a nice bar, not a dive, so wasn't a bad place to work and I enjoyed it. The customers were usually middle- to upper-class professionals, so the tips were good. I made a pot of coffee and showered while it brewed.

Leaving my hair to air-dry, I grabbed two cups of coffee and went next door to Sheila's. I kicked at the door since my hands were full. She was probably asleep after a late night working. I kicked again and waited. Finally, I heard the locks turning and Sheila called through the door.

"That had better be you, Kathleen, and you'd better have coffee."

The door opened and I grinned at her, holding out a steaming cup. She'd wrapped herself in a short silky robe with large red-and-black flowers printed on it. She took the coffee and backed up, letting me into her apartment. Taking a sip, she groaned in appreciation before artfully collapsing onto her couch. I sat in the nearby armchair, curling my legs up underneath me.

It was grossly unfair how she could look so perfect even when she'd just climbed out of bed. Her hair was smooth as it splayed over her shoulders and, even though she wore no makeup, her complexion was flawless and her eyelashes dark and lush. If she weren't so nice, I'd have to hate her on principle alone.

"So," I began, "guess what happened to me yesterday."

Tigger, her cat, jumped up on my lap and I began to pet him. He purred contentedly. I knew I'd be covered in marmalade-colored fur when I left, but I couldn't resist. Tigger was one of the friendliest cats I'd ever known.

She cracked an eye open. "You met a guy?" she asked hopefully. Sheila was always on my case to get out more, go on dates.

"Well," I said, "you could say that. Except he had a knife."

Both her eyes opened now and I told her the story of the crazy guy in the courthouse.

Her mouth was agape when I finished. "Oh my God, Kathleen!" she exclaimed. "You could've been killed!" I shrugged off her concern.

"I don't think he would've killed me. He just wanted to make sure everyone thought he was crazy."

She didn't look convinced, but I changed the subject before she could pursue it. "How was your night?" I asked. "Have you seen Mark?"

Her expression turned grim. "We were supposed to get together last night," she said, taking another sip of coffee. "But I had to cancel. That guy requested me again, so I had to go."

I nodded sympathetically. "How did Mark take it?"

"Not very well," she admitted. "He's supposed to come over tonight. I thought I'd make him dinner or something. Men like that, right?"

I didn't know why she was asking me. My experience with men was vastly inferior to hers. The question must have been rhetorical because she didn't wait for me to answer.

"Anyway, I'll be glad to have a night off. I think this guy is getting a little weird. He was very . . . strange last night."

"Strange how?" I asked.

She shook her head. "It's hard to explain. Moody, maybe?"

She didn't elaborate and I didn't question her further. We talked about her job only sparingly. I think she knew it made me uncomfortable, though I tried to hide that from her out of respect for her feelings.

"What are you going to make for Mark?" I asked, changing the subject.

"No idea," she said with a grin. "Maybe I'll get something from a restaurant and just put it on my plates so he'll think I cooked it." I laughed. That sounded like something Sheila would do.

"What are your plans for today?" she asked me.

"I have to work tonight, so probably just hang out, clean, do laundry. Nothing terribly exciting."

It was on the tip of my tongue to tell her about Blane last night, but something held me back. Talking about it would make it seem too real, and part of me just wanted to forget about it. I didn't want to imagine something where there was nothing. I wasn't exactly his type.

We chatted for a while longer until we'd finished our coffee, then I pushed the orange lump that was Tigger onto the floor and went back to my apartment. Deciding to make good on what I'd said I'd be doing today, I scrubbed my apartment and hauled my laundry down to the basement.

Before long, it was time to get ready for work. I showered and changed into my uniform—black pants and a dark-blue boatneck shirt with sleeves that came down just past my elbows. It was comfortable and easy to work in. It had the added advantage of bringing out my eyes, since the shirt was almost the exact same color. I left my hair down and loose. It would get in the way a bit, but it never hurt to look as good as possible when you were working for tips.

I threw on my jacket and caught a familiar whiff in the air. Pressing my nose to my sleeve, I realized it smelled faintly of Blane's cologne. I wasn't sure if this pleased me or not, but I did take another sniff before heading out the door.

The sun was going down when I emerged from my apartment. I could hear faint strains of music, and the light was on in Sheila's apartment. I smiled. I hoped she and Mark could work it out.

I held my breath as I turned the key in my ignition and released it when the engine turned over easily. The Drop was downtown and it took me only about twenty minutes to drive there.

My shift started at six and I was relieving the day bartender, Abby, a tall blonde who had been working at The Drop for a couple of years.

"Hey, Abby," I greeted her. She was just finishing slicing some limes for the garnish tray when I arrived.

"Hey, Kathleen," she replied.

Stuffing my purse under the bar, I tied a black apron around my waist and started checking the liquor levels in the bottles for tonight.

Abby filled me in on the status of the different customers scattered around the bar before grabbing her purse and leaving. Saturday nights we had two bartenders and four cocktail waitresses. The Drop was owned by Romeo Licavoli and he liked to have both a male and female bartender on busy nights. So tonight my partner was Scott.

Scott attended Butler University downtown, majoring in international business. He was a friendly guy who flirted nonstop, which is probably why Romeo always put him on busy nights. Women loved Scott. He and I worked well together, and while he was constantly flirting with the customers and waitresses, he'd never tried to put the moves on me. Scott treated me more like a little sister and I was glad about that. Mostly.

The pace was steady for a while, then around ten it really picked up. There must have been a concert going on tonight. There always seemed to be something going on downtown, and afterward people wanted to prolong their evening, so they stopped in for a drink.

My hair was really getting in my way now and I took a quick moment to tie it back. I was busy pouring a Tom

Collins when one of the waitresses, Tish, walked up with an order.

"You've got to check out the guy at my table," she said to me. Tish was another one forever trying to set me up, but I thought picking up a guy in a bar wasn't the best idea. Still, I humored her.

"Which table?" I asked, putting the Tom Collins on a tray and grabbing a highball glass for a gin and tonic.

"Eighteen," she answered. "He's with some girl, but check him out anyway."

I finished making the gin and tonic, squeezing a lime into it before setting it on the tray as well. Order complete, Tish took the tray and I looked toward table eighteen. My jaw dropped.

Blane was sitting at the table, a leggy brunette wearing a scrap of a dress at his side. Another couple sat across from them. As if he felt my gaze on him, Blane turned toward me and our eyes met. I saw surprise in his before I turned away.

Orders were waiting to be filled and I was glad to be busy. It's not like I cared that he was here with another woman. What did I expect? That was his lifestyle. Last night had been a mere blip on his radar.

Unlike what it had been for me.

I shoved that thought away and busied myself putting more martini glasses in the freezer under the bar.

I tried not to look back at table eighteen as I worked, but I couldn't seem to help glancing that way. They looked like they were having a good time, laughing and talking. The brunette was so close to him you couldn't have fit a piece of paper between them. She kept touching his arm, her breast brushing against him. I was feeling something too similar to jealousy to be wholly comfortable with it.

"You all right?" I heard Scott ask, and I turned to see him watching me with concern.

"Yeah," I answered. "Why?"

He motioned to the drink I was pouring and I looked down to see that I'd filled it to overflowing.

"Crap," I said, mopping up the mess with a towel. After that, I determinedly did not look at Blane again. A bachelorette party had just come in and they kept me busy for some time as they ordered innuendo-laden drinks for the bride-to-be: "sex on the beach," an "orgasm," and "blow job" shots. I smiled at their teasing, vicariously enjoying their fun.

Out of the corner of my eye, I saw someone sit down at an empty stool at the bar. I turned to take his order and froze. It was Blane.

"So you work here, too," he said, and it was more a statement than a question.

"A few nights a week," I answered stiffly, unsure how to act with him after last night. It wasn't like I had dinner on a regular basis with men like him, not to mention the fact that he was my boss. "Can I get you something? Dewar's and water?"

He smiled slightly and I was absurdly pleased that I'd remembered what he drank.

"Yes," he said, "and something called an appletini, please."

Ah. That must be for the brunette. She looked like an appletini kind of girl. I put more juice than booze in her drink before mixing his. Setting them down on the bar, I took a deep breath.

"Thank you for getting my car fixed," I said, trying to sound grateful. Manners were manners and he'd done me a huge favor. It wasn't his fault that a tiny part of me wished I was the brunette waiting at the table for him to return.

He was wearing a sports jacket and tie tonight and he'd loosened the tie. The color of the jacket was a deep gray and seemed to bring out the gray in his eyes.

"No problem," he said, his smile widening.

I felt my breath catch slightly. It should really be a sin to look that good. He tossed some money down on the bar and I watched him retreat to his table, drinks in hand.

I looked down at the money. He'd left a fifty-dollar bill on the bar. My eyes widened in surprise, then narrowed. Trying to pay me off again. But tonight, I didn't care. Money was money. I scooped it up, ran his tab through the register, and pocketed the hefty tip.

I didn't see when they left and I tried not to think about what they were probably doing at this very moment as I scrubbed down the bar and took glasses back to the dishwasher. What I really needed to do was just forget Blane Kirk. Period. An infatuation with my boss was really the last thing I needed.

It was late when I finally got home, and my feet ached. I smelled like booze and couldn't wait to take a shower. It had been a good night, though. I'd pulled in nearly a hundred and fifty dollars in tips. Of course, nearly a third of that had been from Blane, but I ignored that fact.

Sheila's light was still on and I smiled. That boded well for her and Mark. I flipped on the lights in my apartment as I kicked off my shoes. Ten minutes and a steaming shower later and I was feeling almost human again.

Pulling on a T-shirt and underwear, I crawled under my blankets and let out a contented sigh. I was asleep before I could dwell on anything related to Blane.

I was jerked awake a short while later, sitting up with a start. I was disoriented and I didn't know what had woken me. Then I heard it—loud voices coming from Sheila's apartment. Arguing, it sounded like. I lay back down. I felt bad for her. I guessed it hadn't gone so well with Mark after all.

The shouting went on for a while and then it got quiet. I turned over to go back to sleep but couldn't. I squirmed around for a bit, but finally admitted that I should just get up and go check on Sheila. If Mark and she had gotten in a big fight, chances were she would be pretty upset.

I got up and pulled on my knit shorts. The temperature had dropped, but I was only going next door. I dragged a brush through my hair and grimaced at the dark circles under my eyes. I glanced at the clock. Three thirty.

The night was cold and silent when I stepped outside, and I shivered, wrapping my arms around myself. A light was still burning in Sheila's apartment, so I knew she was awake. I wondered if maybe they'd talked it out. If so, I would be interrupting rather than helping. I stood outside my door, unable to decide what to do. The concrete under my bare feet was like ice, which helped me make my decision. I would just knock once and if no one answered, I'd take that as confirmation that I was interrupting make-up sex.

I crossed over to her door quickly, my feet freezing, and rapped lightly on it. To my surprise, it opened. The door hadn't been closed all the way. That struck me as strange. Sheila knew as well as I did that this part of town wasn't one where you left your door unlocked, especially in the dead of night. Cautiously, I stepped inside.

"Sheila?" I called out.

The apartment was eerily quiet and I felt the hairs stand up on my arms. There were dirty dishes on the kitchen counter and two empty wineglasses. I let out a squeak and nearly jumped a foot when I felt something brush my legs. I looked down. It was Tigger. He meowed and brushed against me again. I tried to breathe normally as my heart pounded in my chest.

"Sheila?" I tried again.

No answer. I peeked into the bathroom, but it was empty. The bedroom door was closed and I walked toward it. I had a sick feeling in the pit of my stomach as I turned the handle and swung the door open.

What I saw made my blood run cold. My knees turned to jelly and I slid down the wall to collapse on the floor.

CHAPTER THREE

Blood was everywhere. I could smell it and it made me want to retch. I could see a leg on the bed, but I couldn't move. My hands were shaking and I couldn't hear properly, for the blood rushing in my ears. The only thing that propelled me to my feet was the fact that Sheila might still be alive.

I stumbled farther into the room, carefully avoiding the bloody streaks on the floor. Moving slowly to the bed, I could see her clearly now and I wished I couldn't. It was obvious she was no longer alive, her eyes staring sightlessly at the ceiling. She was naked and her throat had been violently slashed. Her once-white sheets were now bathed in crimson. Red smeared her stomach and thighs as well.

I could feel a scream coming and I clapped my hand over my mouth in horror. Turning, I sprinted from the apartment into my own. Slamming and locking the door behind me, I tried desperately to think.

Who to call? Grabbing the phone, I tried to dial 911. My hands were shaking so badly, I dropped the phone. Finally able to punch in the numbers, I waited. My breath was coming in gasps, and my heart was pounding.

When the operator answered, I haltingly gave her the address and told her my neighbor had been hurt very badly. I hung up, then wished I hadn't. My aloneness pressed on me like a physical weight, ominous and threatening. I hesitated, then picked up the phone again.

Clarice answered on the third ring.

"Clarice?" I asked, my voice a thin thread.

"Kathleen? Is that you? Are you all right?" Her voice had been groggy, but now I could hear the worry as she came fully awake.

"I . . . I'm not sure," I said shakily. "My neighbor. Her name is Sheila. She's . . . dead. Murdered." The words made it more real and I could feel myself become light-headed. I sank down onto the couch.

"What? Oh my God, Kathleen!" Clarice sounded shocked.

"I called 911." I hesitated. I hated to ask but I didn't know what else to do. "I know the cops are coming, but I'm by myself and . . . I'm scared. I didn't have anyone else to call." It sounded pathetic even to me.

"Don't worry," Clarice said confidently. "If the police are coming and there's been a murder, you'll need a lawyer more than anything else. I'm going to call Blane. He'll take care of you."

"No!" I said frantically, appalled that she wanted to call Blane. "Not him! What about Derrick?" Anyone else, really, would do.

"Blane's the best, Kathleen," Clarice insisted. "I'm hanging up now and calling him. You just sit tight." The line went dead before I could utter another word, and I hung up the phone.

I don't know how much time had passed before I heard a knock on my door. Jerking in fear, it took me a moment to gather myself and go to the door. Peering through the peephole, I saw Blane standing there. I was surprised at how quickly he had come, arriving even before the police.

Opening the door, I stepped back to allow him to enter. He shut the door behind him and I noticed he was still wearing the tie and jacket from earlier this evening. I wondered if he had left the brunette waiting for him somewhere.

He gripped my arm gently and led me to the couch. I sat down and he sat beside me. He took my hands in his and rubbed them.

"Your hands are like ice, Kathleen," he said. "Tell me what happened."

I looked up from our joined hands to his face.

"I was asleep," I said haltingly. "Something woke me. I heard arguing. I thought it was Sheila and her boyfriend, Mark. Then it stopped."

Blane stayed quiet and listened as I talked, his hands still rubbing soothingly over mine.

"I couldn't go back to sleep. I was worried about her. So I got up and went over to her place." The images that I had carefully been keeping at the back of my mind sprang to the fore and I felt tears slipping down my face.

"The door was open, so I went in. And she was in her bed. And blood was everywhere."

I started crying in earnest now and couldn't continue. Blane gathered me into his arms and I sobbed on his shoulder.

After a few moments, I was able to control myself and stop crying. Blane was rubbing my back as though soothing a small child. When he sensed that I was in control again, he spoke.

"You went into the apartment by yourself?" he asked, and I nodded, still leaning against him.

"Did you see anyone?"

"No," I answered. Not that I had been looking.

"So the person who did this could have still been there when you walked in?" That thought had not occurred to me. A shiver ran down my spine, and Blane must have felt it, for his grip tightened on me.

"I'm going to go check things out," he said, easing me from him. My eyes widened.

"No!" I said, gripping his jacket. "They might still be out there!"

"It's all right," Blane assured me, and I watched in stunned surprise as he removed a gun from the back of his pants.

"Why do you have a gun?" I asked.

"Have you met our clients?" he replied dryly. "Don't worry. I know how to use it."

"But . . . how?" I couldn't fathom how a blue blood like Blane would come to know how to use a gun.

"Military," he said shortly, and he rose from the couch. "Stay here," he ordered.

I obeyed wordlessly. Watching him as he slipped out the door, I tried to absorb the fact that, at some point, Blane had been in the military and he was now stalking a possible killer next door. I could hardly wrap my mind around Sheila's death and this completely different side of Blane.

After a few agonizing minutes, he returned.

"No one's around," he told me, tucking the gun back into the small of his back. "They're probably long gone by now."

I could hear sirens now coming progressively closer. Blane looked at me, concern etched on his face.

"Are you going to be able to talk to the police?" he asked kindly.

I'd regained a semblance of calm, the hysteria and panic now receding, and took a deep breath. I nodded and stood, shoving my feet into a pair of flip-flops and following Blane to the door. We reached the parking lot as an ambulance and two police cars pulled up.

One of the policemen saw us and walked over. Motioning to me, he asked, "Are you the 911 caller?" I nodded.

"There's been a homicide upstairs," Blane said.

"And you are?" the cop asked Blane.

"Blane Kirk," he answered. "This is Kathleen Turner. I'm her lawyer."

The cop looked surprised at the presence of a lawyer. "Where's the victim?" he asked.

Blane pointed him in the direction of Sheila's apartment and we watched them climb the stairs. I didn't follow, remaining next to Blane. When they returned, one headed to the car and began talking on the radio while the other cop we'd spoken to earlier came back to us.

He took my name and contact information and I repeated what I had told Blane. When I got to the part about finding Sheila, my voice faltered. I felt Blane slide his arm around my waist and I was grateful for the support. I finished explaining what I had seen.

"So you were only in the apartment for a minute or two?" the cop asked me.

"Probably a bit longer," I said, "but I didn't see anyone."

"Do you know of anyone else that had been with her tonight?"

"She had a boyfriend," I said. "His name is Mark. I don't know his last name. He was some kind of computer guy. He was supposed to come over tonight. She was going to make him dinner."

At that, I remembered my earlier conversation with Sheila and how she'd joked that she was going to put restaurant food on her plates, and I felt tears on my cheeks again.

The cop seemed sympathetic but didn't stop his questions. "Is there anyone else you know of that might have wanted to hurt Sheila?" he asked, and I thought for a moment, blinking back my tears.

"She worked as an escort," I said.

The cop looked mightily interested at this.

"Did she say who she worked for?" he asked.

"No," I answered, "she never said."

"Did she tell you anything else about this escort service?"

Before I could answer, I felt Blane's fingers bite into my waist. I flinched. That was obviously some kind of signal, but I didn't know why he'd want me to stop talking. I hesitated. I felt I should tell the police everything, but also knew that Clarice had been right, Blane was the best at what he did. I should heed his advice.

I shook my head. "No. That's all I know."

Blane's fingers relaxed marginally.

Movement on the stairs distracted me and I saw the EMTs hauling a stretcher down the stairs, the figure on it covered completely with a white sheet. I bit my lip as I felt tears forming again. Blane turned me toward him, away from the scene, and I pressed my head against his chest. I allowed myself, for just a moment, to savor the feeling of someone else being strong so I didn't have to be. I hadn't had that feeling in a very long time.

The shock of Sheila's murder weighed on me as I tried to get a grip. Taking a deep breath, I stepped back from Blane. I seriously doubted he wanted a crying female hanging on him, no matter what the cause, and I reluctantly released him. A flash of orange caught my eye.

"Tigger!" I exclaimed and rushed forward. The cat had been behind some bushes, but he poked his head out when I called. He trotted over and leapt up into my waiting arms. I nuzzled his thick fur and squeezed my eyes shut.

The police were ignoring me now as they went about their jobs, and I saw a photographer head upstairs to take pictures of the crime scene. I went up as well, holding Tigger. Blane followed.

"Why did you want me to stop talking?" I asked Blane, sitting down on my couch with Tigger in my lap.

"You didn't tell me she was a prostitute," Blane answered, sounding irritated.

That got my dander up. "Why should it matter?" I retorted. "She was my friend and someone killed her. It doesn't make her death any more acceptable because of what she did for a living."

"No, but it does make things more dangerous," Blane said firmly. He sat down next to me and rubbed a weary hand over his face.

I felt a pang of guilt. He didn't have to be here at all, and here I was going into bitch mode on him.

"What do you mean?" I asked in a lot less defensive tone.

"There's only one escort service in Indy and, if that's who she worked for, the last thing they're going to want is for that fact to get out. Or any information on who her johns were." He looked pointedly at me. "I want you to keep quiet about what you know, or else you could become a target."

I hadn't thought of that. Absently, I petted Tigger while I mulled this over. It seemed inherently wrong to me not to do everything I could to help the police catch Sheila's killer, just because I was afraid.

"I don't know if I can do that," I said honestly. I had been brought up with a deep sense of justice, thanks to my father, and it went against everything I'd been taught to look the other way, even if it was for my own safety.

"What do you mean?" Blane asked sharply.

"I can't just pretend I don't know anything," I insisted. "Sheila told me she was seeing some guy that kept requesting her. She'd mentioned him several times. The police should know that information. It could have been him and not Mark that killed her."

"You don't know that."

"No, but somehow I can't see Mark doing that to her either," I said. "He just . . . didn't seem the type."

"Ted Bundy didn't look like a homicidal maniac either," Blane said dryly. "If you think this man she talked about might have been involved, then I'll look into it."

This offer took me by surprise. "You will?" I asked.

"Yes," he answered. "Better me than you."

I bristled at this. "Why is that? Because you're a man?"

Blane looked at me strangely. "Yes," he said slowly, as if I were bit of an idiot. "I also have more resources at my disposal than you."

Well, that last part was certainly true.

"Oh," I said, feeling my face heat. It actually did make more sense for him to check it out. I wouldn't even know where to begin hunting down not only Sheila's boss, but the mysterious client as well. "Well, thank you." I strived for a gracious tone, but it had been a really long day.

"Are you going to be all right tonight?" Blane asked, and I looked up at him quizzically. "By yourself," he clarified. "Is there someone I can call to come stay with you?"

The sad part is there really was no one else to call. I hadn't made any close friends in the city yet. Sheila and Clarice were the only friends I'd made that I would have felt comfortable asking to come stay with me. I didn't want to call Clarice because I knew she had kids, so she couldn't just drop everything and come over. I felt uncomfortable telling Blane this, though. It made me sound like a real loser.

"I'll be fine," I said, shrugging off his concern.

He didn't look convinced and I squirmed under his steady gaze.

Glancing at his watch, he said, "Look, it's really late. Why don't I just stay on the couch for a few hours? You can get some sleep and I'll leave in the morning."

I had to quickly turn away, blinking my eyes rapidly against the new tears that had formed. The unexpected kindness of his offer punched another hole in the protective barrier I'd put up. The truth was, I doubted I'd be able to sleep again tonight if I was here by myself. The images in my head were just too fresh. I also had the feeling that Blane knew I had no one else to call.

I cleared my throat before risking speech, not chancing to look at him. "If you wouldn't mind," I said over the lump in my throat, "I would appreciate that."

Then another thought occurred to me. The brunette.

"Um . . ." I started, unsure how to put this. "Unless you have someone . . . waiting for you?" I felt the blood rush to my face and still couldn't look him in the eye.

He didn't say anything for a moment and I think he was trying to decipher my code. I could hardly ask if the leggy slut was waiting in his bed now, could I?

"No," he finally said, his voice expressionless. "Not tonight."

I nodded silently. Rising from the couch, I lifted Tigger into my arms.

"Can I get you anything?" I asked.

It was such an odd sight, Blane sitting on my shabby couch. My grandma's faded patchwork quilt was folded over the side, and her old orange recliner sat in the opposite corner. My TV wasn't one of the new flat kinds and it wasn't that big. Blane looked very out of place with his perfect hair and designer clothes.

"I'm fine," he said dismissively, pulling out his cell phone. "Just going to make some calls." He punched a few buttons and held the phone to his ear.

Feeling summarily dismissed and at a loss as to anything else I might do to make him more comfortable, I retreated to my bedroom.

I deposited Tigger on my bed, stripped off my shorts, and climbed under the sheets. Tigger curled up at my feet and it felt comforting to have him there. But it was more comforting knowing Blane was in my living room. I didn't think I was a wimpy kind of girl, but then again, I'd never before seen anything like what I'd seen tonight.

I shut my eyes tight and tried to think of something else. Picturing Blane covering up with my grandmother's quilt caused my lips to twitch in a smile. Not quite like staying at the Ritz, but he had seemed unaffected by the condition of my apartment, which I appreciated.

I would have sworn that there was no way I was going to be able to sleep after the events of tonight, but that just goes to show you. Your body knows what it needs and I was out within minutes.

Someone was shaking me and I could hear screaming. My eyes flew open and I realized I was the one screaming. Someone was leaning over me, holding my arms. Panicking, I began thrashing, trying to get away. I was drawn toward a male chest as arms wrapped around me, effectively rendering me immobile.

"Kathleen! Wake up!" It was Blane. His voice finally penetrated my terror. "You're okay. It was just a nightmare."

I abruptly stopped struggling and sat, shivering, in his arms. He was sitting beside me on the bed, holding me tightly. Now that I was awake, I remembered the dream I'd been having and I felt another tremor move down my spine. Blane rested his chin on the top of my head and his arms loosened slightly, no longer confining, just soothing.

I'd dreamed of Sheila. She'd been begging me for help and I couldn't reach her. Her throat had been cut and blood was going everywhere. I'd tried to stop it with my hands, but the thick, warm fluid wouldn't quit spilling from her neck. That's when I had woken. I couldn't speak and couldn't seem to stop shaking either.

Blane moved so his back was against the wall at the head of my bed, pulling me with him. I was curled sideways on his lap, my head resting against his chest. It was rare that I felt petite even though I wasn't very tall, but I felt small and protected in his arms. We sat in silence like that for a while as I tried to get the images from my nightmare out of my head. Eventually, Blane spoke, the baritone of his voice rumbling in his chest.

"My family used to vacation every summer at a lake in New Hampshire, Lake Winnipesaukee," he said conversationally, as if we were having a friendly dinner instead of me curled on his lap in my bed. "We had a summer home there and every May I couldn't wait until school was out and we could go." He spoke quietly, his hand rubbing lightly up and down my back.

"The days were filled with things young boys love to do. Hiking through the woods, hunting, tracking bears. I still went after my father died, taking my brother with me. We used to take our boat out on the lake. We'd water-ski or dive. The water was always cold, but we didn't care. The trees were deep green, the sky a brilliant blue, and the water ice-cold."

My trembling began to ease as I listened to his voice, low and soothing in the dark. I could see how a jury could become similarly mesmerized.

"One time we were diving and I wasn't paying enough attention to my brother. He wandered away. I was frantic, trying to find him in the dark water. Nearly exhausted my air supply."

I was completely engrossed in his story now, my nightmare all but forgotten.

"What did you do?" I asked quietly.

"Found him, finally. He was only twelve, maybe thirteen, at the time and since I was older, I was responsible for him. We made it up with moments to spare and then I wanted to kill him for scaring me half to death, though really it was my own fault."

In my mind's eye, I could see Blane, an angry and frightened teenager, terrified that he'd nearly lost his little brother. "I didn't lose track of him again after that."

"Where is he now?" I asked.

"He lives here in Indy," Blane answered.

"It must be nice to have family close," I said wistfully, thinking of my parents. The only family I had was an uncle and his son on my dad's side, and I hadn't seen them for years. Didn't even know where they lived anymore.

"It can be," Blane answered enigmatically.

We sat there quietly for a while. I liked the dark. Most people were afraid of the dark, but to me, the dark had always been comforting. You could be yourself, say anything you wanted to say, and trust the night to keep your secrets. What happened in the long, silent hours from dusk until dawn was like a place out of time. That's how it seemed in my darkened bedroom with me on Blane's lap, huddled against his chest while his arms cradled me. I could smell his faint cologne, and the warmth of his skin seeped through the layers of cloth separating us.

"When were you in the military?" I asked.

"Six years ago," he answered. Blane had removed his jacket and tie and rolled his sleeves up. He shifted, and as he did so, his bare forearm brushed my breast. I shivered and tried to ignore the accidental touch.

"Which branch?" I was curious. Being in the military was the last thing I would have associated with Blane. He had always seemed to me to be very much the aristocratic, blue-blooded type that would never enter the armed forces. This discovery, as well as the personal story he'd told, fascinated me.

"I'm a Navy SEAL."

That shocked me into silence. I felt a new respect for him. My father had drilled into my head that we should always respect and be grateful to the men and women who volunteered for the armed services.

"Surprised?" he asked.

"A little," I answered after a brief hesitation.

"And why is that?"

I didn't want to offend him, so I chose my words carefully.

"It's just that not many men like you join the military."

"And what are 'men like me'?" he asked dryly. I winced and didn't answer.

He sighed.

"I guess I can't blame you for thinking that," he said finally. "My father was furious when I told him I was joining the Navy. But he and I had come to a parting of the ways long before I decided to sign up."

I was about to ask another question, when he heaved another sigh and leaned his head back against the wall. That pang of guilt struck again and I tried to move off his lap. His arms encircling me tightened, holding me in place, though he didn't speak. Resting back against him, I closed my eyes and relaxed.

When I woke again, it was morning, and sunlight was streaming through my bedroom window. I felt deliciously cozy and warm. Then I realized why. Blane was behind me, spooning me against him, his arm draped over me and resting on my stomach.

I came awake quickly when I realized my T-shirt had ridden up to my waist. I'd pulled off my shorts before climbing into bed last night, so the only thing I had on below the waist was underwear. I tried in vain to remember if I had on one of my nicer pairs.

While I frantically pondered what to do, I felt Blane stir. His arm tightened on me, pulling me backward and closer to him. I felt a hardness press against my backside that could only be one thing.

This was a completely unknown situation to me, having a man in my bed. I wasn't a virgin. That had been given up with a lot of furtive groping and sweating in the back of Donny Lester's car when I was sixteen, but my sexual experience since that rather unimpressive encounter had been virtually nonexistent. Which meant I was at a total loss as to how to handle this.

Blane moved again, his hand coming up to cup my breast. My breath caught in my throat. I didn't think he was even awake, actually. I must have made a noise, because he suddenly lifted his head from the pillow as if startled.

I shut my eyes and didn't move. I wasn't sure what Blane's intentions were, and if I were absolutely honest with myself, didn't know what my reaction would be should his intentions be less than pure. My body was having its own enthusiastic reaction to his touch and was quite oblivious to my growing dismay.

As if realizing where he was after his abrupt awakening, Blane lay back down. I could feel his breath on my ear.

"Are you awake?" he said so softly that I almost didn't hear him.

I nodded, barely breathing.

Blane didn't move for a moment, the heat of his palm like a brand on my breast. Then he slowly extricated his arm. My body seemed to hum in disappointment. Moving his hand backward, I felt his fingers graze the exposed skin of my abdomen and move to the curve of my hip, where they lingered. His palm settled into the juncture between hip and thigh, his thumb whispering across my skin.

"I'd better go." His voice was a low rasp in my ear that sent a bolt straight through me.

I wanted to beg him to stay and keep touching me. Instead, I nodded again.

His hand seemed reluctant to move as his palm closed gently on my hip. Then he rose from the bed and walked into the kitchen. Jumping up, I threw on my shorts and finger-combed my hair as I followed him. He had grabbed his jacket and tie by the time I reached him and was pocketing his wallet, keys, and cell phone and shoving his gun in the small of his back. Remembering my braless state, I crossed my arms over my chest.

"Thanks for coming," I said in a quick rush. Our eyes met and held.

"And for staying," I finished lamely. I felt myself blush, but I couldn't look away from him. The stormy gray of his eyes held me transfixed.

"It wasn't a problem," he finally responded. "I'm sorry about your friend. I'll let you know if I find out anything." I nodded.

"If the police contact you, call me," he instructed. "Don't talk to them without me there."

"Okay."

He looked like he wanted to say something else but decided against it. His jaw was locked tight as I watched him leave. I peeked over the railing to the lot below, hoping no one had stolen his expensive car while he had been here. In a few moments, I heard the quiet purr of its engine and tried to ignore the sinking feeling I had when he pulled away.

Yellow police tape covered the door to Sheila's apartment. I stood there looking at it and then felt a brush against my legs. Looking down, I saw Tigger. He meowed forlornly and, with a start, I remembered I needed to feed him. He no doubt needed a litter box as well.

I looked indecisively at Sheila's door again. I knew she kept the things for Tigger in her kitchen. I didn't think she would've minded my taking them if it was to make sure Tigger had what he needed. Going back into my apartment, I grabbed the spare key I had for Sheila's place. We had exchanged keys a few months ago for emergencies and in case we locked ourselves out.

Carefully pulling back the police tape, I unlocked her door and stepped inside. Wanting to go as quickly as possible, I hurried straight to the kitchen and picked up the litter box. I carried it back to my apartment and then returned for his food.

As I was crossing the living room, I heard a phone ring. I stopped in surprise, glancing around. The sound was muffled. Putting down the food, I followed the sound. It seemed to be coming from underneath the couch. Crouching down on my hands and knees, I stretched my arm under it until I felt my fingers brush the metal of the phone. Pulling it out, I looked at the display but it said unknown caller.

I debated for a moment whether or not I should answer, but it stopped ringing before I decided. I quickly shoved the phone into my pocket before I could reconsider. Grabbing the cat food, I locked the door and carefully replaced the police tape.

Hauling everything into my apartment, I set up the litter box and food for Tigger, who appeared quite relieved. Stripping my clothes off to get in the shower, I pulled out the phone and put it on the kitchen counter.

Today was Sunday and the one day a week I had off from both my jobs. After the emotionally and physically exhausting night I'd had, I found myself unwilling to do much except lie around my apartment. It was nice outside, a crisp autumn day, but I felt depressed and lethargic. I knew it was because of Sheila's death, but I tried not to think about it.

I wasn't a person who enjoyed crying. I didn't rent chick flicks just so I could have a good cry. Actually, I hated crying and I despised the fact that I was easily prone to it. So I tried not to dwell on Sheila or the gruesome fashion in which she'd been murdered. Curling on my couch with Tigger, I ate a bowl of cereal and watched sitcom reruns on television until I fell asleep.

Monday morning dawned cloudy and gray. I didn't mind. It suited my mood. The weather had turned cooler, so I wore a favorite sweater today, a teal turtleneck that was soft and comfortable. It hugged my curves and I thought it helped set off my eyes. I put a headband in my hair to keep it out of my face and thought I looked pretty good, which lightened my mood somewhat. I grabbed my coffee travel mug and headed to work, hoping to arrive on time for a change.

I had a small cubicle at the firm where I could keep my things and do other work if there weren't any runs to be made. It had a computer, desk, and not much else. I left my purse and coffee there, then went to make my rounds. Stopping by Diane's office first, I sighed inwardly when I realized she was in today and I'd have to actually speak with her. I pasted a bright fake smile on my face.

"Good morning, Diane," I said pleasantly.

Diane looked up from her computer and didn't smile in return. She looked me up and down for a minute, her lips pursed in an expression of distaste. I tugged self-consciously at the hem of my sweater. It was a common occurrence for her to make some kind of snide comment about my appearance and I waited to see what it would be today.

"Looks like your sweater shrunk," she said with a sneer. "You might want to throw a jacket on over that. I'm not sure it's really appropriate for the office."

I felt my cheeks flame. The sweater hadn't shrunk, she was just implying I'd gotten larger. As if she were one to talk; the chair she sat in creaking under her large proportions. But I bit my tongue from saying what I would have liked to say. She ran the office with an iron fist, only the lawyers and their personal secretaries off-limits to her. If I pissed her off, she could fire me and no one would gainsay her.

"I'll do that," I said sweetly, grabbing the pile of papers waiting for me and retreating back to my desk. I fumed for a moment, trying to get my blood pressure back under control.

Flipping through the stack, I saw that the deliveries were mostly local to other law offices. I gulped down some of my coffee before heading to the elevator to check with Linda and Clarice. As I got in, I saw it was already occupied.

"Hey, Kathleen. Good to see you!" It was James, the associate who had helped me that infamous day when I had fallen all over Blane. He'd found me afterward and introduced himself and we'd been friendly acquaintances since. James was attractive, with dark hair and eyes. He wasn't as tall as Blane, but he still topped me by several inches. Younger than Blane, too, he was only a few years older than me. Whereas Blane's face concealed his thoughts, James didn't have a deceptive bone in his body. He was nice almost to a fault and had manners that would put a southern gentleman to shame.

"Good morning, James," I said with a smile. I hadn't seen him in a few days, and his kindness helped me put Diane to the back of my mind. "Going up to see Mr. Gage?"

James was also the son of the senior partner, William Gage.

"Yeah," he answered, smiling a crooked grin. "Don't want to keep Dad waiting when he calls."

"I bet."

We were quiet for a moment before he spoke again.

"I was wondering, Kathleen, if maybe you'd want to have dinner with me sometime?"

This came out of the blue and I had to struggle to keep the surprise from showing on my face.

"Um . . . sure," I said, then realized that didn't sound very enthusiastic. "I mean, I'd love to." I smiled again and so did James, the relief on his face endearing.

"Fantastic," he said. "How about tomorrow night?"

I quickly checked my work schedule in my head. Tomorrow night was open.

"That sounds great," I answered. The doors dinged open then and he waited for me to exit before he did.

"I'll come by your desk after work tomorrow," he said, and I agreed.

As I watched him head to his dad's office, I was absurdly pleased. I had an honest-to-goodness date with an upstanding guy. James was every mother's dream for her daughter—well educated, good family, exquisite manners, excellent career, and easy on the eyes to boot. What wasn't to like?

A flash of memory hit me—of Blane's arms around me, his hands on me, the hard length of his body pressing against me. A shiver ran down my spine and I resolutely pushed those thoughts away. Blane was dangerous. James was safe. I needed to stop thinking about Blane.

Linda had a few files for me and then I stopped by Clarice's desk. I noticed Blane's door was closed. Trying to ignore the brief sting of disappointment I felt, I sat in a chair by her desk.

"Hey, Clarice," I said.

"Kathleen, I'm so glad you're here," she said, scooting her chair closer to mine. "What happened the other night?"

I told her about Sheila's murder and how Blane had come. I left out the part where he had spent the night.

"Are you okay?" she asked, eyeing me speculatively. I nodded.

"I'm fine. Really."

She looked like she was going to pursue it, so I changed the subject.

"Guess what?" I said. "I have a date!" That worked, as I knew it would.

"That's fantastic news!" she enthused. "With who?"

"You're not going to believe this," I said conspiratorially, "but James asked me out."

"James?" she said, her face showing the same surprise I had felt. "James Gage?"

"The very one," I said, grinning. "We're going out to dinner tomorrow night."

A noise behind us made me pause. I turned to see Blane standing at the corner of Clarice's desk, a stack of folders in his hand. He stared intently at me, a frown creasing his forehead. Clarice and I always chatted, but I didn't want to get her in trouble. Hurriedly getting up from the chair, I cleared my throat.

"Did you have any deliveries for me?" I asked Clarice, all business.

"No, not today, thank you," she answered, turning quickly back to her computer. I think she could sense Blane's displeasure as well.

I wanted to ask Blane if he'd found out anything about Sheila but wasn't sure this was the time or place. The look on his face didn't invite friendly inquiries. I swallowed and moved to pass by him to the elevators. A hand closing around my arm stopped me.

"Can I see you for a moment, Kathleen?" Blane asked. Well, it came out a question, but it was really a command. I saw Clarice look up from her computer.

"Um . . . sure," I said uncertainly, and followed him into his office.

He closed the door behind me and headed to the desk, where he set down the folders he'd been carrying. I stood nervously watching him. After a moment, he rounded to the side of the desk nearest me and leaned back against it, crossing his arms over his chest. He was wearing a charcoal-gray suit today with a white shirt and tie that I'm sure cost more than my entire wardrobe. It made his already broad shoulders look even wider and I noticed how the pants hung low on his lean hips. Appalled at where my gaze had fallen, I jerked my eyes upward.

"How are you doing?" he asked, and his tone had lost its earlier austerity.

"I'm fine," I said. I really didn't want to talk about me. The last thing I wanted was for him to show me kindness, which would probably make me start crying again. I was quite sure he'd seen enough of me crying.

"I was wondering if you'd been able to track down anything on the person Sheila had been seeing," I asked hopefully. It was only Monday, but I was confident that if there was anyone who could track him down, Blane could do it. I'm not sure why I felt this way, I just did. Blane was someone who could be very intimidating and dangerous under certain circumstances—as I had discovered the other night when I'd observed him with a gun held comfortably in his hand—but I also knew him to be the kind of man who got things done.

To my dismay, he shook his head. "No, I'm afraid not."

When he saw the disappointment on my face, he stood and walked closer until he was only an arm's length away.

"I'll keep trying," he said quietly, as he reached out and took a lock of my hair between his fingers like he had

Friday night. With him this close, I could smell a faint trace of his cologne again. I fought to keep my mind on the topic at hand.

"I managed to get Sheila's cell phone," I said. I'd had an idea yesterday. "I was wondering if maybe the person who killed her might have called her. Or, at least, there should be a call on there from the person she worked for. Maybe I could get in touch with her. Or him." I didn't know who it would be. Pimps were usually men, if movies and television were anything to go by, but madams supposedly ran the high-priced escort services, like that Heidi Fleiss.

Blane's hand froze for a moment, then continued threading the strands of my hair through his fingers.

"Why don't you bring it in to me?" he suggested. "I can get the numbers run to see who they are." That sounded like a much better idea than me just randomly calling the numbers. But a whisper of caution made me hesitate.

"I'd better put the phone back," I said, "but I'll write down the numbers first and bring them in." I don't know why I lied, I just did. I had no intention of taking the phone back to Sheila's apartment.

"Okay," he readily agreed. "Good idea. Bring them to me tomorrow."

I waited for him to step back, but he didn't. Instead, he moved slightly closer. Tipping my head back, I looked up at him.

"What's tomorrow night?" he asked, and his voice had dropped lower, making me think things I really shouldn't where he was concerned. He was my boss, I reminded myself, and tried to focus.

His question puzzled me. What was he talking about?

"Um . . . Tuesday?" I answered, my brows knitting in confusion. I saw his mouth curve slightly.

"Yes, Tuesday," he said wryly. "I meant, what were you telling Clarice about tomorrow night?"

Oh. Well, this was slightly uncomfortable. Somehow I doubted Blane would approve of William Gage's son asking the lowly runner on a date. I picked a spot on his suit to look at as I answered.

"James asked me on a date."

Blane didn't respond for a moment, though his fingers stilled in my hair again. When he didn't say anything, I cautiously looked up to find his gray eyes on mine.

"I don't think that's a good idea," he said firmly.

I was surprised at how that hurt, and I responded defensively.

"I'm not good enough for him, right?" I said, my tone heavy with sarcasm. I stepped backward outside his reach. His hand dropped to his side and he watched me.

"I didn't say that," he began, but I cut him off.

"You didn't have to," I retorted. "You think I don't know that you see me as some hick that's far beneath the notice of someone like him?" *Or someone like yourself*, I thought but didn't say.

I saw his jaw clench and his eyes spark with anger.

"James at least respects me enough to ask me out on a date! You just groped me in my bed and left!" My eyes widened in shock at what I'd said. The minute the words were out of my mouth, I regretted them. Not because I didn't think they were true, but because I hadn't wanted to talk about what had happened that night. The flash of anger was back in his eyes and I spun on my heel and ran for the door. Throwing it open, I practically flew out of his office.

"Kathleen, wait!" I heard him call, but I ignored him.

Clarice glanced up at me as I passed, her eyes wide, but I didn't stop. I was already at the stairwell door, not bothering to wait for the elevator, when I heard Blane's door slam shut behind me.

CHAPTER FOUR

I retreated to my cube, grabbed the files I had for delivery, and hurried out of the building. My mind wasn't really on where I was going as I drove. I was reeling from my outburst to Blane. If I'd wanted to prove to him that I wasn't a hick, but a modern, sophisticated woman, I had massively screwed up. I groaned in embarrassment. No doubt he thought I was a young, naive country bumpkin after that scene.

Honking startled me and I realized I'd been sitting at a green light. Glancing in my rearview mirror, I saw a line of cars behind me waiting to turn. I stomped on the gas, and my car lurched forward.

It took me awhile to make all the deliveries and I ended up grabbing a sandwich for lunch to eat in the car. I wasn't looking forward to going back, especially if Diane was around, so I took my time.

The last firm on my list was one I really enjoyed visiting. They were situated farther from the city and nestled in an area surrounded by woods. One of the things I missed most about my hometown was the trees. Autumn was my favorite season and I loved watching the leaves turn color. Although the weather was a bit dreary today, the trees still looked gorgeous with their auburn and burnished gold leaves.

After delivering the envelope I'd had for them, I lingered outside on the way back to my car, letting the peaceful sound of the leaves rustling in the breeze calm my agitation. I leaned back against a tree and shut my eyes. For a few minutes, I just stayed like that, enjoying the fresh air and regaining my equilibrium. I had to get a grip. My fascination with Blane would get me nowhere except even more infatuated. I had to forget about him. After all, I had a date. My lips curved in a smile. Something to look forward to. That was nice.

Pushing away from the tree, I heaved a sigh and headed for my car. As I walked, I noticed someone standing next to it. When I got close enough to see who it was, I froze.

Jimmy was leaning against the side, carelessly playing with a pocketknife. My pulse sped up and I had to fight the urge to turn and run. Looking up at me, his mouth curled into a sneer.

"Kathleen Turner," he said. "It's good to see you again." Pleasant enough words, but the way he said them made my skin crawl.

"How do you know my name?" I asked. I didn't recall Blane giving out anything but my first name to the Santinis.

"We make it a point to find out things about people," he said. He was still playing with the knife and I found it hard to take my eyes off it. It made me think of Sheila and I swallowed hard.

"Blane said for you to stay away from me," I said in as threatening a tone as I could manage. His sneer disappeared and I instinctively took a step back when he moved closer to me, shoving his face near to mine.

"I don't answer to Blane Kirk," he growled, his eyes furious. "And he should remember who I do answer to."

His hand flashed out and I screamed. I expected to feel pain, but I didn't. Cool air touched my skin and I realized he'd sliced through the fabric of my sweater near my neck.

"You tell Kirk to keep you quiet, or next time, it'll be your pretty skin."

He got into a nearby car and drove away. I stood immobilized for several minutes, watching his car shrinking into the distance, before my feet would obey my command to move.

Getting into my car, I took a moment to just breathe and regain control. Finally, when I felt I could drive without crashing, I started the engine and drove back to the firm.

It was late afternoon by now and I wanted to make a quick dash into the building and hit a bathroom first without seeing anyone. My rearview mirror told me I looked less than ideal. My mascara had run when a few tears had escaped on the drive back and there was a long gash in the top of my sweater that left the fabric gaping.

I shot a quick glance around the firm's empty lobby and gratefully slunk into the ladies' room.

I washed my face, sighing at the complete lack of makeup now. I wasn't one of those girls who carried makeup in my purse, but I still wanted to look nice. I pulled off the headband to brush my hair and let it fall around my face. My hair was long enough that it sort of covered the rip if I wore it over my shoulders rather than down my back. I sighed at my reflection. Well, that was about as good as it was going to get. Looking at my watch, I saw I only had another hour before I could go home.

I took care to avoid Diane on my way back to my cube. She'd probably think I'd been getting it on with someone during work hours, the way my clothes were torn. I snorted. As if I would be that lucky.

I had no further deliveries to make today and for that I was grateful. When I had extra time, I usually helped with the typing. The paralegals who worked in the office were forever overloaded with briefs, motions, and the never-ending pile of other paperwork that went hand in hand with the law profession. Peeking into a nearby cube where Lori, one of the paralegals, worked, I asked if she had anything for me to type. Gratefully, she handed me a stack.

"If you could start on this motion, that would be great," she said.

"No problem." Disappearing back to my desk, I went to work.

A little while later, I felt a presence behind me and I turned. Diane was there, watching me.

"When did you get back?" she asked curtly.

Glancing at the clock, I said, "About an hour ago."

"You should always check in with me when you return," she reprimanded me. "I may have more runs for you."

"Do you?" I asked pointedly. Diane was such a control freak; it drove me crazy.

"No," she said. "But I could have," she added snidely. "And they wouldn't have gotten delivered, because you didn't check in."

I'd had a rough few days, and my patience with Diane had reached its limit.

"God forbid you come see for yourself if I've gotten back," I retorted. "Or just put the deliveries here for me when they're ready."

"That's not my job," Diane spat back. "You work for me; I don't cater to you."

"I work for the firm," I gritted out, "and no one else seems to have any problems with me except you."

"That's just because I expect people to actually work when we pay them," she said viciously.

That set my blood boiling and I had opened my mouth to fire back when James suddenly stepped into view.

"Am I interrupting something?" he asked, looking between Diane and me.

Diane's mouth shut with a snap.

"No, sir," she said. "Just reminding Kathleen of her duties." With that, she turned and left.

I still felt like steam was coming out of my ears when James turned toward me.

"Is there a problem?" he asked, his brow furrowing.

I really didn't want to say anything. I was quite sure it would be much easier for me to be replaced than Diane.

"Oh, we just don't get along very well," I said vaguely.

"Is it something I need to address with her?" he asked, concerned.

I'm sure that would go over great with Diane, I thought ruefully, and make her hate me even more. An outcome that would definitely make my life here more difficult.

"No, no," I said, shaking my head. "It's nothing. You know how women can be." That should alleviate his interest. There wasn't a man I'd met yet who didn't want to steer clear of female spats.

"What did you need?" I asked, hoping to change the subject. After all, it wasn't like he just showed up at my cube on a regular basis.

"About tomorrow night," he said, and my stomach clenched. Was he going to break our date?

"I had something come up, so I won't be able to take you to dinner straight from work. Can I pick you up at your place instead?"

"Sure." I smiled through my misgivings, wishing I lived in a nicer part of town, and gave him the address.

"I'll pick you up at seven," he said.

I agreed and, with a parting grin, he left. I worked for another hour or so past the official quitting time just to get the file typed for Lori. It was getting close to seven by the time I gathered up my things to leave.

Walking to my car, I shivered. It had gotten colder and the wind went right through the tear in my sweater. That really upset me. I liked this sweater and now it was ruined. With a sigh, I opened my car door and slid inside, pulling the door with a slam. Then I nearly screamed. Blane was sitting in the passenger seat of my car. I went from tired to highly pissed off in three seconds flat.

"What the hell are you doing?" I yelled at him. "You nearly scared me to death!" My heart was racing in my chest.

"You should lock your doors," he said calmly, unfazed by my yelling. His eyes narrowed as he looked at me and I self-consciously tugged at my sweater, the rip fully visible. "What happened to you?"

I wasn't ready to let go of my anger just yet. "I had a run-in with your friend Jimmy," I said acidly. "He had a message for me."

TIFFANY SNOW

Blane's jaw tightened.

"I'm supposed to keep quiet or else I'll get sliced to ribbons. Any idea what he was talking about?"

"What are you implying?" His voice was icy, and if I'd had more sense at the moment, I would've backed off. But I was too angry to care.

"I'm implying that you're the only one I've said anything to about who Sheila was seeing and who I think might've killed her and now, suddenly today, Jimmy's telling me to keep my mouth shut! Do you want me dead?"

In a flash of movement too fast for me to react, Blane shifted and suddenly I was pinned in my seat, his hand wrapped around my throat. Terrified, I choked, gasping in shock. Although I had accused him of setting Jimmy on me, I hadn't really believed it. My hands had instinctively come up and grabbed hold of his arm, but I couldn't budge him. My eyes squeezed shut and I sat immobile, waiting to see what he'd do. His hand was firmly on my neck, but it wasn't painful. Yet. As I waited, barely breathing, I felt his lips near my ear.

"If I wanted you dead," he whispered into my ear, "you'd be dead. And I wouldn't need Jimmy to do it for me."

I shivered at his words. His hand loosened around my throat but remained there. I opened my eyes and found his face inches from mine. Our eyes locked and neither of us moved. Suddenly, it wasn't just fear that was making my heart race and thickening the air in my lungs. I was sure he could feel my rapid pulse beneath his fingers.

His gaze dropped to my mouth and I knew then what he was going to do. I wasn't sure if it terrified me more or less than his threat.

89

Lowering his head, his lips lightly brushed mine and I felt as though a bolt of electricity had shot through me. His mouth settled gently over mine, his lips pressing softly, urging me to respond. I fought it, unable to turn away because he still held me immobile. He was insistent, though, his tongue lightly tracing the seam of my lips. A whimper escaped me and I caved, opening my mouth beneath him. With a groan of satisfaction, his hand moved from my throat to cradle the back of my neck as he deepened the kiss. My hands crept upward, finding the lapels of his suit coat and sliding under them to touch his hard chest covered by crisp linen.

His mouth was insistent against mine, yet he took his time. Blane was a very good kisser and it seemed I'd only ever been kissed by amateurs before him. I felt heat curl low in my belly. The taste of him was intoxicating to me. He tasted of danger and intimacy, safety and the unknown.

Blane reluctantly pulled back and my blood pounded in my ears. His eyes were focused on mine, their depths now a luminous emerald in the deepening twilight shadows. In the absence of his body heat, I shivered slightly, the cold air seeping into me.

Sitting back, Blane shrugged out of his suit jacket and wrapped it around me. It was still warm from his skin and I could smell his cologne mixed tantalizingly with his own scent on the fabric. Sliding his hand under the collar, he lifted my hair free. The touch of his fingers against my skin sent another tremor through me and I dropped my gaze, my cheeks heating.

"You're blushing," he said quietly, the back of his hand brushing my cheek.

I cursed my fair skin.

"So young and innocent," he murmured, almost to himself.

Not daring to look him in the eye, I focused on the slight bulge of his Adam's apple in his throat.

Fingers under my chin forced me to look up. When my eyes met his, I drew my breath in sharply, taken aback by the intensity with which he gazed at me.

"Be careful," he cautioned. "Don't get involved any further in this." With those curious words, he leaned forward and brushed my lips again.

My eyes slid shut. Then there was a gust of wind and the slam of a car door. He was gone.

My fingers touched my mouth and I realized I was still trembling, but not from cold. Leaning my forehead against the steering wheel, I groaned in frustration. Blane utterly confused me even as he intrigued me. I couldn't deny it. But his words seemed to confirm what I'd already suspected, that he knew more about what had happened to Sheila than he was telling me. What that was, I had no idea. But if he wasn't sharing, then I was going to do what I could on my own to find out who had killed Sheila. While I had faith in the police, I knew better than most how overworked and understaffed police departments were. Sheila had been my friend and I felt I owed it to her to do what I could.

I drove home and took a really long, really hot shower. I let my hair air-dry and dressed in the warmest pair of sweats I had. I carefully hung up Blane's jacket, my fingers lingering on the expensive fabric, and I refused to let myself press my nose against it to smell his scent. Okay, just once, but that was all.

Opening my refrigerator, I sighed. All it contained was some milk, cheese, a couple of eggs, and a loaf of bread that had seen better days, as well as the usual assortment of condiments. I felt the need for comfort food. Throwing on some sneakers, I grabbed my keys and headed to the store.

I wasn't a great cook, but I did all right, and tonight I needed something warm and filling that would remind me of home. Potato soup seemed to fit the bill and—an added bonus—was cheap to make. Loading the necessary items in my cart along with a few other staples, I splurged and grabbed a pint of my favorite flavor of Häagen-Dazs—rocky road. I paid for everything and drove home.

With only two paper sacks, I thought I could probably make it in one trip up to my apartment. Balancing one carefully in each arm, I used my hip to shut my car door. But trudging up the stairs, I tripped and nearly lost a sack.

"Here! Let me help you." Peering around the sack, I was momentarily taken aback. A beautiful black woman stood on the stairs. She was tall, at least five ten, with long black hair that hung straight down her back.

"Oh my God," I mumbled in shock, "you're Tyra Banks."

She laughed, the sound almost musical it was so lovely.

"I get that sometimes," she said, relieving me of one of my sacks. "But trust me, I'm not. 'Cause if I were, I sure as hell wouldn't be living in Indiana." She walked up the stairs and I followed her, still a bit stunned.

"You must be Sheila's neighbor Kathleen," she said when we'd reached the top.

I moved around her to unlock my door. She followed me inside.

"I am," I confirmed, setting my bag on the kitchen counter. She did the same. I had the sinking feeling she didn't know about Sheila's death.

"It's nice to finally meet you," she said. Her smile was wide, and had a touch of mischievousness about it, which only enhanced her beauty. "I'm Gracelyn, but my friends call me Gracie."

"Thanks for helping me, Gracie." I couldn't help smiling back at her, she was so friendly and cheerful. I dreaded what I knew was coming and, sure enough, she confirmed my suspicions.

"Do you know where Sheila is?" she asked. "She was supposed to have dinner with me last night, but she didn't show. I left her a few voice mails and she hasn't called me back."

At that, I turned and looked at the spot on my kitchen counter where I'd left the phone this morning. It was gone. The uncomfortable realization that someone had been in my apartment made me pause before I answered her.

"I'm so sorry to have to tell you this," I said to Gracie, "but Sheila is dead." I flinched inwardly at the abruptness of my words but didn't know how else to put it.

Gracie's face froze in shock for a moment, then she seemed to recover herself. She didn't cry. Actually, she looked more resigned than anything else.

"How did she die?" she asked quietly.

I swallowed heavily before answering. "Someone killed her. I found her late Saturday night in her apartment."

Gracie leaned back against the counter and looked up at the ceiling, blinking her eyes rapidly. I remained silent, letting her absorb the news and regain control of her emotions. Finally, she took a deep, shuddering breath and looked at me again.

Smiling a little, she said, "She talked about you, you know. She really liked you. Said you were sweet and kind and brought her coffee in the mornings."

Now I was the one who felt tears stinging my eyes.

"We got along pretty well," I said, clearing my throat. I began unpacking my bags, and Gracie helped. As I put things in the refrigerator, I had a thought.

"Would you like to stay for dinner?"

Her bright smile appeared again. "I'd love to," she said. "Thank you."

It would be nice to have someone to cook for, for a change, I thought. Usually, it was just me. I felt something brush against me and looked down to see Tigger winding his way around my legs.

"You have Tigger!" Gracie exclaimed, bending down to scoop him up.

I winced. Gracie was wearing dark jeans that fit like a second skin, and a long-sleeved black blouse. Tigger was going to shed all over her.

"I couldn't let him go to the animal shelter," I said, "and I thought Sheila wouldn't mind me taking him."

"Yeah, she would have wanted you to have him," Gracie confirmed, nuzzling Tigger's fur. He purred contentedly in her arms.

I started cooking dinner while we chatted. Finding half a bottle of wine in the refrigerator, I poured two glasses. I found out that Gracie was originally from Ohio and had moved to Indianapolis with a boyfriend, but they had broken up a while ago.

"So how did you know Sheila?" I asked, ladling soup into two bowls.

"We worked together," she answered, as we sat down at my small kitchen table. I thought I knew what that meant even though she clarified. "For the escort service, you know. I don't plan on doing it forever," she said, taking a sip of her wine. "I'm saving my money so I can travel. I've always wanted to go to Ireland."

"My family is Irish," I said, and her eyes brightened with interest. "Well, my dad's side anyway."

"Have you ever been there?" she asked excitedly.

I hated to disappoint her, but I shook my head. "No, but I'd like to go sometime."

She asked what I did for a living and I told her about the firm and working at The Drop.

"You know," she said, eyeing me with interest, "you could probably make pretty good money doing what me and Sheila do—did," she corrected herself. "You're really pretty and you've got gorgeous hair, a real unusual color."

I was embarrassed by her scrutiny and her compliments, though I thought she was being overly kind. I was sure I'd look exactly like a dumpling standing next to her.

"I don't think so," I said. "I don't think I'm . . . cut out . . . for that kind of work."

"You know, it's not always sex," she said, which caught my attention. I thought that was what they did.

At my questioning look, she explained. "Some men really do just want a pretty and entertaining companion for the evening." She shrugged her shoulders. "They pay for someone so they don't have to worry about getting involved or into any entanglements."

Huh. Well, that was interesting. It certainly didn't sound like a bad job. I remembered with more than a little longing what Sheila had told me she made. Then I shook myself out of my reverie.

"No, I couldn't. It's just not me."

"Suit yourself," Gracie said, "but let me know if you ever change your mind."

We finished our meal in companionable silence, both of us lost in our own thoughts. When we'd finished and I was cleaning up, I brought up something that had bothered me.

"Gracie," I said, "you know, you didn't seem all that surprised to hear about Sheila." I turned from the sink to look at her as she stood petting Tigger, who had jumped up on my counter. I shooed him off onto the floor.

"I suppose I'm not," she said. "Sheila had told me about a guy that kept requesting her from the service."

"She did?" I asked, trying to contain my excitement. If Gracie knew about him, she might know who he was.

"Yeah," she said, "but I don't know his name."

My heart sank and she noticed my disappointment. "A lot of them don't even use their real names," she explained. "They're businessmen, political figures. They have a lot to lose if someone were to find out they'd used an escort service."

She thanked me for the meal and gave me a hug. Jotting down her number on a piece of paper, she handed it to me.

"Call me if you change your mind," she said before she left, and I didn't have to ask what she meant.

The next day at work I avoided both Diane and Blane. I had no idea how I was supposed to act with him. My stomach tied itself in knots at the mere thought of going up to his floor. I took the chicken way out and called Clarice from my desk.

"What happened yesterday between you and Blane?" she demanded the minute I said hello. I thought frantically of the kiss in my car before realizing she hadn't meant that, but the scene in his office.

"We just had a slight disagreement," I said weakly.

"Slight, my ass," she retorted. "I got grilled within an inch of my life about you after you ran out of here."

"What?"

"Exactly," she said. "Blane wanted to know everything I knew about you, including what you and I had talked about yesterday."

"You mean my date with James tonight?"

"Yes. He wanted to know if you had been out with James before, if you had dated anyone else in the firm, just everything. I couldn't believe it!"

"What did you tell him?" I demanded.

"Well, I had to tell him the truth," she hedged. "He is my boss, after all. Don't worry, nothing bad. I was just so surprised that he wanted to know." Yeah, Clarice and me both.

"Um . . . Yes, Mr. Galloway, we do have those files you requested," I heard her say. I was briefly confused before I realized Blane must be within earshot.

"He's there, isn't he?" I hissed into the phone.

"Absolutely," she answered. "You're correct about that, sir."

I grinned. "Thanks for running interference for me, Clarice," I said. "He's the last person I want to see right now."

"I assume you mean me and not the aforementioned Mr. Galloway."

Crap! Blane must have taken the phone from Clarice. The jig was up. I winced, leaning over to lightly bang my head on the desk.

"I'd like you in my office, Kathleen," Blane continued. "You have three minutes." The line clicked.

Hanging up, I took a deep breath. I could handle this. So we had kissed, so what? Lots of people did that all the time. It didn't mean anything. But that didn't explain why my heart was racing and butterflies were throwing a party in my stomach.

Nerves jangling, I took the elevator up to Blane's floor. I couldn't resist smoothing my hair in the reflection off the elevator door. Stepping off the elevator, I tugged nervously at the hem of the fuzzy sweater I wore today. It was a deep raspberry color and I thought it brought out the red in my hair. Not that I'd cared what I wore to the office. Okay, so maybe that wasn't precisely true, but I could pretend.

Clarice looked furtively at me as I walked by, and I thought I saw the ghost of a smile on her face. I stuck my tongue out at her. Traitor.

I tapped lightly on Blane's open office door and he glanced up from where he'd been standing behind his desk, bent over studying some papers. He straightened and waved me in.

"Close the door behind you," he ordered, and I did as I was told. He must not have had to go to court today, because he wasn't in a suit, but dressed more casually in black slacks and a black long-sleeved shirt. The cuffs had been folded casually back.

Coming out from behind the desk, he strode toward me. I froze like the proverbial deer in headlights, halfway across the room. He stopped an arm's length from me.

"Did you bring that list for me?" he asked, taking me by surprise. Then I could have kicked myself. Of course this wasn't personal. He'd remembered I was supposed to bring him the numbers off Sheila's cell phone.

"No," I said.

He set his hands on his hips and looked at me, waiting.

"It was gone when I got home last night."

He frowned. "What do you mean?" he asked.

"Just what I said. I left the phone on my kitchen counter yesterday and when I got home last night, it was gone."

Now that I thought about it, it occurred to me that Blane himself might have taken it. He was the only one who'd known I'd had it.

"Was your apartment locked?"

I nodded. "I always lock my apartment."

He didn't say anything to this, seeming to be lost in thought.

After a few moments of silence, I cleared my throat. "Is that all?" I asked, not sure if I hoped it was or wasn't. Looking back at me, he was still frowning.

"I don't like the idea of someone breaking into your apartment," he said.

"Yeah, you and me both," I shot back.

I saw the corners of his mouth twitch in an almost smile. His hands dropped from his hips and he stepped closer. Swallowing, I stood my ground.

"You're so combative," he accused softly. "Are you this way with everyone or just me?"

His question startled me. I was unsure how to answer. On one hand, he had a point, but, from my perspective, I was just trying to guard against him. If anything, the last few interactions between us had shown me how susceptible I was to him.

"I . . . um," I stammered, not knowing what I was going to say. His gaze held me captive as he lifted a hand. The back of his knuckles grazed my jaw, and my breath caught in my throat.

"I like that color on you," he said softly, moving closer to me. I saw his eyes drop to my mouth, and panic flared inside me. I couldn't allow him to kiss me again. It meant something to me, something that I knew it couldn't mean to him. I was just a plaything for him and I had to remember that.

Stepping backward beyond his reach, I blurted, "I have to go. I have a date tonight."

His eyes narrowed and he moved toward me again. I kept walking backward, him stalking me, until I was suddenly stopped by the wall against my back. Placing his hands on either side of my head, he effectively trapped me.

"So you said," he said, his eyes searching mine. "Though somehow I doubt James will be to your liking."

"What do you mean?" I said, disliking the breathlessness in my voice. "James is a nice man." I couldn't stop my gaze from dropping to his mouth and watching as his lips curved in a knowing smile.

"Maybe," Blane murmured. "But I don't think you like nice men."

"That's ridiculous," I protested. "Of course I do." I could feel the heat of his body through his clothes as he towered over me. His shirt was unbuttoned at the top and I could see a glimpse of skin at the base of his throat. I licked my lips and tried not to think of how that skin would taste.

Leaning closer, he placed his lips at my ear. "But I'm not a nice man," he whispered, "and I know you like me." The words slithered into my ear and then I felt his lips touch my neck in a featherlight caress.

A sharp knock on the door shattered the silence and I jumped about a foot. Blane didn't move, his eyes locked on mine. His hand cupped my jaw, his thumb lightly brushing my lips.

The knock came again and I took the opportunity to duck under his arm and escape. I threw the door open on a surprised Derrick Trent.

"I'm sorry, Blane," he said, looking from him to me. "I didn't realize you were in a meeting?" His statement came out as a question as he looked at me. I don't think he even knew who I was.

Smiling brightly, I said, "I was just leaving," and I beat a hasty retreat, not daring to look back at Blane as I hurried down the hall.

CHAPTER FIVE

I drove home, glad to be done for the day. The scene in Blane's office had me rattled. I didn't understand what kind of game he was playing with me. And that's what I'm sure it was. A game. Maybe he just couldn't handle the idea of a woman not eager for his advances. Not that I had shown myself all that uneager, I thought ruefully. I didn't want to think about what might have happened if we'd had another few moments alone in his office. Blane was like the proverbial flame—irresistible even though I knew I'd just get burned.

Shoving thoughts of Blane aside, I took a quick shower so I could blow-dry my hair. It was fluffier and shinier if I blow-dried, but it just took so long I rarely had the patience to do it. This was my first real date since coming to Indy and I thought it was worth the effort.

I surveyed my closet, trying to figure out what to wear. It was chilly, so something warm would be best. I pulled out a black sweater dress that was sexy without being trashy. Black tights, black high-heeled boots, and some silver jewelry and I thought I looked pretty good. The color set off my fair skin and my hair, which hung in waves past my shoulders. The dress hugged my curves without being skintight. I was just putting the final touches on my makeup and adding a spray of perfume when I heard a knock on my door.

Peering through the peephole, I saw that it was James, and I smiled in welcome as I opened the door.

"Wow," he said, grinning appreciatively as he looked me up and down. "You look fantastic."

I was slightly embarrassed but enjoyed his frank admiration.

"Thanks," I said. "You look pretty good yourself." And he did. He was wearing black pants, a gray shirt, and dark sport coat.

I locked my door and he offered his arm as we walked down the stairs. With my heels, he was only an inch or so taller than me. He drove a white BMW, a much more sensible car than Blane's, though certainly not a cheap one. I realized I was thinking about Blane, and deliberately shut those thoughts down.

"Do you like Italian?" James asked as he started the car.

"Love it," I answered. We talked as he drove, chatting about inconsequential things. I had been a bit nervous, but James's warm and unassuming demeanor put me at ease.

He pulled up at a small, exclusive Italian restaurant and gave the car keys to the valet. Another valet opened my door for me and I stepped out. James offered me his arm again as we went inside.

I had, of course, never been to this restaurant before and it was very cozy. The décor was tasteful without seeming pretentious. The maître d' led us to a corner booth far from the kitchen. I scooted into the leather seat and James slid in next to me, situating us side by side in the corner. The maître d' handed us menus, then quietly disappeared.

A waiter came by and James ordered a bottle of wine. Everything on the menu looked delicious and I was having a hard time deciding. James ordered some kind of seafood while I chose the eggplant parmesan.

James was an entertaining date and he had me laughing with stories of past clients and some of the stranger cases the firm had litigated. The wine was excellent and I found I was enjoying myself. Our meal came and the food was delicious. James made a signal to the waiter and a new bottle of wine appeared. He kept refilling my glass, and though I was Irish and could handle my liquor better than most, I could feel that the wine had affected me. I was giggling more easily, rather unconcerned about how close James was sitting to me. His hand had drifted to my thigh as we talked, and I didn't mind.

Someone stopped at our table and we looked up. I sobered up quickly. Frank Santini was standing there.

"James!" Frank exclaimed, his thick lips widening in a smile. "I thought that was you. So good to see you."

"Hi, Frank," James said conversationally. "How are you?"

"I am very well, thank you for asking," Frank replied, his eyes moving to me. "And I see you are doing very well this evening too, judging by the lovely woman at your side."

The alcohol was making my brain fuzzy, but I tried to clear my head.

"Yes, isn't she," James said, smiling at me. "This is Kathleen Turner. Kathleen, this is Frank Santini. He has been a long timeclient of my father's and the firm's."

My lips pulled back from my teeth in a fake smile.

"We have met, Kathleen and I," Frank said. "Though I believe you were with Blane the last time."

I felt James stiffen slightly beside me. Frank turned his attention back to James.

"Have you considered our proposition?" he asked. "You would do very well, you know, and we would support you."

"I am considering it, Frank," James said, his tone somewhat irritated, "and I told you I'd let you know."

The smile disappeared from Frank's face and his eyes narrowed at James. Then he seemed to recollect himself and smiled affably again. "You two have a good evening," he said. "We'll talk later." He walked away.

James took a drink of his wine, saying nothing.

I broke the silence. "What did he mean by a 'proposition'?"

"My dad wants me to run for district attorney," James answered. "He's been pressuring me for a while. Frank has promised the union's support if I do."

"Do you want to?"

"I don't know," he said vaguely. "Maybe."

Frank's visit had put a damper on the evening. James now seemed sullen, which made me uncomfortable.

We didn't speak much as James paid the check and we rose to leave. I found myself still too tipsy for my liking and grateful for James's arm to steady me. After handing me into the car and sliding behind the wheel, he turned to me.

"I need to run by the office for a moment," he said. "Do you mind?"

"Of course not," I answered. "That's fine."

After a few miles, James spoke again. "I didn't realize you were seeing Blane." There was a deceptive offhandedness to his voice that made me wary.

"I'm not seeing Blane," I said firmly. "My car broke down last week and Blane gave me a ride. He had to drop off some papers at Frank's office on the way. That's all."

The ghost of a memory—Blane's lips on mine—flitted through my mind. I wasn't lying. Kissing did not equate to seeing someone, not in the sense James meant.

"Oh," he said, "well, that's good." I saw the flash of his smile in the ambient light from the dash, and his hand reached across the seat to grasp mine.

I smiled feebly and allowed him to hold my hand. Surely he hadn't been jealous?

It was after ten when we pulled into the firm's parking lot. Parking close to the building, he turned toward me.

"You can stay here if you'd like," he said. "I'll just be a few minutes." I agreed and he got out, closing the door behind him.

A good fifteen minutes passed with no sign of James returning. The cold had seeped into the car and I shivered. I didn't know what was taking him so long, but I decided I could wait just as well inside, where it was warm, as opposed to here in the car, where it was not.

Scurrying inside, I sighed with relief as the warm air of the lobby enveloped me. James was an associate in the firm, not a partner, so his office was on the third floor. I decided to go on up and see if everything was okay.

Stepping out of the elevator into the darkened hallway, I glanced around. James's office was at the far end and I could see a light coming from the door. Heading that way, I stopped short when I heard angry voices.

"I told you, I don't like the timing," James was saying. Another voice answered his, but I couldn't make out the words.

That was interesting. I'd had enough booze to make eavesdropping seem like a good idea. Straining to hear, I moved a little closer. What was he talking about? The timing of what? Pondering this, I stepped in front of a darkened office.

A hand shot out of the open doorway and pulled me inside. I drew a breath to scream as I came up forcefully against a hard chest. I struggled in his grip and my head tilted back to look at my assailant. My scream froze in my throat just as his hand clapped down over my mouth.

It was the man from the courthouse—the tall, dark, and handsome stranger who had asked if I was all right after the crazy nut job tried to slice my throat open. I stopped struggling. Faint light from outside filtered through the window, giving him an ethereal quality. My memory of him had not done him justice.

"James is not going to appreciate you spying on him," he whispered, his blue eyes intently locked on mine. "Stay here until he leaves."

Unsure what to do, I hesitantly nodded my head. Although I no longer fought him, his arm remained wrapped around me and his hand stayed over my mouth.

"I would let you go, but I very much don't want you running in there telling Junior about me."

I could feel every inch of him against me, and an unwelcome heat flared in my body. My mind seemed to be working in slow motion, though my hormones were quite pleased to be in this situation. He wore a leather jacket and I could feel its buttery softness against my fingers. The scent of the leather combined with the slightly musky aroma of his skin made my head swim. I was really regretting the wine.

The sudden click of a door being shut caused us both to go still and silent. He pulled me closer to him, melting farther back into the shadows. I could hear someone walk past. A few moments later, another set of footsteps followed. I couldn't see anything except the man, my eyes focusing now on his square, stubble-roughened jaw as he watched behind me.

My captor's attention suddenly returned to me and I felt his hand loosen across my mouth. Instead of dropping his hand, he moved it slightly, his fingers splayed across my cheek as his thumb lightly touched my lips. His eyes had been on mine, but now he looked down at my mouth. Nervously, I licked my lips and tried to focus on anything but the growing tension between us.

"Who are you?" I asked, my voice coming out as a whisper. "What are you doing here?" Both were very valid questions and I was proud to have been able to form coherent thoughts, especially with him touching me. I felt a shiver run down my spine and I knew he felt it, too, when the corner of his mouth lifted in a smirk.

"Ah, an inquisitive female," he said sardonically, his blue eyes intent on mine. "How original." His dry, patronizing tone caused my temper to flare.

"You have no right to be here," I hissed, embarrassed now and trying to ignore the way we were still pressed together. I squirmed, but his arms were like iron bands around me.

"How do you know?" he said, and I was chagrined to see that I was making no progress in breaking his grip.

"You were spying on James!"

"So were you."

Well, I couldn't really argue with that.

"Let me go," I demanded, though my voice wasn't nearly as strong as I would have liked. My stomach was rolling uneasily and the room had begun to spin.

"No need to rush away," he said, still not releasing me. I started wriggling in earnest.

"I think I'm going to be sick," I said frantically.

"On your way then," he quipped, abruptly releasing me.

I stumbled for a moment, then turned and ran out the door and down the hall. I didn't stop until I was in the restroom heaving up the best dinner I'd had in ages.

When I was through, I leaned against the wall, trying to get my breath back. My head was pounding and the room was still spinning. I washed out my mouth in the sink and found some mints in my purse to chew. Suddenly, I remembered James was going to be looking for me, since I was supposed to wait in the car.

"Crap!" Standing fully upright on shaky legs, I walked as quickly as possible in my heels back to the elevator and down. The man in black was nowhere in sight.

The brisk autumn air hit me as I exited the building, and I sucked in a breath as the cold went right through my dress to my overheated skin. Wrapping my arms around myself and keeping my head down, I walked quickly toward James's car and abruptly ran into someone.

Stifling a shriek, I jerked my head up to see James standing there. He'd grabbed my upper arms to stop me and he was looking at me with an expression of irritation.

"Where were you?" he demanded.

Taken aback by his hostility, it took a moment for me to respond.

"I got cold," I replied. "You were gone for a while, so I went inside. I used the ladies' room, then tried to find you." My voice was curt even as I lied. Who the hell was he to interrogate me like I was a misbehaving child? "I didn't realize I was supposed to wait dutifully for you in the cold car." My sarcasm was thick and he immediately backtracked.

"I'm sorry, Kathleen," he said in a much more agreeable tone, "I was just worried when I got back and you were gone." This mollified me somewhat, though I was still leery. James seemed to vacillate wildly between moods.

"Well, I'm all right, just freezing."

"Of course," he said. "Let's get you home." With a hand on my back, he guided me to the car.

In a relatively short time, we were pulling up to my apartment. He walked around to my side and opened the car door for me.

"Thank you for a nice evening," I said as we climbed the stairs. I wasn't sure if he was expecting me to invite him in, but I really didn't want to. Perhaps if I headed him off, he would take the hint.

"You're very welcome," he said politely, and the affable gentleman was back. We'd reached my door by this time and I had my keys in my hand. I unlocked the door but didn't step inside.

"May I ask you out again?" he asked, and I couldn't help smiling at his manners. I wasn't feeling fireworks with James, but then again, fireworks can burn you. James was nice, comfortable, and safe. I should want that and forget about womanizing Lotharios.

"I would like that," I said, and when he bent to kiss me lightly on the lips, I didn't resist but I didn't encourage him, either. In the back of my mind, I had the sneaking suspicion that perhaps kissing two men in one day was bordering on slut territory. Technically, I hadn't kissed Blane, but I thought that might be splitting hairs. Regardless, with James, I didn't feel the spark and energy I did with Blane. It was nice . . . and that was all.

With a parting smile, I stepped into my apartment and watched as he went back down the stairs. Closing and locking the door, I turned and leaned against it, sighing.

Well, that had been interesting. James was such a nice guy, I really couldn't fathom that he had any deep, dark secrets he was hiding, no matter what Mr. Tall, Dark, and Mysterious had said. What had he been doing at the firm anyway? Honestly, I thought the deepest secret James had was that he probably needed a prescription.

I headed to the bedroom to change and noticed my ancient answering machine flashing that I had a message. Pushing the button, I waited and heard . . . nothing. It must have been a sales call and they'd hung up when the machine had answered. Except there were four messages, all silent. That was really strange and it kind of gave me a creepy feeling. I ignored it and changed into my flannel pants— they had seen better days, but they were so warm—and a long-sleeved T-shirt. After washing my face and brushing my teeth, I hit the sack.

The jangling of the telephone roused me and I blearily looked at my clock. I'd only been asleep an hour. Stumbling to my feet, I grabbed the phone.

"Hello?" I mumbled, still half-asleep.

There was silence for a minute and I almost hung up.

"Kathleen?" A man spoke hesitantly. I frowned.

"Yeah?" I answered. "Who is this?"

"Kathleen, it's Mark." That woke me up.

"Mark, are you all right?" I had no idea why he'd be calling me, especially this late at night.

"Um . . . no, actually . . . I don't think so," he said haltingly. His voice was anxious.

"What's wrong?"

"I can't talk about it over the phone. But I need to see you, Kathleen," he said. "Can I meet you somewhere tomorrow?"

"Of course," I said, and thought for a moment. "I'll probably be at the courthouse tomorrow around eleven. Can you meet me there?"

"Yeah, that'll work. I'll find you." And with barely more than an assent from me, he hung up.

I chewed my lip in worry. Mark hadn't sounded like himself at all. If I didn't know better, I'd say he'd sounded scared. But that didn't make any sense. And neither did him calling me. Mark and I were merely passing acquaintances. Why he would come to me if he was in trouble, I had no idea. Although I suppose technically he was a murder suspect, I couldn't believe he'd killed Sheila.

Shrugging off the disturbing conversation, I replayed the events of tonight. I wondered who the man in the dark had been. Piercing blue eyes that took my breath away flashed through my mind. I groaned and buried my suddenly flushed face in my hands. I was never drinking again.

The run-ins I'd had with Blane had no doubt influenced my libido and not in a good way. I was simultaneously embarrassed and frustrated. Embarrassed that I'd nearly thrown up on a man whose name I didn't even know. A very attractive man at that, and one who practically oozed sex. And I was frustrated because Blane's cat-and-mouse game with me had left my hormones working overtime tonight, which James's light kiss hadn't come close to sating.

I was too tired to think and I didn't like where my thoughts were leading me, which was basically around in circles with nibbles of worry at the edges when I thought of Mark. I went back to bed, hoping everything would look slightly better in the light of day.

It didn't, but I decided not to think anymore about the Man in Black (original, I know) and to just focus on my work and my meeting with Mark.

I was gathering up the documents and files I needed to take to the courthouse when a deliveryman stepped into my cube. He was holding a vase of flowers.

"Kathleen Turner?" he asked, to my surprise.

"Yes," I answered, and he held the flowers out to me.

"Delivery for you," he said, and was gone before I could open my mouth to ask who had sent them.

It was a beautiful arrangement and quite large. A few white and pink roses were mixed in with snapdragons, eucalyptus, forget-me-nots, and lilies. The effect was very lovely and smelled divine. It had been so long since someone had sent me flowers that I took a moment to bask in the pleasure. I thought, a little smugly, that James was really laying it on thick. I dug for the card. Pulling it open, I read the printed words.

I can be nice.

My eyes widened. No. It couldn't be. But I couldn't help remembering what Blane had said yesterday, right before I'd beat a hasty retreat from his office.

"I'm not a nice man."

Lori's head poked around the corner. "Wow," she said, her eyes alight with curiosity. "Who sent those?"

I crumpled the card in my fist. There's no way I could tell anyone that one of the partners had sent me flowers. Especially not that it had been Blane. Everyone would immediately assume I was sleeping with him.

"No idea," I lied. "Strange, huh?"

Before she could question me further, I jumped up and grabbed my purse and papers.

"Gotta get to the courthouse," I said. "See you later." I heard her call a good-bye to me as I headed out the doors, and I breathed a sigh of relief. I really did not want anyone to know about Blane. Not that there was anything to know, I thought irritably. He was bored and playing a game with me and it needed to stop. I'd deal with him after I met with Mark.

"Kathleen!" Hank said jovially as I stepped through the courthouse metal detector. "Ain't seen you in a few days. You doin' all right?" Beneath his grin was real concern and I knew he probably still felt guilty about the incident last Friday.

I smiled at him. I couldn't be angry. If someone was determined to get a weapon into the courthouse, I didn't believe there was much that could be done to stop them.

"I'm fine, Hank," I said. "No worries." Relief washed across his face as he handed my things back to me.

By the time I finished my deliveries, it was nearing eleven and I was glad I'd timed that well. Now I just had to find Mark and maybe we could grab some lunch. The problem was, he hadn't stayed on the phone long enough last night for us to set up a specific meeting place.

I wandered around the courthouse for a while, but it was crowded and difficult to pick one person out of the many. Glancing at my watch nervously, I saw that it was fifteen minutes past the time we were supposed to meet. I stepped outside and shaded my eyes from the glaring sunshine.

Suddenly, a hand closed over my wrist and pulled. Whirling, I breathed a sigh of relief when I saw it was Mark. Then my eyes widened as I took in his appearance.

Mark had always been meticulous in his personal grooming and I had often teased Sheila about the sharp creases on his pressed shirts and pants. That was nowhere in evidence today. He was wearing clothes that were so wrinkled they looked like they'd been slept in, and he was sporting several days' growth of beard. His eyes were darting around and his grip tightened on my arm as he tugged.

"C'mon," he said urgently. "We need to get out of the open."

"What?" I asked, confused. "Why?"

"Too many eyes and ears," he said, which only increased my bewilderment, but I allowed him to lead me.

He took us away from the courthouse and down a side street, moving so quickly I had to half-jog to keep up. Glancing behind us every few steps, he seemed to expect someone to be following. It unnerved me so much that I, too, started turning to look when he did.

Mark stopped in front of a small diner, peering through the window, then he pulled me inside. He sat at a small table facing the door and I sat across from him. Mark was carrying a backpack that he left hooked over his arm rather than laying it down on an extra chair.

"Mark," I said once I sat down. "What is going on? Are you all right?" My first thought in taking a good look at him was that Sheila's death had hit him hard. I felt bad for him. I knew what it was like to lose someone in a sudden and violent way. Thoughts of my dad flashed through my mind.

"No, I am most definitely not all right," he said, sparing a glance at me before his eyes again moved to the windows. "I wanted to tell you, warn you—I think you might be in danger." His eyes were on me again, intent and serious.

I might have laughed at the melodrama, his words were right out of a movie script, but I could see he believed them. "What are you talking about?" I asked. "Why would I be in danger?"

"It's the people I work for," he said, "or really, the people they work for. I think"—he faltered for a moment and had to clear his throat before he continued, speaking quietly—"I think they might have been the ones who killed Sheila."

The shock must have shown on my face.

"I was there that night," he continued, his eyes intent on mine. "Sheila and I argued and I left. But I hated to leave it like that. So I came back . . ." His voice faltered and he rubbed a weary hand across his face. Clearing his throat, he continued, his voice thick. "When I came back, she was dead. And I ran. I was terrified they were coming for me, too. Kathleen, it's my fault Sheila's dead."

It was difficult to watch the pain on his face and I reached out to take his hand, giving it a comforting squeeze. I had no idea what to say. I was in shock and still didn't know why someone would want to kill him.

"But why would they kill Sheila?" I asked, confused.

"To try and get to me, I think," he answered. Before I could ask why, he gripped my hand tightly. "And you can't trust that firm you work for, Kathleen. They're involved, too. I don't know how far exactly, but they can't be trusted."

A chill went through me as I remembered telling Blane about Sheila's cell phone and how, hours later, it had disappeared from my apartment.

"Involved in what?" I asked. I was confused. Mark was being vague and if Blane was involved or, more importantly, I was in danger, I wanted more information. "Who do you work for?"

"I work for a software company," he explained. "Called TecSol."

"Why would someone at a software company kill someone?" None of it made any sense.

"It's about Eve," he said. "I knew about the problems and I went to your firm for help. Someone betrayed me. They told me to keep quiet or I'd regret it. I didn't believe them. I thought I was doing the right thing. But Sheila paid the price and now they're after me."

I wanted to ask him who Eve was, and he looked like he would have said more, but something out the window caught his eye. Then his hand was like a vise on my arm as he dragged me out of my seat. I had just enough time to see a man come through the diner's door before Mark pulled me back behind the counter.

We ran through the kitchen, Mark shoving a couple of cooks and a waitress out of the way as we barreled past. I winced when a stack of plates went crashing to the floor. Mark pulled me on relentlessly until we burst out of the back door into an alley. A glance right before the door shut behind us showed me that the man had followed us through the kitchen.

"Run!" Mark shouted, shoving me forward.

I didn't need to be told twice and sprinted down the deserted alley, Mark hot on my heels. The door crashed open behind us, slamming into the brick wall. I didn't turn around but redoubled my efforts, lungs burning for air as my knees pumped.

A gunshot rang out and I shrieked, ducking around a corner. Mark followed me as we collapsed against a wall, breathing heavily.

"Kathleen," he gasped. "Take this." He thrust his backpack at me. "We'll split up. It's me they want. I'll be in touch. Now go!"

"What?" I practically screeched. "I'm not leaving you!" I could feel tears stinging my eyes and I blinked them away. I was not leaving him alone. With surprising strength, he shoved me away.

"Go!" he said, and before I could utter another protest, he took off in the opposite direction.

I was frozen for a moment in shock before I was able to command my feet to move. Then I took off down the alley, his backpack slung over my shoulder.

What I saw at the end of the alley made me slide to a stunned stop. It was him. My Man in Black. He was facing my direction, pointing a gun at me.

Well. That was certainly disappointing. I filed that emotion away for later.

Instinctively, I spun and started back the direction I'd come and then skidded to a stop again. The man who had been chasing Mark and me had appeared at the other end of the alley. I was trapped.

My head swiveled back and forth, trying to decide what to do. I spied a door off to my left and flung myself at it, praying it was unlocked. The gods must have been feeling pity for me because, miracle of miracles, the knob turned under my hand. I burst through the doorway just as I heard the sound of a bullet ricocheting off the brick wall near where my head had just been. Turning, I twisted the deadbolt on the door.

I was in what appeared to be a small, deserted store, empty save for a few boxes. My harsh breathing was loud in the quiet room. I looked around frantically for another way out, but when I didn't immediately see one, I started searching for anything that could be a weapon. A rickety wooden chair caught my eye and I ran to it. Grasping its legs, I tried to pry one off. It always looked easy when they did it in the movies, but rickety though it may have looked, this chair was sturdy enough to withstand my fruitless attempt to break it apart. I called it a few choice words under my breath.

A scraping noise behind me made my breath freeze in my lungs. I grabbed my still fully intact chair and moved back into the shadows, holding it over my head. The door I'd come through burst open and slammed against the wall. I heard footsteps coming closer and I bided my time. Taking a deep breath, I closed my eyes and swung the chair.

"Ow! Damn it! Stop, Kathleen!"

Hearing my name startled me and I dropped the chair, then ran forward into the meager light. It was my Man in Black. I had knocked him down to the floor and he was rubbing the back of his head. He'd dropped his gun and I quickly picked it up, moving a safe distance away. Sitting up, he looked at me.

The gun felt strange in my hand. I hadn't held one since my dad had died. Nonetheless, I pointed it at him with steady hands.

"How do you know my name?" I demanded. "And why were you chasing me?"

"I wasn't chasing you," he said calmly. Too calmly for someone with a gun pointed at him, if you asked me. "I was trying to help you." He got to his feet and I stepped back, eyeing him warily.

"You have a funny way of showing it," I said. Even to my ears I sounded bitchy, but I thought I had the right. "Why should I believe you? And you still haven't told me how you know my name."

He smirked and I had to ignore the way my stomach tightened in response. No man should be allowed to look that good after getting cracked across the head.

"I made it a point to find out your name after the incident at the courthouse."

Oh. Well, that made some sense. I felt an embarrassing flush of pleasure that he'd wanted to know about me.

"Who are you?"

"You seem to have a knack for getting into trouble," he said, ignoring my question. "First the crazy loon at the courthouse, then you're spying on Junior." He rolled his eyes when he said "Junior" and I took that to mean he didn't think much of James. "And today you have a man chasing you with a gun."

When he put it like that, it did seem rather bizarre. And he didn't even know about Sheila.

"This isn't how my life usually is," I protested, then wondered why I was defending myself to a man who wouldn't even tell me his name.

"Who are you?" I demanded again, using the gun for emphasis. He looked at me and for a moment I thought he wasn't going to answer.

"Dennon," he finally said. "Kade Dennon. Now why don't you tell me why you're here?"

"I'm here because some freak was chasing me with a gun," I said. I didn't say anything about Mark. Mark had said not to trust anyone at the firm and I didn't really know anything about this guy, just that I'd seen him at the court-house and the firm, albeit after hours.

The gaze he leveled at me said he didn't believe me for a second, but I resolutely pressed my lips together. He'd moved closer without me noticing, and in a flash he ripped the gun from my hand. A cry of dismay fell from my lips.

"Let's get out of here," he said, shoving the gun in the small of his back and taking my arm. His manhandling didn't sit well with me, especially with my pride hurting over how easily he'd taken the gun from me. I pulled away from him.

"I can walk, thank you," I said stiffly.

I was suspicious of him, even though he claimed he had been trying to help me. We made our way to the front of the building, which was as dark and deserted as the back.

"What happened to the other guy?" I asked, wondering if Kade had killed him. He seemed to read my mind.

"He's alive," he answered, but didn't offer anything further.

Unlocking the front door, we stepped out onto the street and I was struck by how normal everything looked. A few minutes ago, I'd been terrified and running for my life. And yet the sun was still shining and people passed by on their way to do normal everyday things. It felt like I was stepping out of the twilight zone.

"Let me help you with that," Kade said, reaching for Mark's backpack, which I still had slung over my shoulder.

I quickly stepped beyond his reach. "No, thanks. I'm fine."

Our eyes met, and in that instant, I knew that he wanted whatever was in the backpack. He must've seen Mark give it to me, which meant he was lying to me. I felt fear again in the pit of my stomach. I'd almost rather have someone chasing me. At least then I knew which side they were on. Kade was trying to gain my trust, which scared me. I turned and started walking back toward the courthouse, Kade falling into step beside me. His hand gripped my arm, tighter this time, so I couldn't easily pull away.

I didn't know what to do. He had a gun. That pretty much trumped anything I might do to get away from him. I thought of Mark and worried about what kind of trouble he was in and if he'd pulled me into it as well.

As we neared the courthouse, we ran into a group of high school kids on a field trip. There had to be at least a hundred of them crowding the sidewalk and steps around us. That's when I had an idea.

I stopped abruptly in my tracks and Kade jerked to a halt beside me. As he turned, a questioning look on his face, I pointed at him and said as loudly as I could manage, "Oh my God! It's that guy on TV!" I added a high-pitched squeal just to seal the deal.

The effect was instantaneous. Girls close to me turned, got one good look at him, and started screaming. A wave of bodies surged toward us. I saw a brief look of horror on Kade's face before he was mobbed. He couldn't maintain his grip on my arm as the girls pushed between us, and I quickly took advantage, sliding into the crowd.

I headed toward the courthouse door, glancing behind me only once to see all the cameras and cell phones extended toward Kade. He raised his head, and our eyes locked. He did not look happy. At all. He looked coldly furious, actually. But he tipped his head slightly to me, as if to acknowledge he'd been outmaneuvered, and I knew I hadn't seen the last of him.

CHAPTER SIX

I hurried around the courthouse to the other side, where I'd parked my car. As I was passing by security, I had a thought. Peering through the crowds, I saw Hank, and made my way toward him.

"Hank, you have a minute?" I asked him and he glanced around in surprise. A grin creased his face when he realized it was me.

"For you? You bet," he answered, and motioned toward another guard, Carl, to take his place. I retreated to a less crowded part of the foyer and Hank followed me.

"What can I do for you, Kathleen?" he asked cheerfully. It had occurred to me that Hank, who knew nearly everyone who passed through these doors on a regular basis, might know who Kade was.

"I was wondering if you knew someone," I asked. "His name is Kade Dennon. Ever heard of him?"

Hank's grin faded. "What do you want to know about him for, Kathleen?" His brows had drawn together in a frown.

"I just ran into him, that's all," I answered vaguely. "He seemed . . . different." *Sexy, secretive, dangerous, and scary,* I also thought but didn't say.

Hank's lips pressed together disapprovingly. He seemed to see through me.

"You don't want to be gettin' involved with Kade, Kathleen," he said seriously. "He's bad news."

Duh. As if I couldn't figure that part out on my own.

"What do you mean?" I pressed. Details, please.

"Kade's nothin' but a hired gun," Hank said, and now he looked downright disgusted, but his distaste wasn't directed at me. "He stays just beyond the reach of the law, and works for whoever will pay him the most to get the job done."

I thought of the creepy Jimmy, who worked for the Santini brothers.

"You mean like Jimmy Quicksilver?"

Hank barked a short laugh. "Jimmy's an amateur compared to Kade," he said. "You send Jimmy when you want to send a message. You send Kade"—his voice lowered—"when you want someone to just disappear."

I didn't like the sound of that. "So he works for the Santini brothers, too?" Somehow, I couldn't imagine Kade answering to anyone.

Hank shook his head. "Kade works for himself. The Santini brothers may hire him, but he don't work for them."

"Okay, thanks for the information, Hank," I said hurriedly. My inner clock had been ticking and I wanted to get away from the courthouse before Kade freed himself from the teenage mob. "I'll talk to you later." I walked away, but not before I saw the worried look on Hank's face as he stared after me.

The rest of the afternoon was uneventful as I went back to the firm and finished out the day, trying unsuccessfully to ignore the two gorillas in my cube: the flowers from Blane, and Mark's backpack. I wouldn't say I chickened out of confronting Blane, but I'd had enough stress for one day. Since I didn't want any more questions from coworkers, I took the flowers home with me.

I had to work at The Drop tonight, and for once I was glad for the diversion. I plaited my hair in a French braid and hurriedly donned my uniform. Uncomfortable leaving Mark's backpack in my apartment after Sheila's phone had disappeared, I stowed it in the trunk of my car. I thought about opening it, but Mark had trusted me to keep it safe, not to pry.

As I locked my door, I noticed a moving truck outside. Someone was moving into Sheila's apartment. It took me by surprise and I had to swallow back the sorrow that threatened. As I walked to my car, I saw a girl carrying a box upstairs. She was about my height and dressed all in black. Her jet black hair hung raggedly down her back. One streak had been dyed red. Hmm. I didn't think she and I were going to be buddies, if appearances were anything to go by. I would have introduced myself anyway, just to be neighborly, but I was already running late. Sliding behind the wheel, I headed downtown.

I was bartending alone tonight, Wednesdays not being usually very busy, and Tish and Jill were waitressing. Romeo was throwing a big Halloween bash in a couple of days, since Halloween fell on a Friday this year, so we spent our downtime putting up decorations. I was glad to have pulled the Halloween shift—I knew from previous experience that tips were usually pretty good that night.

"So, what are you dressing as, Kathleen?" Tish asked me as we hung a strand of mini lighted jack-o'-lanterns over the window.

The question took me by surprise. I hadn't thought we were supposed to dress up.

"We have to wear a costume?" I asked, and she nodded.

"Romeo thinks it'll bring in more customers," she answered. "And I was told the girls should try to sex it up a little." She rolled her eyes at this and so did I. I doubted Romeo had told Scott to "sex up" his costume.

"I have no idea what to wear," I said honestly. "What are you dressing as?"

She brightened then and I had a feeling of foreboding.

"Well," she said excitedly, "I had this idea. You know how you do such a great Britney Spears?"

Okay, don't judge me, but I love Britney. Not everyone can be a Pavarotti fan. I'd realized back in high school that I could do a dead-on impression of Britney. They'd found that out at The Drop one night when I'd been a little too enthusiastic in singing along when one of her songs came on.

"Yeah . . ." I said slowly, wondering where Tish was going with this and sure I wasn't going to like it.

"I thought it would be pretty neat if you dressed as Britney and I dressed as Madonna! I already talked to Jill and she's coming as Christina. Deirdre's going to be Beyoncé. What do you think?"

I'd stopped stringing the lights, my jaw agape as I stared at her in horror. "You can't be serious," I said when I finally found my voice. "There's no way I can pull that off!"

Tish waved her hand dismissively at me. "Of course you can! I even have an outfit you can use." When I still stared at her, speechless, she explained with a shrug. "I dressed as Britney a few years ago. It's in the back. I'll give it to you so you'll have it for Friday."

There was no way I was going to be able to talk her out of this. Tish was nice but could be like a bulldog when she got something in her head. I had misgivings, but maybe it would be fun. After all, I hadn't dressed up for Halloween in years.

"Fine," I said, giving in with ill grace. "But I am *not* kissing you."

She laughed and I made a face at her before going in the storeroom for the box of black-and-orange candles that were to be the table centerpieces.

The bar looked very festive by the time we were done and I felt my spirits lift. I was a holiday junkie. Any holiday would do. I celebrated everything from Fat Tuesday to Flag Day.

Customers were slow but steady tonight and they had cleared out by the time we closed, which was always nice, since we had to clean and set up the bar for the next day before we left.

I was finishing drying some bar glasses when Tish set a paper bag on the bar.

"Don't forget the braids," she reminded me, and I rolled my eyes at her.

"You leaving?" I asked, and she nodded.

"Unless you want me to wait for you?"

"No, that's fine," I said. The bar was in a decent neighborhood and I was parked close. I'd never felt uncomfortable leaving late at night and told Tish she could go on and I would lock up.

Fifteen minutes later, I was locking the door, juggling my purse and the paper bag in my arms. I checked to make sure the deadbolt was secure. When I turned around, I was startled to see a man standing in the shadows. A flash of fear went through me before I processed the fact that his silhouette was familiar.

Blane.

He was leaning against his car, which was parked against the curb. My heart raced from his sudden appearance, but I couldn't resist drinking him in. He'd opted for casual again and his jeans hugged his legs, tapering to his casually crossed ankles and boots. He wore a dark shirt that I couldn't see clearly due to his leather jacket. His arms were crossed as he watched me.

"If you could stop scaring me half to death when you show up, I'd appreciate it," I said dryly, sensing a pattern in how he'd gotten the drop on me yet again.

"Did you get the flowers?" he asked, ignoring my reprimand.

I immediately felt guilty for not thanking him. My mother had taught me better manners than that and I was sure they had cost a small fortune. Flowers had been a rare luxury for my mother when my father was alive. Though she had always chastised him when he bought them for her, saying they were too expensive, she'd secretly loved them. The specialness of the treat had rubbed off on me.

"I did, thank you," I said stiffly. "They were beautiful." I took a small step back, careful to maintain a safe distance away from him. His lips twitched, suppressing a smile as he observed me.

"Is it just killing you to thank me?" he asked, and I bristled.

"Of course not," I lied, my cheeks growing hot from embarrassment that he would assume my manners were lacking. "I just don't know why you sent them, that's all."

He pushed away from the car and suddenly was standing much closer to me than was comfortable for my heart rate. I instinctively took another step backward only to run into the wall. Blane moved closer until I had to tip my head back to look at him. The faint light from the streetlamp at his back illuminated me even as it threw his face into shadows. He was close enough now for me to smell his cologne as it mingled with the scent of leather from his coat.

"How was your date?" he asked in a soft voice.

His hand reached out to snag my braided hair and he slowly slipped off the band holding it. I felt my breath seize in my chest. I knew he'd asked something, but I was having a hard time remembering what it was as his fingers started loosening the plaited strands of my hair. Then I remembered and blurted out an answer.

"Fine, it was fine." My voice was too breathless. I searched the darkness of his face, trying in vain to see his eyes. His fingers kept methodically unbraiding my hair.

"Sounds thrilling," he said dryly, and I had the fleeting thought that I should defend James.

"Wh-what are you doing?" I stammered.

He'd completely undone my hair and was now letting the wavy strands slide through his fingers. I'd always been a sucker for someone touching my hair. Add to it Blane's overwhelming sensuality and natural charisma and I felt like I was going to melt into a puddle of goo on the sidewalk.

"Touching you," he replied in a low voice, and I think my heart rate tripled. Those two words conjured up all kinds of images that I had no business thinking about. I tried to remember why I needed to stay away from him.

"Stop," I said, and it was a truly pathetic protest. Really, I was surprised that he didn't laugh at me.

"Do you want me to stop?" he asked in that same raspy tone that went through me like an electric current.

I couldn't think with him so close, with his hand in my hair, his other hand now closing over my hip. I blurted out the first thing I could think of that would help me get back behind my defenses.

"Did you find out anything with those numbers on Sheila's phone?"

His hand stilled in my hair.

"I know you're the one who took it," I persisted. "Which was really low of you, you know?"

"How do you know I took it?" he asked, and this time his voice had an edge to it.

It made me shiver and not in a good way. I belatedly realized I was in an extremely vulnerable position. Blane had a way of getting past my suspicions and defenses and I was kicking myself for being such a stereotypically gullible female.

"I don't . . . I mean, you could've . . . but maybe not," I backtracked nervously. "I guess anyone could've broken in and taken it. Hey, what do I know?" I was babbling and forced myself to shut up.

After a few moments, he responded. "You're right," he said, "I did take the phone."

Part of me exulted that my instincts had been right. The other part—the more sensible and realistic part—thought that I may have just put myself in a bad situation. Mark's warning about not trusting Blane and the firm echoed in my head. We were alone on the street, late at night. What an idiot I was. I vividly remembered Blane's hand around my throat in my car.

Blane's fingers moved in my hair again and I instinctively jerked back in fear. He towered over me and suddenly the shadows of his face no longer looked mysterious, but threatening instead. I felt a shiver run through me. He must have felt it too, because his hand moved up to the back of my head and he forced me to look up at him.

"I'm not going to hurt you," he said firmly. "I took that phone because I'm trying to protect you."

I must not have looked convinced, because he continued. "The people who killed your neighbor, they wouldn't think twice about doing the same thing to you."

Many things about what he said bothered me but one stood out more than the others. "You know who killed Sheila?" I searched his face, hoping I could tell whether he was lying.

He shook his head. "Stay out of it, Kathleen," he ordered. "Or you'll end up the same way."

My temper flared again. "Is that a threat?" I demanded, my eyes narrowing in anger. I was sick of this game. I needed to know who was my friend and, more importantly, who was my enemy.

Blane's hand fisted in my hair, and my head was tugged backward, the slight pain making me gasp. He wrapped his arm around my waist and jerked me to him, until I was fully pressed against him. I dropped the bag as my hands came up to try and push against his chest, but I couldn't get any leverage. He lowered his face until it was mere inches from mine, his eyes boring into mine and shining silver in the night.

"You're like a cornered kitten, Kathleen," he said, shaking his head. "Still hissing and pretending you can fight your way out. I'm trying to protect you. Let me."

I wasn't sure I appreciated being compared to a kitten, but I suppose there were worse things. I wavered. He seemed so sincere. I could feel his heart beating in his chest, and mine seemed to have taken on the same rhythm.

"But . . . why?" I asked, confused. It didn't make sense. Why would Blane give me a second glance, much less try to protect me? What was I to him? Nothing, really.

I sucked in a jagged breath when I felt his lips touch my jaw. His hand tugged again and my head was forced farther back, giving him access to my throat. I felt his mouth graze the skin on my neck and I shivered.

"I don't know," he whispered against my skin. "I can't seem to stay away."

I had a hard time following his words when I felt his tongue touch the place where my neck met my shoulder. My eyes slid shut and my lips parted as my breath came in small pants. My arms slid around his neck and I buried my fingers in his hair, greedily combing through the soft locks. His mouth fastened onto the skin of my neck and he sucked lightly. The heat from his touch flashed through my entire body.

"Ma'am, are you all right?"

The sudden loud voice was like a bucket of cold water. Blane quickly released me, pushing me behind him as he turned to face the police officer a few feet away. My head was still spinning when the officer spoke again.

"Ma'am, do you need some help?"

TIFFANY SNOW

I stepped out from behind Blane and my knees felt like jelly. The policeman was watching Blane suspiciously, his hand resting lightly on his holster.

"I'm fine," I answered. "Just heading home for the night." I stole a furtive glance at Blane whose face was unreadable, save for the clenching of his jaw.

"I'll see you later, Blane," I said quietly, and walked to my car, the officer eyeing me with concern. My eyes met Blane's one more time, then with a confusing mixture of relief and disappointment, I started my car and drove home.

I reached my apartment building with no real memory of driving there. My mind was too full of Blane. What he'd said. What he'd done. I had to stop giving in to him. Obviously, he liked the chase. The problem, as it always was with men like him, was once the chase ended, they lost interest. I knew myself well enough to know I could never have a casual fling with Blane. I'd end up with a broken heart and a parting gift, no doubt thoughtfully picked out by Clarice.

It wasn't until I was walking up the stairs to my apartment that I remembered I'd dropped Tish's Britney costume and forgotten to pick it back up.

"Crap!" I exclaimed, stopping in my tracks. I really didn't want to go back.

"What's the matter?"

I glanced up. The girl who'd moved in to Sheila's apartment was leaning against the railing outside her door. It was dark up there, so I hadn't initially seen her. Now that I looked more closely, I could see she was smoking a cigar.

"Nothing," I finally replied. "Just forgot something." I finished climbing the stairs and hesitated. I felt like I should say something else.

"I'm Kathleen," I said, by way of introduction, holding out my hand.

She looked at it for a moment and I thought maybe she wasn't going to take it, then she stuck the cigar in her teeth and shook my hand. Now that I was closer to her, I could see she was about my height. Her face looked very young.

"CJ," she said. "Nice to meet you." Then she resumed leaning on the railing, puffing on the cigar. I wasn't sure I'd heard her name correctly.

"CJ?" I repeated, and she nodded.

"Well, nice to meet you as well," I said formally.

CJ didn't seem very talkative. I moved toward my door. "Good night," I said, and thought I heard a mumbled "good night" from her general direction.

Unlocking my door, I stepped inside. The day had caught up to me and I was exhausted. And, apparently, I had to find a new Britney Spears costume before Friday. I groaned and fell into bed.

~

Thursday was busy and I was grateful for that. It left me less time to worry about Mark and obsess about Blane. Not that I was obsessing, really—I just kept replaying his kisses over and over in my head. Not healthy, I knew, or good for my resolve to resist him. I was taken by surprise when the object of my obsession suddenly showed up in my cube around midafternoon.

"We need to go downtown," he said curtly.

My heart had started beating double-time the minute I laid eyes on him, and I could feel my face flush. His words didn't immediately register. All I could think about was when he'd kissed me and said he couldn't stay away. He'd even left a little mark on my skin, which I refused to call a hickey. My cube, which wasn't that big to begin with, felt much too small with him standing in it.

"Why do we need to go downtown?" I finally blurted, when my mind had processed what he'd said. He was dressed for court today, full suit, gray pinstripe, with a white shirt and burgundy patterned tie. I felt rather dumpy in my khaki pants and navy sweater.

"The police want to meet with you," he answered.

"What for?"

"They wouldn't say."

He turned to leave, not giving me a chance to question him further, and I grabbed my purse and hurried after him. As we passed Diane's office, I saw her watching us. Crap. Me leaving with Blane. Yep, I bet I knew what she was thinking. Fantastic.

Blane led me to his car and opened the door for me. I slid inside and he shut the door behind me. Then he was driving us toward downtown. I'd forgotten how small the interior of the car was, or maybe it was just Blane's size that made it seem small, but we were very close and I tried not to be distracted by that.

"You didn't have to come," I said. "I could have gone by myself."

He glanced at me before returning his eyes to the road. "I'm your lawyer," he said firmly. "It's my job to go with you."

"Then I need to pay you," I said stubbornly, though I wondered how I'd ever be able to afford to do so. I knew the firm charged upward of five hundred dollars an hour for Blane's time. I saw the corners of his mouth twitch.

"You can pay me by wearing what's in the backseat."

Bemused, I twisted in my seat and saw my brown paper bag sitting behind me. I groaned and heard Blane chuckle softly.

"I'd hoped I'd lost it," I said, disappointed that wasn't the case. My cheeks heated, thinking of how little there was to the costume.

"Dare I hope it's an example of your usual taste in non-working-hours apparel?" Blane asked.

His words made butterflies dance in my stomach. Damn. "No," I retorted, "it's not. The staff at the bar are all dressing as pop divas Friday night." I hesitated. This was embarrassing. "I'm supposed to be Britney," I grumbled.

I jumped in surprise when Blane laughed outright, and while I loved the sound, I felt myself turn even redder.

"Gee, thanks," I mumbled sullenly, crossing my arms over my chest and slinking down in my seat.

He managed to quell his laughter, but his grin remained. "I just can't imagine you pretending to be Britney," he said, glancing at me. His grin made his eyes sparkle, I noticed absently. "You don't seem the type."

I bristled at his impugning of my beloved pop princess. "Hey, she's very successful," I said defensively, "especially for how young she is." In some part of my mind, I couldn't believe I was talking to Blane about Britney Spears. It seemed surreal.

He laughed softly and shook his head. "I'm not saying she isn't," he said, and I could hear the amusement lacing his voice. "I'm sure she's a very talented young woman."

I harrumphed at this, but at least he'd respected my Britney-love.

We arrived at the station all too soon. I'd been enjoying these rare tension-free moments between Blane and me. Taking my elbow, he hustled me inside. Blane gave our names to the officer sitting behind the front counter, who told us to have a seat in the waiting area. We obediently sat in the blue plastic chairs and waited in silence.

A few minutes later, a man stepped through the doorway and walked over to us. He was about five ten and looked to be in his early forties. His hair was brown and thinning on top and he wore nondescript brown pants, a white shirt, and a too-short tie.

"Kathleen Turner?" he asked, as Blane and I stood. I nodded and he extended his hand.

"Detective Frank Milano," he said, shaking my hand firmly. Blane introduced himself as well and they also shook hands.

"What's this about?" Blane asked. He'd told me in the car to let him do the talking.

"We'd like Miss Turner to help us identify a body," Detective Milano replied.

My mouth dropped open in shock. "A body?" I repeated.

Blane gave me a look. I shut my mouth with a snap.

"Yes," the detective answered. "We think we may have found the person who killed your neighbor, Sheila Montgomery, but need to make sure. We thought you might know him."

I was surprised for a moment, but then realized that this was good news. Maybe Mark had been wrong about shadowy people being after him and Sheila. But I didn't know why the police would think I knew who it was.

"We'll need to take you down to the morgue," he continued, and I nodded.

"Okay." The detective turned and led the way, Blane and I falling into step behind him.

"Have you ever seen a dead body before?" Blane asked me quietly.

I thought of my mom and dad and nodded.

"Have you seen a dead body that hasn't been prepared by a mortician?" Blane persisted.

I could see where he was going. I knew dead bodies were awful, but I thought I had a pretty strong disposition. "I'm not going to get sick or pass out, if that's what you're wondering," I hissed in exasperation, rolling my eyes. Please. It's not like I was some kind of fragile flower.

Blane didn't say anything more and I hoped I'd made my point.

A few minutes later we were in a chilly room that smelled strongly of antiseptic and something else. My imagination said it was death and decay. I told my imagination to shut the hell up.

A tech met us and took us to an even colder room, where the cabinets were. It looked eerily familiar—not because I'd been in a morgue before, but because it looked just like what you'd see on TV. I shivered and I didn't think it was just because of the cold.

The tech and Detective Milano stood on one side of the cabinet and Blane and I on the other. My earlier bravado to Blane was fading quickly and I shifted nervously from one foot to the other. When the tech opened the door and pulled out the body tray, I started to feel a little light-headed.

There was a very still figure on the tray, covered with a white sheet. I couldn't look away. The smell was much stronger now and my stomach rolled. I swallowed heavily, determined not to throw up.

The tech pulled down the sheet. It was Mark. He looked perfectly peaceful, as if he could be sleeping. Except the entire back of his head was missing.

The room seemed to grow dim before my eyes. I stumbled backward, needing to get away from the horrifying remains of Mark's body. I reached out blindly for Blane, unable to tear my gaze away from the gruesome sight.

The next thing I became aware of was the sound of angry voices. They seemed to come from far away, like my ears were full of cotton. I felt very floaty. And cold. Cold and floaty. The voices were louder now and I could make out the words.

". . . the fuck you think you're doing, detective," Blane was saying, and the fury in his voice made me want to cringe. "Some warning would have been nice."

I couldn't hear the detective's response.

It felt like I was moving. Opening my eyes, I looked up into Blane's face and realized he was carrying me. I squeezed my eyes shut, immediately wishing I could pass out again just to spare myself the humiliation of being carried by Blane.

Before I could ask to be put down, he was laying me carefully on a sofa. Behind him I could see Milano hovering, a somewhat anxious expression on his face. No doubt he was wondering if I was going to throw up. I took a mental inventory but didn't hurt anywhere, which struck me as odd.

"Didn't I hit the floor?" I asked Blane, confused. He'd taken off his suit coat and laid it over me. Since I was still shivering, I was grateful for it. His face was set in anger, his lips pressed together in a thin line. At my question, though, they softened.

"You think I'd let you fall?" he replied in a soft, teasing voice that only I could hear. "I have to keep you uninjured so I can remind you that you were quite sure you wouldn't pass out."

Okay, I had that coming.

I sat up and Blane moved his jacket behind me to rest over my shoulders. Looking up, I saw Milano. I glared at him accusingly.

"Why didn't you tell me it was Mark?" I demanded. He looked uncomfortable at my accusation.

"We weren't sure he was the same person as the one you said was Sheila's boyfriend," he answered defensively. "We needed you to identify him as the same man."

"What happened to him?" Blane asked. He had been crouched in front of me, but now he moved to sit beside me on the small sofa.

Glancing around, I saw we were in what looked like an employee break room. Besides the sofa and a few mismatched chairs, the room contained a refrigerator, a microwave, and a TV.

"Neighbors found him," Milano said. "He wrote a suicide note confessing to the murder before he shot himself."

The image of Mark's poor head came back to me and the room seemed to tilt. Blane must have sensed my distress, because he slid his arm around my back and gripped me tightly.

"Breathe slow," he said in my ear. "Breathe deep."

I closed my eyes and concentrated on my breathing. I felt the world right itself again after a few moments. When I opened my eyes again, I saw Milano watching us suspiciously. I knew what he probably thought, seeing Blane's arm around me, but I didn't care.

"You're saying he killed himself?" I asked. That just didn't make sense. Mark had been scared and trying to keep himself alive yesterday. He had not seemed like a man in the throes of depression and guilt.

"That's how it appears," he answered.

"You've got it wrong," I said firmly. "There's no way he could have murdered Sheila, and he didn't kill himself either. He was murdered, too."

I could see the skepticism in Milano's eyes, then pity, which just infuriated me.

"Believe me," I insisted. "You've got to find whoever did this. They killed Sheila and now Mark."

Milano was already shaking his head. "I'm sorry, but the case has been closed. Mark was her boyfriend. You yourself said they argued that night, which places him at the scene of the crime. His note was his confession."

"But you're wrong!" My voice was getting shrill and Blane pulled me tighter against his side. Whether to comfort me or quiet me, I didn't know.

"I'm sorry," Milano said, and to his credit, he seemed sincere. "There's nothing more I can do." With a last look at Blane and me, he left.

"Are you all right?" Blane asked.

I sniffed. My eyes were wet and my nose had begun to run. Angrily, I swiped at my eyes with my sleeve.

"Fine," I said curtly. "Can we go?"

In answer, Blane stood and helped me to my feet. I shrugged off his coat and handed it back to him. We headed to the car and I crossed my arms over my chest. The sunlight was fading and the wind had picked up. After we'd gotten in the car, Blane turned up the heat.

"Don't you ever wear a coat?" he asked.

I grimaced. I hated wearing coats. Usually, I wore layers and sweaters until there was snow on the ground. Only then did I concede to winter and wore a coat.

"Not usually," I answered. It wasn't until we were halfway there that I realized we weren't going back to the firm, but were headed to my apartment.

"Why are you taking me home?"

"You've had a shock," Blane said matter-of-factly. "You're taking the rest of the day off. You need to rest."

I opened my mouth to protest, but a glance from him made me close it. It was nearly five anyway. It wasn't worth arguing about.

We pulled into my parking lot as dusk was falling. I turned toward Blane to thank him, but he was already getting out of the car. In a moment, he was helping me out of the car. We climbed the stairs in silence. I hated to admit it, but he was right. I felt shell-shocked.

Pulling my keys from my purse, I went to unlock the door to my apartment and froze. It wasn't locked. Blane, standing behind me, noticed something was wrong.

"What is it?" he asked.

I turned toward him, my eyes wide. "I always lock my door," I said.

Understanding dawned immediately in his eyes and he abruptly pulled me away from the door, pushing me behind him. Reaching for his back, he pulled out his gun. I blanched. I hadn't seen that.

"Stay here," he ordered.

I nodded obediently, but I was thinking, *Fat chance, buddy.* Tigger was in there.

Quickly pushing open the door, Blane took a glance inside. If anyone was waiting on the other side, they didn't show themselves. Carefully stepping into the apartment, he held the gun out in front of him. He disappeared from my view and I counted to ten—okay, five—before following him. The scene that met my eyes made me gasp.

My apartment had been thoroughly trashed. I couldn't believe what I was seeing. My couch was flipped over, the cushions shredded. The glass of my television screen had been smashed. The few potted plants I'd managed to not yet kill had been dumped on my carpet.

I could see into the kitchen, and the refrigerator door was standing wide open, its meager contents dumped out on the linoleum. Dishes and glasses lay in broken shards on the floor.

As I stood in shock and dismay, Blane came back into view from my bedroom, tucking the gun back in his waistband. His face was grim.

"Did you find Tigger?" I asked frantically. I knew I absolutely could not handle it if something had happened to him.

Blane shook his head. "No. We can keep looking, though."

But I knew that he thought Tigger was probably dead or gone, and Blane's image blurred as my eyes filled with tears.

145

Carefully stepping over the broken glass, I stood in the doorway of my bedroom. My clothes had been pulled out of the closet and lay in disarray on the floor. I could see they'd been torn. Unable to stomach any more, I turned away.

A knock from the living room made us both spin around. My new neighbor, CJ, was standing there. Her mouth was shaped in an O as she peered around, wide-eyed. But I didn't notice that so much as what she was holding.

"Tigger!" I shrieked, stumbling forward to take him. Thank God. Tears leaked from my eyes as I felt his familiar rumbling purr. I looked at CJ.

"Thank you so much," I said. "How did you find him?"

"He was wandering around outside," she answered. "I thought he might be yours." She paused. "So, what the hell happened in here?"

"Did you see or hear anything unusual today?" Blane asked.

CJ shook her head. "Nah. I work at night, so I sleep during the day. Didn't hear a thing. Sorry."

I was disappointed, but at least I had Tigger back. "Well, thank you so much for taking care of my cat," I said gratefully.

"No problem. Catch you later."

After she left, I looked around and sighed. What had already been a long day was promising to be an even longer night. And I didn't even want to think about how I was going to replace all of my things. I didn't have any renter's insurance.

"Come on," Blane said, picking his way through the living room to the door.

I frowned in confusion. "What do you mean?" I asked. "I can't leave. I need to call the cops and start cleaning this mess up."

"No, you're not," he said curtly. "We'll call the cops from my place. You're staying there tonight."

That was such a bad idea. Tempting, in that way that makes you know you'll love every minute and hate yourself in the morning, but still a bad idea.

"I don't think so," I stated firmly. "I can go stay with Clarice or something."

Blane's jaw set and I grew wary.

"You can come willingly or unwillingly," he threatened. "But like it or not, you're coming with me." The look on his face made me think he wasn't bluffing.

Somehow I knew that if I went with him, there would be no turning back, a line in the sand would have been crossed. But despite that inner voice shouting at me, telling me going with Blane would be much more dangerous to my well-being than staying here, I gave in and followed him out my apartment door.

CHAPTER SEVEN

I held Tigger in my arms as Blane drove. I felt numb. Mark had been murdered, and it appeared I might be next on the list. I held Tigger closer to me. Suddenly, he seemed like all I had.

The car stopped, Blane turned off the engine, and I looked around curiously. Not having paid attention to where we were driving, I hadn't realized we had arrived. Glancing out the window, I found myself gaping.

We were stopped in a circular driveway, and my side faced the house. And what a house it was—a gorgeous two-story colonial-style house with huge pillars in front. A long sidewalk led to the enormous front door, and discreetly placed floodlights lit the house at strategic spots. The lights were on inside, on the bottom floor, and I wondered if Blane lived with other family members. Or a new girlfriend.

I was so caught up staring wonderingly at the house that Blane was already at my door before I even knew he'd gotten out. I gripped Tigger tightly as I stepped out of the car and turned to the pathway. Blane reached over, lifting my purse strap off my shoulder and carrying it by his fingers. His other hand settled on the small of my back as he guided me up the walk.

Even in the deepening twilight shadows, I could see the grounds were spacious and landscaped. We passed carefully tended shrubs, and although the yard was full of trees, I didn't see more than a handful of stray leaves on the ground. And those seemed to be an almost artistic touch rather than normal autumn debris. As we neared the door, it opened and I paused, hesitant.

"It's all right," Blane said reassuringly. "It's just Mona, my housekeeper."

Sure enough, a woman stepped into the doorway, smiling widely. She was a bit taller than me and appeared to be in her late fifties or early sixties. Her hair was a shiny silver-gray and styled in a sleek bob. Her clothes were very nice and conservative, yet still practical. For some reason, she reminded me of a piano teacher.

"Good evening, Blane," she said, as we neared and passed by her into the house. She shut the door and turned to us, her eyes resting expectantly on Blane.

"Good evening, Mona," Blane said. "This is Kathleen Turner. She works at the firm. Someone broke into her apartment, so she and her cat are staying here."

Mona frowned. I smiled nervously, hoping Mona didn't think I was one of Blane's flavors-of-the-month.

"I'm so sorry to hear that, dear," she said, and her eyes were kind.

I let out the breath I'd been holding. She glanced down at Tigger, clutched in my arms. "Of course you're welcome here. What is your cat's name?"

"Tigger," I answered. "His name is Tigger." Said cat was still snoozing, his purring so loud it was almost embarrassing.

Mona reached over to scratch Tigger's ears, which made him purr louder.

"Perhaps Tigger would like some dinner?" she asked, and I nodded. She reached for him, and as I handed over my precious orange lump of pampered feline, Blane spoke to Mona.

"Where's Gerard?" he asked.

"Oh, he's upstairs," she said casually. "One of the bathrooms has a leaky faucet." Tigger seemed content in Mona's arms as she stroked his fur. "It'll be good to have a cat around here again," she said.

My eyes widened a bit. This was just for tonight. I opened my mouth to correct her, but she kept talking. "My own cat, Morris, died a few years ago. We still have his litter box and things. You won't mind, will you, Tigger?" she said to the oblivious cat.

Well, crap. Now I didn't have the heart to tell her we weren't staying long.

"Will you let him know that I'm in for the evening?" Blane said.

"Of course," Mona replied. "Let me get Tigger settled and I'll get you two some dinner."

"I'm putting Kathleen in the Garden Room," Blane called after her as she walked away. "Is it suitable?"

Mona stopped abruptly, turning around to look at Blane, and her face registered surprise before she masked it. "Quite" was all she said before resuming her path to the kitchen.

I tried not to gape like a complete hick as I cast furtive glances around the foyer. The whole house had beautiful wood floors with rugs tossed lavishly throughout. A grand staircase, straight out of *Gone with the Wind*, led to the upper floor. Off to my right on the main level was a grand piano under a chandelier, and an archway leading to yet another room. To my left was an identical towering arch that led to a dining room with a dark mahogany table that easily seated twelve.

"This way," Blane said, taking my elbow. My arms suddenly felt bereft without Tigger.

"Mona and her husband Gerard take care of the house and grounds," Blane explained as we climbed the stairs. "They live in a house that adjoins the property. They decided to come with us when we moved here from back East when I was a child."

"How long have they worked for you?" I asked.

"As long as I can remember," Blane answered. "Mona was also my nanny when I was a child."

He'd had a nanny. I'd had after-school specials on the television. I was yet again reminded of the vast differences between Blane's station in life and my own.

The upstairs was just as awe-inspiring as the downstairs. A long Persian runner lay on the floor of the hallway and I nearly couldn't bring myself to walk on it, it was so pretty. Blane walked to the end of the hallway and opened a door, pulling me inside. He flipped on the lights and I stared in awe once again.

Now I understood why he'd called it the Garden Room. All four walls featured a magnificent continuous mural. Impressionist painters had always been a favorite of mine and I recognized Monet's garden at Giverny. Even the bed linen fit the theme. The overall effect was that you were standing in the middle of a beautiful sun-dappled garden with lavender flowers and a pond with water lilies.

"Do you like it?" Blane asked.

"It's . . . amazing," I said wonderingly.

"My mother was an artist. She decorated each of the bedrooms in a different style. This room she painted herself."

I turned to Blane. "Your mother painted this?" I said, amazed.

He smiled, nodding. "She was quite talented," he replied, and I thought I detected a hint of pride in his voice. He gestured to a doorway in the far corner.

"There's a bathroom through there," he said. "In case you want to freshen up before dinner." His kindness suddenly hit me and I was humbled by it.

"Blane," I began, "I don't know how to thank—" but I was cut off when he placed a finger on my lips.

"Don't thank me yet," he said, and his voice had taken on an edge that made me wary. "When it comes to you, my motives aren't exactly"—he paused, his eyes skimming down my body and back up—"altruistic."

My mouth went dry.

"I'll be back to get you shortly," he said, pulling the door closed as he left.

I sank down onto the bed and nearly groaned. The beautiful quilt was soft and luxurious, the mattress perfect—not too soft and not too hard. I felt a bit like Goldilocks and I couldn't resist scooting back and lying down. A sigh escaped me as my head hit the down pillow. Blane hadn't said how long he'd be and I thought maybe I could rest for just a few minutes.

When I opened my eyes, I knew instantly that it had been more than a few minutes. The room was cloaked in the deep shadows of night and someone had covered me with a blanket. I rubbed my eyes, then glanced at my watch. It was after midnight. I'd slept for over six hours. Some guest I was, I thought with chagrin. I'd slept through dinner and hadn't even gone to see about Tigger.

Speaking of dinner, I realized I was starving. And sleeping in my clothes, which I hated doing. The house was pretty big, maybe it wouldn't disturb anyone if I snuck down to the kitchen and got a snack. I had no idea how many people lived here with Blane.

Swinging my legs out of bed, I realized someone had removed my shoes as well. I tried not to think about who that might have been as I searched for them in the dark. I couldn't find them. Oh well. Less dirt to get on the Persian rug.

A quick stop in a bathroom, no less luxurious and as pretty as the bedroom, to brush my teeth and splash some water on my face and I was ready to go.

The house was like a well-oiled machine—no doors squeaked when opened and no floorboards creaked under my footsteps. It was dark, but there was enough ambient light for me to see. I crept down the stairs and through the dining room to where I thought the kitchen might be. Jackpot! And, like every other kitchen I'd ever been in, a small light had been left on.

A huge stainless-steel refrigerator stood in the corner and I went right to it, my stomach grumbling along the way, as if sensing food was near. I pulled open the door to survey the contents and was somewhat disappointed with what I saw. It was a very healthy refrigerator, with lots of vegetables, cheese, yogurt, and eggs. I wondered if I should dare to try and make eggs, but then decided that would be too much trouble.

I opened the freezer and peered inside, grinning in delight at what I saw. As luck would have it, and I'd had precious little luck lately, a pint of rocky road sat on the shelf, just waiting for me. Without thinking twice, I grabbed it, fished a spoon out of a nearby drawer, plunked myself down in a chair at the small kitchen table, and dug in.

My eyes closed in pleasure as the first bite of chocolatey gooeyness hit my tongue, and I sighed. I ate slowly, savoring each spoonful. This was turning out to be the best part of my rotten day. My thoughts turned to Mark and I felt embarrassed and guilty at my own self-pity. He'd certainly had a much worse day than I'd had.

I thought about the things he had told me yesterday. Something kept niggling at the back of my mind, but I couldn't put my finger on it. Trying to focus on what was bothering me made it more elusive and finally I gave up. With a jolt, I remembered that he'd given me his backpack. I'd forgotten about it after everything that had happened today. Now I was thankful that I'd left it in the trunk of my car and not in my apartment. My car was still at the firm, so I figured it should be safe.

"I see you woke up," Blane said, and I nearly choked on my ice cream.

He moved into my field of vision and leaned against the granite counter in his favorite pose, arms and ankles crossed as he surveyed me. My hand automatically reached up to smooth my hair and then I self-consciously jerked it back down. The last thing I wanted was him thinking I was preening for him, though I knew his eyes had missed nothing.

"Ice cream?" he asked, gesturing to the nearly empty container.

"Sorry," I said sheepishly. "I've eaten nearly all of it." I'd considered getting a bowl, but realistically had known I would probably finish the whole pint.

It was dark, but I thought I saw his lips twitch slightly.

"It was rocky road," I elaborated, as if that explained everything.

"Rocky road," he repeated.

I took another mouthful, swallowing before I spoke again.

"Chocolate-covered nuts wrapped in marshmallowy goodness in chocolate ice cream. What's not to love?"

"Indeed."

I ate in silence for a few minutes. He surprised me by pulling out a chair and sitting opposite me. The loaded spoonful I'd taken stuck in my throat and I swallowed heavily. Feeling the need to fill the silence, I started talking.

"You have a really beautiful home," I said. "Do you live alone?" I wondered where his parents were or if they were no longer around.

"Thank you," he replied. "And yes, I live alone."

I scooped up some more ice cream.

"Your brother?" I asked, but he shook his head. "Your . . . parents?" I said hesitantly, and left the rest of the question unasked. He shook his head again.

"They're no longer with me."

I felt a twinge of sympathy for Blane and thought, ruefully, that we finally had something in common. I, too, was without my parents.

"Do you know why anyone would have done that to your apartment?" Blane asked.

I attempted to ignore the emotion that surged inside me at the mention of my apartment and tried to think. It occurred to me then that the only new thing in my possession was Mark's backpack, but considering how easily Blane had taken Sheila's phone from me, I wasn't about to tell him about it.

"No, I don't," I answered. "I don't really have any enemies here and I don't own anything of any real value." I thought of Diane but dismissed her. She wasn't the type to do something like that, even disliking me as much as she did.

"Maybe someone with a vendetta," Blane persisted. "A jilted lover?"

My cheeks flamed in the dark and it seemed the tension in the room notched upward at his words. I cleared my throat before answering.

"Um . . . no, that couldn't be, I mean, there's not . . . just . . . no." I winced at my stammering explanation, really not wanting to go into details that my last "lover," if you could even call him that, had been years ago and I was quite sure he was not carrying a torch for me.

Blane didn't say anything to that and I busied myself licking the spoon clean.

Blane took the empty container and spoon from me, tossing the container away before putting my spoon in the sink. I faced Blane awkwardly, unsure of what to do next. He didn't help matters, merely watching me as I made to move past him.

"Well, good night," I said, but his hand closed on my arm.

"I'll walk you back upstairs," he said. "It's dark and I don't want you to trip and fall."

I could feel my skin tingling where his fingers touched me. I swallowed and allowed him to lead me from the kitchen.

"I'm sorry I fell asleep and missed dinner," I said as we walked. "That was rude of me."

"You were tired," he responded in an emotionless voice. I couldn't tell if he was upset or couldn't care less. He was so difficult to read, it was frustrating. His thoughts and emotions always seemed to be kept very carefully under wraps, whereas I felt like I was an open book.

The house seemed darker now, perhaps because I'd been in the brighter kitchen, and I was glad Blane was guiding me. We walked up the stairs and to my bedroom door.

"Mona put some clothes for you in the bureau and closet," Blane said. "They should fit well enough until your apartment is back together."

At his words, I felt my eyes sting with tears, and this time I didn't have the strength to fight it. I'd been unwilling to deal with the feelings of violation and fear that filled me when I thought about what had happened. Now that came rushing in and I fought to maintain control. I didn't want to cry in front of Blane. He'd leave in a minute and I could have my emotional breakdown in privacy.

"Thank you," I squeezed past my throat thickened with tears, blinking my eyes rapidly to press them back.

"I'm sorry," he said quietly, sensing my distress. His hand came up to touch my cheek, his thumb lightly brushing my skin.

"It's all right," I managed, fighting the urge to tilt my head toward his hand and the comfort he offered.

"It's not all right," he said fiercely, and my eyes widened in surprise at his tone. "You need someone to take care of you."

Those words shocked the hell out of me and also ignited my independent streak. I drew back from him and his arm fell to his side.

"I don't need anyone to take care of me," I said stiffly. "I can take care of myself." Blane's eyes narrowed and I instinctively stepped back farther.

"Because you're doing such a great job?" he said wryly. I ignored his words. A small, frightened part of me thought he might be right, but I refused to acknowledge it. It wasn't like he was volunteering for the job. That thought took the heat from my anger and depressed me. I was alone, whether I liked it or not.

I didn't have anything more to say and didn't want to hear anything he might say, so I warily slipped past him into the room. He allowed me to pass, his eyes intent on mine as I closed the door. After a moment, I heard his footsteps moving down the hall and I breathed a quiet sigh of relief.

I decided I would feel and sleep better if I showered, so after a quick examination of the drawers and closets, I turned up a few underthings and a T-shirt that would work for me. The choice of panties made me blush. I didn't want to think about whose they were or why Blane had them in his house when he'd said he lived alone. I grabbed the one plain white satin pair I found and headed into the bathroom.

I took my time in the shower, enjoying the fantastic water pressure, and felt a bit better when I was through. I managed to find a brush, and worked the tangles from my wet hair. Pulling on the T-shirt and underwear, I slipped under the covers and pulled the quilt up to my chin.

However, I couldn't sleep. The long nap assured that my mind was now running in circles, refusing to let me sink into peaceful oblivion. I thought about Mark and Sheila and the horrible ways in which each had died. I thought of the things Mark had told me and I wondered if I was the next target. I had no doubt that the murders were linked. It was too much of a coincidence for them not to be. I thought about my apartment, all my possessions in the world, now broken or destroyed. This time I didn't bother trying to stop the tears from sliding down my cheeks. It surprised me that I felt not only fear, but also an overwhelming anger.

Allowing myself to wallow a bit in self-pity, I turned my face into the pillow to muffle my sobs. I had no idea how I was going to recover from what had been done to my belongings. I didn't have enough savings to replace everything.

I suddenly felt arms slide underneath me and I was lifted upward. I didn't resist. I knew who it was and I couldn't make myself deny him. Blane lifted me onto his lap, just as he had the night Sheila died. I curled into him, burying my face against his shoulder as I cried. His arms wrapped around me, his hand stroking my damp hair.

We stayed like that for a long while and I could hear him speaking quietly as he tried to soothe me. Over my ragged breathing, I could barely make out his words.

"Shh, it's all right," he was murmuring. "Don't worry. I'll take care of you."

I couldn't say precisely what effect those words had on me, but the tightness in my chest eased somewhat, my earlier bravado gone. My tears were waning now and Blane's fingers lifted my chin so I was looking at him. I knew I must look horrible after the crying jag and I was glad for the room's darkness. His eyes glittered and I found myself unable to look away. A thumb brushed my cheek as he wiped the tracks of my tears, and I felt my resolve crumble.

Stretching upward, I settled my lips on his and wrapped my arms around his neck. He momentarily stiffened in surprise and I wondered if I'd presumed too much. That thought was driven from my mind when he clutched me to him, his mouth greedily devouring mine. His desire for me was a heady thing and I reveled in it, opening my lips so he could deepen our kiss. Throwing caution and inhibitions to the wind, I shifted, wrapping my legs around him and resettling myself on his lap. His erection pressed against me and he groaned as his fingers tangled in my hair.

My hands worked feverishly at the buttons on his shirt and I sighed in pleasure when I finally reached the warm skin of his chest. I pushed the shirt over his shoulders and down his arms and he jerked his hands free. His hands slipped under my shirt to settle on my waist, digging into my skin as he gripped me tightly.

My brain turned off as my hormones kicked into high gear. It had been a long time since the backseat of Donny Lester's car. I had never felt as much charged sexual tension as I did with Blane. I couldn't stop touching him. My fingers traced the contours of his chest and shoulders. Blane was warm and gloriously hard all over. His hand came up to cradle the curve of my cheek as he kissed me.

Pressing closer to him, I ached for him to touch me. His hand returned to grip my waist and I whimpered, hoping he'd move his hands upward. Finally, impatient and wanting more, I reached for the hem of my shirt and dragged it up over my head. Barely had the fabric fallen from my fingers than Blane's hands were on my breasts. I gasped at the sensation, my head falling backward as my body seemed to hum with pleasure and anticipation. I wanted Blane with a desperation that would have frightened me if I'd been in any condition to think clearly. Blindly, I reached downward, finding Blane's belt and tugging on its fastenings.

I suddenly found my wrist caught in an iron grip. Blane's other hand gripped my waist, pushing slightly and putting a few inches of space between our skin. Confused, I looked up at him. He was breathing as heavily as I was, his lips glistening in the dark from our kisses. The look in his eyes made the throbbing between my legs intensify and I settled myself more firmly against the hard length of him beneath me.

"Stop," he bit out through clenched teeth, his fingers almost painful against my skin. I froze, uncomprehending. Why would he want me to stop? Unsure what to do, I leaned forward, my breasts resting against his chest as I pressed my lips against his jaw.

"I said stop," he commanded, putting both hands on my waist and pushing me backward onto the bed and off his lap entirely. Following me, he pinned my arms above my head, immobilizing me. My legs instinctively parted as he crouched between them. I was completely confused, and yet acutely aware of him. Everywhere his skin touched mine, I burned.

"Make love to me," I begged, unable to stop the words tumbling from my mouth, a thread of need in the dark night. All the defenses I'd put in place against Blane, all the warnings about getting involved with him, were tossed aside. Suddenly, I needed nothing as urgently and as desperately as I needed him.

His eyes were locked with mine and I couldn't fathom their depths. The clenching of his jaw and the tightening of his fingers around my wrists were his only reaction. I was about to repeat myself, shamelessly beg him again, when he spoke.

"I . . . can't," he finally said. "I won't." Shock and dismay warred in me. I didn't know what to do or say. Although I'd never baldly asked a man to make love to me before, the idea of Blane turning me down would never have crossed my mind. But it seemed he was.

"What? Why?" I managed to gasp. His hands moved down my arms from my wrists and I bit back a moan as the calluses on his fingers brushed my skin. Although his mouth was telling me no, his hands seemed to have trouble obeying the command and I felt flames lick at me again as he caressed me.

"You're beautiful, Kat. Perfect," he said. I focused on the fact he'd said I was beautiful and barely registered the nickname, my mind preoccupied with the journey his hands were taking to my hips. "And I thought I could, but I can't. You're too young and innocent and I'm not going to do that to you."

I felt my face heat as I realized Blane must think I was a virgin. Apparently, I'd been wrong in assuming seduction was instinctual if my woeful lack of experience was so readily apparent to him. Images of the many beautiful, sophisticated women I'd seen with him flashed through my mind and I wanted to cringe. I almost blurted out that I wasn't innocent, but sensed this was going nowhere fast. If I wanted to salvage any of my self-respect, I had to end this quickly. My resolve didn't make it to my mouth though, because I heard myself say, "You're Blane Kirk. Since when do you care?" I could hear the bitterness, and to my humiliation, jealousy in my voice.

"Usually, I don't," he replied in the cold, hard voice. His fingers bit into my waist and my breath froze in my chest as I felt his fingers hook the thin straps across my hips and pull them taut. For a moment, I rejoiced, thinking I had won after all. It would only take a sharp tug from him and the fragile fabric would tear.

"I doubt you're on any sort of birth control either, are you?" he asked, in the same hard tone. His cold practicality was like a slap in the face and I felt my own naïveté as a physical pain. I couldn't speak.

He cursed viciously and sat abruptly back, releasing me. Before I could do or say anything, he'd grabbed his shirt and tucked it across me, covering my bare chest and stomach. His mouth was again on mine, brutal in his intensity, and I tasted the sharp tang of blood as my teeth cut the inside of my lip. Then he was gone, slamming the door shut behind him.

I didn't think I'd ever been so humiliated in my life. I didn't sleep around, so putting myself in this vulnerable position with Blane was a first for me. And considering how I'd been rejected, I doubted I'd be repeating the experience anytime soon.

Too stricken to put my clothes back on, I crawled back under the covers, clutching Blane's shirt to me. I refused to cry over Blane—my pride wouldn't let me—and eventually I fell into a fitful sleep. My dreams were filled with images of Blane, always just out of my reach, a stony expression on his face, devoid of emotion.

~

I was awakened by the sunlight streaming through the windows and realized someone was in the room, opening the blinds. Sitting up abruptly, I realized I was still naked and clutched the quilt to my chest. Mona was in the room and she turned at my movement, a warm smile on her face.

"Good morning, dear," she said. If she was surprised to see me half-naked in bed, Blane's shirt peeking out of the covers beside me, she didn't show it. "Blane has left for work, but he had Gerard bring your car by this morning for you. I brought some breakfast." She gestured to a tray on the nearby bureau. "I wasn't sure what you preferred, so I hope you don't mind I brought a bit of everything."

I finally found my tongue. "Thank you," I said, shoving a hand roughly through my tangled hair, pushing it away from my face. "I appreciate that." I really did. I couldn't remember the last time someone had fixed me breakfast. It had been years. Mona moved to the door, and before she could close it, I asked, "Wait, can you tell me what time it is?"

"Of course, dear," she said. "It's a bit after nine o'clock." The door closed. Dismay filled me and I leapt out of bed. I was so late for work. Diane was going to have my head on a platter.

I showered and dried my hair in record time. Scrambling through the closet, I found a pair of sleek black pants that fit me perfectly and a teal sweater that I was afraid might be real cashmere. I had no choice, really, since my clothes were nowhere to be found.

There was no makeup in the bathroom and I grimaced at my reflection. My lower lip was a bit swollen from where it had been cut when Blane kissed me. The memory of last night simultaneously made me shiver with longing and blush in embarrassment. I was grateful to whatever gods there were that Blane was gone this morning and I could put off having to face him.

I regretted not being able to enjoy a real breakfast in bed. Mona had made eggs and bacon, and I looked longingly at them. There was also a basket of muffins, Danish, and bagels. Juice and coffee sat next to the tray and I gulped down a cup of coffee, not taking time to put cream or sugar in it, and grabbed half a bagel. Then I was out the door and downstairs.

Mona met me at the bottom of the stairs, carrying a long black coat and my purse. "Here you are," she said, handing them to me.

"That's not my coat," I said, taking my purse from her.

"Oh yes, I know," she said, laying it across my shoulders and holding it expectantly.

"Blane mentioned you didn't have your coat with you yesterday, so you can wear this," she explained. "It's much too cold to be without a coat today." Not knowing how to refuse her without looking churlish, I pushed my arms into the sleeves.

My lips thinned. Blane's whispered words came back to me from last night. "I'll take care of you." This had to stop. I couldn't get more attached, or more dependent, on Blane. I had to get out of here.

"Thank you so much, Mona," I said. "Will you keep Tigger a little longer for me until I can get my apartment sorted out?" I didn't want to leave Tigger in my apartment alone during the day. He'd been lucky yesterday and I didn't want to chance something happening to him, even though it seemed he really did have nine lives.

"We'll be glad to," Mona said. "Don't worry about him. He's settled in nicely."

With a last smile at her, I headed for the door. She followed me, saying just before I walked out, "Did you like your room?"

Bemused, I stopped. The way she'd said it was strange, like my answer was portentous or something.

"It's lovely," I said truthfully. "I've never seen anything like it."

She smiled even wider. "It is, isn't it? It's a shame so few people are allowed to see it. That room was such a particular favorite of his mother's. And Blane's."

Our eyes met briefly before I looked away. I didn't want to hear any more. Scrambling for the keys in my purse, I walked down the path to my car, waiting in the circular drive. I climbed in, and with one last look at the beautiful home, even more breathtaking in the morning sunshine, drove away.

It was after ten when I finally made it to the office. I glanced around nervously as I hurried inside, hoping to avoid Diane. It might just be possible to sneak to my cube without being seen.

My plan seemed to be working when I scuttled past Diane's empty office and I breathed a sigh of relief. That relief turned to dismay when I rounded the corner into my cube and nearly ran into her. She took in my appearance in a quick glance, her eyes lingering on the expensive sweater and my swollen lips.

"Diane," I began, "I'm really sorry I'm late—"

"I was just cleaning out your things," she said frostily, shoving a small box into my arms. It held my coffee cup, a framed picture of my parents, and a few odds and ends. I stared at her, mouth agape.

"Wh-what do you mean?" I stammered as my heart sank. I thought I knew what she meant.

"You're fired, Kathleen," she said simply. "Don't make me call security."

"But I was just late this once!" I protested. And it was true. Mostly. I didn't really count the occasional five or ten minutes, especially when I worked past closing so often.

"It's not just that," she hissed. "You're white trash and have no business being here." Her eyes looked over me again and her lip curled in distaste. "God knows what he sees in you." I felt myself pale under her haughty inspection.

Drawing myself up, I refused to be cowed by her. "I don't know what you're talking about," I said stiffly. Then I remembered—James! Surely he would take my side and help me keep my job. I couldn't bring myself to even think of Blane. Somehow, invoking Blane when Diane thought I was sleeping with him felt beneath me, even if I wasn't actually sleeping with him.

"James may have something to say about this," I threatened, hoping it was true.

"James is the one who told me to do it," she said, smiling thinly now. "After I told him I'd seen you leaving with Blane yesterday in the middle of the afternoon, he agreed with me that we don't need . . . distractions . . . like you around here." She managed to convey a world of loathing into her words.

Inside, I was dismayed. I couldn't believe James could be so vindictive. We'd only had one date. Then I remembered how he'd reacted when he'd thought Blane and I were together and my hopes crumbled.

We'd gathered an audience by now and I refused to show how shaken I was. With as much dignity as I could muster, I turned and walked away and out the doors. It wasn't until I reached the safety of my car that I allowed myself to succumb to fear of what I was going to do now, embarrassment at the scene with Diane, and anger over the unfairness of it all. Somehow I managed to get the key in the ignition, and I drove away from the firm.

I reached my apartment and turned off the car, struck by what I saw. A huge truck had backed up to my building, and two men were carrying my ruined sofa down the stairs. Jumping out of the car, I ran over to them.

"Hey, what are you doing?" I asked in alarm. "What's going on?"

They ignored me as a third man came up, clipboard in hand. "Are you Kathleen Turner?" he asked.

"Yes," I answered. "Why are those men taking my sofa?" By now they'd shoved it in the back of their truck. Peering in, I could see the rest of my ruined furniture as well.

"We were told to take the old things when we delivered the new," the man with the clipboard said.

"That's all of it," one of the guys called out to him, and he nodded.

"We'll be going then," he said, turning back to me. "The locksmith is still upstairs. He'll give you the new key. Have a good day." He was already climbing in the truck's cab.

"Wait!" I called out to him, but he either ignored me or couldn't hear me over the truck's engine rumbling to life. In a few moments, they were gone, my furniture with them.

Aghast, I ran up the stairs, and sure enough, there was another stranger working on the locks on my door. The back of his shirt said Ted's Lock and Key.

"What are you doing?" I asked, panic now wearing on my nerves at the strangers invading my apartment.

He glanced over his shoulder at me. "Just installing a new deadbolt," he said. "You the resident?"

"Yes."

"Well, I'm almost done and I'll be out of your way."

"But," I stammered, "who told you to do this?"

He shrugged. "Don't know. Call comes in, I get sent out. Didn't take the order. Just told to install a new lock." With that, he put his tools away, closed and reopened the door to check the fitting, and stood.

"Here's the new key," he said, dropping a pair of keys in my hand. "Have a good day now."

Still in shock, I watched him walk down the stairs. A noise made me turn my head and I saw that CJ had opened her door and was leaning against the jamb. She was wearing all black again and I could see she had an eyebrow pierced with a silver hoop.

"They gone?" she asked.

"Yeah." I assumed she meant the truck guys.

"Finally," she said, heaving a sigh. "I couldn't sleep with all the noise they were making."

"When did they come?" I asked, and she glanced at a watch on her wrist.

"About an hour ago, but people have been coming and going since you left last night."

"What?" I was alarmed. I hadn't told anyone what had happened to my place. "Who came and went?"

"I don't know who they were," she said, shrugging. "I thought you'd gotten someone to come clean the place up." She paused. "Your boyfriend was here this morning. I assumed you knew."

My mind was reeling. "What boyfriend?" I asked, though I could guess what she was going to say before she said it.

"That guy you were with last night," she answered. "Isn't he your boyfriend?"

Blane.

I closed my eyes, shaking my head. "No. He's not my boyfriend." I had a sinking feeling I knew what he'd done. With hands that shook slightly, I eased open my apartment door. Stepping inside, I froze in astonishment.

You would never have guessed what had happened here the day before judging by how it looked now. The apartment had been completely cleaned up. The food on the floor, broken glass, dirt from the plants, everything was spotless. My torn furniture had not only been removed, it had been replaced. A matching leather sofa and loveseat filled the living room, both a deep burgundy. A new flat-screen television hung on the wall. The carpet was pristine, as if it had been steam-cleaned.

I walked through to the kitchen almost as if I were in a trance. Opening the cabinets, I saw that the dishes had been replaced as well. And not by the cheap stuff I'd gotten at Walmart. Nice, heavy dishes with a pretty pattern were neatly stacked on the shelves. Opening the refrigerator, I saw that it had been restocked, with more food than I think I'd ever had in it.

Not even the bathroom had been neglected. What had remained of my torn shower curtain had been replaced with a different one. Matching towels hung on the rack; even new shampoo and conditioner bottles sat on a shelf in the shower.

My bedroom was what finally broke me. The ruined quilt on the bed had been replaced with one nearly identical to the one on the bed in which I'd slept last night, shattering all doubt about who had orchestrated this. The empty rods from which my curtains had been torn had been refitted with matching drapes. Opening my closet, I saw that an entire new wardrobe had been purchased and carefully sorted into pants, skirts, and blouses, casual and formal.

Sinking down to the floor, I curled my arms around my legs and laid my head on my knees. It was too much. Overwhelming. I couldn't begin to process what I was feeling. Blane had taken out of my hands the choice of either accepting or rejecting his assistance. His assumptions and high-handedness angered me. I'd been taking care of myself for years. I didn't suddenly need him to do it for me.

However, I wasn't stupid enough to not be fervently grateful for his thoughtfulness and generosity.

What had me in knots, what confused me utterly and left me unable to process what to do next, was the why of it. Two days ago, I would have assumed Blane expected me to sleep with him in return for doing something like this. Now . . . well, judging by last night, that obviously was not the case. His contradictory actions baffled me. He'd said he would take care of me, but he wouldn't have sex with me. It didn't make any sense. A man like Blane didn't do things just for the sake of doing them, there had to be something in it for him. I just couldn't fathom what it was.

Well, regardless of his motives, I had a call to make. Gathering myself, I got off the floor and found my phone, also new and one of those high-end brand-name cordless kinds. I dialed the firm, asking for Clarice's extension.

"Blane Kirk's office," she answered.

"Hi, Clarice," I said. "It's Kathleen."

"Kathleen!" she exclaimed. "Oh my God, Kathleen, what happened? It's all over the building!"

"What's all over the building?"

"That you're having an affair with Blane, and James was jealous, so he had Diane fire you," she hissed into the phone, trying to be quiet, it seemed.

I winced in embarrassment. Sheesh. Word traveled fast.

"I am not having an affair with Blane," I said firmly, though the little voice in the back of my head reminded me that I would be if Blane hadn't stopped last night.

"You're not?" She sounded disappointed and I wanted to groan in exasperation.

"No, I'm not," I repeated, and she sighed.

"Well, damn. What are you going to do now?" she asked.

"I don't know," I answered, reminded that now I needed to look for another job. Obviously, I wouldn't be able to put down the firm as a reference, and that would make it more difficult. I absently rubbed the back of my neck, stress and tension getting to me.

"I'm sorry, Kathleen," Clarice said. "The way Blane reacted when he heard . . . I just thought the rumors were true."

My pulse sped up at that.

"What did . . . how did he react?" I asked, hating the fact that I was dying to know.

"Oh, he got into it big time with James, I thought they were going to come to blows and James looked ready to pee his pants, but then he left. I think he had a court appointment or something. He seemed in a big hurry."

Something flashed in my mind as I spoke with Clarice, and my breath caught. TecSol. The company where Mark had worked. He'd been afraid of them. Now I remembered where I'd heard that company name before. Well, read it, actually. The night I'd helped Clarice finish her work. The brief I had typed up and Blane had delivered to the Santini brothers had concerned TecSol. But for the life of me I could not remember the details in the brief.

I froze at the knock on my door.

CHAPTER EIGHT

"Clarice," I said into the phone, "I've got to go. I'll call you later." I hung up over her protests. My palms were sweaty. I thought for sure it was Blane at my door, and my feelings were divided on whether or not I wanted to see him. I didn't think I was ready to face him after last night.

The knock came again and I hurried to the door, pausing to take a deep breath and brace myself and my emotions. He'd made it perfectly clear last night that while he had a weird protective thing going on with me, that's as far as he would take it, regardless of the physical attraction between us. I wondered if I could keep my thoughts from painting themselves on my face. Embarrassment warred with gratitude and I didn't know what I was going to say to Blane.

When I opened the door, I was surprised to find James standing there. I felt a stab of disappointment that it wasn't Blane, but then I recalled what Clarice had told me and was immediately wary. And angry. He was responsible for me losing my job. James may not need to worry about where his next meal was coming from, but I certainly did.

"What do you want?" I asked, my voice frosty. I didn't move from the doorway, blocking his entry.

The malice in James's smile sent a shiver down my spine. He moved closer but I stood my ground, tipping my head back to look at him.

"Heard you lost your job today," he said, and I caught a whiff of alcohol on his breath.

"Thanks to you," I snapped.

"It's not good for business to have sluts parading around the office," he sneered. "Tell me, did he have to work to get between your legs, or were you panting after him like a bitch in heat?"

The blood left my face in a rush. I couldn't believe what he'd just said to me. In spite of myself, tears stung my eyes at his crudeness. Then anger came to my defense. My hand came up and slapped him hard across the cheek.

"Don't talk to me like that," I spat at him, fury and dismay making my voice shake.

In a flash, he struck me with his fist, landing a blow to the side of my face that slammed my head against the door and left me reeling in pain. Grabbing my hair, he yanked me toward him and I cried out in pain.

"Blane will be through with you within the month and he'll toss you aside like the used garbage you are," he hissed. "Then you'll be sorry you chose him over me. And I'll make sure you're very, very sorry."

Tears of pain stung my eyes as I struggled to remove his hand from my hair.

"Let her go." The voice startled both of us and James whipped around. CJ stood in front of her door, a gun in her hand. I nearly fainted with relief.

"Let her go," she repeated and I was glad to see her hand was steady as she pointed the gun at James.

James's lips curved in a frightening smile that seemed half-crazy. He shoved me aside and I fell hard against the doorframe, wincing as my shoulder took the brunt of it. I just managed to keep to my feet.

"No problem," he said, "I was through with her anyway."

We both watched him as he walked down the stairs, and didn't move until we heard his car pull out of the lot.

"Thanks," I managed to get out, and CJ hurried over to me.

"Let's get some ice on that," she said matter-of-factly, helping me into my apartment.

I was too stunned and in too much pain to resist as she pulled me inside. She helped me to the couch and went to my kitchen for the ice. When she came back, she handed me the bundle of ice wrapped in a dish towel and sat down beside me. Gingerly, I held it to my throbbing cheek.

"Who the hell was that guy?" she asked. I grimaced.

"A guy I used to work with," I answered. I was still reeling from the bizarre confrontation; I had trouble wrapping my mind around James's reaction. He'd acted like he'd caught me cheating on him. While I had been upset that he'd gotten me fired, I hadn't in a million years thought he'd hit me.

"What an asshole," she said with a disgusted snort. She looked around the apartment now with undisguised curiosity. "Looks like they did a pretty good job cleaning this place up."

"Yeah," I said noncommittally. I didn't want to think of Blane right now. Getting up from the couch, I went to the kitchen, tossing my makeshift ice pack into the sink. My head was pounding, so I swallowed two pain-relief capsules.

"Can I get you something to drink?" I called to CJ.

"Sure." Digging through the unknown contents of my refrigerator, I unearthed some kind of bottled tea beverage and poured her a glass. Instant tea from a bottle was kind of icky, in my opinion, but I guess a lot of people liked it.

"Thanks again for helping me out," I said, returning to the living room and handing her the glass. "I'm surprised you were up," I continued, sinking back down onto the couch. "Didn't you say you sleep during the day and work at night?"

CJ took a swig of the tea before answering. "Yeah, usually I wouldn't have heard, but I had trouble falling asleep."

"So what do you do for a living that you work at night?" I asked, curious. "And why do you have a gun?"

"I'm a computer programmer," she said, completely surprising me. "I work for a company in Japan, so I have to keep their hours. And I have a gun for protection, of course."

She said this last part like I was an idiot for even asking. And after the scene with James, I couldn't disagree.

"That's impressive," I said. And it really was. She seemed very young. "Why don't you move to Japan if you already have a job there?"

CJ shook her head. "No way. Have you seen some of the crazy shit they eat over there? No, thanks. I'm staying right here in the good ol' US of A." Reaching in the pocket of her black jacket, she pulled out a cigar.

"You mind?" she asked, and I grimaced. I hated cigarette and cigar smoke, though strangely, pipes didn't bother me. She caught my look and put the cigar away with a slight sigh.

"Aren't you a bit young to smoke cigars?" I asked. She just cocked an eyebrow at me.

"I've been programming computers since I was ten and on my own since I was sixteen. I figure if I want to smoke a cigar, I'm going to smoke a cigar."

Well, I couldn't argue with that and I had to admire her independent attitude.

"What do you do?" she asked, and I hesitated. In view of her obvious talents, my life seemed downright pathetic.

"Well, this morning I just got fired," I said reluctantly.

"That sucks," she said, sounding sympathetic.

"But I still have my night job, so I guess that's not too bad." Speaking of which, I'd better see if my Britney outfit was still in the car. I'd need the tips I'd hopefully get from showing some skin tonight.

"What do you do at night?"

"I'm a bartender at The Drop." I wondered if that was all I was destined to be, if my aspirations for an actual career had disintegrated.

"That's cool," she said, and it was a testament to her age that she seemed to actually think it was. "Well, I'm going to get some shut-eye," she said, getting to her feet and setting the now-empty glass down on a nearby table. "Nice talking to you."

I smiled at her and walked her to the door. "Same here. And thanks again."

"Don't mention it." With a cocky grin that made her seem far friendlier than she had appeared the first time I'd seen her, she retreated to her apartment. Heading downstairs, I retrieved my paper bag and Mark's backpack from the trunk of my car.

It felt like I was invading Mark's privacy by opening his backpack. It briefly crossed my mind that, since he was dead, he probably wouldn't mind. Embarrassed at my tactless thoughts, I pushed them aside and pulled out the contents.

There wasn't much in there. A few blank papers, a key chain with two keys on it, and a DVD. I turned the DVD over in my hands, studying it. I didn't have a computer, or a DVD player either.

Wait. I didn't *used* to have a DVD player. I hurried over to inspect the new television. Sure enough, there was a DVD slot down below the screen. Turning it on, I slid the DVD in and stood back so I could see the picture fully.

My breath caught as Mark came on the screen. He was obviously filming himself, because I could see him fiddling with the camera. After he seemed satisfied, he moved back so the camera could capture his image. Then he began speaking.

"If you're watching this, Kathleen," he said, and my eyes widened, "then I must be dead." His face was grim but he continued. "I can't say I'm happy about that, but I'm not surprised. There are some pretty big stakes involved in what I've discovered. I just wish I could have found a way out." He rubbed a tired hand over his eyes, then looked back at the camera.

"I'm sorry to involve you, Kathleen, but I didn't know where else to turn or who to trust. I can't tell you everything on here, in case this falls into the wrong hands, but please, Kathleen. Please help me."

I swallowed heavily, my vision blurring slightly with tears. It was horrible. I'd known all along he hadn't killed Sheila and committed suicide, but hearing the helplessness and fear in his voice made it so much worse. Someone had murdered both of them because of something Mark had known. My attention was riveted to the screen as he kept speaking.

"I left what you'll need at my house," he said and then gave an address. I hurriedly grabbed some paper and jotted it down. "It's hidden," he warned, "and I can only give you a clue as to where to find it."

He had to be joking. A clue? Seriously? My heart sank. I had never been particularly good at puzzles.

Mark stared intently at the camera, as if measuring his next words.

"Think like a smuggler, Kathleen."

That was it. The video was over and the picture turned dark. I stared at the empty screen. How was that clue supposed to help me? A smuggler hid things and Mark had hidden the information in his house. The clue was like circular logic; it made no sense and wasn't a clue at all. I drove a hand through my hair in frustration.

Well, it didn't matter if I couldn't understand. I had to go to his house and see if I could find what he'd hidden anyway. I could no more turn my back on Mark's request to help him and Sheila than I could have turned my back on my dying mother. It just wasn't in me.

Grabbing the keys he'd left in the backpack, on the assumption I'd need them to get into his house, I tore the page with his address from my notepad, grabbed my purse, and left, making sure to lock the door behind me.

One good thing had come from my getting fired, I thought as I drove. I now had time to try to figure this out. On the other hand, I suspected that I might end up like Mark and Sheila, which made me grip the steering wheel tight enough to turn my knuckles white.

Mark lived across town in a nice middle-income neighborhood. The yards were all neatly tended and a few had

Halloween decorations up. It was midafternoon and the neighbors were all at work. It was quiet save for a dog barking in the backyard of a house a few doors down. I thought it would be wise not to park directly in front of Mark's house, so I parked on the street behind it, walking through his neighbors' yards until I came to his back door.

I had to try twice to get a key in the lock. I took a deep breath to calm down. Finally, the knob turned, and I eased the door open and stepped into Mark's kitchen.

It was eerily quiet. I stood still for a moment, just listening, and I heard nothing to make me think I wasn't alone. I tucked the keys in my pocket and started walking through his house.

It was your typical bachelor's place, functional without being particularly homey. I kept repeating what Mark had said—"Think like a smuggler"—but I was still drawing a blank. It didn't help that I didn't even know what I was looking for.

I couldn't see Mark hiding anything in the kitchen, so I moved on through the house. Upstairs, I saw nothing remarkable in his bedroom—only a bed, a dresser, and a lamp. Opening his closet, I moved aside his clothes, searching for any cabinets hidden in the walls. I crouched on the floor and peered under the bed and even lifted up the mattress. Nothing. I searched through his drawers, knocking on the backs of them like I'd seen people do in the movies, but they all sounded pretty solid to me.

After about an hour, I decided there was nothing hidden in the bedroom. Following the hallway, I came to another room, where apparently Mark had expended all his decorative energies.

The room was filled with science-fiction paraphernalia. I'd watched as much television as the next person, but I had no idea what some of the stuff was. Complete sets of action figures sat on shelves throughout the room, in various scenes and poses. Computer equipment was piled in the corners, along with books on programming. I had to duck to avoid the spaceships that were hung from the ceiling with transparent wire, simulating various flight patterns. I didn't know where to begin searching in here, but I had a gut feeling that this was the room he'd meant by his clue.

Glancing at my watch, I knew I didn't have a lot of time. I had to be at The Drop by six, and I still had to get back to my apartment and get dressed first. Fighting against my inherently tidy nature, I delved in, moving as fast as I could. I pulled apart stacks of computer equipment and flipped through books to see if he'd hollowed one out, like that guy in *The Shawshank Redemption*. I took shelves off the walls, sending the tiny figures so carefully placed on them falling heedlessly to the floor.

After another hour, I wanted to scream in frustration. It seemed hopeless and I thought Mark had greatly overestimated my ability to solve his puzzle. Sitting on the floor, surrounded by the mayhem I'd created, I heaved a sigh of defeat. Apparently, I wasn't able to think like a smuggler.

Getting to my feet, I inadvertently cracked my head on one of the overhanging spaceships and I cursed. It was a big ship. Reaching up in frustration, I grabbed it with both hands and yanked it down from the ceiling. I was about to hurl it across the room in a fit of temper when I paused and realized what I was holding.

I'm not a huge sci-fi fan but even I knew *Star Wars* backward and forward. I was holding a replica of the *Millennium Falcon.* I gasped. Of course! Han Solo had been a smuggler! And where had he smuggled things? Inside his ship!

I just knew I was right. I eagerly inspected the ship, looking for a way to open it, but it had been glued tightly shut. Grabbing something heavy and metallic from one of the piles on the floor, I hammered at the plastic until I felt it give way. Pulling it apart, I was able to see inside the replica ship.

Taped to the inside was a small rectangular object, a little smaller than the size of my palm and only about a quarter inch thick. I pulled it out to take a good look. It was some sort of computer equipment, and I thought it must be a hard drive.

Shoving it into my pocket, I stepped into the hallway and froze. I could hear voices coming from downstairs. Men's voices. I looked around, but there was no fast way out. On my left was the bathroom, and without thinking, I ran inside, pushing the door nearly shut behind me. Moving as fast and as quietly as I could, I climbed behind the shower curtain into the shower, thankful that Mark had a dark opaque curtain and not glass doors. I tried to be still and breathe as quietly as humanly possible.

I could hear the men's voices getting louder, but I couldn't make out what they were saying. The door to the bathroom suddenly flew open, bouncing against the wall, and I nearly screamed. The voices were clear now, from the hallway.

". . . know what we're doing here. We've already searched this place." The man sounded angry and affronted.

"You obviously didn't search it good enough." The second voice sounded vaguely familiar to me but I couldn't place it.

"Gimme a break, Jimmy. Just because you tore that girl's apartment apart like a hurricane went through doesn't mean we're any closer to finding it. You think it's here? Then you find it."

"Frank sent me to watch and make sure you're thorough. Not to do your work for you."

I did know that voice, and if I had been scared before, now I was terrified. It was Jimmy Quicksilver. I remembered how coldly inhuman and deadly he had been on the two occasions I'd had the misfortune of meeting him. Without consciously making the decision to do so, I drew back farther, pressing myself against the shower wall, hardly daring to breathe. I didn't want to consider what would happen to me if they found me.

"Make yourself useful before I decide you're worth more to us dead than alive," Jimmy replied, with a condescending sneer in his voice.

To my relief, they moved farther down the hall and I sucked in a lungful of air. My heart was pounding like it would leap out of my chest and I felt light-headed. I recognized the classic signs of fight-or-flight and I tried to slow my breathing.

"What the fuck happened here?" They must have gotten to the office and seen the mess my searching had caused.

I closed my eyes and prayed, hoping they'd think whoever had done it was already gone.

"Looks like someone else was better than you," said Jimmy coldly.

I heard a hard thump against the wall, and a grunt, then nothing. I strained to listen.

I heard footsteps pass the bathroom on their way downstairs. After a while, I heard the front door open and close.

Even though they were supposedly gone, I didn't move. It could be a trap. They could be waiting for someone to come out of the house. I looked at my watch and waited. Thirty minutes should be good.

After about fifteen, I smelled something funny. Sniffing the air, I realized what it was. Smoke. Tearing through the shower curtain, I ran to the hallway and stopped short, a small shriek escaping my lips before I clamped them shut.

A man was lying faceup on the floor. Although his eyes were open, he was very obviously dead. His throat had been slit from ear to ear so deeply it was a wonder that his head was still attached to his neck. Blood pooled in a dark red puddle beneath him. Bile rose in my throat but I swallowed it down. I didn't have time to be sick.

Smoke billowed up the stairs. My eyes were watering and I started coughing. Jimmy must have started a fire. Dropping to my knees and carefully avoiding the dead body, I tried to see through my now-streaming eyes. I crept down the stairs, hoping to reach the back door, but the heat and smoke became too intense. I had to turn back.

Scrambling up the stairs and down the hall, I thought furiously. There were windows in both Mark's bedroom and his office, and I thought there was a tree in the backyard. That would probably be my best bet.

I got to my feet and ran into the office, shutting the door behind me. Swiping at my eyes to clear them, I ran right over the junk on the floor and rushed to unlatch the window. But when I tried to shove it upward, it didn't budge. I tried again, putting all I had into it, but it still didn't move.

Frantically glancing around the room, I grabbed a piece of computer equipment that looked heavy enough to do some damage. Taking it in both hands, I smashed it against the glass until I saw, with relief, a spidery web appear in the window. Three more times and the glass had given way. I made as big a hole as I could, trying to clear as many shards as possible, then reached through to shove the screen out.

I was right. There was a big oak tree growing beside the house, but it wasn't close. I would have to jump to it. I looked down at the ground and gulped. If I missed, I would break a leg, or worse.

I climbed out of the window and straddled the frame, wincing as the glass shards cut into my hands and legs. Taking a deep breath, I leapt for the tree.

My fingers just managed to grab a branch, though the weight of my body made the muscles in my arms scream with pain and I nearly slipped. Wrapping my legs around the branch, I shimmied closer to the trunk. Twigs caught at my hair and I hurriedly yanked myself free. I had climbed trees since I was very young, so I was down the tree in no time flat. The sound of an explosion and glass shattering came from the house and I saw flames leaping out of a window. Without another glance, I ran for my car.

I raced home and made a beeline for the shower. I reeked of smoke and my hands were bloody from myriad tiny cuts. The beautiful new sweater and slacks were beyond repair and I grimly tossed them aside. After blowing my hair dry, I braided it in pigtails, complete with fluffy white bands, just like Britney's. As I got ready, I thought about the conversation between Jimmy and the other man. "The girl's apartment," he'd said. Well, I guess now I knew who had trashed my place looking for Mark's backpack.

I put Band-Aids on my hands and taped a couple of larger bandages to a few deeper cuts on the inside of my thighs, where I'd straddled the broken window frame. Ruefully, I realized I'd have to wear latex gloves tonight while making drinks. I couldn't risk bleeding into someone's glass.

Inspecting my face in the mirror, I saw that I had a livid bruise on my cheekbone, from where James had hit me, that was slowly seeping underneath my eye. By tomorrow, I'd look even worse. Fantastic. Tonight I figured I could hide it with a thick layer of makeup. The low lighting at the bar would help.

Dumping out the paper bag Tish had given me, I chewed my lip uncertainly. A black sports bra, white shirt, gray cardigan, schoolgirl miniskirt, and kneesocks lay on my bed. It wasn't terribly skimpy, but it would definitely show more skin than I felt comfortable revealing.

Glancing at the clock, I realized I didn't have time to be picky. I threw on the costume, knotting the shirt between my breasts and rolling up the sleeves. I didn't need a picture—I knew exactly how Britney had worn this costume, though I didn't have the heart to look in the mirror to see how I compared. I had a larger chest than Britney and the amount of my cleavage on display was considerable, but there was no time to do anything about it. Putting a tiny pair of silver hoop earrings in my ears, I grabbed the hard drive I'd retrieved from Mark's house and hurried out. Scant seconds later, I was pounding on CJ's door.

It took a few bouts of persistent knocking before I finally heard the locks turning, then CJ opened the door. Her mouth fell open when she saw me.

"You have got to be kidding me," she said flatly, eyeing my costume, but I waved my hand to interrupt her. She didn't seem the type to appreciate Britney Spears anyway.

"It's for work," I explained. "Listen, I need your help."

"I'm listening," she said carefully.

I handed her the drive. "A friend of mine . . . gave . . . me this," I said. "Can you figure out what's on it?"

CJ turned it in her hands, looking it over. "Sure," she said, shrugging. "No problem."

I felt a niggle of guilt. I couldn't help it, I had to warn her.

"Listen," I said, "whatever's on here, I think it might be dangerous. Two people may have been killed because of it."

CJ looked at me like I was nuts.

"I'm serious," I said earnestly. "I just . . . want you to be fully informed before you say you'll look at it."

She examined me for a moment, a frown creasing between her brows.

"I can tell you're serious," she finally said. "It's just a little hard to believe, that's all." Pocketing the drive, she pulled out a cigar and lit it, still examining me as if deciding whether or not to believe me.

"Please be careful," I said, "and don't tell anyone. I'll stop by when I get home tonight."

CJ took a puff of the cigar and nodded. "All right," she agreed. "See you then."

With a quick smile, I jogged to my car.

I arrived at The Drop only a few minutes late, parked around back, and hurried inside. The place was already busy. I did a double take when I saw Scott. He'd dressed as a Navy officer in dress whites, complete with mirrored shades. I was briefly reminded of one of my favorite movies of all time, *Top Gun.* Yum.

"About time you showed up," he snapped. But I felt a little satisfaction when he did his own double take. He let out a low whistle as he looked me up and down. "Holy shit, Kathleen," he said. "You look good enough to eat."

The smile he gave me made me blush and I quickly turned away to shove my purse in a cubbyhole under the bar. Well, at least I knew I looked good, even if I did feel like I was about to fall out of my top.

"Kathleen!"

I turned and saw Tish standing there. She was wearing a Madonna outfit, complete with cone bra.

"Oh my God!" I exclaimed, laughing. "Where did you get that? You look fantastic!"

She was wearing a platinum-blonde wig done in a Marilyn Monroe style, along with platform heels and fishnet stockings. Tish preened for me.

"Thank you," she said, winking at me. "Just something I had stashed away in the closet." She grinned. "And you look perfect, Kathleen! That outfit suits you. We'll be pulling in the bucks tonight!"

I hoped she was right. I caught glimpses of Jill and Deirdre out of the corner of my eye as I hurried to get my station set up. They both looked amazing. Jill was beautifully—and scantily—dressed as Christina Aguilera, and Deirdre looked exotic in her skintight Beyoncé outfit. Romeo would be pleased, I was sure.

The crowd grew until it was practically shoulder-to-shoulder and I was mixing drinks as fast as possible, so I barely had time to think. Most of the customers were dressed up as well, and we had repeated requests to sing and dance. Thankfully, we were all too busy to oblige. Romeo had brought in a karaoke machine for the night and set up a stage at one end of the room. It was very popular and I tried not to wince at some of the drunken revelers who took the stage, belting out tuneless numbers.

It was after nine when I heard my name being called from the crowd around the bar. Glancing up from the three martinis I was pouring, I saw Clarice and her boyfriend, Jack. They'd managed to push their way to the bar and I hurried to finish the drinks, setting them on a tray before going over to them.

"Hey, Clarice!" I said, reaching over the bar to give her a brief hug. I was glad to see her. It had made me a bit sad that I hadn't been able to say good-bye to her this morning when I was fired. "What are you doing here?"

"The kids are trick-or-treating with Grandma," she said, "so we thought we'd come here and see you."

"Fantastic," I said, smiling. "What can I get you to drink?"

Clarice ordered a rum and coke while Jack had a beer. I was just setting the drinks down in front of them when Clarice's smile faded from her face.

"Oh my God," she breathed, looking behind me. "I can't believe it."

I threw a quick glance over my shoulder but couldn't tell what she saw.

"What?" I asked her. "What is it?"

Her lips thinned. "It's Blane," she said, still looking behind me. "Remember me telling you about Facebook girl?"

I nodded. I remembered Clarice and me laughing about Blane's last breakup.

"Well, she's here. With him, the idiot."

I didn't want to turn around this time. I didn't want to see. But I couldn't help it.

Glancing quickly behind me again, I searched the crowd until I saw them. The bar was packed with people, but Blane and his date stood out like two beacons. Blane couldn't be missed, because he was taller than most other people around and just had a presence about him that made him jump out in a crowd. The girl stood out because . . . well, because she was drop-dead gorgeous. She had long, shimmering blonde hair that hung down her back and she was wearing a glittering fairy costume that must have cost a fortune. A matching mask covered her eyes. She was currently wrapped in Blane's arms, her lips whispering something in his ear.

I turned back around, feeling sick to my stomach. Clarice looked like a mad momma bear wanting to defend her cub. I made my lips curve in a false smile.

"It's not a big deal," I said. "Those were just rumors, remember? I'm not with him."

She looked at me with doubt in her eyes and I knew she didn't believe me. I hated that I was such a terrible liar. No, I wasn't "with" Blane, but I wasn't used to being as intimate with someone as we had been last night only to see him with someone else the next day. My gut twisted and I had to deliberately push my feeling aside. It didn't matter who Blane was here with anyway. I had no time to dwell on it.

I didn't get a chance to talk to Clarice and Jack again, as the orders came fast and furious. It was hard to be friendly and flirt for tips when I was concentrating on moving drinks as quickly as possible. Scott and I had a good rhythm down, though, and nobody got mad about their drink taking too long.

"I hear you've set your sights on Blane."

I looked up from the drink I was pouring and saw Blane's date standing at the bar. She was at least a head taller than me and even more beautiful up close. I felt like a kiddy dumpling next to her in my pigtails and kneesocks.

"Excuse me?" I said, speaking loudly to be heard over the current wannabe singer on the karaoke stage.

"You can forget about him," she said, leaning toward me. "He may go slumming with you for a night or two"—she looked at me like I was a piece of gum stuck to her shoe— "but he'll always come back to someone of his own . . . class."

I curled my hands into fists, the nails biting through the gloves into my palms.

"Someone like you, you mean," I said stiffly.

She smiled without humor. "Especially someone like me," she replied. With one last contemptuous look, she turned away and disappeared into the crowd.

"You all right?" I heard Scott ask.

Without a word, I grabbed two shot glasses and filled them with tequila. Grabbing the salt and some lime wedges, I held a glass out to Scott.

"Want one?" I asked, and he grinned.

"Only if I get to do a body shot." His eyes raked over me again, lingering on my cleavage.

Some of the customers around the bar heard and started cheering. I tossed back the tequila and bit into the lime, its tang cutting through the bite of the alcohol. When I was done, I smiled tightly at Scott. He certainly seemed to appreciate my costume tonight, as did the other men surrounding the bar. I might as well enjoy it.

"Why not?" I said, handing over the salt.

His grin widened and the crowd cheered louder. Moving close, he positioned the glass between my breasts, taking his time doing so. Even after working for hours, he still smelled nice. I could see my own reflection in his mirrored sunglasses. Reaching up, I took them off so I could see his eyes. They twinkled at me and I smiled for real this time. Scott's charm was irresistible.

"Where do you want the salt?" he asked in my ear as his arms slid around my waist. Although I appreciated his consideration, I decided I didn't care.

"You decide," I replied. His gaze dropped to my chest and he leaned forward. But instead of feeling his tongue above my breast, where I'd half-expected it, he licked my neck where it met my shoulder. Cold air hit the warm spot and I felt the slight tickle of the salt, then he licked me again. This time I shivered.

Then his mouth was taking the glass from between my breasts as he tossed the liquid back. I put the lime between my teeth, and Scott's lips met mine before he pulled it away from me. Wolf whistles and more cheering erupted from the crowd. Scott pulled me close for a hug and he and I grinned at each other.

When I turned away to get back to work, I suddenly stopped, my smile fading.

Blane was watching me. His face looked like it had been carved in granite. The fury in his eyes made me want to run and hide. For a moment, no one existed but the two of us as our gazes stayed locked together.

A raucous laugh nearby broke the spell and I stiffened my spine, my eyes narrowing at him and hopefully sending a message. I wasn't a child and if he didn't want me, there were others who did. Turning on my heel, I headed to the other side of the bar to take orders. Scott looked at me quizzically, since he'd been working this end, but didn't argue and just went and took my spot.

I resolutely refused to look for Blane again and kept working with a smile plastered to my face. A cluster of drunken college guys hogged my end of the bar, seeming to think I was now available to do body shots for just anyone. I tried to stay pleasant as I fended them off, moving to take orders from those around them. Hopefully, they'd take the hint and find someone else to pester.

Tish appeared and leaned heavily against the bar. I could tell she'd about had enough as well. Our eyes met and I knew we were both thinking the same thing. This night was never going to end.

"Pour me a shot, Kathleen," she said wearily, "I need it."

I poured us two shots of bourbon, straight up. I figured with the week I'd had, I deserved to let my hair down. We tossed them back in unison, then she took a deep breath, plastering a smile on her face as she dove back into the crowd.

Finally, after what seemed an eternity, the crowd started to thin. Glancing at my watch, I saw it was nearly one in the morning. A few minutes later, Scott signaled the waitresses for last call. People really started clearing out after that and finally I felt like I could stop and take a breath. I'd had another couple of shots and was starting to feel it. Scott and I started to clean up the bar area as the waitresses cleared tables.

Only a handful of people remained after another half hour and we'd nearly finished. Scott called everyone over to the bar for one last celebratory drink—we'd all done very well tonight. I'd made over two hundred dollars in tips, and that was without the percentages the waitresses would give Scott and me.

I sipped at the vodka martini Scott had made for me, aware that I still had to drive home after this. I was already a bit unsteady on my feet.

"Hey, Kathleen," Jill said, "you're gonna sing for us, right?"

I snorted. "Yeah, right," I said. "As if I'm not tired enough from tonight?"

"I know, but you're all dressed for it and everything," she protested. The others joined in, cajoling me.

"C'mon, Kathleen," Tish implored. "You can't let that karaoke machine go without trying it out just once."

Okay, she had a point there. It had been calling my name all night. Maybe every girl had an inner diva just dying to get out.

"All right, all right," I gave in, waving down their applause with a grin. I finished my martini—liquid courage, as my mother used to say—and headed for the stage.

"I need backup singers," I called out. Tish and Jill ran over, giggling. Scott and Deirdre sauntered closer and leaned against one of the tables to watch. The few customers left turned our way as well, curious as to what was going on. A quick glance reassured me that Blane was no longer here—or anyone else I knew, for that matter.

I scrolled through the list of songs until I found the one I wanted. A big hit for Britney, it struck a chord with me now. When the strains of "Toxic" filled the room, Tish and Jill cheered.

"Love this one!" Jill exclaimed, as she and Tish positioned themselves behind me.

I didn't need to follow the lyrics that scrolled on the screen, and I'd had enough booze to ensure that my performance was completely uninhibited. Throwing myself into the song, I duplicated a few of Britney's dance moves. Jill and Tish got into it, too, dancing with me in ways I was sure I would be blushing about tomorrow, though Scott and the other men left in the bar seemed to appreciate it, hooting catcalls at us.

We finished to wild applause and Scott let loose several whistles. Grinning and exhilarated, I hopped down off the stage, laughing with Jill and Tish. I was glad they'd talked me into it, having some fun for a change. The past few days I'd felt like the weight of the world had been on my shoulders, and it was so nice just to let loose and be young and carefree.

I noticed a mask someone had dropped on the floor by a table in the corner and detoured to pick it up. As I neared, a customer who had been standing in the shadows approached me. Glancing toward him, I stumbled and would have fallen if his hand hadn't shot out to steady me.

"That was some performance," Kade Dennon said, tugging me toward him.

Again dressed in all black, he wore the same cocky half grin on his face. In my inebriated state, his eyes seemed bluer, the dark lashes longer than I remembered.

"Self-appointed detective by day, pop princess by night," he jeered softly. He pulled me close, wrapping his arms around my waist, and I felt the evidence of his appreciation pressed against my stomach. Against my will, I felt an answering heat curl low in my own body.

Leaning down, he put his lips to my ear and I shivered, my eyes sliding shut.

"I know where you went today, princess."

That sobered me right up, my eyes jerking open in shock. I was only at one place of note today and that had been Mark's. Trying to bluff my way out, I stammered, "I . . . I don't know what you're talking about. I've been at home today."

"I was trying to decide whether to come in after you or let you burn to a crisp, when I saw you climb out the window." His eyes bored into mine and his smile melted away. "I want what you found in there today."

"Kathleen, you need some help?" Scott was coming out from behind the bar, a look of concern on his face. "Is that guy bothering you?"

Kade gave a minute shake of his head and looked downward. I followed his gaze and saw the glint of metal against his side. My eyes jerked back up to his. I didn't doubt for a moment that he was serious.

"I wouldn't let him come over here if I were you," he said softly.

"I'm fine, Scott," I called out, trying to keep my voice steady. "Really. Thanks, though."

Scott stopped. Although he still looked unsure, he retreated back to the bar.

"Very good," Kade said. "Now let's see if you can follow more instructions." His hands were caressing me as he spoke, distracting me as he touched the bare skin of my back above the skirt. My mind sluggishly tried to keep up with what he was saying. "Meet me tomorrow night in Monument Circle."

"I have to work tomorrow night," I said quickly, trying to think.

"I'll wait," he retorted. "So far, I'm the only one who knows you have it." He paused, then added, "But that can change."

The thought of Jimmy and the dead body made me feel light-headed.

Kade bent down so his face was only inches from mine. "Might as well put on a good show," he murmured, his eyes dropping to my mouth.

Then he was kissing me and I was too stunned to do anything. His tongue tangled with mine and my hands fisted in his jacket. Distantly, through the roaring in my ears, I heard someone give a wolf whistle. Finally, Kade released me and I gasped for breath. Whatever he saw in my eyes must have amused him, because he laughed softly.

He leaned back to whisper in my ear, his warm breath again sending a shiver through me. "I like the braids."

Then he was gone, the front door swinging shut behind him.

Shaken, I grabbed my purse from under the counter and said a hasty good-bye to Scott. Deirdre had already gone. Tish and Jill were nearly done as well. Tish winked at me as I walked by and I gave her a weak smile in return. She no doubt thought I was in a hurry to leave so I could continue my evening festivities with Kade. She couldn't have been more wrong.

CHAPTER NINE

I felt battered and worn as I drove home. My hands stung and itched from the cuts and then from wearing latex all evening. The cuts on my thighs hurt and my arms ached from hanging from the tree as well as from all the work I'd done tonight. I could feel that my cheek was very tender and my eye was starting to throb.

And, to top it off, I was embarrassed and ashamed of my reaction to Kade. He was a dangerous man, a killer, and I'd melted in his arms like a lovesick teenager a mere twenty-four hours after begging Blane to make love to me. I'd never thought of myself as someone who could be labeled as "easy," but it seemed I was veering close to that territory. My head was filled with silent recriminations.

I couldn't wait to take a shower and go to bed, stress and alcohol making my head throb. Before I could do that, I had to stop and see if CJ had found anything.

I knocked on her door, the frigid air making me shiver. The temperature had dropped and I could see my breath. My hand was poised to knock again when the door opened, revealing CJ wreathed in a cloud of cigar smoke.

"Thought that was you," she said around the cigar clenched between her teeth. "Come in."

She stepped back and I scooted inside gratefully. Smoke or not, it was warmer inside than out.

The apartment looked completely different from when Sheila had lived there, and I looked around curiously. CJ seemed to really like black. All her furniture was black leather, her tables a mix of black lacquer and glass. I saw a desk with a black marble top in the corner. She had a laptop sitting on it as well as three large flat-screen computer monitors.

CJ plopped herself down on the couch and gestured for me to do the same. "I'm still copying the drive, so I haven't had much of a chance to look at the data," she said, surprising me.

"Really?" I asked. "I didn't think it would take so long."

"The drive was damaged and wouldn't spin up," she replied. "I put it in the freezer for a while and now it's working, but the copy is going real slow. It'll probably take another couple of hours."

"Okay, thanks," I said. Then I remembered Kade. "Um... is there any way to erase the data on the disk after you're done? Someone else wants it and I don't want them to have whatever is on there."

CJ eyed me speculatively for a moment, then nodded. "Yeah. The only sure way to really get rid of the data is to overwrite the drive. An erase doesn't really delete anything. The sectors are recoverable, especially if you know what you're doing. I can fix that, if you want."

"Thanks," I said gratefully. I felt grungy and was tiring quickly, so I asked to use the bathroom. After scrubbing my face free of the thick makeup, I felt much better and more awake.

"That asshole left quite a shiner," CJ said when I returned. I grimaced. The bruising on my cheek and eye from James this morning was very noticeable now. "So," she said, taking another puff of her cigar, "are you going to tell me what's going on or what?"

She was right. I'd dragged her into this—she should know about Mark and Sheila. I sighed.

"I think I need a drink first," I said wearily.

Without a word, CJ got up and went to the kitchen, returning with two glasses and a bottle of bourbon. Splashing some into each glass, she handed me one. I sipped it for a minute or two, then launched into my story, telling her about Sheila and how I'd found her dead. Then I told her about Mark and how the cops had decided he'd killed her and committed suicide, ending with my near escape from his house today and Kade demanding I turn over the drive tomorrow night.

When I finished, I tipped the bottle and gave myself another generous pour, drinking it down quickly. I rationalized that I needed it to help me sleep tonight. Otherwise, thinking about Kade, Jimmy, and the dead man in Mark's house would keep me up all night.

"I'll go with you," CJ said abruptly.

"What?" I asked, surprised.

"Tomorrow night," she said. "I don't think it's a good idea for you to go alone. You need someone to watch your back."

At first I was glad; it would be great to not be alone. Then I remembered Sheila and Mark, and knew I couldn't let anything happen to CJ. Regretfully, I shook my head.

"I can't let you do that," I said. "I shouldn't even have involved you this much. It's dangerous."

CJ snorted. "Of course it's dangerous, which is why we should help each other."

I started shaking my head again and opened my mouth to speak, but she interrupted me.

"You're tired. Go home and go to bed. Come over in the morning. I'll know more and we can argue about it then."

I smiled. She sounded as stubborn as me, but the part about going to bed sounded good.

"All right," I said, getting to my feet. "See you in the morning." The room tilted a bit and I saw CJ smirk.

"You a lightweight, eh, Britney?" she joked, and I couldn't help laughing.

"Nice," I retorted. "I'll have you know I make a damn fine Britney Spears. And I can hold my liquor just fine, thank you very much. I've just had a long night."

"I bet," CJ said, walking me out.

A few moments later, I was locking my door, leaning against it gratefully and closing my eyes. I hadn't been exaggerating. It seemed like forever since I'd woken up this morning in Blane's house. I wondered bitterly if the fairy girl was there with him now.

Hands closed over my upper arms. "Where the hell have you been?"

I started violently, my eyes flying open. Blane stood in front of me, his eyes blazing with fury.

"You should have been home an hour ago," he bit out. "Where were you? With that pretty-boy bartender who had his hands all over you?"

My shock gave way to anger. "What is it to you?" I spat at him. "Shouldn't you be fucking your fairy about now?"

"Don't talk like that," he gritted out. "I didn't know Kandi was going to be there tonight."

So that was her, the Kandi-with-an-i girl. Yeah, that fit the snobby bitch, I thought, not caring if I was being petty.

"That didn't stop her from telling me exactly what she thought of me," I said bitterly. "As if I haven't had enough of that today."

That seemed to take the heat from his anger and I felt his grip on my arms loosen.

"So I heard," he said grimly. "You shouldn't have lost your job," he said more gently, and now his hands moved slowly up and down my arms in a soothing way. "I've taken care of things. You can come back to work on Monday."

The part of me that had been worried about what I was going to do without that job sighed in relief. But the part of me that knew you couldn't get something for nothing raised its head suspiciously.

"Why?" I asked him.

Blane looked momentarily confused.

"Why?" I repeated. I stepped away, feeling the need to put some space between him and me. His arms fell to his sides as he watched me. "Why are you doing this?"

The questions that had hammered at the back of my mind all day now tumbled from my mouth in a torrent. "Why the apartment makeover? The new clothes? New furniture? Why are you even here?"

Blane's posture stiffened as I spoke, his eyes narrowing. Normally, that would have warned me, but I was too confused and angry to stop.

205

"Am I some sort of project?" I continued. "A charity case for you? Just tell me, because I don't know what you want from me." I crossed my arms over my chest and waited for an answer, bracing myself for words I probably didn't want to hear.

"I don't want anything from you," he said stiffly. "I told you last night that I would take care of you and that's what I'm doing."

I hated being reminded of last night and I felt my cheeks heat. "But why?" I persisted, exasperated that he kept dodging my question. "It doesn't make any sense. I'm nothing, no one to you, so why would you care what happens to me?"

"Because I like you," he finally said, and he sounded almost surprised at the admission. "And because you needed help and I'm in a position to offer it."

"And you want nothing in return?" I asked skeptically.

"Nothing."

"Right," I scoffed. "Because life really works like that." I knew better. I didn't know what Blane wanted, but I wasn't naive enough to believe that, eventually, he wouldn't expect me to pay up.

The stinging in my hands recaptured my attention and I decided I was done with Blane, whether or not he was done with me. I hadn't invited him here and didn't even know how he'd gotten in, but I was ready for him to leave. Hoping he'd catch the hint, I turned my back on him to go into the kitchen. The room spun and I stumbled, my arm flying out to catch myself so I wouldn't fall and be humiliated even further.

Blane had his arm around me, steadying me, before I even had time to blink. "You're drunk," he said, a slight accusation in his tone that made me bristle.

"I've had a really bad day," I shot back defensively. "I thought I deserved a drink." Or two. Maybe five. Whatever.

Blane's hand moved up to my shoulder and he squeezed. I thought it was probably meant to be comforting, but he had hit upon the spot where James had shoved me against the door and I yelped in pain.

"What?" he said in alarm. "What's wrong?"

I just shook my head. "It's nothing. Just a bruise." Reaching over, Blane flicked on the kitchen light and I blinked in the sudden brightness, raising my hand up to shield my eyes.

"What happened to you?"

I winced at the tightly leashed fury in Blane's voice. Crap. He'd seen my face, and since I'd washed off my makeup in CJ's apartment, I knew my bruised cheek now showed up in the stark kitchen light. It didn't help that I had such fair skin anyway.

"It looks worse than it feels," I said quickly, turning away. I had reached the sink and started peeling the limp Band-Aids from my hands.

Blane's hands settled on my waist and I could feel him behind me. His arms reached around to grasp my hands so he could turn them palm up. He didn't move for a moment and I closed my hands over the myriad small, angry red cuts.

"You went to Mark's," he observed in a flat voice.

I caught my breath. "How did you—"

"I saw his message to you on the DVD," he said simply, as if it was of no consequence that he'd come uninvited into my apartment and then gone through my things.

Turning so my back was to the sink, I faced him. "That was a private message," I hissed angrily. "You have no right to go through my things!"

"Don't I?" he said, and his eyes moved to my cheek. His hand came up, the fingers touching the bruised skin so gently it felt like the wings of a moth. My breath caught in my throat and our eyes locked.

"Tell me what happened today," he coaxed, and suddenly the urge to lay my burdens on him was overwhelming. I argued with myself that I wasn't supposed to trust him. Yet he said he wanted to help me, and looking around my apartment, he already had helped me, much more than I could ever repay. So, with a sigh, I told him the story.

His hands returned to my waist and we stood there, our bodies inches apart, as I told him about Diane firing me at James's behest, then about James showing up here. As dispassionately as I could, I stumbled over how he had attacked me and how CJ had scared him off. Blane's face gradually turned stony as I talked and I nervously looked away.

Since he'd seen Mark's message and already knew I'd gone to his house, I told him about finding the hard drive and nearly getting caught by Jimmy. His fingers bit into my hips when I got to that part. I finally finished the story with seeing the dead guy and having to escape the burning house from the second-floor window.

"What did you do with the drive?" he asked. I hesitated. I didn't want to involve CJ in this.

"I hid it somewhere safe," I hedged.

"You should give it to me," he said, and I rolled my eyes.

"You'll have to get in line," I said grimly. "Kade's already said I have to give it to him tomorrow."

"Kade?" Surprise edged Blane's voice and I remembered that I hadn't told him about Kade. "Kade Dennon?"

"Yeah," I said, "you know him?"

His lips thinned and he gave a curt nod.

"We've met." He didn't elaborate. Grasping my hands, he looked at them, then turned me toward the faucet again, running warm water over the cuts. It felt good, and soothed the burning.

Gently toweling my hands dry, he asked, "Were your hands all that got cut?" I hesitated for an instant before nodding my head. It was an instant too long.

"Where else?" Blane asked in a tone that brooked no disobedience.

"My . . . legs," I said halfheartedly. "But it's fine, not a big deal. I'll just take a shower and they'll be fine."

This wasn't quite true. I'd checked the bandages on my thighs tonight when I'd gone to the employees' restroom, and several of them had been bright red from blood seeping through. I just wanted to clean up and put new bandages on. They'd be fine in a couple of days.

"You're not showering in this condition," Blane said.

"And what condition is that?" I retorted.

"Drunk," he said flatly. "You're liable to fall and break your neck. Go sit down," he ordered, pushing me toward a chair at the table.

"I'll be fine," I insisted, but he shot me a look that had me scooting hurriedly toward a chair.

Blane filled up a bowl with warm water and grabbed a kitchen towel. Crouching down in front of me, he quickly removed my heeled Mary Janes. With businesslike efficiency, he peeled the tall socks down my legs. The room was really spinning now and I didn't think it was all due to the alcohol I'd drunk. His fingers were warm and rough against my legs as he searched for the elusive cuts.

"Where?" he asked.

"Hmm?" I had lost track of the conversation, my senses going into overload with him so near and touching me. Glancing up at me, whatever he saw in my face must have clued him in as to the directions my thoughts were taking because his jaw clenched tightly.

"Where are the other cuts?" he asked again, speaking slowly. The words penetrated my numbed brain and I felt blood heat my cheeks.

"Um . . . higher," I muttered, unable to look him in the eye.

His hands moved hesitantly upward, as if waiting for me to protest, but I kept my lips pressed firmly closed. It wasn't my fault. He had been the one who wanted to play doctor.

Slowly brushing my miniskirt up my thighs, his fingers touched the bandages. His hands closed over my knees, pushing them apart, and I felt a flash of desire arc through me. But judging by what he said next, he wasn't feeling the same.

"Do you have any idea," he ground out as he pulled off the reddened gauze, "how close you came to cutting your femoral artery?"

Well, that was a bucket of cold water if I'd ever felt one. I sighed and rubbed my tired eyes.

"Biology wasn't really my strongest subject," I said dryly, then hissed in pain as the water touched the open cuts. "Crap, that hurts!"

To his credit, Blane was quick and efficient. He had the cuts cleaned, medicated, and bandaged much more quickly than if I had done it myself. Getting to his feet, he pulled me upward as well, turning the room into a Tilt-A-Whirl once again.

"Let's get you to bed," he said, and to my addled brain, it sounded like an invitation.

"Only if you're joining me," I said, hooking my fingers into his belt and tugging.

In the part of my brain that still retained a semblance of common sense in spite of the alcohol, I was shocked at my proposition. It appeared he felt the same, for his lips pressed together in a look I was starting to know well.

"Fine," I retorted, spinning away from his grip and stomping into my bedroom.

He followed me, more to make sure I didn't fall on my face, I think, than anything else. I decided that since he had no interest in having sex with me, then it wouldn't bother him if I changed my clothes. I peeled off my sweater and shirt, dropping them carelessly on the floor. Glancing over my shoulder, I saw he'd paused right inside the doorway, his eyes riveted on me.

Conscious of the lack of my usual inhibitions, I flashed him a smirk. Keeping my back to him, I crossed my arms over my chest, pulling the black sports bra over my head. My braided pigtails brushed the bare skin of my back, but I didn't look at Blane. Instead, I slowly slid down the zipper on the back of my miniskirt. Hooking my fingers inside the waistband, I dragged it and my panties down over my hips, needlessly bending at the waist as I slid the material down my legs. When the fabric puddled at my feet, I stepped out and walked to my bureau. I'd never done a striptease before, but it hadn't seemed very hard.

I wasn't brave enough to look at Blane as I searched through unfamiliar piles of satin and lace for pajamas. Finally, I gave up and pulled out a blue satin shorts-and-camisole set. I slipped them on and turned to face Blane. He hadn't moved from where he stood, but his eyes blazed and his hands were fisted at his sides. I felt a surge of satisfaction. So he wasn't immune to me after all.

Grabbing my brush off the bureau, I walked until I stood mere inches from him, tipping my head back to meet his eyes as I held out the brush.

"Will you help me with my hair?" I asked as innocently as I could.

He hesitated, then gave a curt nod. I climbed into the center of the bed with my back to him and started undoing the braids. After a moment, I felt the bed dip as he moved behind me. My hair was down and I combed through it with my fingers as a sigh escaped me. It felt good to have the braids out. I waited and finally felt the bristles pull tentatively through my hair.

It was immediately clear that Blane was unaccustomed to combing a girl's hair. He was slow and exceedingly careful when he hit tangles. I couldn't repress a small smile. It struck me as sweet, actually, that he didn't want to hurt me. I could have told him he could pull all he wanted—I had a pretty hard head—but I kept my silence. After the many women I knew he'd been with, it meant something that this was a task unfamiliar to him. What had been a ploy on my part to get him to touch me was turning into something tender and sweet.

I closed my eyes and enjoyed the gentle tugging of the bristles and the feel of his hands smoothing the strands as he brushed. I felt a warm tightness in my chest and knew I was in dangerous territory. Although my head knew I couldn't risk getting more attached to Blane, it seemed I was powerless to stop it. Feeling the need to get back on more familiar footing, I cleared my throat.

"I remembered there's a case pending with the firm regarding TecSol," I said, and the brush paused for a moment before continuing. "I need to know what it's about."

"Why do you need to know?" Blane asked guardedly.

"Mark worked for them," I said. "He was afraid of them. Afraid they were after him. That Sheila was killed because of him."

"What else did he say?" The brush combed through the strands effortlessly now, the tangles gone.

I thought. "He said it might have something to do with Eve." Mark had also said someone at the firm had betrayed him, but I kept that to myself. I wondered who Eve was and what part she had played in Mark's death. "Is there someone named Eve involved with the case?"

"No," Blane said. "EVE's not a person, EVE's a thing. They call it Electronic Voting Evaluation. TecSol wrote the software that the city is using for the first election where all voting will be done online."

I frowned. "The case with TecSol—wasn't it about election fraud?" I asked, trying to remember what I had read that night.

"Yes," Blane confirmed, still brushing my hair as he spoke. "Six months ago, someone came forward from TecSol claiming to be a whistleblower, saying that the software had security flaws. They were terminated and sued for disclosure of proprietary information. They countersued for wrongful termination under the Whistleblower Protection Act."

"What do the Santini brothers have to do with any of this?" I remembered Blane and I having to deliver those documents to them that evening.

"They own TecSol through a front company," Blane answered.

"What's the status of the case now?"

"The case is no longer pending, as the plaintiff is dead," he said flatly.

Startled, I turned around to face him. "The whistleblower is dead?"

Blane nodded, his face grim. "Car wreck," he explained.

I felt a flash of fury. "You know they were killed," I insisted, and he nodded again. "But," I sputtered, "they can't do that. They just can't go around killing people!"

"I know," he said calmly, "and I'm working on it. But you need to stay out of it. It doesn't concern you."

"It concerns me now," I retorted. "Mark said he knew about the problems with EVE, and that he'd come forward. He said someone at the firm betrayed him and now Mark's dead. But he gave that information to me. I can't just ignore that. And you!" My eyes narrowed at him and I quickly pushed backward on the bed, away from him. "You work for them! Whose side are you on? Did you betray him?"

Blane's hand flashed out and snagged my waist, dragging me back toward him. I struggled briefly, but it was embarrassing how quickly Blane subdued me. My arms were pinned to my sides as he loomed over me.

"I didn't betray him, Kathleen, I'm on your side," he said curtly, "but you're not helping me protect you. I don't want them to know about you or what Mark told you. You could very well end up dead."

My face paled at the reminder as Blane's eyes searched mine intently. "I think they might already know," I said weakly, "or will soon." My anger had dissipated in a cloud of anxiety.

"What do you mean?" he asked.

"Kade," I answered, my voice small. "He threatened to tell them if I didn't bring him the drive."

Growling a curse, Blane sat up, releasing me.

"I was going to give it to him," I said, sitting up. "He said to meet him tomorrow night at Monument Circle."

"Good," Blane said. "He'll leave you out of it so long as he gets what he wants. Kade's number one priority is himself." His eyes focused on my bruised cheek again. "And I'll take care of James," he said grimly.

Alarm shot through me. "No! You can't!" I said, latching onto his arm and tugging as he made to stand.

Blane paused, though not because of my ineffectual pulling on him. "Don't tell me you have feelings for him," he said with disgust. "Not after what he did to you?"

"Of course not!" I protested, still hanging on to his arm. "He's a bully and a jerk!"

"Then why are you stopping me?"

"Because he's crazy!" I said, dismayed. "Really crazy. And he has this weird competition thing with you and I don't want you to get hurt!"

Our eyes caught and held.

"I couldn't handle . . ." I had to stop and take a breath. "Please," I finally managed, "just . . . stay. With me. Please stay." My eyes pleaded with him and I could tell when he relented.

"This isn't a good idea," he muttered, his eyes dragging down my body. Still, he turned off the light and kicked off his shoes, leaving his jeans and shirt on. He turned to climb into bed, but I was on my knees, stopping him. He looked at me questioningly, but I didn't say anything; I just started undoing the buttons of his shirt. He didn't stop me and I tugged it from his waistband and pushed it off his shoulders and down his arms, sighing in pleasure as I did so.

"You're still drunk," he said gruffly, and I shrugged, scooting back on the bed and under the covers.

After a moment he followed me. I unabashedly snuggled up to his side, resting my head on his chest as his arms encircled me. I remembered what he'd said last night, about me being innocent, and the words fell out of my mouth before I could think better of it.

"I'm not a virgin, you know," I said baldly.

Blane went very still. After a moment, he spoke.

"Tell me about your lovers," he said lightly, his hand stroking my back.

I moved closer. "Not lovers, plural," I corrected. "Lover, singular. Men," I groused, "are always thinking women are as promiscuous as they are."

"I stand corrected," he said. "Tell me about your lover."

"That's really too romantic a title for him," I said, remembering the groping in the confines of the car. "I was sixteen. It was homecoming and his father had a big sedan. End of story."

Blane's hand paused on my back. "How was it?" he asked carefully. I tried to concentrate. Sleep was crowding into my brain along with the booze, and my thoughts were fuzzy. I consciously had to make my mouth move to answer him.

"Quick. Painful. Embarrassing." Those were the feelings I would forever associate with that encounter. And that was my last thought before sleep claimed me.

When I woke, weak light cast a dim glow in the room and I realized it must be morning. I lay on my back, Blane's arm beneath my head. He lay on his side against me, his other arm across my stomach. Closing my eyes, I relaxed, enjoying the moment.

Blane's hand moved down my stomach and underneath the waistband of my shorts. "I knew this was a bad idea," he whispered in my ear. "I can't seem to keep my hands off you."

Without another word, his hand parted my thighs and a long finger slipped inside me. I gasped at the intrusion, and his mouth covered mine. Our tongues dueled even as he stroked me and I felt like I was on fire from the inside out. My arms lifted and wound themselves around his neck.

Blane added a second finger to the first and I bit back a moan. My hips rose of their own volition to meet his thrusting fingers, and my breath came in pants. Heat flared between my legs as his thumb slid over a spot that made my body jerk against his hand.

"God, I want you, Kat," he groaned against my lips.

A pounding on my apartment door shattered the cocoon around us. Blane's hand stilled and I wanted to cry in disappointment. The pounding came again and Blane was up and out of the bed, heading to the front door. Scrambling up on legs that were shaking, I grabbed his shirt and stuffed my arms into the sleeves. I didn't have a robe, but it was long enough to serve as one.

Blane pulled open the front door, gun in hand, and I nearly collapsed in relief to see CJ standing there. I had been afraid it might be James.

CJ eyed the two of us and Blane's gun, her hand still poised to knock, and I saw her eyebrows climb skyward.

"Er, sorry to interrupt," she said uncomfortably, looking past Blane to me.

"Not a problem," I said quickly. "Blane, this is my neighbor, CJ. CJ, this is Blane."

CJ gave Blane a curt nod.

"I was just wondering if you saw this." She held up today's newspaper. Stepping around Blane, I took it from her, read the headline, and gasped.

"What is it?" Blane said, looking over my shoulder at the page.

"It's James," I said numbly. "He's entered the race for district attorney."

I frantically skimmed the article below. "It says here the previous candidate pulled out of the race citing the need to spend more time with his family. He's endorsed James in his place."

Blane took the paper from my fingers, reading the article himself as I tried to absorb this information.

"Come by when you have a minute," CJ said, giving me a meaningful look.

"Yeah . . . um . . . okay," I said nervously. "I'll be over in a bit. Just need to get dressed."

With a nod and one last glance at Blane, still absorbed in the paper, she retreated to her apartment and I closed the door. Blane dropped the paper on the couch and turned toward me. My mind flashed to what CJ had interrupted and I could feel myself blushing furiously.

"I'd better get going," he said, eyeing me with regret. He glanced at his watch and tucked his gun into the small of his back.

I looked up when he stood in front of me.

"I'm going to need that," he said softly, and I didn't resist as he pushed the shirt down my arms, my breath catching when he touched me.

Putting it on, he rolled up the sleeves and carelessly did up a couple of buttons, his eyes never leaving mine. His fingers came up to softly brush the bruised skin of my cheek and I saw his eyes turn cold and hard. Then he was kissing me again, his arms crushing me to him. When we finally broke apart, I was gasping for air. He rested his forehead against mine.

"I'll see you tonight," he said softly and I nodded, unable to speak. Then he was gone.

I hurried through a shower, throwing on some sweats and leaving my hair wet before going over to CJ's. She answered quickly, pulling open the door for me.

"Want some coffee?" she asked, and I gratefully accepted. A slight pounding in the back of my head told me I hadn't escaped last night's imbibing unscathed.

"What did you find out?" I asked, sipping the scalding liquid as I curled up on her couch. She plopped down beside me, again in unrelenting black, though today she'd opted to leave the eyebrow ring out.

"An extremely complex encryption algorithm," she said simply.

I looked at her blankly, uncomprehending, waiting for the rest.

Rolling her eyes, she explained. "It's like the key to a lock, only not just one lock, but lots of locks."

Okay, that was easier to follow.

"But what is the lock for?" I asked, and she shrugged.

"There wasn't a way to tell," she replied. "I'd say it was for secure communications, but it wasn't the right kind for that. You said it belonged to Mark, right? Any idea where he might have gotten it?"

I didn't want to involve her any further, but at this point, I didn't see how I could help it. I needed her expertise. "I think it came from where he worked," I said, "a company called TecSol."

Her eyes widened, in fear or awe, I couldn't tell. "The company that did the cutting-edge online voting software," she breathed.

"You've heard of them?" I asked, surprised.

She nodded jerkily. "Everyone has," she replied.

Except me, apparently, I thought grumpily.

"What they've done is groundbreaking. They supposedly created an unbreakable method of encryption that solved the performance problem of true random number generators without compromising the integrity of the encryption. They haven't said exactly how they solved it because it's proprietary and they're patenting it."

"Okay, you lost me," I said, holding up a hand to stop her. "Layman's terms, okay?"

"When you want to send information over the Internet securely, it has to be encrypted—you know that much, right?" I nodded. Everyone knew that. "Each site has its own encryption code generated for them to use and only they have the key—that's what makes it secure. But everything is hackable, given enough time and talent. TecSol created a way for each individual transaction to be encrypted using a different key. The problem was, it was too slow to be able to handle the traffic generated by something like a nationwide online election, because the encryption process used a true random number generator."

"What's that?"

"Someone may think it's easy for a computer to randomly generate numbers," she said, and I silently agreed, "but it's not. A computer that just spat out random numbers would be, by definition, broken. There's really only two ways a computer can generate random numbers and that's a pseudo random number generator or a true random number generator."

"What's the difference?" I asked, sipping my now-tepid coffee.

"I'll give you an example," she said. "If you wanted a random number, how would you go about getting it?" I thought about it for a moment.

"I guess I'd roll some dice," I answered.

She grinned. "Exactly. So, imagine rolling dice for your random number, but then writing down all the results you get. You'd get a list of random numbers, but it would be a predetermined list. That's a pseudo random generator, and algorithms like the one I found are used to create them. You give the formula a beginning number, or seed, and then it puts it through the formula to generate the random number. Random, yes, but predetermined and calculable, if you know the seed."

"Then what's a true random number generator?" I was caught up in her explanations in spite of myself.

"It's where you use something truly unpredictable to generate the numbers, kind of like a virtual die attached to a computer, and it's the only real way to get a random number. Unfortunately, it's not as fast as the other method, so not practical for what TecSol was trying to do."

"What's truly random?" I asked, curious.

"Oh, lots of things," she said. "Atmospheric noise, radioactive decay. Things like that. Unpredictable and without a pattern is the key."

I struggled to make sense of all this given what I now knew. "So Mark had a drive with an encryption algorithm on it. And that's the one, we think, TecSol is using to encrypt their online voting software?"

CJ nodded, her face losing its excited animation and becoming grim.

"So they didn't really solve the problem, did they?" I asked. "They're just saying they did and using the pseudo generator thing instead."

"I think so," she said. "Which give us a serious problem, as well as tells us why Mark was killed."

"They can't let anyone know," I finished for her. "If it leaked out their software wasn't secure, they'd lose their contract with the city as well as any pending contracts, and probably get sued on top of it. The whole business would be sunk."

"Everyone's going to be watching how this software performs," CJ said. "And that's not the worst of it."

I looked at her questioningly. That part sounded pretty bad to me and reason enough for them to kill us.

"You're assuming they know about the flaw and can't fix it. It's possible—probable, actually—that the flaw is by design."

"By design?"

"If they know the encryption key for every transaction, then those packets can be intercepted, decrypted, and modified," she explained.

Our eyes met in mutual understanding. "To steal an election," I said. We sat in silence for a moment, processing this.

"Does anyone else besides that guy, Kade, know you have this?" CJ finally asked, and I shook my head.

"No, wait," I corrected myself. "Blane knows, too, though he doesn't know I gave it to you. I told him I hid it. But I trust him."

CJ gripped my arm tightly. "Don't trust anyone, Kathleen," she said in earnest. "There are people that would pay millions for access to what we found and they won't let us stand in their way. They'd kill us as quickly as TecSol would if they knew we had it."

I searched her eyes and knew she was right. A chill went through me. We were sitting on a powder keg and I didn't know what we were going to do about it. A thought struck me.

"Oh my God," I gasped in dismay. "The election! It's in three days. And now James is running for DA."

I thought for a moment. "James and the Santini brothers are tied together somehow. They wanted him to run. They're going to use the software to make sure he wins."

"Who are the Santini brothers?" CJ asked, and I quickly explained their ownership of TecSol and the now-dormant case Blane had told me about.

"If James is district attorney, then he'll be able to run interference for any further cases against TecSol for election fraud," I said, "paving the way for them to go nationwide with the software."

Tampering with an election went against everything I believed. My father had taught me respect for my country and its history. The fact that someone would try to put in place a way to engineer election results in the "good ol' US of A," as CJ had put it, made me angry. "We have to do something," I said.

CJ's eyes had the same fire I knew was in mine and I thought I'd found a kindred soul.

"Damn straight, we're going to do something," she said.

And we began to plan.

CHAPTER TEN

It was several hours later that I finally went back to my apartment, though the plan CJ and I had come up with seemed far-fetched. I didn't know if we could pull it off—it wasn't like I was a *Mission: Impossible* kind of girl.

I'd argued for a long while that we should go to the police. CJ had been vehemently against that, though her reasons seemed more paranoid and conspiracy-rampant than logical to me. The whole thing seemed bizarre. This wasn't how my life was supposed to go. Murder, fraud, and conspiracy were the things of fiction, not reality. At least, not my reality.

CJ said she would get the drive ready and I was supposed to pick it up from her on my way to work. Not only was she going to overwrite the data, but she was going to affix a minuscule GPS transmitter to it so we could follow where Kade took it. She'd been adamant about wanting to come with me tonight, but I'd been steadfast in refusing her. Only my explanation that Blane said he'd be there tonight persuaded her not to come. She didn't trust him with the information, but I think she thought he'd keep me safe. I hoped she was right.

The thought of Blane made me cover my face with my hands and groan in embarrassment. I couldn't believe that I had stripped in front of him last night. I swore I was never drinking again (yeah, right).

Although, it hadn't seemed like he'd minded my little striptease. I wondered what would have happened if CJ hadn't knocked on my door.

Who was I kidding? I knew what would have happened. I should be grateful she'd interrupted, but I wasn't. I'd tried not to become emotionally involved with Blane, but it had been a futile effort. I was self-aware enough to know that I was teetering on the edge of falling for him, which scared me utterly.

As I glanced around my apartment, taking in all the new furniture and things that Blane had bought for me, I wondered whether he might feel something for me, too. It seemed too much to hope for. I knew what a player Blane was, but I couldn't help myself. I was cursed as an eternal optimist. The thought of seeing him again tonight made me feel good and eased the weight of worry about what CJ and I were planning.

I was getting ready for work when there was a knock on my door. Toweling my hair dry, I hurried to the door, careful this time to look through the peephole first before answering.

"Gracie!" I said, throwing open the door and smiling in welcome. Gracie still looked like a runway model, even wearing low-slung jeans and an oversized sweater, like she was now. She smiled back and I gestured for her to come inside.

"What are you doing here?" I asked, closing the door behind her.

"I— What happened to you?" she interrupted herself, eyeing the bruise on my cheek. I grimaced.

"Nothing," I answered, not wanting to talk about it. "Just a misunderstanding."

Gracie looked like she didn't believe a word of it. "Yeah," she said grimly, "I've had those kind of misunderstandings before."

"So what's going on?" I asked, anxious to change the subject. I headed toward the kitchen. "Would you like something to drink?"

"Sure," she said, following me. "Looks like you redecorated," she commented, glancing around.

I didn't say anything to that. I could barely understand Blane's generosity myself, much less try to explain it to someone else.

Grabbing a couple of mugs, I filled each with some coffee I'd brewed. I offered one to Gracie, pointing out the cream and sugar on the table. After we'd fixed our coffee to our satisfaction, we sat side by side on the couch. I tucked my bare feet up underneath me.

"I wanted to let you know about some information I found," Gracie said, sipping slowly at her coffee. At my questioning look, she clarified, "About Sheila's client."

"You found out who he is?" I asked eagerly, but she shook her head.

"I couldn't find out an actual name, but I heard he's looking for someone new and he's going to be at a party tomorrow night."

"What kind of party?" I asked.

"It's a special kind of party," she answered. "Every once in a while, my employer will throw one of these. They're to introduce the girls to new clients and to old ones who may be looking for someone different."

"And he'll be there?"

"That's what I've heard," she said. "I was wondering if you wanted to come. I could tell Simone—that's my boss—that you're thinking of getting into the business. So you wouldn't be obligated to be with anyone, but maybe you'd learn something that would help us track down who killed Sheila."

It sounded safe enough but I was wary of the circumstances.

"Are you sure I wouldn't have to"—I searched for the right words—"be hired by anyone?"

"Absolutely," Gracie reassured me. "I promise. You'll only go with somebody if you want to." She hesitated. "Have you given any more thought to trying it out?"

I shook my head. "I just don't think it's for me."

Gracie shrugged. "Okay, if you're sure," she said. "So do you want to come to the party?"

"Let me think about it," I said. The prospect of going to a party to be looked over like I was a piece of meat was rather daunting, even if I was just posing as an escort. We chatted some more while we finished our coffee, then Gracie glanced at her watch.

"I've got to get going," she said, "but here, let me give you this." Reaching into her purse, she scrawled something on a piece of paper. "This is my address. If you ever need a place to stay"—her eyes flicked back to the bruise on my face—"just come. I won't ask any questions."

I really appreciated her thoughtfulness and I impulsively hugged her. "Thanks, Gracie," I said sincerely.

She seemed a bit surprised, but returned the hug.

After she left, I had to hustle to get ready. I was grateful to be able to return to my usual work uniform of pants and a long-sleeved boatneck T-shirt, leaving the Britney outfit at home. Hurriedly locking my door, I knocked at CJ's and waited.

Opening her door, she handed me a small package. "Here's the drive. Be careful and don't drop it," she admonished.

"I won't," I assured her.

"Give me your cell number so I can reach you later," she said, and I watched as she punched it into her cell phone.

"Good luck," she called out as I headed down the stairs. I hoped I wouldn't need it.

Scott was bartending with me again tonight and I gave him a friendly smile as I stowed my purse under the bar.

"How's it going?" he asked as he wiped down the bar.

"Good," I said.

I noticed out of the corner of my eye that he was still looking at me. Looking the way I'd seen him look at the waitresses. I cursed my luck. Of course he would be interested now, when I was with someone else.

Wait, *was* I with someone else? It felt like it, though Blane hadn't actually said anything concrete. Maybe that's the way it was with someone like Blane, I thought cynically. He didn't have to make it official because it wouldn't be lasting very long.

It wasn't very busy tonight, which was nice after the chaos of Halloween. The time went a bit slowly, though. I was finishing serving a couple sitting at the bar when Scott came up behind me.

"Hey, Kathleen," he said, and I turned toward him. He looked nervous, which was endearing, and I smiled at him, though I thought I knew what was coming. "I was wondering if you'd like to go out sometime."

A sheepish grin curved his mouth. Scott looked good tonight. A lock of his hair fell over his forehead and I reached forward to push it back. But I saw him differently now. If he'd asked me out a couple of weeks ago, I would have been ecstatic. But now, he seemed very young. Probably a stupid thing to think since he was my age. I tried not to compare him to Blane.

"I'm sorry," I said, "I'm sort of . . . with someone." Maybe. "But thank you for the invitation." I gave him a quick peck on the cheek and he smiled ruefully.

"Guess I waited too long," he said. "You'll tell me, right, if you become . . . uninvolved?"

I nodded. That little awkward scene over, I turned back to my side of the bar, glancing around for any new orders, or customers who may have come in.

Blane stood in the shadows, watching me. I smiled in welcome. My heart leapt in my chest as he strode to the bar, sliding onto a stool. He wore jeans and a long-sleeved black henley and, as was his habit, he'd pushed the sleeves a few inches up his arms. His hands caught my eye as he sat down and I blushed furiously, remembering what had happened between us this morning. Then my brows furrowed as I noticed that his knuckles were raw and scraped.

I made him a Dewar's and water, setting it on the bar in front of him. His hand curved around the glass and I jerked my eyes up, from looking at his hands to his face. He smiled, as if he knew what I was thinking.

"Who is he?" he asked, gesturing slightly with his head toward Scott, busy at the other end of the bar.

"Scott," I said uneasily. Blane seemed to have a possessive streak that I didn't want to antagonize. "We work together a lot." I hurriedly changed the subject. "You're here early." I didn't get off work for another two hours.

My breath caught at the look in his eyes. "I wanted to see you," he said softly. His eyes skimmed over me before he reached up, his fingers resting under my chin as he turned my face slightly away. I squirmed uncomfortably as he inspected my cheek. I had taken a great deal of care, and makeup, to cover the bruises. Moving backward so his hand fell away, I met his eyes again.

"James won't be bothering you anymore," he said firmly.

My stomach clenched. "Why?" I asked. "What happened?"

"I spoke with him," Blane said evenly, "and was able to convey how . . . displeased . . . I would be if there was a repeat of his behavior yesterday."

Okay, so I know I probably should have been mad at his interference. I was a liberated woman and could take care of myself, right? I didn't need some big, burly man to heap violence on those who would hurt me, and I thought I probably knew now why Blane's knuckles were in the shape they were.

I should have felt that way, but I didn't. In reality, I was not only grateful for Blane's protection, I was also touched that he cared enough to fight for me. Then a thought occurred to me and I frowned.

"Won't that make things difficult for you at work?" I asked. James was Mr. Gage's son. He might be able to get Blane fired as easily as he had me.

"No," Blane answered, taking a sip of his drink. "I'm a partner. Since I'm an owner, I actually have more of a say in that business than James does, regardless of his family connection."

"You warned me about him," I said, remembering the scene in Blane's office. "How did you know?"

"I've heard things," he said curtly, and I knew he wasn't going to elaborate.

I nodded. Then someone called my name and I had to get back to work.

A little while later, I was able to get back to Blane, and I saw that he'd finished his drink. But when I asked him if he'd like another, he declined.

"I've got to do something first and then I'll be back," he said, tossing some money down on the bar. My eyes followed him as he stood. The shirt and jeans hugged him in all the right places and I enjoyed the view. I felt warmth between my thighs as I thought about taking his clothes off. My eyes caught his and he cursed softly under his breath. Leaning across the bar, he stroked my ponytail, pulling it over my shoulder and tugging slightly until I leaned toward him.

"Keep looking at me like that and I won't be held responsible for my actions," he said roughly.

My tongue darted out to wet my suddenly dry lips and I saw his gaze drop to my mouth. His lips met mine for the briefest of kisses, his tongue brushing gently against mine and sending an electric current through me, before he pulled back.

"I'll be back," he said, and headed for the door.

I watched him leave, not moving until Scott startled me.

"So that's him, huh," he said from beside me.

"Um . . . yeah," I said, clearing my throat.

"Where'd you meet him?" he asked, and I hesitated. Telling Scott that I was dating my boss would probably make me sound like a total tramp.

I was saved from answering by Tish, who needed an order filled. Scott didn't bring it up again after that and I was glad. I didn't really know what I would have said if he had. Dating your boss was always frowned upon, no matter who you were.

I tried to keep busy and not watch the clock. About thirty minutes before closing, Tish came up to me.

"Kathleen," she said, a mischievous grin on her face, "that guy is waiting out back for you."

My heart leapt and I grinned happily. I glanced eagerly at Scott, who rolled his eyes.

"Fine, go," he said, "but you owe me one."

I smiled wider. "Thanks, Scott," I said, grabbing my purse. It had slowed down even more and I'd already gotten a lot of my prep work done, so didn't feel too badly about sneaking out early.

I made my way through to the back door and stepped outside. It was really cold and I shivered, wishing I hadn't been in too much of a hurry to bother with a coat this afternoon. I looked around, but it seemed deserted.

"Looking for someone?"

I spun around and my stomach lurched. Kade was standing a few feet from me, leaning casually against the wall in the shadows of the building next door.

Of course. Tish hadn't seen Blane tonight. She'd just seen me with Kade last night. I cursed my stupidity. If I hadn't been so eager to see Blane, I might've realized Tish's mistake.

I reached for the door, but before I could open it, Kade pulled open his leather jacket slightly, revealing the same gun he'd had last night in a holster on his hip. I swallowed.

"Let's take a walk," he said. The feeble light from the streetlamps made his dark hair seem black in the night, his deeply set eyes shadowed. Taking my elbow, he started walking me deeper into the darkness.

The streets were quiet tonight and we seemed to be the only ones out. I walked stiffly beside Kade, his grip tight on my arm.

"Did you bring it?" he finally said.

I hesitated. There was no one to back me up, no one who even knew where I'd gone or with whom. No one at the bar knew Kade's name. I felt fear seize me. There was nothing stopping Kade from first taking the hard drive, then killing me. Or the other way around, whichever he preferred.

"How do I know you won't kill me if I give it to you?" I asked, trying to keep my voice even. I had nothing to bargain with, but I thought frantically, trying to buy time.

Kade stopped, pushing me against the nearest wall. His gun was in his hand now, so quickly I hadn't even seen him pull it, and he pressed it lightly underneath my jaw. One corner of his mouth lifted upward in his version of a humorless smile. His eyes were cold.

"You don't," he said simply.

My lips thinned. It didn't seem like I had a lot of options. I had the small satisfaction of knowing that, if he did kill me, he still didn't have what he wanted, since CJ had wiped the drive. Keeping my head as still as possible, I dug in my purse, pulling out the small package and handing it to him.

"Here," I said. Kade didn't look down, but just took it, pushing it into his pocket. The gun disappeared and I took a shuddering breath.

"Now, that wasn't so hard, was it?" he asked.

I felt my eyes stinging and I angrily blinked back traitorous tears. God, I hated my habit of crying when I was mad. It made me look weak.

"I thought you were a decent guy," I hissed at him. "Not some gun-for-hire that gets off on threatening women."

In a flash, his smile disappeared and he moved closer, his face inches from mine. I sucked in my breath sharply.

"You don't know anything about me," he bit out, his jaw clenching in anger. "And you're involved in something way over your head. Be glad I'm the one who found you and not someone else." His eyes stared intently into mine, and despite myself, I became aware of our bodies pressed tightly together.

"I know what I'm doing," I insisted, trying to be brave in the face of his anger. "What's your part in this?"

His bitter smile reappeared. "Why should I tell you that?"

My heart skipped a beat and then pounded double-time when I felt his hands settle on my hips. I bit my lip, hard, and saw Kade looking at my mouth.

"Let me go," I said with as much calm as I could muster. Kade didn't move and I started to feel desperate. "If you're going to kill me, then do it," I demanded. "Otherwise, let me go." I swallowed hard. "Please."

"You're too pretty to kill," Kade said lightly, "and you've been very helpful." He sighed. "Mostly." His eyes took on a calculating look. "How did a bartender get involved in this anyway?" he asked scornfully.

I immediately bristled. "I'm not just a bartender," I protested, though why I cared what he thought, I couldn't say. "That's just my second job."

"Oh really," he said, his eyes narrowing. "What's your real job then, princess?"

"I'm a . . ." I hesitated. It sounded so ridiculous to say I was a runner, barely a step up from bartender. I decided to stretch the truth. "I work at a law firm." Technically, that was true. Sort of. I'd been fired, but then Blane rehired me.

"The same one as Junior?" His pet name for James. I nodded.

His forehead creased in a frown and he opened his mouth to say something, but he didn't get the chance.

A loud gunshot startled a scream from me as brick shattered close to my head. In an instant, Kade had shoved me to the ground and drawn his gun. Another shot shattered more brick and I covered my head with my arms. My ears rang when Kade fired a couple of shots back at our assailant. Then his iron grip was on my arm again as he dragged me to my feet.

"C'mon," he said, pulling me after him. "I thought I told you to come alone."

I stumbled and he jerked me upward.

"I did," I replied, breathing heavily as we rushed down an alley. "I swear."

Another gunshot. This time there was no shattering brick, but a blinding pain in my side. I cried out and fell against Kade. Wrapping an arm around my waist, he dragged me with him. I clutched at my side, trying desperately to stay on my feet. Kade turned slightly, firing more shots behind us. I heard the sound of an engine and squeal of tires.

"I think they're gone," Kade said, lowering me to the ground. He pulled my hands away from the burning in my side and lifted my shirt. "It's not that bad," he said, "the bullet just grazed you."

I bit my tongue to keep from telling him what he could do with his "not that bad" diagnosis. It hurt like hell.

"I need to press on it to stop the bleeding," he said.

"Why aren't you just leaving me here?" I asked through gritted teeth, determined not to moan in pain like I wanted. "I thought you were going to kill me anyway."

He grinned and I was momentarily distracted from the pain. It was a real smile, which reached his eyes and made a dimple appear next to his mouth.

"It would ruin my reputation," he said. "I wouldn't have missed." Then he was pressing on my side and I bit my lip hard so I wouldn't make any noise.

"I need to put a quick bandage on this," he said, and I barely had time to comprehend what he was saying before he'd pulled out a knife and slit the front of my shirt from neck to hem.

"What are you doing?" I squeaked in alarm as he pulled the ruined shirt off my arms. My back made contact with the freezing pavement and I started to shiver.

Kade ignored me as he cut off one of the sleeves. Lifting me slightly, he wrapped it around my chest right underneath my bra to cover the wound in my side. He tied it together so it wouldn't slip but wasn't uncomfortably tight.

Despite being in pain, I immediately crossed my arms over my chest, though I knew he'd already gotten an eyeful.

Kade quickly removed his leather jacket and unbuttoned his long-sleeved shirt. I watched, my eyes getting larger and larger, as he stripped off the shirt and shrugged back into his jacket.

"Can you stand?" he asked, and I did so, grimacing only slightly.

The tight makeshift bandage seemed to help. Kade draped the shirt over my shoulders and I pushed my arms into the too-long sleeves. It still held the warmth from his body. My eyes were on level with his bare chest peeking through the leather of his jacket and I swallowed. His fingers moved to button the shirt when I gathered my courage and looked up into his eyes.

The tension between us was suddenly palpable and I felt as if I could barely breathe. Our eyes stayed locked and I felt his knuckles brush against my skin as he gradually did up the shirt's buttons. When he reached the one between my breasts he paused, and I felt the merest brush of his fingers in my cleavage.

In a flash of movement, Kade suddenly spun around, drawing his gun and stepping in front of me. My heart leapt into my throat. I hadn't heard anything, but obviously he had. My hands felt like ice as I waited.

"What are you doing here, Kade?"

I released my breath in a gust, relief pouring through me. Blane had found me. I peeked out from behind Kade and flinched. Blane was standing about twenty feet away, also holding a gun.

"Blane!" I called out, "I'm here."

I stepped from behind Kade, but he grabbed my arm tightly.

"You know Blane?" he asked suspiciously.

I decided to fudge the truth a little. Okay, more than a little.

"He's my boyfriend," I answered, which was stretching the truth to a ridiculous degree, but I hoped it would deter Kade from keeping hold of me.

The effect of those words was instantaneous. Kade looked nearly stricken and seemed to freeze in place.

Not understanding, but still wanting to get away, I looked down at his hand on my arm and said, "Let me go."

He jerked as if I'd slapped him and immediately released me. I walked toward Blane, careful to not get in the line of fire. When I got close enough, Blane reached out and pulled me to him, wrapping an arm around my waist. I gratefully leaned against his chest.

"What are you doing out here with him?" Blane asked quietly, his voice like ice.

"I thought it was you," I tried to explain. "He . . . surprised me."

Glancing down at me, he frowned.

"What happened?" he asked.

"I got shot," I said. "Sort of. Just a graze, I guess."

I could tell Blane was suddenly and dangerously furious.

"You shot her?" he bit out at Kade, and I began to seriously worry that Blane might shoot him.

Kade's eyes narrowed and the tension in the alley notched upward.

"No, no!" I said quickly. "Someone else was following us. Kade didn't shoot me. He helped me."

Blane didn't say anything to that. He and Kade were caught up in a staring match. I tugged on his arm. It was like trying to move granite.

"Please, let's just go," I said, glancing uneasily at Kade, who also hadn't lowered his gun.

Finally, Blane walked us backward until we could round the corner of the building. Kade did not follow. Blane lowered his gun and took my arm. A few minutes later, we were in his car. I leaned back against the heated seat and closed my eyes, sighing with relief.

"Tell me what happened," Blane demanded, and I obeyed, sticking just to the highlights of Kade demanding the drive and someone shooting at us. I didn't really want to go into details and tell him about what Kade and I had talked about, or how he'd bandaged me.

"Do you need to go to the hospital?" he asked, and I shook my head.

"No, it's not that bad," I said. Now that the initial shock had passed, the pain was manageable.

A few minutes later, we were pulling up to his house. Mona had left a light burning downstairs for Blane.

"Why are we here?" I asked. "You should have taken me back to my apartment."

"I'll feel better with you here," he answered as he got out of the car.

I wasn't sure what that meant, but got out when he opened the door.

"Can you make it to your room by yourself?" Blane asked, and I nodded. "I'll be up in a while. I have a phone call to make."

I went silently up the stairs to what was apparently "my" room. I wasn't sure what to think of that. On one hand, it established a level of comfort and suggested something more than temporary. On the other hand, he hadn't invited me to his room.

Which, of course, I didn't want him to do. Right.

The tub in the bathroom looked particularly inviting and I ran the water while I stripped. For some reason I couldn't just toss Kade's shirt on the floor with my pants, and instead found myself folding it carefully.

The bandage Kade had made for me stuck to the dried blood and I gritted my teeth in pain as I took it off. I sank gratefully into the hot water and sighed in relief as it enveloped me.

I took special care with my side and the healing cuts on my thighs as I washed, but I didn't bother with my hair. Leaning my head back on the tub, I closed my eyes and tried to relax. I must have dozed off, because the next thing I knew I opened my eyes to see Blane leaning against the sink, watching me. I sat up with a gasp.

Blane couldn't help but see my exposed chest and I quickly sank back down in the water, my cheeks flaming.

"I want to see your injury," he said, "and how your cuts are healing." Grabbing a towel, he stepped forward and held it open for me.

I felt my face heat as I pulled the plug and stood. Wrapping the towel around me, Blane helped me out onto the bathroom floor, keeping his hands on my waist. His eyes drifted downward.

"I wonder how far down the blush goes," he said quietly, a smile playing at the corners of his lips.

I blushed even more at this and he gave a soft laugh. Scooping me up in his arms, he carried me in to the bed and laid me on it, sitting down beside me.

"Let's take a look," he said. His hands moved to part the edges of the towel, and in a blind panic, I grabbed them. My hands felt small and inadequate trying to hold on to his, though he did humor me and pause.

"Shy tonight, Kat?" he teased lightly. "I don't recall you being shy last night."

I groaned at the memory, my hands flying up to cover my face, unable to look him in the eye.

"A gentleman doesn't remind a lady of her embarrassing behavior," I said reproachfully through my fingers.

"Ah yes," he said softly, and I felt his touch trace my skin under the towel, "but I'm not a gentleman, am I?"

Cold air hit my body as I felt him pull the towel away. Embarrassed as I was, I decided to act like an adult and put my arms down by my sides. My elbow brushed the raw skin and I flinched.

Blane frowned and pushed my arm up above my head, turning me slightly so he could see the wound on my side. I tried not to notice how his touch made me shiver. Grabbing a small box by the bed, he squeezed some ointment on the angry red skin and rubbed lightly. My breath hissed between my teeth. The closest thing I could compare it to was a really bad skinned knee. The skin had been torn away but it wasn't very deep. Blane placed a bandage over the area and gently laid my arm back down at my side.

His hand drifted lightly across my rib cage and my breath caught. He was looking at his hand on me and the expression on his face was difficult to decipher. If it were anyone else, I would say he looked guilty. But it was Blane, and that didn't make sense.

"What is it?" I asked, not realizing my voice was barely above a whisper. "What's wrong?"

His eyes lifted to mine, but he didn't answer right away.

"Four inches," he finally said. "The difference between life and death for you tonight was four inches."

My blood ran colder at his bald assessment and I could think of nothing to say.

His hand drifted down to rest on my hip. "May I see how the cuts are doing?" he asked.

My mouth went dry and I shook my head on the pillow. "They're fine," I managed in a strangled voice.

He didn't answer me, his lips twisting slightly in a crooked smile. Reaching up, he grasped the band holding my ponytail and slowly slid it down until my hair was released. His fingers combed through the strands, gently resting them over my shoulder.

I was acutely aware of all my senses. The faint smell of his cologne as he bent toward me. The cotton of his shirt that felt rough against my skin as it brushed my stomach. The quiet in the room save for the pounding of blood in my ears and the quickness of my breath. The air seemed thick in my lungs as I watched him watch me. I felt very vulnerable lying there naked in front of him while he was still fully clothed. It felt submissive, but not in a bad way.

His hand slid slowly down my leg until he reached my knee. Hooking his fingers under the joint, he slowly bent my leg upward, pushing my knee out. My eyes widened in surprise, but I didn't have the strength of will to deny him.

Blane moved farther onto the bed between my legs, then he did the same thing to the other knee, until my inner thighs were exposed. His eyes never left mine and it seemed I was held captive by them. It wasn't until his gaze dropped that I felt another incriminating blush stain my cheeks. I had never been so exposed to a man before and embarrassment made me wish for something to cover myself.

Blane traced the healing cuts lightly and I tried to remember to breathe, which was a completely futile exercise when he gently pressed his lips to the inside of my knee. His mouth traveled slowly up my thigh, softly brushing the damaged flesh as he passed. My legs trembled and his hands caressed the outside of my thighs, much as someone would gentle a terrified animal.

"I want to kiss you, Kat," he murmured against my thigh, the roughness of his jaw abrading my sensitive skin.

Okay, that was odd. He'd never asked my permission before.

He must have taken my silence as acquiescence, but he didn't move to kiss me. Instead, his head lowered between my legs and I squeaked in surprise, instinctively scooting backward away from him.

Blane's hands closed over my thighs, holding me in place. His warm breath caressed my thigh and then his mouth was on me and I couldn't breathe. The intimacy of it shocked me and then pleasure spiked in my senses and my eyes slammed shut. I whimpered and clutched the blanket. Blane gently nudged my legs farther apart and I couldn't resist him.

The same sensations Blane had stirred in me last night built again, only this time he didn't stop but took me right over the edge. Stars exploded behind my eyes and Blane's name fell from my lips as I came apart.

When I could open my eyes, it was to find he'd kissed his way up my body and was nuzzling my neck. My breath came in pants as I tangled my hands in his hair, holding him close to me.

"You're beautiful," he whispered, and he pressed his lips against mine for a kiss I felt clear down to my toes.

After a moment, he pulled back and I mewled in disappointment, thinking he was leaving me. But instead of going, he scooped me into his arms and walked out the door.

"What are you doing?" I asked, stretching upward so I could taste the tantalizing exposed skin of his neck.

"Taking you to bed," he said, carrying me down the darkened hallway.

I smiled. "We were just in bed," I said while sucking gently at the skin under his jaw.

"Not my bed," he answered, pushing open another door and shutting it behind him.

He laid me down in the center of a massive four-poster bed, but I was up on my knees and reaching to catch his sleeve as he stood. Pulling him toward me, I started on his shirt, tugging it out of his jeans and undoing the buttons. His hands tangled in my hair as it hung in waves down my back and then he was kissing me. Shoving the shirt down and off his arms, I moved to his belt, but he pushed me backward onto the bed, climbing on top of me and recapturing my lips.

I tugged at his belt, moaning in relief when I was finally able to get it and the button underneath it undone. Then my hands were brushed aside as Blane moved his mouth from my lips to my breasts. I lost my train of thought, able to focus only on the delicious torture he was inflicting on me. His hand moved between my legs and he slid two fingers inside me. I cried out and his hand stilled.

"Am I hurting you?" he asked, and I frantically shook my head.

"More!" I gasped, and he complied, making me moan and writhe underneath him. "Please," I managed to breathe in his ear. I didn't have enough coherence to string together two actual words, so hoped he'd get the message with just one.

He pulled away from me and quickly shed his pants. I heard the crinkle of a wrapper and then he was gathering me in his arms again as he lay between my thighs.

"Tell me if anything hurts you," he said and I nodded— beyond speech now, I wanted him so badly. I felt him at my entrance and a flicker of unease went through me; it had been a long time, after all. But then he was pushing inside and all I could think was how incredible it felt, him filling me. He went agonizingly slow and I could see his jaw was clenched as he held tightly to his control.

"God, Kat," he breathed, "you feel incredible. So tight."

Okay, well, that certainly was a confidence builder. I wrapped my legs around his hips and arched upward, delighted when he groaned.

"Make love to me," I whispered against his lips, then his mouth was on mine, our tongues tangling together as he thrust inside me again and again.

Blane was much larger than Donny had been and he stretched and filled me. I felt the delicious pressure building again and clung to Blane, my fingernails digging into his shoulders. My release crashed over me and I cried out.

A bare moment later, Blane shuddered in my arms, his lips finding mine again.

Afterward, I couldn't move. I felt boneless and sated. Blane lay on top of me, but after a moment he moved to the side, turning away from me. I was touched that he'd not only thought to protect me, but that he was also trying to be discreet about it. When he turned back, he gathered me in, pressing kisses to my eyes, my cheeks, and finally my lips. Our skin was slightly damp with sweat, but he didn't seem to care and I certainly didn't.

Brushing my hair back from where it was clinging to my damp forehead, he leaned over me. Our eyes met and held. He placed a gentle kiss on my lips, and my heart turned over in my chest. He gazed once more into my eyes, and a small smile curved his lips as a finger grazed lightly down the side of my face. I smiled shyly back.

Turning on his side, he tucked me against him back-to-front and draped his arm over my waist. I lay there for a while and just savored the feel of him holding me. It was the sensation of feeling cherished and protected that had me reeling. No one else had ever made me feel the way Blane did. I smiled sleepily and nestled closer to him.

I was jerked awake by the sound of a phone ringing. For a moment, I was completely disoriented. Then I remembered where I was and sat up, glancing around for the ringing phone.

Blane was no longer in bed with me, but it was still dark outside. I had no idea what time it was, and where was that damn phone? Scrambling out of bed, I promptly stubbed my toe and cursed. Limping, I followed the sound to my purse. Blane must have brought it in for me. I dug inside and jerked out the still-ringing phone.

"Hello?"

"Kathleen, is that you? It's CJ."

Oh my God, I had completely forgotten that she was going to call me if she managed to track the hard drive with the GPS device.

"Kathleen?"

"Yeah, yeah, I'm here," I said quickly, shoving a hand through my hair.

"Where are you?" she asked.

"I'm at Blane's," I answered. "What's going on? Did you trace where Kade took the drive?"

"He's at some house," she said. "I'm sitting in my car outside of it now, thought there might be something to be seen."

"What house?" I asked, curious, and she gave me an address.

I went very still. "What was the address again?"

She repeated it for me.

"Oh my God," I breathed.

"What? What's wrong, Kathleen?" CJ's voice was anxious in my ear.

"That's Blane's address. It's here."

CHAPTER ELEVEN

I t took me a moment to process this, as stunned as I was, and I felt fear ice my veins.

"Kathleen? Are you there?"

"Yeah, I'm here," I answered, my mind spinning.

"Listen," she continued, "I'm outside in my car. I parked on the street on the west side of the house. You have to get out of there."

"But if Kade's here," I argued, "Blane might be in danger. I can't just leave him." My pulse was racing now as I wondered where Blane was. Maybe he'd heard an intruder and had gotten up to check it out.

"Kathleen," CJ said, her voice sad, "I'm sorry but I think you need to realize that Blane probably knows that Kade is there. He might even be the one who sent Kade to get it from you."

My stomach clenched at this and a shaft of pain pierced my chest. "You're wrong," I said, shaking my head even though I knew she couldn't see me. "Blane wouldn't betray me like that. He wouldn't put me in danger."

I heard CJ sigh. "Fine," she said curtly, "but I'll still wait for you. I'll give you fifteen minutes to get out of there."

"Okay," I agreed. "I'm going to try to find Blane."

I hung up the phone and grabbed my purse. Carefully opening Blane's bedroom door, I peered down the darkened hallway and listened. All was silent. As quietly as I could, I went back to my bedroom, hurrying into the bathroom and yanking on my clothes and shoes.

I was about to step on the stairs when I realized I had nothing I could use to defend myself or Blane, should I need it. Thinking quickly, I retraced my steps to Blane's room, searching the walls blindly for a light switch. Flicking it on, I saw what I needed on the table next to the bed. Blane's gun. I grabbed it, checked that it was loaded, and flicked the safety off. Now I was ready.

I crept down the stairs, pausing every couple of steps to listen. I didn't hear anything until I reached the bottom. Voices were coming from the den. Stepping as lightly as I could through the dining room, I paused outside the door to the den, which was open a bare inch. Golden light appeared through the crack, sending a shaft of light into the shadowed dining room. Now I could plainly hear the voices, and my heart sank as I recognized them. Blane and Kade.

". . . you not to come here," I heard Blane say. "It's too dangerous if you're seen. No one can know we're working together."

"You have so little faith in me that you'd think I'd let someone see me?" Kade scoffed. "Please."

There was quiet for a moment.

"Did you find it?" Blane asked.

"No," Kade answered, "it wasn't on there. And I think your pretty little girlfriend is hiding something from you."

"What? Why?" Blane sounded irritated.

"Because all that was on that drive was gay porn. More than I ever wanted or needed to see."

My mouth twisted in a bitter smile and I had to appreciate CJ's style.

"Are you fucking kidding me?" Blane said, and now I could hear the anger in his voice.

"Would I kid about this?" Kade said, sounding angry as well. "Maybe you don't know her as well as you think. And why the hell didn't you tell me you were involved with her? I could have shot you in that alley."

"Because it wasn't any of your business," Blane retorted. "She doesn't even own a computer, Kade, and I doubt she'd know what to do with it if she did. You probably just missed something."

"I didn't miss anything," Kade said evenly. "And we need that code or we're screwed."

"I'm well aware of that," Blane answered curtly. "Has Frank contacted you about it yet?"

"Yes. He said he's getting impatient. There's too much riding on this election. You and I both know that."

Blane didn't reply to that.

My gut was twisting inside me and I felt like I was going to throw up. I had been wrong, so wrong. Mark had been right to warn me. I shouldn't have trusted Blane.

"So let's go see your girlfriend and make her tell us what she knows," Kade said.

I stopped breathing, panic flaring inside me.

"You know where she lives, right?"

"She's not there," said Blane flatly.

"Then where is she?"

A pause, and then, "In my bed."

Kade laughed derisively. I cringed.

"I swear, you're more ruthless than I am sometimes, Blane," he said. "I guess those scratches on your shoulders must be from her. I trust now she'll tell you anything you want to know?"

I didn't want to hear Blane's answer. Without realizing, I was backing away from the door, my hand pressed tightly to my mouth so I wouldn't betray my presence with any sound of the anguish that I was currently feeling.

Something crashed behind me and I spun around in horror. I'd inadvertently bumped into the table and sent a crystal candelabra clattering to the surface. For a moment, I was frozen, then realized the men had stopped talking. I jerked my head around in time to see the door fly open, temporarily blinding me with the light that spilled out. Kade stood there looking at me, his gaze malevolent.

I didn't waste another moment. Fear was a great motivator. I turned and ran. I knew there was a door in the kitchen that opened to the grounds and would ultimately lead me to the street where, hopefully, CJ was still parked. I heard cursing behind me but didn't pause, running as if my life depended on it, which it actually did.

Scrambling through the kitchen, I threw open the door and tore through the yard. It was dark but I ran heedlessly.

"Kat! Wait!" I heard Blane call from not very far behind me. I kept running.

Both Kade and Blane were taller and faster than me and I knew I wasn't going to make it. Turning quickly, I aimed the gun high—I knew I wouldn't kill them but hopefully they didn't—and fired off a couple of rounds. Kade and Blane hit the ground and I took off again.

I saw the street ahead and tried to run faster, the cold air searing my chest as I gasped for breath. To my relief, CJ's car was idling at the curb, the lights off. I ran to it, yanking open the passenger door and diving inside.

"Go! Go!" I yelled at her, turning to see Blane and Kade closing in. CJ stomped on the gas and we pulled away from the curb. Turning around, I saw Kade raise his gun. I flinched, but Blane shoved Kade's arm down before he could get off a shot. Then I saw nothing as they were lost in the darkness of the street behind us.

"Holy shit!" CJ exclaimed, her eyes wide as she stole quick glances at me. "Hey, point that thing somewhere else, would you?" She gestured to the gun I was still holding in my shaking hands.

"Sorry," I said, quickly thumbing the safety on and putting the gun in my purse.

"Where'd you get a gun?" she asked.

"It's Blane's," I answered, trying to catch my breath. My heart was still pounding in my chest.

"You took Blane's gun?" CJ said, smiling widely now. "Sweet."

I didn't think it was sweet. My eyes stung, but I blinked back the tears. I refused to cry. I had known that it was dangerous to get involved with Blane. I had no one to blame but myself.

And yet the thought of his lies and how he'd used me, been planning on using me, caused my stomach to tighten painfully. A surge of nausea made me clutch at my middle.

"Stop the car!" I said, and CJ must have heard the urgency in my voice because she pulled over immediately. I was out before it had completely stopped, my stomach heaving. I threw up its meager contents in the grass, wiping my mouth on my sleeve—Kade's sleeve, actually—and I grimaced.

Getting back in the car, I dug in my purse. I knew I couldn't go home. That would be the first place they'd look. Finding the scrap of paper I needed, I held it up so I could read it.

"Take me here," I said, giving CJ the address. "I can't go home, they'll be there. But you should be okay. They know nothing about your involvement."

"Where am I taking you?" she asked, looking over the paper.

"A friend offered to let me stay with her if I needed to," I said, thinking of Gracie and hoping she'd meant it.

"Are we still on for Monday?" she asked and I nodded.

"Absolutely." My resolve to thwart whatever plan was in place hadn't weakened. If anything, it was stronger now. If Blane thought I was some stupid little girl who "didn't even own a computer," well, he had another think coming, even if it was true that I didn't own a computer.

"Nice job on the gay porn," I complimented her, and she grinned. "They really hated that."

"So tell me what happened?" she asked and I repeated the conversation I'd overheard.

"I don't know how they're involved exactly," I said, "but I think Kade works for the Santini brothers. Blane works for the firm, and I know he has no love for James, but they must be working together to get James elected."

"It makes sense," CJ mused. "Blane's the brains and Kade's the gun. Blane must have realized your connection to Mark and wanted to gain your trust so you'd tell him what

Mark knew. So he played good cop while sending Kade to play bad cop."

I closed my eyes, dismayed at how easily I'd been played. CJ must have sensed how upset I was, because she didn't say anything else.

Gracie lived in a much nicer apartment complex than I did and I thought again of how much money she made as an escort. I would have to figure out something soon. Obviously, I couldn't go back to the law firm on Monday. Rent was due and I had just enough in my checking account to pay it, but I had to get another job quick.

I told CJ to stay in the car. I wanted as few people to know about our association as possible. Should something happen to me, I didn't want anyone to be able to link her to me and go after her as well. She said she'd wait to make sure it was all right for me to stay.

Tentatively, I knocked on Gracie's door. It was very late and I hated to wake her, but I didn't know what else to do. I waited a few minutes and then knocked again. Finally, I heard the lock turn.

"Kathleen?" she said in surprise when the door opened. She was wearing a beautiful red satin negligee and I belatedly hoped she was alone.

"Hey, Gracie," I said, smiling weakly. "I was hoping you meant it when you said I could stay with you."

She didn't say anything and I hastened to add, "It'll only be for a day or so."

"Of course!" she said. "You can stay as long as you like! I was just surprised, that's all. Come in!"

Stepping back to the railing overlooking the parking lot, I flicked a wave at CJ, who flashed her lights at me and pulled out of the lot.

"Just letting my ride know they could go," I explained as I entered her apartment.

It seemed Gracie was fond of the tropics, for her whole apartment was decorated in that theme. Bamboo and bright colors adorned the space as well as lots of live plants. Gracie must have a green thumb.

"C'mon," she said, "I have a spare bedroom you can use." I followed her down the hall to a bedroom with a twin bed. It was decorated sparsely and I could tell it was rarely used.

"The bathroom is over there," she said, pointing across the hall. "I have my own, so no worries there. Let me get you some things."

She left and I sank down on the bed, suddenly bone-tired. When she reappeared, she was carrying a small bundle.

"Here's a nightgown for you," she said, "as well as some toiletries. Toothbrush, hairbrush, that sort of thing."

I accepted the pile gratefully. "Thank you so much, Gracie," I said and she just smiled. I could see the questions in her eyes, but true to her word, she didn't ask me why I was there.

"See you in the morning," she said, leaving me alone.

When the door had closed behind her, I wasted no time in ridding myself of the hated shirt, restraining myself from childishly stomping on it, but just barely. My jeans quickly followed and I slipped on the nightgown she'd given me to wear. It wasn't really my style, but I didn't care. After using the bathroom and brushing my teeth, I fell into bed, falling asleep almost instantly and ignoring the wetness on my cheeks.

Morning came all too soon. It took me a moment to remember where I was and the events of last night. My heart plummeted in my chest when I recalled the vivid details in my mind. It didn't help that the soreness between my legs reminded me of just how much of an idiot I'd let myself become with Blane. He must be laughing himself silly at how easy it had been to get me into bed. Suddenly, I felt no better than the parade of women that Clarice and I used to make fun of—the ones who never had a clue how transitory and interchangeable they were in Blane's life.

Moping and feeling sorry for myself wasn't going to get me anywhere. I had other problems that needed to be addressed. Hauling myself out of bed, I padded across the hall to the bathroom. I brushed the snarls from my hair and splashed some water on my face, then went in search of coffee.

To my surprise and dismay, I found that Gracie had company. I stopped short in the kitchen as I saw her and another woman sitting at the table.

"I'm so sorry," I apologized. "I didn't realize you had a guest." I turned to leave, but Gracie stopped me.

"Kathleen, wait. There's someone I'd like you to meet."

I reluctantly turned back around, my cheeks burning. The nightgown Gracie had given me left little to the imagination. Indigo with spaghetti straps, and nearly backless, it only came down to midthigh.

"Can I get dressed first?" I asked and she just laughed.

I noticed she was still in her nightgown as well, though she'd thrown on a matching robe over it.

"Simone won't mind," she said, beckoning to me. The name rang a bell, but I couldn't quite place it. I walked forward, plastering a smile on my face as I turned to the woman sitting with Gracie.

She was older, perhaps in her forties, but beautifully made up. I knew immediately that she had money. Her makeup was flawless, her hair perfectly coiffed in a stylish French twist, and she wore smart black trousers with a pinstriped blouse. Heavy silver earrings hung from her ears while a matching necklace circled her throat. Smiling, she held her hand out to me.

"Good morning, Kathleen," she said, and I realized she had an accent. French, maybe. "I've heard a lot about you."

I turned questioningly to Gracie, who just smiled.

"It's a pleasure to meet you, Simone," I said politely, grasping her hand.

"Sit down, Kathleen," Gracie said as she jumped up. "I'll get you some coffee."

I thanked her and pulled out a chair, noticing as I did so that Simone was looking me over with a critical eye. Nervously I sat, clasping my hands in my lap. Gracie set a cup of coffee in front of me and I took a small sip as she sat back down.

"I work for Simone," Gracie explained, and then it clicked.

The escort service. Simone was the madam. I eyed her curiously. She didn't fit my mental image of what a madam would look like, which was something more along the lines of Dolly Parton in *The Best Little Whorehouse in Texas.*

"Gracie mentioned that you might be interested in coming to work for me," Simone said. "Are you?"

I bit my lip in indecision. I'd had no time to prepare for this, and part of me wanted to give Gracie a good wallop for springing Simone on me.

I wasn't naive enough to think that I wouldn't be expected to have sex with someone, no matter what Gracie had said. But I knew I couldn't do that. I couldn't imagine doing what Blane and I had done last night with just some random guy. On the other hand, this might be my only chance to get a lead on who had killed Sheila. If I went to the party, maybe I could get a line on Sheila's killer. Somehow I would just have to find a way to avoid the sex part of the job.

I nodded my assent. "Yes, I would."

Simone laughed quietly. "That's wonderful, my dear," she said. "We provide sophisticated, discreet, and beautiful companions to very wealthy, very powerful men. I'm delighted to add you to our ranks."

"I don't know about the sophisticated and beautiful part," I said ruefully.

"My dear, you will do quite nicely," she said, exchanging a knowing smile with Gracie. "Gracie will take you today to get you outfitted for my party this evening. You will come, won't you? And I promise, you will be a lovely addition to our little family."

I swallowed and forced a smile, unsure what I was getting myself into. Getting up to leave, Simone kissed both of my cheeks, European style, and did the same to Gracie, who returned the gesture. After she'd left, Gracie came back and sat at the table again, beaming at me.

"I'm so excited!" she said enthusiastically. "You are going to love it! I promise. And today, we get to fix you up!" She rubbed her hands together gleefully.

"What do you mean by fix me up?" I asked, my trepidation growing.

"Fun stuff," she said with a dismissive wave of her hand. "We'll get your hair styled and your makeup done. And I know just the place to go for your gown. You're going to look amazing!"

Gracie was like a persistent mother hen. She made me eat some breakfast, though I could barely choke it down. My stomach was still in knots whenever I thought of Blane, which happened more frequently than I wished. I'd warned myself against getting involved with him because I'd known what would happen, and I'd been right. The feelings I had for him had only strengthened and solidified after we'd made love, making his betrayal even more difficult to take.

I showered and changed into some clothes that Gracie loaned me from her own wardrobe—a pair of Capri pants that were so long they fit nearly like regular pants, and a button-down shirt. Gracie said it had to be a shirt with buttons because we wouldn't want to pull anything over my hair once it had been fixed.

She drove us to a tiny boutique called Helen of Troy, greeting the woman inside with a warm hug and the kiss-kiss gesture Simone had done.

"Helena, it's so good to see you!" Gracie said. "This is Kathleen. She's going to Simone's party tonight and needs a dress."

Helena was a tiny woman with long red hair, haphazardly braided, hanging down her back. If I had to guess, she must have been in her fifties, and going by the way she was dressed, I was dubious as to whether or not she was a good judge of clothing.

Looking me over with an appraising eye, she pushed me toward a changing room.

"Strip!" she commanded, and I was surprised at her forcefulness as she shoved me into a room and yanked the curtain shut behind me.

Gracie poked her head in. "I know she's odd," she said in a conspiratorial whisper, "but she knows what she's doing. Promise." With a last grin at me, she disappeared.

I shrugged off my clothes and stood there in my borrowed underwear until Helena reappeared.

"Take your bra off and try this on," she said, helping me into a dress. When it was zipped, a wide smile broke out on her face. "Ah, perfect." She spun me around to face the mirror and my jaw dropped.

The dress was a deep iridescent aqua, the fabric seeming to flow and change color as the light hit it when I moved, almost like water. It was a strapless corset gown with a sweetheart neckline and an empire waist adorned with crystals, beads, and sequins. Fitted to mid-thigh, it then flared out into a small train behind me, the front skirt cut away to reveal white lace. The color of the dress brought out the blue in my eyes and contrasted perfectly with my strawberry blonde hair. The neckline made my cleavage look voluptuous, and the tightly fitted waist and skirt turned my figure into the perfect hourglass.

"Wow," breathed Gracie, and I noticed she'd poked her head in again. "That looks amazing on you!"

I couldn't stop looking in the mirror. I could hardly believe it was me staring back.

"What will she be?" asked Gracie, speaking to Helena, and I glanced around, frowning.

"What do you mean?" I asked.

"Oh, it's something Simone does," Gracie explained. "It's kind of like a costume ball. Everyone wears masks, doesn't use their real names, that sort of thing."

"She will be a mermaid, of course," answered Helena, as if it were obvious.

A little while later, she'd outfitted me with shoes, a matching clutch purse, and a beautiful mask, the real elaborate kind I'd seen for Mardi Gras. It completely covered my face except for my mouth and chin. I couldn't help getting a little excited about tonight, if only because of the clothes I'd be wearing.

Next we went to a salon and I gulped when we entered. It was one of those really nice ones that offer you something to drink while you waited. As we sat waiting our turn, I leaned over to Gracie.

"I can't afford this," I whispered urgently in her ear. She just waved me away.

"Simone has an account here," she said as she flipped through a magazine. "All of us come here. Don't worry about it."

They called my name and I was primped, poked, waxed, and made up to within an inch of my life. I wanted to draw the line at the bikini wax, but Gracie insisted. I did, however, put my foot down when they wanted to cut my hair. And no, I wasn't putting up a fight because I knew Blane liked my long hair. At least, that's what I told myself.

"It's not a problem," the stylist said. "We will arrange it in beautiful waves and curls so it hangs down your back and tantalizes. Just so." He held my hair in his hands to approximate the style and showed me in the mirror.

When I was done, I'd had a manicure and pedicure. My makeup was done in a natural way that somehow managed to emphasize the blue of my eyes while still making them look smoky and mysterious. My hair was pulled back with two elegant combs and then cascaded in waves down my back. I had to admit, the stylist had done a nice job.

"You look fantastic!" Gracie exclaimed in delight.

"So what will you go as tonight?" I asked.

"I'm going as a tigress," she said, winking at me, and I laughed. I could easily imagine Gracie as a tiger.

When she stepped out of her bedroom later, dressed in a gold gown with a slit in the side up to her thigh, it was enough to take my breath away in awe. Her black hair hung absolutely straight and the gold made a beautiful contrast to her cocoa skin. I almost felt dowdy again standing next to her, even in my blue dress.

"Let's go!" she said, and we made our way downstairs to find a long limousine waiting.

"To welcome you properly as one of us," Gracie explained with a smile.

I smiled back uncomfortably. I wondered what Simone would do when I didn't fulfill my side of the deal tonight.

We settled into the plush leather interior and Gracie poured us each a drink from the crystal decanter inside filled with an amber whiskey.

"To settle your nerves," she said, handing me a glass. The scotch was a good vintage and I swallowed it gratefully, my stomach doing butterflies.

I wondered if I'd be able to figure out which man had been with Sheila. Her death lingered on my conscience and I felt slightly depressed that nothing had been done to bring her and Mark's killer to justice. How much the firm and Blane were involved, I didn't know. Hopefully tonight would bring answers.

"How will I know if it's him or not?" I asked Gracie.

She didn't ask what I meant. She knew.

"I heard he goes by 'Enigma,'" she said. "I've never met him, so I don't know what he looks like."

Enigma. Okay. That didn't send a chill up my spine or anything.

"Code names?" I questioned. Gracie nodded.

"I told you that no one uses their real names at these things," she reminded me. "The men included."

I took another gulp of my liquid courage. It flashed through my mind that Blane would like how I looked tonight, then I banished the thought as quickly as it had come. I couldn't afford to get emotional, though a part of me did wish for his solid, reassuring presence, even if he was a liar.

"We're here," Gracie said as we stopped, and I downed the rest of my drink.

The door opened and we got out. I was momentarily taken aback. I don't know what I had been expecting, but it hadn't been this. We were in front of a very large stone Victorian mansion. I felt like I'd stepped into a gothic novel.

"Follow me," Gracie said in an undertone.

She raised her chin and walked to the gate as if the sidewalk were a runway. I followed, mustering as much courage and confidence as I could. Gracie muttered something to the man at the gate, who scrutinized her and me before allowing us to pass.

"What was that about?" I breathed to her.

"Password," she whispered back.

No one greeted us at the door as we walked inside. It was very dim, only a few scattered candelabras giving off any light. All lamps and overhead lights were turned off. Uneasily, I followed Gracie down the hallway, our heels on the marble floor making the only sound.

We finally came to a set of double doors at least twelve feet tall, where two men dressed in tuxedos and black masks stood as sentinels. Gracie didn't acknowledge them, so I tried not to stare. She drifted inside, and taking a deep breath, I followed.

The room I stepped into must have been a ballroom at one time, with its easily twenty-foot ceiling. Now, however, it was very different. It had been decorated and redone to seem like a very luxurious outdoor lounge. Groups of chairs, sofas, settees, and chaises were scattered around, all in jewel-tone colors and soft, plush fabrics. Small tables held more candelabras, and heavy curtains and tapestries hung from the walls. The carpet under my feet was thick, muffling my footsteps. Private alcoves had been created using folding wooden screens, though I didn't have a view into any of them to see what they contained. But most surprising of all were the trees that had been brought indoors, in huge urns that housed their roots. The trees created even more privacy and shadows.

People were scattered around the room, their conversations muted by the furniture and tapestries. Music played softly in the background—jazz, I thought. I caught sight of several other women dressed as splendidly as Gracie and me. Everyone was wearing a mask. There were easily twice as many men as women and they were all in white-tie tuxedos with the same simple black masks that had covered the guards' faces. Looking around anxiously, I tried to see Gracie, but she'd melted into the crowd.

"So good to see you, my dear," a voice said, and I turned to see a woman, I supposed she was Simone, gliding toward me. She was dressed in long silver gown with a matching mask. "Tell me, Helena dubbed you the Mermaid, did she not?"

I swallowed. "She did," I replied, my voice barely audible. The weirdness of the situation was starting to freak me out and I wondered, a bit anxiously, what I'd gotten myself into.

"Well," she said, "we'll call you Lorelei. Please, don't be nervous," Simone said, grasping my arm and tugging. "Come, let me introduce you to some gentlemen who I think would find you most intriguing."

I allowed her to lead me to a group a ways from the door. Two men and a woman sat talking, one man in a chair and the other on a couch while the woman was artfully arranged on a chaise. Her hair was a platinum blonde and she wore a red velvet gown with a slit up the side that had been draped to reveal a long, smooth leg.

"Gentlemen," Simone said, "I'd like you to meet Lorelei, the Mermaid. Lorelei, this is the Scarlet Ibis." She gestured to the woman on the couch, who inclined her head slightly to me.

Both men stood, taking it in turns to grasp my fingers and press their lips to the back of my hand. I automatically smiled, though I was trembling inside. Neither one introduced himself, though they both graciously invited me to sit. Simone drifted away and I found myself talking to one of the men.

"You are quite lovely," he said quietly, and I noticed that the other man had begun conversing in an undertone with the Scarlet Ibis.

What the heck was an ibis anyway, I thought. And why was Simone calling me Lorelei?

"Thank you," I said just as quietly. I didn't know what else to say so remained silent.

"I do believe you're new," he said in a somewhat bemused tone.

"Is it that obvious?" I asked and he smiled.

"A bit," he answered. "But don't worry. We're really all quite harmless." Then he seemed to think that over. "Well, most of us are harmless." His lips curved in another smile. He had dark eyes and dark hair and seemed familiar, but I brushed it off. He fit the description of a lot of men.

He was quite charming, talking to me of inconsequential things and even making me laugh a bit. I was beginning to relax and I ventured to ask his name.

"I'm called Mercury," he answered. I wasn't sure if I was relieved or disappointed. My purpose here was to try to find Enigma, but I wasn't sure what I was going to do if and when I actually did.

Mercury gently laid his hand on my shoulder and I jumped. I hadn't been expecting him to touch me. His fingers trailed lightly down my arm.

"I would like very much to get to know you better," he said. "Would you like that?"

I thought I knew what he was asking and I panicked. I didn't want to refuse him outright without knowing what the consequences would be. Would he get angry and tell Simone? Would she make me leave? So I thought of an excuse.

"I just need to get something to drink," I improvised, standing quickly. "I'll be right back." Not waiting to hear what he had to say, I quickly walked away. Glancing around, I noticed people with drinks in their hands, so there must be a bar around somewhere.

I wandered aimlessly through the darkened room, trying not to look too closely into shadowy alcoves, especially after in one I saw a woman with her dress around her waist as she straddled a man. It didn't take a genius to figure out what they were doing. I quickly rushed by, my cheeks flaming in embarrassment.

Finally, I found the bar. Sighing in relief, I asked for a glass of champagne. I didn't want to cloud my head with any more hard liquor, and champagne didn't have much of an effect on me.

"Well, hello, beautiful. What's your name?" The voice made me choke on the champagne.

A hand appeared with a handkerchief and I gratefully took it, dabbing at my mouth. Reluctantly turning, I saw Kade behind me. He was wearing a mask, but I would have known those eyes anywhere. I wondered why a man like him would need to be at a place like this.

"Sorry about that," he said with a crooked smile. "Didn't mean to startle you."

I searched his eyes for any sign of recognition, but couldn't tell if he knew who I was or not.

"I'm Omen," he said. "And you are?"

I decided to try and disguise my voice as much as possible, so when I replied, I poured on the southern accent, trying to make it more *Designing Women* than *The Beverly Hill-billies.* "They call me Lorelei."

"Ah," he mused, his eyes raking me up and down, "the fatal mermaid siren, luring unwary sailors to their deaths with her irresistible song. It seems fitting.

"Are you here with someone?" he asked, taking a sip of his own drink as he glanced around the room.

I shook my head. "No, but I'm looking for someone." I decided to chance it. Finding Enigma was going to be a needle-in-a-haystack search. Maybe if I just asked, someone could point him out.

"Who is that, Lorelei?" he said, sounding slightly amused. He eyed my lips when I nervously wet them.

"Enigma."

Kade's eyes narrowed slightly and he didn't answer. I felt myself break out into a cold sweat under his scrutiny. Finally, he moved so he stood beside me.

"Look over there," he said in my ear. "He's standing in the corner by the fireplace, watching you."

I looked where he said and felt my blood run cold. Even from a distance, I recognized the frame. Wide shoulders, blond hair, and even the way he stood were all too familiar to me.

It was Blane. My hand started to shake and I hurriedly put down my champagne glass before I spilled it everywhere. My mind reeled. It couldn't be. Gracie had to have been wrong. I turned and ducked into the nearest path away from him, relieved to see that Kade did not follow.

I walked quickly, my head down, as I tried to regain control of my emotions and think logically. Both Kade and Blane were here, which only emphasized my suspicions that the firm and Blane were in league with the Santini brothers. I sincerely doubted they were here to pick up escorts, though I was at a loss as to what the election fraud software had to do with prostitutes. Gracie had said the man who had been seeing Sheila was code named Enigma. And according to Kade, that was Blane.

I wasn't looking where I was going and I was brought up short when I collided headlong into someone. Jerking my head up in alarm, I would have stumbled had he not grabbed my upper arms, steadying me. I closed my eyes in relief when I saw it was the man who had called himself Mercury.

"There you are, Lorelei," he said. "I was afraid you'd gotten lost on your way back to me."

And just like that, I realized why he seemed so familiar. It was James, of all people. "I . . . I'm sorry," I stammered, trying to conceal my surprise. "I got a bit turned around."

"Let's find somewhere private where we can . . . talk," he said with satisfaction in his voice. I gulped and plastered a smile on my face. I didn't see how I could refuse without making a scene. He didn't seem to know who I was, but I couldn't believe I hadn't recognized him earlier. Though, to be fair, it's not like I'd been expecting to actually know anyone besides Gracie here tonight.

He led me through the maze of trees until we came to an empty private alcove. A wide loveseat and a table with a few candles scattered on it occupied the space. Uneasily, I sat on the couch while he sat close beside me. I decided talking would be better than anything else he might have in mind.

"So how long have you been coming here?" I asked, my voice too breathless for my liking. I tried to steady my nerves.

"A while," he said vaguely, sliding his arm over my shoulders and touching my bare arm.

"Do you see a lot of different women?"

"Not usually," he answered. "I like to find one I really like and stick with her." He pressed his lips to my shoulder and I clenched my fists. I focused on a silver candlestick on the coffee table in front of me. Its candle had burned low and the flame flickered out as I watched.

"Maybe I should go," I said. I tried to squirm away from him, but his arm tightened around me.

"No, don't go," he insisted, mistaking my reluctance. "I'm not with anyone now. The last woman I liked a lot is no longer with us. I'm looking for someone new. I would be quite, quite content with you." His fingers bit into my shoulder as his mouth moved to my neck.

I was so intent on trying to push him away that it took a moment to realize what he had said. When I did, I went utterly still in shock.

"No longer with us?" I repeated dumbly.

"Mmm," he murmured against my skin. "It seems her boyfriend didn't like her . . . occupation. Jealousy is a powerful emotion, Lorelei."

I didn't know what this meant, but I knew he was talking about Sheila. How Blane fit into this, if they both had been paying for her services, I didn't know yet. But I did know I had to find out more. I slid my hands inside his tuxedo jacket to touch his chest, pretending to be as wrapped up in the moment as he was. James's lips moved to mine. I evaded him so they ended on my cheek.

"What happened to her?" I asked.

But before he could answer, we were interrupted.

"Mercury."

I jerked back in surprise. Blane stood in the alcove with us. My heart stuttered, then started to pound.

"Mercury," Blane repeated, and James reluctantly lifted his head from my neck.

"What do you want?" he said snidely. "Can't you see I'm busy?" He made to pull me close and kiss me again, but I quickly turned my head away, pushing against him. I heard a snarl of anger and then Mercury was lifted bodily from me.

"The Patron wants to speak with you," Blane growled at him, giving him a shove out of the alcove.

James's eyes shot daggers at him, but he left. Then Blane turned to me and I inwardly quaked at the look in his eyes, while trying not to admire how amazing he looked in his tuxedo. The coat was cut perfectly, emphasizing his broad shoulders, and the black mask only served to enhance the green of his eyes and the strong curve of his jaw.

"Lorelei, I believe?" he asked cordially, his tone belying the anger in his eyes, and I nodded. A spark of hope ignited inside me that he didn't recognize me.

"I was told you were looking for me," he said, moving to take Mercury's spot beside me on the couch, his arm draping behind me. The loveseat suddenly felt much smaller than when its previous occupant had been there.

I adopted my accent again when speaking, hurriedly trying to think up an excuse for why I'd been looking for him. "Yes, I was. I was told you might be looking for someone with whom you could spend some . . . quality . . . time." I didn't know how well I was pulling off the femme fatale thing, but I was giving it the best I had.

"Are you offering?" he said, his eyes sliding to my mouth and farther down to where the curves of my breasts were revealed by the cut of my dress.

"Perhaps," I said ambiguously, smiling as flirtatiously as I could manage.

"I can be quite demanding," he cautioned, and my breath caught and held as he lowered his head. "And I don't share."

This last was a low growl before his lips met mine. My arms lifted to curve around his neck as I buried my fingers in his thick blond hair. His tongue touched my lips and I willingly opened my mouth, sighing with pleasure as he deepened the kiss.

I couldn't think of anything but Blane as he kissed me, his arms wrapping around my waist. His mouth trailed kisses down my neck, and unlike with Mercury, this time I burned. Blane's tongue dipped into my cleavage and I gasped, wanting more. I felt him tug the bodice of my dress down, my breasts spilling over the top. He groaned and tugged one nipple into his mouth, palming my other breast. I bit my lip to keep from making any noise.

The heat between us grew in intensity as Blane's mouth and tongue traced my skin. His hand drifted under my skirt and between my thighs. I whimpered when I felt his hand slip under my panties, and his fingers part my folds to slide inside me. His slick fingers stroked the tight bundle of nerves that set my veins on fire and I parted my legs wider, wanting to feel him inside me.

"God, Kat, what you do to me," he murmured in a pained voice as his lips reclaimed mine.

My eyes flew open. He knew who I was. I tore my mouth from his, struggling against him as his weight pressed me into the couch.

"Let me go, Blane," I hissed, pushing ineffectually at his shoulders.

"Did you think I wouldn't know it was you?" he whispered in my ear, ignoring my struggles. His hand stroked me again, his fingers leisurely moving in and out of me, and I dug my fingernails into his shoulders. My traitorous body responded to him as more wetness pooled between my legs, and my hips lifted to meet his fingers.

"Did you think I wouldn't recognize this body?" he continued, his words slithering inside my ear. "The way your skin tastes, the softness of you against my fingers, the sounds you make when I touch you?"

Bending his head again to my breasts, he took me in his mouth, his teeth gently tugging on my nipple. Against my will, I gasped again and I felt his mouth curve in a smile. His hand moved fast and sure inside me, stroking me knowingly. I was rapidly losing any will to get away and it made me want to cry in frustration. I couldn't let him do this, not after he'd lied to me, betrayed me, and used me.

My arm reached out blindly and my hand fell on the candlestick I'd observed earlier. With a quick motion, and trying not to think too much about what I was about to do, I grabbed it and hit it against the back of Blane's head. He immediately went limp on top of me.

He was heavy and it took some squirming and pushing before I was able to get out from under him. I hurriedly re-adjusted my dress and combed my fingers through my hair. Blane still wasn't moving and a niggle of worry made me lean over and press my fingers to the pulse in his neck. Its beat was strong under my fingers and I released a breath I hadn't realized I'd been holding. Grabbing my purse, I knew I had to get out of there. Now.

CHAPTER TWELVE

I made my way as quickly as possible to the two doors through which I'd entered, slipping out in relief. The two sentries were still there, though still neither spoke to me. It was eerie and I shivered.

I walked down the hall and turned a corner, stopping abruptly when I saw James standing mere feet away.

"There you are," he said with a smile, walking toward me. "I was just coming back to find you. Let's get to know each other better, shall we?"

He took hold of my elbow, guiding me toward a door. I resisted, trying to pull myself loose.

"Let me go, James," I demanded, then cursed my own stupidity.

He froze. "You know me?" he asked.

I kept my mouth firmly shut this time.

He abruptly pulled me inside a nearby room, closing the door behind us. It was some kind of den or library. A large mahogany desk sat in one corner, and an entire wall was covered in shelves filled with books. A curved window ranging from the ceiling to the floor looked out onto the darkened grounds.

James gave me a shove and I stumbled forward, quickly turning so my back wouldn't be toward him. I was wary now, realizing that I was in the presence of the man who had most likely killed Sheila. I recalled how James's moods changed so rapidly—charming and gentle one moment, furious the next—and it struck me how apt his Mercury moniker was.

I knew Blane hadn't done it, no matter what Gracie had said. I may not have trusted him, but I knew he wasn't responsible for the horrendous scene I saw that night.

Leisurely taking off his mask, James moved toward me and the smile he wore made a chill run down my spine. As he stepped into the light, I was taken aback to see that his mask had been hiding a black eye, and with a jolt, I remembered Blane's raw knuckles.

"I think you have some explaining to do," he said quietly.

I shook my head, backing away from him. "I don't know what you're talking about." I was proud that my voice didn't shake. My eyes darted around the room frantically for anything I could use as a weapon.

James stalked me, his eyes taking on that unhinged look that was terrifying. I looked for a way past him to escape out the door, but there wasn't a path beyond his reach. I decided to try my luck anyway. Grabbing a stack of books from the shelf, I threw them at his head and darted to the door. I heard him curse.

The door was inches away when his hand grabbed hold of my hair, bringing me up short. I yelped in pain. He dragged me backward toward him and I was helpless to do anything about it. He ripped the mask off my face and paused before a short, humorless laugh issued from him.

"Kathleen. I must say, you've surprised me. I didn't know this was your sort of thing." Releasing my hair, he turned me to face him, his hands closing with brutal force on my upper arms.

"Why are you here?" he demanded.

I raised my face to his, anger building inside me. I was tired of being pushed around by James and if he was going to kill me, and I was pretty sure that was on the agenda, then he was going to tell me the truth first.

"I'm here because I wanted to know who killed my friend, Sheila," I said through gritted teeth. "Why did you do it, James?" I asked. "What did she ever do to you that made you think she deserved to be killed like that?"

Whatever he thought I was going to say, that obviously wasn't it. "What are you talking about?" he said, his face creasing in confusion. "Sheila's dead?" His hands loosened slightly on my arms. "They told me that her boyfriend made her quit."

"She was murdered," I said accusingly. I wasn't sure if I believed that this was new information to him. It was too convenient.

"And you think I did it?" he said angrily. "What kind of screwed-up fuck do you think I am, Kathleen?" He shook me roughly.

"The kind of screwed-up fuck who gave me a black eye," I shot back, refusing to be cowed.

He abruptly released me as if he'd been burned, stepping away from me slightly.

"I didn't mean to do that," he said roughly. "I was . . . upset."

"What else do you do when you're upset?" I persisted, pressing my advantage. "Do you slit someone's throat, James? Because that's how I found Sheila."

"I didn't kill her!" he insisted angrily, shoving his fingers through his hair. "I'm running for office, Kathleen. Why would I screw that up by killing someone?"

"I would think that might be exactly why you'd kill her," I replied.

James was suddenly in my face again as he grabbed my arms, making me wince in pain.

"You can't think that," he said urgently, shaking me again. "You're going to ruin everything. You have to believe me!"

"You're hurting me," I managed to say, trying to pull away from him.

"What's going on here?"

We both turned and I sagged in relief to see someone else had entered the room. Another man, mask still intact, stood in the open doorway. James immediately removed his hands from my arms.

"Dad," he said, "it's nothing. Kathleen and I were just having a disagreement." As if I couldn't get any more shocks tonight, I watched as William Gage Sr. calmly shut the door and walked forward, removing his mask.

"Good evening, Kathleen," he said cordially.

I nervously acknowledged his greeting with a nod, not knowing what else to do in a strange situation that was becoming even stranger. I wondered, a little hysterically, if the entire firm was here.

"What kind of disagreement?" he asked, turning toward James, who was obviously still rattled. He paced the floor, repeatedly pushing his hand through his hair.

"She thinks I killed Sheila!" he burst out, pointing an accusing finger at me.

I didn't say anything.

"Sheila who?" Mr. Gage asked, unperturbed.

"That whore I was with a few weeks ago," James clarified, and before I could think better of it, I'd marched forward and slapped him.

"Don't call her that," I spat at him. "She was a good friend and just trying to make it the best she could. She didn't deserve to die like she did."

James grabbed my arm again, fury in his eyes. I flinched, expecting a blow, but his father brought him up short.

"James," he said, steel in his voice. "Release her."

I waited. After a moment, James reluctantly let me go. I breathed a sigh of relief, hurriedly stepping beyond his reach.

"Kathleen," Mr. Gage said politely, "of course James didn't kill that woman. He may be a bully, but he's certainly not a murderer."

"Then who did?" I asked him, still not wanting to let go of my suspicions.

Mr. Gage smiled and I felt a chill go through me.

"She was collateral damage, my dear. A warning, if you will."

My jaw dropped and I stumbled backward, away from him. James appeared to share my shock as he looked at his father in horror.

"What?" I stammered. "A warning for what? But why? I don't understand." I couldn't believe the nice gentleman I'd known and respected as the head of the firm could be behind something so heinous. Mark's suspicion that Sheila had been killed because of him echoed in my ears.

"There are lots of things you don't understand, Kathleen," he said condescendingly. "My son is in a very unique position. About to be elected as district attorney, as I'm sure you've heard. Sheila's death was necessary to help keep . . . certain people . . . in line. People who would try to thwart those plans."

"You killed Sheila and framed Mark," I accused, furious. Mark had been right after all. Sheila's murder had been a message to him. "And then when he didn't do what you wanted, you had him killed, too."

"Of course not," Mr. Gage replied, "Mark committed suicide. The police were quite sure about that."

I swallowed heavily, my mouth suddenly dry. Whereas James was scary because of his lack of control, his father was terrifying because he was so controlled. He told me all this as if he were talking about the weather. The only emotion in his voice was when he allowed his feelings for James to show. I'd seen enough movies to know what happens when the killer finally confesses. I wasn't going to be allowed to leave the room alive.

"Jimmy!" Mr. Gage called, and the door behind him opened.

I sucked in a breath when I saw Jimmy Quicksilver standing there.

"Yes, sir?" he said, taking in the scene in the room with a quick cold glance.

"Jimmy, this lovely lady has been too inquisitive for her own good. Would you be so kind as to . . . assist . . . her from the premises?"

Jimmy's eyes flicked to mine and my palms started to sweat. "Absolutely," he said with a leer, entering the room and heading toward me.

"No!" James shouted. "Dad, you can't—!" James was cut off by a loud crack as Mr. Gates backhanded him across the face.

"Shut up, Junior," Mr. Gage hissed at him. "This is for your benefit, you know."

I tried easing slowly toward the door while their attention was diverted but was abruptly stopped by Jimmy.

"Touch me and I'll scream," I threatened.

He laughed. "Well, we can take care of that."

Pulling off his bow tie, he handed it to Mr. Gage. "Gag her. I'll hold her."

That's when I began fighting for my life, kicking and scratching anything within reach, screaming bloody murder.

Jimmy twisted my arm up behind me and I cried out in pain. "That's enough of that," he hissed in my ear. "Now be a good girl and hold still."

I pressed my lips firmly closed, but Mr. Gage was able to yank the fabric into my mouth, my teeth cutting my lip when he did so. I tried to meet James's eyes, begging for his help, but he turned away. Bitter despair rose inside me.

"Give me your tie, James," Mr. Gage demanded.

A moment later, Jimmy was tying my hands behind my back, cinching the knots so tightly that numbness set in almost immediately.

"That should do it," Mr. Gage said. "Now take care of her and let me know when it's been done." He turned away, dismissing us.

Jimmy dragged me out the door and down the dimly lit hall.

We reached the front door and stepped outside. I tried to think. As much as I could, I dragged my feet, but he was too strong. Once we were on the porch, he pulled me away from the door, backing me up against the wall.

"Out of sight, out of mind," he breathed quietly, leering at me. His eyes focused on my bleeding lip. "I don't think I'll kill you right away," he mused, almost as if he were talking to himself. "We can have some fun first."

His tongue darted out, licking the blood off my lip, and I shivered in revulsion.

"If you're really good," he said, "I may even keep you alive for a day or two."

I looked at him with hatred in my eyes. I was not going to let him rape me before he killed me, and certainly not for days on end. Snapping my head forward, I made contact with the bridge of his nose and he yelped in pain. I braced myself for retaliation and it came swiftly, as he buried his fist in my stomach. I doubled over, the pain excruciating and nausea bubbling inside me. I thought somewhat hysterically that if I threw up now I'd die from asphyxiation, which might be better than whatever Jimmy had planned for me.

"Let the girl go."

I heard the words and tried to straighten up even though my insides felt like they were on fire. Jimmy was frozen in place by the gun Blane had pressed to his temple.

"I said, let her go." Blane's voice was colder than ice and I heard the distinctive click of the gun's hammer being cocked.

"Kirk," Jimmy said, "you're messing with stuff you should leave alone. Walk away and I'll forget we had this little conversation."

"Not gonna happen, Jimmy," Blane said. "Let her go or you die."

Jimmy's eyes were still on mine and I saw him smile. It sent chills through me. In a sudden movement, he spun toward Blane, knocking the gun away. It clattered to the ground. Instantly, a knife was in his hand. I tried to scream around the gag as he went after Blane, who leapt backward out of the way. They grappled and Jimmy let out a cackle of laughter.

I watched in horror, barely breathing, as Blane twisted and dodged the glittering knife. I winced when he didn't move fast enough and the knife came away red. Blane's hand locked around Jimmy's wrist and I heard a sickening crack. Jimmy cried out in pain, and the knife clattered to the ground. Blane's fist landed in Jimmy's face, and blood spurted from his nose. Without the knife, Jimmy was no match for Blane, though he did land a few hits. Within moments, Blane had pummeled Jimmy until he'd collapsed facedown on the cold ground. Blane quickly retrieved his gun and headed toward the spot I stood, now several feet away.

"Time to go," Blane said, breathing heavily from the exertion. I noticed the arm of his tuxedo had been sliced.

A movement behind him caught my eye. I desperately tried to scream around the gag, my eyes wide.

Without turning, Blane dove into me, shoving me to the ground. My head cracked painfully on the concrete as I heard Jimmy's knife whiz by overhead and bury itself in a tree. Flipping over onto his back, Blane squeezed off a single shot and Jimmy didn't move anymore.

"You all right?" Blane asked, helping me to my feet.

I nodded, deciding the pain in the back of my head was well worth it to avoid being stabbed. He took my arm, hustling me down the stairs to the sidewalk. A car pulled up and I stopped, afraid of who it might contain.

"That's our ride," Blane said, tugging me forward. Pulling open the back door, he helped me climb inside, then sat beside me.

"Go," he ordered the driver, who wasted no time in complying.

"It's about fucking time. Thought you were going to need help."

Somehow, I wasn't surprised to see that Kade was driving.

"Not likely," Blane retorted.

I watched as Blane pulled out a switchblade, flicking it open to reveal a wicked-looking knife. He leaned toward me and I flinched away. My heart was still pounding and I was a hair's breadth away from complete hysterics. He stopped and our eyes met in the darkness.

"I'm not going to hurt you, Kat," he said softly. "I just want to get the gag off. Will you let me do that?"

He blurred a bit and I blinked back tears, nodding. Leaning forward again, he quickly cut the gag, pulling it out of my mouth.

"Turn around," he said, and I obediently shifted so my back was to him. He cut the bonds on my wrists and I could feel the blood rushing back into my hands. He studied me while I resolutely kept my eyes focused on my hands in my lap.

I felt the brush of a cloth against my lip. Blane was wiping away the blood from my cut mouth. After a moment, his hand was beneath my chin, urging me to look at him. Reluctantly, I did, expecting to see anger there, especially because

I'd hit him over the head with a candlestick. Instead, I saw nothing but worry.

"Are you all right?" he asked, tracing my jaw with his thumb. "Did he hurt you?"

His concern was my undoing, and tears began streaming from my eyes. Blane gathered me in his arms, shifting me onto his lap, and I pressed my face into the crook between his neck and shoulder. I tried to stifle my sobs. At this point, I didn't care if Blane was a bad guy or not. He'd saved me.

Blane held me close and the feel of his arms around me made me finally feel safe. After a few minutes, I was able to regain control of myself, my breathing shaky and scattered.

"Is she done yet?" Kade asked impatiently.

"Shut the fuck up, Kade," Blane retorted.

"Blane, you're such a bleeding heart," Kade shot back. "Remember, this is the same chick that coldcocked you less than an hour ago."

"I'm really sorry about that," I whispered in Blane's ear.

And I was. It had seemed like a good idea at the time, but of course hindsight is twenty-twenty. I was very lucky indeed that I hadn't hurt him too badly. His arms tightened around me and he pressed a light kiss to my lips.

"It did take me by surprise," he said, smiling a little, "and hurt like a son of a bitch."

My smile back was tremulous. I curved a hand behind his neck and pulled him down for another kiss. Our lips met and clung together and I parted mine with a sigh. His tongue met mine and then we were kissing with a frenzied passion, the adrenaline turning to fire in my veins as I clutched him to me. I felt the hard length of him pressing beneath me and I moaned, wanting to straddle his hips and bury him inside me.

"Not in my backseat, please," Kade interrupted dryly. "I just had it cleaned."

I could feel myself blushing bright red as I pulled back from Blane, who didn't even bother glancing at Kade. He was studying my face as if bidden to memorize it, lightly tracing my brow, eyes, cheek, and lips.

"So, what were you doing there tonight, if I may ask?" Kade said belligerently.

I figured I owed Blane an explanation so I directed my answer at him.

"I was trying to find out who killed Sheila."

"By becoming a prostitute?" Kade asked incredulously, and I turned toward him, irritated.

"I wasn't a prostitute," I said angrily, sitting forward so I could grasp the front seat. "I wasn't going to have sex with anyone."

Kade laughed at me. "Your innocence is charming," he said, "and also incredibly stupid. You were almost killed tonight, and nearly got Blane killed as well."

His unvarnished criticism stung, because it was a little too close to the truth.

"Well, I could ask you the same question," I threw back at him. "Why were you two there? I know Mr. Gage had Sheila killed because of her involvement with Mark. Were you the one he sent to murder her?"

Kade's cold eyes met mine in the rearview mirror and I inwardly flinched, the thought crossing my mind that perhaps I shouldn't antagonize him.

"Kat," Blane said, pulling me back against his chest, "Kade didn't kill her."

I turned to him, frustrated with his denial.

"I know he's a gun-for-hire," I said. "And he works for the Santini brothers. Mr. Gage is obviously in cahoots with them. It only makes sense that Kade is the one who killed her."

"It may make sense to you, but he didn't kill her," Blane repeated. "I'm sure they sent Jimmy to take care of Sheila."

I crossed my arms stubbornly over my chest.

"How do you know?" I persisted. "Kade's a liar. You can't trust what he says." My eyes narrowed at Kade, still silent in the front seat. "You see? He doesn't even deny it."

"I know he didn't kill Sheila," Blane said quietly, "because he's my brother."

Time seemed to stop for a moment as those words reverberated inside my head. I stared at Blane in disbelief. Kade was his brother? It didn't seem possible. Kade was a bad guy, Hank had said so. He'd threatened me numerous times. Blane couldn't possibly be related to someone like that.

A memory rose in my mind of Blane telling me about going diving with his brother and nearly losing him. His frantic search and vow to never lose track of him again. He'd said that same brother lived here, in Indy.

Another memory flashed and I cringed inwardly. Kade kissing me. Me kissing him back. My eyes jerked to meet Kade's again in the mirror and his flashed a warning at me, as if we were both thinking the same thing.

I hurriedly shifted off Blane's lap into the seat and he didn't stop me. "Why didn't you tell me?" I asked him, my voice low and accusing.

His jaw tightened, but it was Kade who answered. "You didn't give us much of a chance, did you? Dramatically running off in the middle of the night. And firing a gun at us."

"I ran off, as you put it, because I heard you two talking," I sneered at Kade, my earlier fear now manifesting itself in anger directed at him. "You both wanted that code and neither of you seemed to care how you got it. God knows what you planned to do to me, Kade, whereas you"—I directed my anger at Blane now—"apparently your idea was to fuck me for it."

Kade let out a low whistle. "And the kitty has claws," he chided.

His condescension made me want to climb over the seat and scratch his eyes out. The intensity of my anger shocked me. I didn't view myself as a violent person, but if Kade had been in the backseat with me, I don't know if I could have stopped myself from trying to inflict as much physical damage as possible on him.

It occurred to me then that Blane hadn't saved me from Jimmy because of any feelings he might have for me, but because they still needed me for something. The code. It appeared that was my last bargaining chip. And it didn't help that Blane didn't deny what I'd said to him.

"Do you have the code?" Blane asked.

I felt a stab of pain that I'd been right. Ruthlessly, I shoved the feeling aside. He wanted to be all business? No problem.

"Not on me, no," I lied in a snide tone, and I felt a childish glee when I saw that my response had irritated him, his jaw clenching again.

290

"You know," I said breezily, "you should see someone about that whole jaw-clenching thing. That can't be good for your teeth."

A bark of laughter erupted from the front seat and I narrowed my eyes at Kade's back.

"I need that code," Blane said evenly, ignoring my comment entirely.

"Why?" I shot back. I wanted the truth, and by God, I was going to get it.

I was startled by the abrupt stop of the car and I glanced out the window to see where we were. They'd taken me to Blane's house. The door next to me flew open and Kade was standing there.

"Let's go," he said. The thought went through my mind that if I went inside, I might not come back out again.

"Take me home," I demanded, not budging from the car.

He bent down so his face was on level with mine. "I thought you wanted answers," he mocked me, and my palm itched to wipe the sneer from his face. "They're inside. Not to mention," he leaned closer, "you're not in much of a position to argue."

The threat was implied and I exited the car with as much dignity as I could muster.

"After you, princess," Kade said with exaggerated courtesy. "Or should I call you Lorelei?"

I ignored him, raising my chin in the air, and preceded him up the sidewalk. Blane fell into step with Kade behind me and I struggled not to feel self-conscious with both their eyes on me.

"At least this one is more entertaining than the others," Kade said to Blane just loudly enough for me to overhear. "It's like Hooker Barbie masquerading as Nancy Drew."

My cheeks burned with anger, but I pretended I hadn't heard.

"Enough," Blane said roughly, and Kade shut up.

They took me inside to the den, where they'd been conversing last night. I sat uneasily in one of the leather chairs. I watched as Kade sat in my chair's twin, leaning forward and resting his elbows on his knees. Blane shed his tuxedo jacket and untied his bow tie before he sat on the edge of the desk, crossing his arms in front of him.

My eyes caught on the red stain and rip in his shirt sleeve. "You're hurt," I said with alarm and Blane glanced down at his arm.

"Just a scratch," he dismissed before turning his unflinching gaze on me. "Now what do you want to know?" he asked.

I licked my lips nervously, studiously ignoring Kade.

"Who do you really work for?" I thought that was the pertinent information, at least as it regarded my continued good health.

"No one," he answered. "You could say this situation happened by accident."

I regarded him with suspicion. "How could it be by accident?"

"Kade and I don't usually work together," he said with a sigh.

My glance moved unwillingly to Kade, who was watching me, his lips curved in an insincere smile. I quickly looked back at Blane, who said, "Kade used to be FBI."

"Used to be?" I asked. Kade as law enforcement was difficult to wrap my head around.

"They had a lot of rules that got in the way," Kade said dismissively.

"Those are called laws, Kade," Blane said stiffly.

"Whatever they are," Kade continued unperturbed, "I decided I would enjoy myself more as a . . . freelancer."

"Vigilante, you mean," Blane clarified.

"You say tomato . . ." Kade sighed in mock frustration.

"People hire him to find lawbreakers and be judge and jury."

"And executioner," Kade added lightly, eyeing me. "You'd be surprised how good business is." I doubted it.

"Last year," Blane continued, ignoring Kade, "I realized something was amiss with the firm and its relationship with TecSol. I needed someone on the inside with the Santini family, so I asked Kade to move back to town and help me."

"And I'm not even charging him," Kade threw in.

"And why do you need the code?" I asked.

"Because of this."

Blane walked behind the desk and hit a few keys on the computer sitting there. A light flickered behind me and I turned. A map had been projected onto the wall. I got up and walked over to examine it more closely.

It was a US map and it looked like all the states had been broken down into counties. About eighty-five percent of them were black, including Indianapolis and the surrounding areas.

"What's this?" I asked, turning to face Blane.

"It's all the elections that will be encrypted using that code in two days."

I froze in shock, stunned at what I was seeing.

"But . . . that's not possible," I stammered. "It's only supposed to be used in Indy."

"That's what you think, princess," Kade said, standing up and striding toward me.

I was beginning to detest that nickname.

"What you don't know is that TecSol is just one front company. There are dozens more, all using the same software to encrypt the returns. All going live on Tuesday."

"The Santini brothers—" I began, only to be cut off by Kade.

"They're little fish," he dismissed. "This is much bigger. The problem is we haven't found the ones who are really behind this yet. The code would help us track this to them." His confidence and patronizing attitude toward me pricked my anger again.

"How will that help you? What do you know about computers, codes, and encryption?"

Kade just smiled infuriatingly at me as Blane sighed.

"Quite a bit, actually," Blane answered. "Kade's job in the FBI was in the cyber crime division."

Kade was staring intently at me, still grinning crookedly as if daring me to question his competence further. He arched an eyebrow. My mouth closed with a snap as I tore my eyes from his, walking around him toward Blane.

"Will you give us the code?" Blane asked quietly.

I looked at him, wanting to trust him more than I'd wanted anything in a long time, but a part of me couldn't let go of my suspicions. Suspicions of him, of us, of what he'd told me.

"Do I have a choice?" I answered.

"You always have a choice."

"Though you may not like the consequences," Kade chimed in from behind me.

I spun around. "Is that a threat?" I asked, my eyes narrowing.

His answering smile only infuriated me more.

"It's a fact," he said.

I didn't see a way out of this. I didn't think Blane would actually harm me. But Kade might. The very fact that they were brothers would impede anything Blane might try to do to help me—blood is thicker than water, or so my dad had always said. And I was definitely the water in this scenario.

"Fine," I spat. My capitulation could not be termed gracious.

I turned toward a nearby chair and put my right foot on the seat, high heel and all. As I pulled up my skirt, I realized both men were watching me avidly. Inwardly, I smiled in satisfaction. It appeared men the world over had the same weaknesses. Running my hands up my nylon-encased leg, I inched the skirt up until the top of my thigh-high stocking showed. Both Kade and Blane were still.

Reaching inside the top of the stocking, I pulled out the tiny thumb drive CJ had given me. "A precaution," she'd said, and I could only be grateful for her foresight.

"Sorry your hands were too busy elsewhere to search me properly, Blane?" I asked innocently, brows raised.

His eyes jerked to mine and the look in them said I was playing with fire. *Show's over,* I thought grimly, removing my foot and dropping my skirt. I tossed the drive onto Blane's desk with a clatter and he quickly scooped it up.

"How are you going to trace it?" I asked.

Kade answered. "We need to get into their infrastructure, but I'm working on that."

I raised an eyebrow at Blane, silently asking him to elaborate. I didn't bother responding directly to Kade.

"He hasn't been able to hack into their network yet," Blane said.

"*Yet* being the key word," Kade said arrogantly.

"Your time is running out," I said. "Wouldn't it be better if you had someone on the inside?"

"That would make things a lot easier, yes," Blane said, "but our last lead died with your friend Mark."

"Maybe I could help you," I offered.

Kade laughed out loud and my cheeks flushed.

"What are you going to do, princess?" he asked snidely, stepping closer to me. "Fuck the information out of Santini?"

The crack of my hand against his jaw sounded loud in the room, and for a moment, no one moved. Kade's furious eyes locked on mine and neither of us spoke, the tension in the room so thick I could barely breathe.

"Kade," Blane barked, "take a walk."

Kade didn't move. I stood my ground, but was shaking inside. Finally, after an endless moment, Kade turned and stalked out of the room. My knees nearly buckled in relief and I grasped the back of the chair next to me to steady myself.

"I apologize for him," Blane said quietly. He'd come around the desk to stand next to me. "You didn't deserve that."

My eyes stung but I blinked back the tears. Why should I care what vile things Kade said about me?

"Is he always such a charmer?" I asked dryly.

"He's just . . . a bit of a cynic," Blane answered.

Sliding his arms around my waist, he pulled me toward him and I didn't resist. I knew I shouldn't allow myself to believe that he felt anything more than a passing interest in me, but my heart refused to listen to reason. It felt good, it felt right, to be in his arms.

"Not that I'm going to complain that you two don't get along," Blane continued, and I looked up questioningly. He lowered his head until his lips were millimeters from mine before whispering, "I don't like competition."

His mouth slanted across mine in a kiss that brought back the memory of his body on top of me, inside me. My hands lifted of their own volition to clutch his shoulders, the muscles strong and solid under my fingers.

Blane's hands moved to cup my rear, pressing me to him, and I felt his arousal against my stomach. I gasped when his mouth moved to my neck, my head dropping to the side to give him better access. He moved a hand to my hair, trailing in waves down my back, and fisted some in his hand.

"So beautiful," he murmured against my skin.

His breath was hot and my hands were itching to touch him. I couldn't think when he did this and I struggled to hear the whisper of caution in the back of my mind. This wasn't real. Not in the way I wanted it to be. I was only useful for one thing, apparently.

"No, stop," I said breathlessly, pushing against him. He didn't seem to hear, his tongue flicking wetly against my earlobe, sending a spike of pleasure through me. I pushed harder.

"Blane, stop!"

This seemed to finally get through to him and he abruptly released me. I stumbled backward.

"What's the matter?" he asked. His eyes burned with desire and I wanted to tell the little voice in my head to shut the hell up so I could dive back into his arms.

"I can't do this," I said, trying to sound more resolved than I felt. "I can't be your"—I searched for the words I wanted—"flavor of the month."

His eyes glittered. "I never said you were," he countered.

"Then what am I?" I asked, trying not to betray my hope.

His lips pressed thinly together and I had my answer.

"Thought so," I said grimly. I grabbed my purse and turned to go.

"Kathleen, wait," he said, grasping my arm.

I looked up hopefully. He looked like he was about to say something. Then his jaw clenched tightly shut and my heart sank. Turning my hand palm up, he deposited something in my hand. Looking down, I saw it was a set of car keys.

"To get home," he explained, and I closed my fist around the cold metal. He was standing so close I could smell him and I inhaled greedily, keeping my head down so he wouldn't see the disappointment on my face.

"Thanks," I managed. I pulled away and he released me. Turning to leave felt like I was swimming against the tide, and it wasn't until I'd reached the door that something struck me.

"Wait," I said, turning back to find him still watching me. "Aren't these the keys to Kade's car?" I asked, frowning.

Blane's lips curved in a grin. "Yeah," he answered. "It'll really piss him off."

I laughed. *That* I would be glad to do.

"Blane," I began hesitantly, looking up at him. "Why were you there tonight? Are you a . . . customer?" I had a hard time getting the word out.

His smile faded. "I know I haven't given you much reason to trust me," he said, "but believe me when I tell you that no, I'm not a customer."

Relief filled me. I hadn't wanted to believe that Blane could so willfully participate in paying prostitutes for sex.

"Then why did Gracie tell me that Enigma was the one Sheila was seeing?" Gracie had seemed very sure about that.

"She lied," he answered flatly. "She probably told you whatever they wanted her to say. I'd assume so you wouldn't trust me."

"Why were you even there?" I persisted.

"It's safer for you if you don't know that."

My lips thinned in disappointment, but I knew I'd get nothing more out of him.

"Bye, Blane," I said simply.

"Bye, Kat."

I walked out of the house and didn't look back.

CHAPTER THIRTEEN

I drove home feeling physically and emotionally spent. I tried not to cry, I was sick of crying, and it seemed overly emotional anyway to cry over Blane. How could we break up when we hadn't even been together? But despite appealing to my logical analysis of the situation, my heart wasn't having any of it.

I tried to regret sleeping with Blane, but I just couldn't. I doubted I'd ever again meet a man like him and I couldn't bring myself to regret our short time together, and the greedy part of me wished it wasn't at an end. For the first time, I wished I was more like the other women Blane dated. They thought nothing of getting involved in a relationship that was doomed before it even began, having fun for as long as it lasted. I knew Blane wasn't a commitment kind of guy, but unfortunately, I couldn't pretend that didn't matter to me.

As I locked Kade's car, a very nice black Mercedes with tinted windows, I realized I needed to tell CJ what had happened. When I knocked on her door, she opened it quickly. Cigar stuck between her teeth, she surveyed my gown.

"You dress very . . . unusually," she finally said with a puff of smoke.

I laughed, the first time I'd done so in a while, and she pulled the door open so I could go inside.

"Thanks so much for helping me last night," I said, collapsing in a heap of blue fabric on her couch. "I found out some things today." I told her about having to give the code to Blane and Kade, how they were working to track the code, and how it was much more widespread than we'd thought.

Her eyes widened and she took quick puffs on her cigar as she listened.

"Do you trust them?" she asked me when I was through. I thought about it.

"I want to," I finally said, "but I'm not sure." I did believe that they knew about the code and were trying to trace it, but I wasn't sure their motives were as selfless as they'd implied.

"You still want to go tomorrow?" she asked and I nodded.

"I think we should do what we'd planned," I said. "Speaking of which, were you able to get me inside?"

CJ had said she would be able to hack into a local temp agency and make sure I was not only assigned to TecSol, but also scheduled to work there come tomorrow morning.

"Of course," she said. "Once you're inside, you'll need to hook this up to a network port." She handed me a square box with a short antenna on top. "This is a wireless access point. I've already configured it so all you have to do is plug it in. Once it's working, I can access their network."

"Where will you be?" I asked.

"I'll be in my car outside. Once I get to the network, I'll need you to get me to a computer there. Will you be able to get access to someone else's computer?"

"If I have to, I will," I said simply. I'd have to make it up as I went along. We couldn't plan everything.

302

"We'll only have about ten minutes from the time you plug in the access point to when they track it down and disable it. Once I get on a computer, hopefully that will be enough time to find where they're housing the code program."

"What then?" I asked. "Are you going to fix it?"

"I don't think I can," she said regretfully. "We'll just have to break it." She handed me another of those little thumb drives like the one I'd given Blane.

"What's this?"

"It's a last-ditch emergency," she said grimly. "If I can't upload the program to the right server or if I get disconnected, this will install a worm that will do it."

"Why is it last-ditch?" I asked, taking the drive.

"Because it has to be plugged in to the actual server," she explained. "It won't work over the network. But if it gets plugged in to the right server, it'll do what it needs to do."

"Got it," I said, closing my fist over the drive. "I'll be at TecSol by eight thirty. Give me until nine thirty to find a port and a computer. I'll call you right before I plug in the device."

"Sounds like a plan," CJ said as I got up to leave. "And don't forget," she said as I opened the door. "Make sure you're not in the same room as the access point when they find it or you're toast."

"I'll be fine," I said with more confidence than I really felt. "I'll call you when everything's in place."

"Good luck," she said and I smiled tightly. I had to finish this. Mark and Sheila were counting on me and I couldn't just give up now because I was afraid. My dad hadn't raised a coward.

I retreated to my apartment, stowing the access point and the thumb drive in my purse and regretfully examining my gown as I undressed. Somehow I doubted I'd ever have the need to wear it again. But I carefully folded it and set it aside so I could have it cleaned. After showering the grime and makeup off, I felt more like myself. Cinderella turned back into a plain working girl. Pulling on a pair of underwear and donning one of the few T-shirts I could find, I set my alarm and fell into bed.

I wasn't sure what woke me. My eyes flew open but I lay still. It was very early, the darkness of the room just beginning to fade with the onset of dawn. A slight noise made me sit bolt upright in bed and I choked back a scream. Kade was sitting in a chair opposite my bed staring at me, his usual cocky grin unfazed by my surprise.

"What the hell are you doing here?" I said, angry and alarmed at his intrusion.

"I see you helped yourself to my car," he said.

Of course. He'd come for his car. No problem. I'd give him his keys and he would leave.

"Blane let me borrow it to drive home last night," I explained, quickly leaping out of bed and grabbing my purse, digging inside for the keys. When I turned to give them to him, I noticed his eyes were taking in my appearance, and when they met mine, they glittered with an emotion that made my hand start to shake. I clenched my fist around the cold metal.

"Here's your keys," I managed to say. I held them out to him, unwilling to step closer and fervently wishing I had more clothes on.

"We have a problem," he said, making no move to take the keys. My arm dropped back to my side.

"What kind of problem?" I asked, my stomach tightening in a knot.

"Gage found Jimmy's body last night. Not yours. They know he didn't kill you."

I swallowed. "Does that mean they'll send someone else after me?" I asked weakly.

Kade's eyes met mine again, and now they were cold. "They already did," he answered.

I felt my heart begin to pound and my knees turn to jelly as realization struck. "You," I breathed.

Kade smiled but it was without humor. "You're smarter than you look," he said, but I ignored the insult. "And worth more, too. They gave me twenty thousand in cash to take care of you."

"Twenty thousand dollars?" I squeaked in alarm. Crap. I might even be tempted to off somebody for that kind of money.

"Murder doesn't come cheap, princess," Kade said.

My mouth was dry as sawdust. I had nothing to bargain with now, no reason to give him to not kill me. I wasn't even with his brother anymore. But that didn't stop me from trying.

"Blane—" I began, but he interrupted me.

"Blane doesn't know."

My heart sank at his words. Panic struck and I ran to my bedside table, where I'd stored Blane's gun. Yanking open the drawer, I scrabbled inside until my shaking hands touched the cold metal.

Kade's arms closed around me, his hands like iron bands on my wrists, the fabric of his jeans rough against the backs of my thighs. I watched helplessly as he pried open my fingers and took the gun.

Fear iced my veins. I couldn't move, his arms effectively pinning mine to my sides. Would he make it quick? He hadn't shied away last night from letting me know how much he loathed me. I despised how terrified I was, but I wasn't a big fan of pain.

"Let me go," I managed to grit out, struggling to get out of his grip.

"Believe it or not," he said, "I'm not here for you. I was looking for Blane and thought he might be here."

I went still.

"Isn't he at his house?" I asked stupidly, and could practically hear Kade roll his eyes.

"If he was, do you think I'd be wasting my time here with you?" Kade abruptly released me and I stumbled forward before turning around to face him.

"Then where is he?" I asked, anxiety welling inside me. "I left him last night in the study. You were there. Where could he have gone?"

"That's the point," he said like I was an idiot. "I. Don't. Know."

I shoved a hand through my hair, worry gnawing at me. Then I felt like I was being ridiculous. Blane was certainly capable of taking care of himself. "He's probably fine," I said, not sure if I was trying to convince Kade or myself. "He's probably at work or the courthouse or something."

"I thought so, too," Kade said, "until I found these on his desk."

He tossed a large manila envelope onto the bed, and some photos spilled out. I picked them up, shock going through me. They were pictures of him and me last night. We were on the couch together in a "private" alcove, and my dress was pulled down, his mouth on my breast. Face flaming and feeling slightly nauseated, I flipped through the rest. Blane with his hand up my skirt, my head thrown back in desire, his lips on mine. Each moment of our interlude stared up at me in relentless black and white.

"Why would someone do this?" I whispered in dismay. The thought that someone had been there watching, taking pictures, sickened me.

"Blackmail," Kade said shortly.

I looked at him questioningly. He grinned mirthlessly.

"You were a prostitute last night, remember?"

I paled. The thought of someone using me to hurt Blane was difficult to absorb. Anger flashed through me as I realized Simone, at least, had to have known. Was that why she'd been so anxious to welcome me into the fold? Because she'd somehow found out about my connection to Blane?

"Why would someone want to blackmail him?" I asked. "He's just a lawyer. And single. Why would anyone care?"

"You are incredibly naive," he said scathingly. "Blane's not 'just a lawyer,' as you put it. He's one of the best and most well-known lawyers in this city, and his family's reputation goes back generations. Blane's great-grandfather was a judge on the supreme court of Massachusetts. His grandfather was lieutenant governor. If Blane has political aspirations, these"—he gestured to the pictures—"could put an end to that."

My mouth formed a little O. I hadn't known all that. Then realization hit me.

"This was what he wouldn't tell me," I breathed, looking back down at the pictures.

"What?" Kade asked.

"Last night," I explained. "Blane wouldn't tell me why you two were there at that party. He must've known they were going to blackmail him." Then something else about what Kade had said struck me as odd.

"Wait," I said, "Blane said you're brothers. But you said 'Blane's grandfather.' Wasn't he your grandfather, too?"

Something flickered briefly in Kade's eyes before they turned hard again.

"Let's just say I was born on the wrong side of the blanket," he said coolly. My eyes widened. As if answering my question, he continued, "Our father wasn't exactly the most faithful of men. I don't claim any of them."

"Except Blane," I said.

"Except Blane," he echoed evenly.

"Why?" I asked, fascinated at the story in spite of myself.

His eyes narrowed and he moved a step closer until we were nearly touching. My breathing hitched.

"Just know that I won't let anything happen to Blane," he hissed. "And the last thing I'm going to do is let some random woman come between us."

I swallowed heavily, shaking my head.

"I'm not trying to come between anyone," I protested. The very idea was absurd.

Kade just looked at me intently, as if trying to verify the truth of my words. The tension notched up another level between us as his blue eyes bored into mine. I jumped in surprise when his hands moved under my shirt to settle on the bare skin of my hips. A shiver danced across my skin. He leaned forward, putting his lips at my ear.

"You didn't tell him about us," he whispered, and my face paled. I abruptly remembered Kade kissing me in the bar on Halloween night.

"There is no 'us.'"

"You sure about that, princess?"

I couldn't answer him, my stomach twisting itself into knots. Abruptly, he stepped back, releasing me.

"I put my number in your cell," Kade said. "Call me if you hear from Blane." Then he was gone.

My knees gave and I slid down the wall until I sat on the floor. Worry for Blane crowded out thoughts of Kade and I chewed my lip, trying to think where he could be. A quick glance at the clock and I realized I had to get going, whether Blane was missing or not.

An hour later, I was pulling up to the TecSol building, and parking in the lot. It was a big building downtown in the business district, and the parking lot was nearly full. I got out of the car, nervously smoothing my blouse and skirt. I'd opted for as professional an appearance as I could manage, even putting my hair up in a French twist. Realizing it was now or never, I steeled my nerves and headed inside.

The girl at the reception desk couldn't have been older than twenty. I smiled as I told her I was the new temp, Lucy Tanner (fake name courtesy of CJ). She told me to have a seat and she'd call the HR manager.

I did as she suggested, taking in the lobby as I did so. It was large and open, with a few scattered sofas and chairs. The whole area was surrounded with windows that showed the street, though they were tinted so those outside couldn't see in. I watched people walking by in the early morning sunshine on their way to work.

"Good morning! You must be Lucy." I turned around and saw a woman in her midforties walking toward me. She stopped and held out her hand, which I shook. Her smile was infectious and I smiled back.

"Yes, the temp agency sent me," I answered.

"Excellent! I'm so glad they had someone with the right qualifications available on such short notice."

A frisson of alarm went through me. Qualifications? CJ hadn't mentioned anything about special qualifications. My smile was forced now.

"I'm Dana Arnold," she said. "If you'll follow me, I'll show you where you'll be working today." She turned toward the elevators and I fell in step behind her, frantically wondering what skills I was going to need to fake today.

"You'll be working for our vice president of system design," Dana said, punching the button for the tenth floor. "His secretary is out for the next six weeks on maternity leave."

"Here, you'll need this," she said, handing me a small plastic card. "A security badge," she explained. "Just hook it onto your belt and it'll get you around the building."

Obeying, I clipped it to my waist as the elevator doors slid silently open. We stepped out into a hallway where you could turn right or left. She turned left, using her own badge to open the set of double doors ahead of us. Glancing behind me, I saw an identical set of doors down the other side.

"What's over there?" I asked.

"That's the software engineering department," Dana answered. I filed that information away for later.

We walked into a large open office area with huge curved windows. It was very quiet and the carpet was plush, muffling the sound of my heels. Dana walked me toward a nice desk with a large flat-screen monitor and a small Tiffany-style lamp. The desk faced the windows and sat catty-corner to an enclosed office.

"Here's where you'll be working," she said, motioning to the desk. I felt a pang of regret that this wasn't a real job. It would have been nice to work in such a luxurious space.

"Mr. Avery will be in shortly," she said, gesturing to the office. "He'll be traveling to Chicago tonight to prepare for the election tomorrow. All you need to do is make sure he has everything he needs. His secretary, Molly, had everything pretty caught up before she left. I think there are some translations that need to be done, but that's all for now."

She moved to the computer and missed the widening of my eyes. Translations?

"Here's the log-in for the computer," she said, handing me a Post-it note with a password scrawled on it. "Do you need anything else right now?"

I shook my head. "I'll get to work," I said with more confidence than I felt. Dana left and I settled myself into the leather chair behind the desk. I smiled at my luck. No one was around and the vice-president guy wouldn't be in for a while yet.

A stack of papers sat on the desk and I picked up the top one curiously. It was all in Spanish. I guess these were what Dana was talking about when she said I was supposed to translate. I groaned in dismay, vowing to kill CJ when I got out of here. A little warning that I was supposed to be bilingual would have been nice.

The phone at my elbow rang and I jumped. Hesitantly, I picked it up.

"Mr. Avery's office," I answered.

No one said anything, so I repeated myself.

"Who is this?" a man's voice demanded.

"My name is Lucy. I'm Mr. Avery's secretary. May I help you?"

"Oh. You must be the new temp," he said. "This is Mr. Avery. I need something off my computer. Put me on hold and go into my office. Pick the line up there."

"Yes, sir," I said, quickly obeying. His office door was un-locked and I let myself inside, hurrying to the far side of a large desk and credenza before picking up the phone.

"What would you like me to do, sir?" I asked.

"Log on to my computer and e-mail me a document." He gave me his password, which I jotted down on a piece of paper before typing it into the computer. He guided me to the right location and I e-mailed him the file.

"Is that all?" I asked.

"Yes, thank you," he answered. "I should be in within the hour." He disconnected.

My hands were shaking now and I quickly dialed CJ.

"I'm in," I said when she answered. "The vice president of system design just gave me his computer password and he's not in yet."

"Awesome," CJ said. "That's incredibly good luck. This may actually work."

"By the way," I said sarcastically, "you could have told me I was supposed to know Spanish."

"I thought you might be more nervous if I told you that," she said matter-of-factly.

I couldn't really disagree with that. I wasn't the world's greatest actress.

"Have you plugged the WAP in yet?" she asked.

"No," I said, "I'm the only one here and it would be a dead giveaway if I plugged it in where I'm at now. I'm going to have to go to another floor or something."

"Okay. But watch out for the security cameras."

"What? What security cameras?"

But she'd already hung up. I cursed under my breath. The list of things she hadn't told me was growing.

Leaving the office, I grabbed my purse and headed across the hall to what Dana had said was the software engineering department. I took a deep breath and opened the door.

The space was the same size as the other side of the hall-way, but this area had been segmented into cubicles. I hesi-tantly walked down the path between cubes, trying unob-trusively to look in them as I passed. Most had men in them working on their computers. I didn't spot a single woman.

Rounding the corner, I nearly barreled into someone.

"I'm so sorry," I said, backpedaling a couple of steps. A squat, bald man with a sour-looking expression on his face looked up at me.

"Who are you?" he asked gruffly, still frowning.

I smiled in what I hoped was a winsome way.

"I'm Lucy, the new secretary for Mr. Avery," I answered.

"What are you doing over here?"

I scrambled for a reason. "Uh . . . I was . . . um . . . just looking for a cup of coffee," I improvised. "Is there a kitchen around here somewhere?" I glanced around, as if a kitchen would suddenly materialize in front of us.

He grumbled something under his breath before jerking his finger over his shoulder. "That way," he said.

"Thanks!" I said brightly, easing past him. I kept walking until I reached the kitchen, where I poured a cup of coffee. Retracing my steps, I saw an empty cube in what looked to be a mostly deserted area. Looking around quickly, I ducked into it.

My hands were shaking again as I tore open my purse, pulling out the device CJ had given me. I crawled under the desk and plugged it in to a power outlet, then yanked the network cable from the computer and pushed it into the access point instead.

I jumped up, brushed myself off, and grabbed my purse and the mug of coffee. Walking quickly, I went back to my desk, thankfully not running into anyone along the way this time. Letting myself back in Avery's office, I released a pent-up breath and called CJ.

"It's in," I said.

"I know," she responded and I bit back a retort. My nerves were on edge. "What's his password?" she asked and I told her. "Okay, give me a minute." I watched the screen, and in a few moments, the mouse started moving on its own.

"Are you doing that?" I asked, and CJ grunted an affirmative. I watched for a few minutes as she opened windows and typed what I assumed was code. My heart was pounding madly and I knew I was not cut out for this cloak-and-dagger stuff.

"How much longer are you going to be?" I asked nervously.

"I need a few more minutes," she said. I glanced at my watch.

"He's going to be here any minute. I need to get back to my desk. If he catches me in his office—"

"That's fine," CJ cut in, "just buy me as much time as you can before he gets there."

Relieved, I hurried back to my desk, sinking into the leather chair. I decided to try and look busy while I waited so I logged on to my computer and propped some of the pages of incomprehensible Spanish up on the document holder next to the screen.

The click of the lock on the door startled me and I dropped my cell phone, which clattered to the desk. Grabbing it, I hissed, "He's here," and hung up.

The door opened and a tall man in a dark suit stepped inside. He was carrying a leather briefcase. Spying me, his long strides ate up the space quickly before stopping in front of my desk. Jumping to my feet, I started to panic, wondering if CJ had had enough time yet. I couldn't let him go into his office and see the stuff she had open on the screen.

"Good morning," he said, holding out his hand. "I'm Stephen Avery." I shook his hand and forced a smile.

"Good morning," I answered. "I'm Lucy Tanner. Dana said I'd be working for you for a while."

Avery looked to be somewhere in his late forties to early fifties, his hair dark but with touches of silver at the temples. He was handsome in an austere sort of way. His demeanor, though friendly, gave the impression of someone you wouldn't want to cross.

"It's nice to meet you," he said, his hand still holding mine. "Do you prefer Lucy or Ms. Tanner?" His eyes took in my appearance in a frank way and he seemed to like what he saw.

"Lucy is fine, thanks," I said.

"My secretary had to leave a week early," he said. "She wasn't expected to deliver her baby until next week. But I expect you know those things can't always be scheduled." He smiled engagingly.

"Of course," I responded automatically. "Um . . . I mean, not . . . you know . . . personally," I stammered like an idiot. I felt myself blush furiously and Avery's smile grew. Deciding I should just quit while I was ahead, I pressed my lips together and smiled back, pulling my hand out of his.

"I know this is a bit last-minute," he said, "but I need an assistant to come with me to Chicago. We leave tonight. Would you be available to do that?"

My eyes widened. This could either be a really good thing or a really bad thing, depending on what CJ had been able to do.

"Um . . . sure," I said. "I should be able to do that."

"You don't need to . . . let someone know? A husband or boyfriend perhaps?"

I shook my head, then belatedly realized I probably should have lied when a glint appeared in his eyes.

"We'll be back Wednesday," he continued. "So you only need to pack for a couple of days."

"Okay," I said, nodding, "I can do that."

Avery made to move past me and I panicked, thinking I needed to stall him and give CJ more time.

"Wait!" I said, and Avery turned questioningly. I thought frantically. "What sort of things should I pack?"

"Business attire is fine," he said. His eyes brushed down my body and back up again. "And perhaps something a bit more . . . informal," he added. "Chances are good we'll be celebrating tomorrow night."

His eyes had a look in them that made me feel slightly sick, but I covered my dismay with what I hoped was a flirtatious smile. At the moment, I had no compunction against using any means at my disposal to stall him.

"What kind of celebrating?" I flirted. Avery took a few steps back toward me.

"How old are you?" he asked curiously, reaching out to brush some nonexistent lint off my shoulder. His hand lingered. I swallowed nervously but wanted to keep his attention. The longer he was out here with me and not in his office, the better.

"Twenty-five," I lied. He just looked at me. "Twenty-three," I relented.

God, I was such a terrible liar. I never could get away with lying to my dad. He had always known when I was fibbing.

"Old enough," he said cryptically, before turning away again.

My courage failed and I racked my brain for a way to stall him further. Then a memory of Blane came back to me. Quickly brushing my hand against the stack of papers on my desk, they fell to the floor in a scattered pile.

"Dang it," I said, and saw Avery pause out of the corner of my eye. Heaving a sigh, I quickly got down on all fours but took my time gathering up the papers. I could feel my skirt hitch upward on my legs as I moved, but I didn't pull it down. I also didn't hear Avery's office door open.

"Let me help you," he said, crouching down in front of me.

Leaning over, I felt his eyes on my blouse as it gaped from my neck. After a couple of minutes, and despite how slowly I worked, we had gathered up the papers. Rising, Avery helped me to my feet. I smoothed my skirt down over my stomach and hips, and his gaze followed the path my hands took.

"Thank you, Mr. Avery," I said with another smile.

"Anytime," he replied. "And please, call me Stephen." My gaze dropped from his eyes to an unmistakable bulge in his pants. Apparently, my little ploy had worked, even if it had left a bad taste in my mouth.

Avery retreated to his office and I breathed a sigh of relief, hoping I had given CJ had enough time. Sitting back at my desk, I picked up my cell and called her.

"Was that enough time?" I asked as quietly as I could.

"Just finished a few seconds ago," she said, and my eyes slipped shut in relief. "But I've got bad news."

My eyes flew open. "What?" I asked.

"The server we need access to isn't hooked to the network there anymore. They've already moved it or are in the process of moving it."

"Moving it? Moving it where?"

"Something like this, it has to be hooked up to an Internet backbone. Closest to us is probably Chicago," she answered. Dread filled the pit of my stomach as she kept talking. "Unless we can find it, there's nothing we can do."

"Lucky for us, my boss is taking me with him on a business trip," I said. "Guess where he's going?"

"No shit?" she said. "He's taking you to Chicago?"

"Yeah. We leave tonight."

"You still have the thumb drive I gave you?" she asked.

"Yes, but what am I supposed to do with it?" I rubbed my hands across my forehead, disappointed that our plan hadn't worked so far.

"The server name is EVE0928," CJ said. "That's 'EVE'—E-V-E—and then zero-nine-two-eight. It will be labeled. You just have to find it and stick the thumb drive in it."

"You make it sound easy," I grumbled.

"Hell no, it won't be easy," she huffed in exasperation. "There will be hundreds of servers there. I think you should forget this whole thing and get out of there."

"I don't know if I can do that," I said, thinking of Sheila and how brutally she'd been murdered. "This is our only shot, right?"

CJ sighed. "Yeah, pretty much. But Kathleen, it's not your job to stop them. You can just walk away. No one knows but you and me, and I certainly won't blame you. Hell, I would've been out of there by now."

I thought about it. No one, besides CJ, even knew where I was or what I was doing. There would be no one to save me if I got in over my head. Three people had already been killed, and those were just the ones I knew about. A part of me really, really wanted to do what CJ said and just leave. But the other part of me, the part that knew what my father would have done given the same situation, overruled it.

"I'm going to stay," I said firmly. "Just tell me what I need to do."

"Fine," she said in resignation. "If you're going with them, chances are you're going to see the server. If you get that far, you'll be in good shape. You're just going to have to improvise. Don't let them see you plug it in. It has to have at least thirty seconds to upload the worm to the server's hard drive. If someone pulls it out before then, it's over."

"All right. I'll do what I can."

"Be careful, Kathleen," CJ warned.

"I will," I assured her. "I'll see you Wednesday." And I really hoped I would.

I'd just hung up my phone when the double doors opened again and a man came barreling into the office. He didn't even pause by my desk, just passed me by. I jumped up.

"Wait! You can't just go in there!" Barely glancing at me, he pushed open Stephen's office door.

"There's been a security breach," the man told Stephen. "Unauthorized access via an access point someone plugged in." I lingered behind him, listening.

"What did they access?" I heard Stephen ask. The man shook his head.

"Unknown as of yet. Whoever it was, they covered their tracks." I entered the room and Stephen glanced up.

"Did you need something, Lucy?" he asked.

"I was wondering if I could get you a cup of coffee. And your visitor?" I looked expectantly at the man.

"That would be great, Lucy," Stephen said. "This is Brian. He's head of network security."

Brian didn't bother doing more than giving me a brief nod.

"Hi, Brian," I said, smiling and turning up the accent a bit.

If there's one thing I knew about men, it's that they assumed most women were dumber than they were. Add blonde hair and a southern accent and it wasn't even a question anymore. I thought I'd play it up the dumb factor. It's always better to be underestimated than overestimated. "I'll get that coffee right away."

I returned in a few minutes bearing the mugs. Not stopping to knock, I opened the door to the office and walked in. Neither of the men stopped talking, which is exactly what I'd hoped they would do. I was just the secretary, after all.

"How did an access point get installed without anyone noticing?" Stephen was saying, his voice like ice.

"I don't know, sir," Brian answered. "We're having the footage reviewed as we speak, but there weren't any cameras in that immediate vicinity. It could have been installed yesterday or last night, for all we know."

I thanked whatever gods were looking out for me today and prayed my luck would continue.

"Have it dusted for fingerprints," Stephen said. "And don't tell anyone. Find out what they accessed." Brian nodded as I set the coffee on the table next to him.

Fingerprints. Crap. I hadn't even thought about that. I wondered how long it took to check for fingerprints. My fingerprints had been taken and catalogued as a security measure when I'd begun working for the firm. The clock was already ticking on my charade.

"I hope we won't have any security problems tomorrow?" Stephen said curtly. I set his coffee next to his elbow on his desk.

"No, sir. Things will be locked down tight."

With no more excuses to linger, I left his office and resumed my seat at my desk.

A little while later, Brian came out of the office and left. I was in the middle of using a website I'd Googled to translate the pile of Spanish. It was slowgoing, but I thought I was making some progress.

The day passed uneventfully, almost lulling me into a sense of complacency. The place seemed so normal. It was hard to believe they were behind such a scheme as rigging an election. I left at lunch for something to eat, but couldn't stomach more than a few bites of a sandwich. My nerves were frazzled and I briefly longed for a shot of bourbon to steady them. Finally, around four thirty, Stephen came out of his office and I hurriedly shut down my translator website.

"Go ahead and take off, Lucy," he said. "Pack a bag and meet us at the airport at seven. We'll be taking the corporate jet, so go to hangar 18."

"Okay," I agreed.

He left and I saved my file before gathering up my purse. As I was getting ready to leave, I remembered the coffee mugs in his office. If we were going to be gone for two days, I should probably put those back in the kitchen to be cleaned.

The cups were sitting on a table near the window and I lingered for a moment, watching the sun begin its downward journey to the horizon. The days were getting shorter now. Not that I minded. I briefly wondered about the weather in Chicago. I rarely watched the news and hadn't thought to look on the Internet today. Autumn was a strange time of year. Here in Indianapolis, it could be fifty degrees one day and seventy-five the next. Chicago was no exception.

Spotting a small television in the far corner of the office, I went over and flipped it on, hoping Stephen had cable in his office so I could catch The Weather Channel. To my surprise, a television station didn't appear. Instead, the screen was segmented into many different blocks, each block showing a different image. As I watched, perplexed, I realized it was a feed from the security cameras around the building.

My heart rate shot up and I studied each of the blocks avidly, hoping Brian had been telling the truth when he'd said there hadn't been any cameras near where I'd plugged in the wireless device. It was hard to tell. A lot of the shots were very similar and I realized the layout of the cubes was probably the same on the different floors. Each of the boxes had labels, though, and by process of elimination, I was able to figure out which location each indicated. I breathed easier. He hadn't been lying. I hadn't seen any security cameras this morning by that cube because there weren't any.

I was just about to flick off the television when something in the corner caught my eye. A man—but his clothes appeared to be half off. How strange. Unthinkingly, I touched the block where that image resided and it immediately expanded into a larger window. Hmm. A touch screen, I guessed. I looked closer at the image and gasped.

It was Blane. He appeared to be in a room, pacing its length. His shirt was ripped and torn, and blood stained one side of it. When his face turned briefly toward the camera, I saw blood on his face.

Oh my God. I stood still for a moment, frozen in horror. Blane was here. And while I'd been whiling away the hours up here in a cushy office, he'd been beaten and held prisoner somewhere in the building.

Frantically, I tapped the screen again so I could see the window's label. Sub2–Area5. This place must have a sub-basement. I had to get Blane out of there. Flicking off the television, I grabbed my purse and hurried to the elevator.

Looking at the buttons, I was momentarily stymied. There was only one level showing below the ground floor. I'd have to get there and see if there were stairs or something.

Pulling out my cell phone, I dialed Kade. When he picked up, I didn't waste time with preliminaries.

"I found him," I said. "Meet me with a car behind the TecSol building downtown in fifteen minutes."

I flipped the phone closed without waiting to see if he said anything. I had no idea what I was going to do in the next fifteen minutes to get Blane out, I just knew I had to do something. CJ had said to improvise. I was about to see how well I did that.

CHAPTER FOURTEEN

The elevator opened onto what appeared to be a deserted basement, complete with concrete floors and walls. Cautiously, I stepped out into the dimly lit hallway, glancing around. The ceiling was tall, maybe ten feet, with bare pipes crisscrossing overhead. The elevator doors slid shut, startling me.

I thought longingly of the gun Kade had taken from me this morning. What I wouldn't give to have it right now. I wasn't getting much done just standing there, so I picked a direction and started walking.

My steps echoed on the concrete floor and I cursed my decision to wear heels this morning. Stepping gingerly, I turned a corner. The next hallway was just as dark and empty as the one I was in. Suppressing a shiver of apprehension, I eased forward.

About halfway along, there was a door marked Custodial. An idea came to me and I held my breath as I tried the knob. It was unlocked, the door swinging open easily.

Fumbling for a switch inside, I flipped on the light. My face broke into a wide smile. The small room was filled with janitorial equipment and supplies. Yes, this might just work. A large metal shelving unit stood against the wall and on it were stacked mounds of blue overalls, all with TecSol embroidered in small letters on the front.

I quickly pulled a pair of overalls on over my clothes, hiking my skirt up as I did so. The outfit was big and I rolled up the sleeves and legs of the pants. Grabbing a TecSol ball cap off the shelf, I tucked my hair up into it and pulled it down low over my forehead.

A cleaning cart was shoved in the corner and I hid my purse under a pile of folded trash bags. Checking to make sure the cart had supplies, I added a mop, a bucket of water, and a plunger for added authenticity before pushing it out into the hallway.

Hoping I was going the right way, I resumed walking. At the end of the hall, I was rewarded with what looked like a loading elevator. Taking a deep breath to calm my jangling nerves, I hit the call button.

The groan and grinding of the elevator through the open-mesh metal door made me cringe. Whoever was down below would certainly know someone was coming. When the cage arrived, I slid open the door, my fingers finding handholds in the cold metal. I pushed my cart inside and hit the button for the only place you could go, which was down.

The bottom floor was a stark contrast to where I'd just been. Bright fluorescent light flooded the elevator as I pushed the mesh cage open and wheeled my cart into the glaringly white hallway. Glancing from under the brim of my cap, I saw a man sitting in a chair about thirty feet away. He was watching me. I pretended not to notice.

As nonchalantly as my racing pulse and sweaty palms would allow, I pushed the cart closer to him, keeping my head down. I hadn't seen any cameras, but I was sure at least one was around. My heart rate picked up even more when I saw he was sitting in front of a windowless door. I prayed that Blane was behind it.

When I was a few feet away, the man stood and I gulped. He towered over me—all six-plus feet of him, built like a linebacker. I closed my hands in fists to stop them from shaking.

"What are you doing here?" the man asked gruffly.

I bent over my cart, picking up a random can and a cloth. "Ah wuz told ta clean the bathrooms down heah," I said, nodding toward the door behind him and laying the hick accent on thick. I was careful not to meet his eyes.

"Well, this isn't the bathroom," he retorted. "It's at the end of the hall, so get moving."

I nodded like I was listening to him and turned away. Suddenly, I clutched my stomach and bent over, moaning in pain.

"Hey, what's going on? What are you doing?" he said anxiously, bending toward where I was hunched over.

Spinning around, I aimed the can in his face and pressed the nozzle. A white foam hit him right in the eyes and he yelled in pain, clapping his hands to his face. Grabbing the plunger off my cart, I wielded the long wooden handle like it was a baseball bat and swung as hard as I could. It bounced off his ribs like it was a toy and he reached one hand blindly inside his jacket.

Terrified that he was reaching for a gun, I swung again, but before it could make contact, he ripped the plunger out of my hands. Grabbing the front of my overalls, he threw me hard against the wall, my head cracking painfully against the stone, and I slid to the floor. Shaking my head to try and clear my now-blurry vision, I saw him move toward me again.

Scrabbling on the floor away from him, I grabbed the cart for leverage and then watched in horror as it tipped over on its side. The bucket of soapy water spilled across the floor and I rolled to avoid it.

The man stepped toward me and I watched as his foot slipped in the water, sending him crashing to the ground. His head knocked hard on the floor and he was still.

Gasping for air, I lay there for a moment, shaking uncontrollably. Crawling over to him, I felt for a pulse, relief flooding me when I felt one. I certainly hadn't wanted to kill him; unconscious was good enough. Reaching inside his jacket, I took his gun. I pushed my hands into his pants pockets and found the keys I was hoping he would have.

Leaping to my feet, I tried to unlock the door. It took a couple of attempts, but I finally heard the lock tumble. Pushing open the door, a scream caught in my throat as I was unceremoniously dragged inside and shoved against the wall, knocking the hat off my head.

"Kathleen?"

The shock on Blane's face might've been amusing if our situation weren't so dire. Then all thought was driven out of my head when his mouth landed hard on mine. It wasn't a sensual kiss or even tender. It was desperation and hunger poured from him into me. When he pulled away, I was gasping for air. His bound hands cupped my face.

"They told me you were dead," he said hoarsely, his eyes intent on mine. I struggled to keep my wits about me when really I just wanted to fall into his arms and kiss him back with equal urgency.

"'Reports of my death have been greatly exaggerated,'" I quoted, still a bit breathless.

Blane's lips tipped up like he was thinking about smiling.

"I'm here to bust you out," I continued. "Let me go now?"

He abruptly released me and I could almost see him regaining his usual mask of detachment.

"How did you get in here?" he asked.

I tugged at the knots on the cords tying his hands together, impressed that he'd still managed to grab me even with that handicap.

"I'm temping here today and I saw you on the security cameras," I said, unwinding the cord from his arms.

Once it was loosened, he pulled the rest of it off himself. His shirt was hanging open and I saw what had caused the bloodstain now. A shallow cut ran across his chest, crusted with dried blood. My fingers reached out to touch him, but stopped when he grabbed my wrist.

"Are you all right?" I said anxiously, inspecting the marks on his face and relieved to find they were mostly superficial.

"I'm fine," he answered curtly. "Though I have a serious problem with you being within a mile of this place." His jaw clenched in anger and I pressed my lips together in a stubborn line.

"I don't recall asking your permission," I said evenly. How typical! Here I was, saving him, and he was going to argue with me about it!

Before I could say anything further, Blane had plucked the gun out of my hand.

"Hey!" I protested.

"Stay behind me," he ordered, opening the door into the hallway. A quick check revealed we were still alone, except for the guard lying motionless on the floor.

"Is he dead?" Blane asked.

"Of course not!" I retorted, stung that he'd think I'd just decide to kill someone willy-nilly. "I wasn't trying to kill him. Just knock him out."

"And how did you manage that?" Blane asked, tugging the body into the room as I held the door.

"I hit him with a plunger."

He froze, his eyes meeting mine in disbelief.

I shrugged. "Then he slipped and hit his head. I got lucky."

Blane raised an eyebrow before shaking his head. "Let's hope your luck holds," he muttered as he removed the man's jacket and threw it on over his ruined shirt. It fit well enough. "Let's go."

I grabbed my purse from where it had fallen off the cart and we headed back down the hall to the elevator, Blane leading the way. My heart was in my throat, but we didn't meet anyone else. It had to be past five now. People would be leaving for the day. I hoped we could blend in with the rest of the crowd and walk out the front door.

Not seeing any cameras in the freight elevator, I hurriedly took off the overalls, tugging down my skirt, which had bunched around my waist. I was a little wrinkly, but overall not too bad. I tried to repair my French twist, but it had completely fallen out, so I made do by smoothing my hair and combing it with my fingers. Blane's eyes were on me, but I tried to ignore him, my cheeks flushing under his watchful gaze.

Reaching the basement, we headed down the hallway toward the main elevator. I was beginning to breathe easier now. Freedom was very close.

I should have known better.

"What are you doing down here?" a man called from behind us. I reflexively looked back, gasping when I saw the man pull out a gun.

"Stop right there!" he called out, breaking into a jog.

Blane's hand wrapped around my upper arm in an iron grip and he pulled me into a run. The sound of a gunshot made me cry out as it ricocheted off the concrete wall. I tried to keep up with Blane, but my skirt and heels slowed me down.

We reached the elevator and Blane slammed his hand on the call button. Hooking an arm around my waist, he dragged me in front of him, pressing me between the closed elevator door and his body. I heard another gunshot and cringed into him. His body jerked slightly and he grunted. Turning but still shielding me, he aimed and fired off a shot. I heard a thud and a clatter and hoped he'd hit the guy.

The elevator doors opened and we fell inside. Hurriedly, I pressed the button for the lobby and repeatedly jabbed at the button to close the doors, melting against the wall in relief when they finally slid closed.

Turning toward Blane, my breath caught in my throat. I pulled his jacket aside to see a red stain spreading on his shirt as he leaned against the back wall.

"Oh my God, Blane! You were hit!" I felt light-headed as I took in the angry, pulsing wound in his shoulder.

"I'll be fine," he said, wincing. "It looks worse than it feels."

I remembered saying the same thing to him about my black eye.

"Good, because it looks horrible," I retorted past the lump in my throat. It didn't escape my notice that what had hit him in the shoulder would have hit me in the head if he hadn't been shielding me.

The elevator opened and I struggled to look calm and normal as we exited, focusing on the doors ahead of us. They were only fifty feet away.

We walked behind the other people leaving as they talked and laughed with one another. A few glances came our way, but I deliberately avoided eye contact. Instinctively, I reached for Blane's hand, drawing comfort from his large, warm grip. Thirty feet.

Motion caught the corner of my eye, and I saw two men rushing toward the elevator we had just left. Fear iced the blood in my veins and I clutched Blane's hand.

"It's all right," he murmured quietly to me. "Keep moving."

I tried to stay calm and keep it together. Twenty feet. Fifteen. It was all I could do to keep my pace even with Blane's measured steps when every fiber of my body wanted to run. Ten feet. Five.

Then we were outside and I wanted simultaneously to laugh and weep from relief. Blane gave in to my tugging and we walked faster. Glancing up, I saw his lips pressed tightly together, his face pale under his tan. A grimace of pain was carved into his mouth. Taking his arm, I pulled it over my shoulder as I slid an arm beneath his jacket and behind his back. He didn't say anything, but he leaned on me.

Rounding the corner of the building, I was grateful night had almost fallen. We'd taken only a few steps when Kade materialized in front of us.

"What the fuck did you do?" he bit out at me, taking in Blane's wound.

"Not her fault," Blane said, wincing again as Kade took over, helping Blane walk to his car.

I rushed to open the passenger door and Blane got inside, leaning back against the seat and closing his eyes.

"Is he going to be okay?" I asked Kade, biting my lip nervously. Blane had said it wasn't bad, but it looked like a lot of blood. Guilt and worry ate at me. If only I'd been faster running down the hallway, Blane wouldn't have gotten hit.

"He will be. As soon as I get him to a hospital," Kade said. "You coming?"

I shook my head. "No. I have to be at the airport by seven."

Blane's eyes flew open and his gaze narrowed on me. "Why?" he asked.

"They're going to Chicago tonight," I quickly explained. "I'm working for one of the vice presidents, Stephen Avery. I'm hoping I'll be able to find the right server on-site."

Blane and Kade exchanged a meaningful look.

"What?" I asked, watching them communicate silently.

"Grab her," Blane said, and before I could even react, Kade had wrapped an arm around me, pinning my arms to my sides. Pulling me toward the car, he opened the back door.

"What the hell are you doing?" I cried out, furious. "Let me go! Blane! Why are you doing this?" I felt humiliated and betrayed. Kade pulled me in such a way that I couldn't regain my footing, and my shoes scrabbled uselessly against the concrete.

"Knock it off, Kathleen," Kade ordered, "I've got to get Blane to the hospital and I don't have time to deal with your tantrum."

"Then go!" I said. "Just leave me alone!"

"Forget it," he said, manhandling me into the backseat. "You have no business going to Chicago. You'll only get yourself killed. And, for some reason that's utterly beyond me, Blane wants you alive."

"Please, Kade," I begged, "I've come this far. They murdered my friend. I can't let them get away with doing that. I have to finish this."

Something I said or in the way I said it must have penetrated. He paused in shoving me in the car and I stopped fighting too. Our eyes caught and held.

"Please," I whispered. His lips pressed together.

"What can you do, Kathleen?" he asked. "You're one woman. You can't take them down alone."

I knew it was the truth even as he said it and yet I said simply, "I have to try."

There was a pregnant pause while I held my breath, waiting to see what he'd do. Finally, he slid his eyes to Blane in the front seat. I looked as well and saw that Blane had passed out.

"Get him to the hospital, Kade," I said urgently. "Forget about me."

"That's probably the smartest thing I've heard you say yet," he muttered grimly, and to my relief, he let me go. Kade wasted no time climbing into the driver's seat and driving away. He didn't look back.

Reaching my car in TecSol's lot, I drove home as quickly as I dared. I grabbed a small suitcase and started throwing things in it. It was nearly six and I knew it would take me forty-five minutes or more to get to the airport. My stomach was complaining about the fact that I hadn't really eaten anything since breakfast, but I didn't have time.

Running into the bathroom for my curling iron and makeup, I glanced in the mirror. My blouse was stained with Blane's blood. I froze, staring at the reflection. I was having a hard time processing what he had done to protect me. Guilt weighed heavily on me. I could only be grateful he hadn't been fatally injured.

Forcing myself into motion again, I took off my blouse and skirt, opting instead for a pair of warm wool slacks and an ivory cowl-necked sweater that was soft to the touch. I wasn't a big fan of white since it tended to wash me out, but the ivory shade of this outfit was flattering on me. With no time to redo my hair, I just brushed it out and let it fall over my shoulders. I'd learned my lesson with the heels and found a pair of flats in my closet instead. I shrugged into the black coat Blane had given me and ran out the door with my purse and suitcase.

Fifteen minutes after I'd arrived at home, I was back in the car. I had wanted to knock on CJ's door but resisted the urge. She might have tried to talk me out of going, and given how afraid I was, it wouldn't take much urging.

Pointing my car toward the airport, I tried to breathe calmly even though it felt like I was jumping from the frying pan into the fire. Kade's words echoed in my head and I tried not to let the overwhelming fear and despair drown me. I would do what I could and the rest was in the hands of Fate, the fickle bitch.

I arrived at the airport with only a few minutes to spare, hurriedly parking my car in the lot for the hangar before wheeling my luggage inside. Remembering my fake name at the last second, I gave it to the man waiting inside, who checked a list and took my luggage.

"Right this way," he said, and I followed him over to a small jet. The steps were lowered and we walked toward them. He handed my luggage to someone else who was loading bags into the bowels of the plane.

"Have a nice flight," he said, nodding at me.

I plastered a smile on my face, and taking a deep breath, climbed the stairs and stepped inside.

I was momentarily stunned speechless. I had never been inside a private jet before and it was as different from a commercial plane as water is from wine. The tiny seats squeezed together to fit as many people as possible weren't to be found here. Instead, several leather armchairs hugged the walls, and an actual couch curved from the wall in an L shape. Throw pillows in various shades decorated the seats, and small wooden tables were placed within easy reach. The floor was carpeted with a long rug that matched the pillows. All in all, it was more luxurious than I had imagined.

Three men were already seated in a group, talking earnestly with one another. Unsure what to do, I stood indecisively right inside the doorway. A voice from behind me made me jump.

"Lucy, so glad you made it," Stephen said. "I was wondering if you were having a hard time finding us. Please, have a seat."

We walked down the center of the aisle and Stephen acknowledged the men we passed. I noticed that one of them was Brian, who I'd met earlier today. I kept going until I got to the couch, where I sank down into the buttery soft leather. I know it was completely idiotic, but I was absurdly pleased to be able to sit on a couch while flying.

Stephen followed, joining me on the couch. As he took in my clothing, there was frank appreciation in his eyes. He'd removed his jacket and loosened his tie, and he sat back against the leather with a sigh, resting his arm across the back of the couch. This put his body in close proximity to mine and I had to resist the urge to scoot farther away. My eyes caught on the security badge clipped to his belt.

Someone else came through the door and I looked up, distracted. My eyes widened and my jaw dropped when I saw who it was.

Kade had stepped onto the plane.

Stephen saw where I was looking and glanced over too. He hurriedly got to his feet. Kade's eyes landed on me briefly before he looked at Stephen. He showed no signs of acknowledging me, so I quickly tore my gaze away. In a moment, he stood in front of Stephen.

"Dennon," Stephen said quietly by way of greeting. "I didn't know you were traveling with us tonight." An unspoken question hung in the air and I tried to pretend I wasn't avidly listening.

"Good evening, Stephen," Kade replied. "My . . . employers . . . thought it would be a good idea if I came along. To protect their investment, you understand." While his words were friendly, it was impossible to miss the implied threat underneath them.

"Of course," Stephen said agreeably, seemingly unfazed by Kade's words. "Please make yourself comfortable." He gestured behind us, but Kade ignored him, choosing instead a chair that was directly across from me.

"And who do we have here?" he asked lightly, his eyes on me. I swallowed heavily, unsure of what game he was playing. Stephen's jaw clenched at this and I was sure he wouldn't have introduced me if he could've helped it.

"This is my new assistant, Lucy," he said, resuming his seat next to me. "Lucy, this is Kade Dennon."

"Nice to meet you, Lucy," Kade said, one corner of his lips quirking up in a smirk.

"Likewise," I replied.

A woman came out from the front of the plane—the flight attendant, I supposed—and told us we were readying for departure. She asked Stephen if he wanted something to drink and he asked for a glass of wine.

"Would you care for a glass as well?" he asked me solicitously and I nodded. Kade, I noticed, declined anything to drink. A few moments later, the woman handed Stephen and me each a cold glass of chardonnay.

We were airborne shortly after that and Stephen informed me it would be only about a ninety-minute flight. I sipped my wine and tried to be unobtrusive, though I could feel Kade's eyes on me. This seemed to irritate Stephen and he leaned toward me and twisted so his back was to Kade, effectively blocking me from view.

Stephen talked quietly to me, asking me questions and chatting. I tried to stick to the truth as much as possible. Too many lies are hard to keep straight. As we talked, he put his hand on my knee, his palm lightly brushing up and down my thigh. It made me tense, but I tried to ignore it. It seemed nothing that had transpired this afternoon while helping Blane escape had been traced back to me, thank God.

"That color is lovely on you, Lucy," Stephen said, his knuckles touching the draped neck of my sweater. Perhaps accidentally, perhaps on purpose, his hand brushed against my breast. I plastered a smile on my face as I thanked him.

"Stephen," Brian called from the front of the plane. "Do you have a minute?" Stephen's eyes tightened in irritation, but he voice was placid when he said, "I'll be right back."

I nodded, relieved to be given a respite from his attentions. He got up and walked away and my eyes slid closed.

My nerves were stretched tight as bands of rubber and I felt like I might snap at any moment. A headache was starting to pound in my skull and I thought maybe it hadn't been a good idea to have a glass of wine on an empty stomach.

"How you holding up, princess?" Kade had slid into the now-vacant seat next to me and my eyes popped open.

"I'm fine," I said in a low voice, brushing aside his inquiry. "How's Blane? Why are you here? Is he going to be all right?" My questions came out in a rush.

"Blane's fine," he said. "I left him in good hands. Thought you needed me more tonight."

"Who are your employers?" I asked, remembering what he'd told Stephen.

"Ah, that," he said with a sigh. "A little white lie." He shrugged.

"You lied?" I hissed, anxiety gnawing at me. "What if he checks?"

"Relax," he said dismissively. "He won't." He paused for a moment. "So what's your plan?" he asked.

I glanced at Stephen out of the corner of my eye. He was still deeply in conversation with the other men.

"I was going to try to lift his badge," I said under my breath. "Thought it might get me where I need to go."

"And how are you going to lift his badge without him knowing?" Kade said sarcastically.

I just turned and looked at him, waiting for him to get to the obvious conclusion. I could tell when he did, for the amusement vanished from his eyes and his lips thinned.

"You're going to fuck him," he said matter-of-factly. I winced at his crudity.

"It won't get that far," I hissed. "Just far enough for me to get his badge."

"Your plan sucks," Kade said, his own anger coming to the surface now.

"Do you have a better one?" I demanded, narrowing my eyes at him.

"We could just kill him," Kade suggested, smirking when he saw me blanch. When I didn't respond, he sighed and said, "Fine. Have it your way."

Stephen returned then, his eyebrows lifting when he saw Kade sitting beside me. Kade stood, saying, "Just getting to know your assistant better, Stephen."

Stephen's smile was a bit forced as he resumed his place next to me. Kade drifted toward the back of the plane. I saw him pour himself a drink from a nearby decanter. It looked like scotch or bourbon.

"We'll be landing in a few minutes," Stephen said, his finger tracing lightly from my jaw down my neck to the edge of the top of my sweater. I noticed he wore a wedding ring, and my revulsion grew. I tried to disguise it with a smile. "Would you have dinner with me?" he asked.

"I'd love to," I said. "Maybe a private dinner with just us?" I suggested, placing my hand on his thigh. I was rewarded with an answering gleam in his eyes.

"That can be arranged," he said softly. Leaning forward, he kissed me. I responded, trying to block out the thought that he most likely had been involved with keeping Blane a hostage today.

Opening my eyes, I saw Kade watching us, his eyes unreadable. Tipping his glass back, he downed the rest of the contents and I watched the movement of his throat as he swallowed.

We landed and rode in waiting limousines to a downtown hotel. It was right off Lake Shore Drive, overlooking Lake Michigan. The city lights were beautiful, but it was a relief that I wasn't the one driving in the traffic.

I waited in the hotel lobby while Stephen checked us in, the concierge hastening to get someone to carry our luggage as Stephen passed out room keys to the men in our group. We rode the elevator up, but all the men got out on a lower floor. Kade caught my eye briefly as he stepped out of the elevator, and then the doors slid shut again and it was just Stephen and me.

When we reached the third floor from the top, Stephen got out and I followed. Handing me a key, he said, "Our rooms are next to each other."

"That's . . . convenient," I said with a small smile. Leading me to my door, Stephen pulled me toward him and kissed me again before I could get the key card in the slot.

"Maybe we could have dinner . . . later," he breathed in my ear. I thought frantically. I wasn't ready to do this yet. I needed more time.

"I'd really like to freshen up," I said breathlessly. "Change into something else. Give me an hour?" I stretched upward to kiss him. "I promise I'll make it worth the wait." That seemed to do the trick.

"All right," he agreed. "One hour and I'll be back."

I smiled and watched him as he retreated to his room across the hall. Sliding my key into the slot, I gratefully hurried inside, letting the door click shut behind me.

I was amazed at how large the room was. It wasn't like I was some hick who hadn't ever stayed in a hotel before, but I had never been able to afford a place like this. It had a separate living room area with a sofa, and flat-screen television on the wall. A small table with two dining chairs was in an alcove next to windows that stretched from the floor to the ceiling. Beyond them, I could see the lights of the city and Lake Shore Drive below.

In the bedroom, which was separated from the living area by a set of French doors, was a king-size four-poster bed that stood high off the floor. I thought with chagrin that I'd probably need a step stool to get into it.

The bathroom featured ceramic tile and a marble tub, and the sight of it made me long to turn on the water and relax. My head was throbbing from tension. Giving in to my impulse, I started filling the tub, delighted to find some complimentary bath oils that I added to the water. The room filled with a lovely floral scent.

I stripped off my clothes, being sure to fold them carefully. My mouth felt gross after kissing Stephen, so I brushed

my teeth before pinning up my hair and lowering myself
into the steaming water. I felt my muscles relax and let out
a long sigh, the tension easing from me. My eyes slid shut in
bliss and I enjoyed the small respite to my tumultuous day.

"Well, this is a nice surprise."

My eyes flew open. Stephen was standing in the bathroom watching me. I must not have heard the door open
over the water running.

"Stephen," I said, blushing furiously and grabbing for a
towel. "What are you doing in here?"

"I just had an interesting phone call from our head of
security back in Indy," he said, and now I noticed the hardness in his eyes and the cruel twist to his lips. "It seems they
were able to pull some prints off that access point that was
planted this morning."

I abruptly stopped struggling with the towel, my eyes flying to his, and I knew the jig was up.

"Damn it," he said, his hand closing on my upper arm as
he hauled me dripping out of the water. "You lying bitch. I
was willing to overlook helping Kirk escape, but not compromising our network." He shook me roughly and I clenched
my teeth together to keep from biting my tongue. "What the
hell did you do?"

The floor was wet and I slipped, falling against the door.
In an instant he had me pressed against it, his hand at my
throat. He squeezed and I couldn't breathe.

"You probably thought I didn't know about Kirk, didn't
you," he spat furiously at me. "I've got news for you, Kathleen," he hissed my name. "We let him escape. Do you think
he'd have gotten away so easily if we hadn't wanted him to?
You stupid cunt."

I was starting to see spots now as I pulled uselessly at his arm.

"Speaking of which," he said, and his voice had changed from furious to menacing, "I guess there is something you're good for before I kill you."

The pressure on my throat suddenly eased and I gasped, sucking in a lungful of air.

Snagging me around the waist, Stephen yanked me up, hauling me out of the bathroom and tossing me onto the bed. The cold air hit my wet skin. Rolling quickly away, I tried to cross the bed away from him but he caught my leg, pulling me backward.

"Good idea," he said. "I didn't want to see your ugly face anyway."

I could hear the jingling of his belt as he undid it. Panic clawed at me. Grabbing hold of one of the bedposts, I tried to use it pull myself away. Since I was still wet, Stephen lost his grip. But my freedom was short-lived. With a growl of fury, he grabbed my hips, his fingers bruising my flesh.

"No!" I cried out. "Let me go!" I struggled but was no match for him as he pulled me back onto my knees.

"Shut the fuck up," he commanded, shoving my face down into the comforter and holding me there, his hand tightly gripping the back of my neck. He straddled me, pinning my legs in place.

I struggled to breathe and knew I was about to be raped and killed, not necessarily in that order. The hard crack of his leather belt hitting me made me scream in pain. He hit me twice more and my skin felt on fire.

Suddenly, he released me. I fell to the side, struggling to breathe and crying at the same time. I knew I had to move, had to get away before he grabbed me again, and I tried to crawl across the bed.

Hands again touched my waist and I screamed, adrenaline surging through me. I struck out blindly as I was flipped onto my back. My wrists were caught and I sobbed in helpless fury.

"Kathleen, stop, it's all right. You're safe now."

The words didn't immediately penetrate my fear, but when they did, I cautiously stopped fighting and opened my eyes.

Kade was leaning over me, gently but firmly holding my wrists so I wouldn't hit him. The usual mocking gleam in his eyes was gone. In its place was rage and an emotion I couldn't name. My relief was so profound, I could do nothing more than sob. He released my arms and I turned on my side, pulling my knees up and curling into myself.

Sliding his arms underneath me, Kade lifted me in his arms and carried me out of the bedroom. I clung to him, my face buried in his shoulder as I tried to regain control. He sat on the couch with me in his lap, pulling a blanket over me. My hair was half up and half down and he methodically began removing the remaining pins as my tears drenched his shirt.

I finally made myself stop crying and took deep, cleansing breaths. It felt so good to breathe. The pins were out of my hair now and Kade was gently stroking my head.

Clearing my throat, I asked hoarsely, "What happened to him?"

"Dead," Kade said shortly, his hand not ceasing its motion.

I wasn't surprised and I couldn't bring myself to be sorry that Stephen was dead. I shuddered, thinking if Kade hadn't come, it would have been me.

"Thank you," I said roughly. "I don't know what I would've done . . ."

I couldn't continue, the tears clogging my throat again. It was quiet for a few moments as Kade let me regain control.

"Are you all right?" he asked quietly. "He didn't—"

I cut him off before he could finish the question. "No."

Another shudder ran through me and Kade pressed me closer. His hands were warm against my skin under the blanket and I curled further into him, savoring the feeling of safety after believing I was going to die.

I shifted so I could see his face, and the blanket slipped down past my shoulder. Kade's eyes dropped to my chest. I felt the surge of his response underneath me.

"Sorry, princess," he murmured after a moment, dragging his eyes back up to mine. "I'm just a man with a very beautiful, and very naked, woman on his lap."

Our eyes met and held and my breath caught in my throat.

"You should move now," he commanded, his voice rough, and I felt his hands curl into fists.

Abruptly I sat up, moving off his lap and taking the blanket with me. I didn't meet his eyes as I wrapped myself up and moved to the other end of the couch.

"He said they *let* Blane escape today," I said, and merely speaking Blane's name made it feel like he was a presence in the room with us. "And they know it was me."

"That's unfortunate," he said, "but not unexpected." The look in his eyes was gone as if it had never been, his usual smirk in its place. "We have his key card now, though I think it would have gone better if we'd just done things my way."

The slight mockery in his tone made me wince but I couldn't argue with him.

"I'm going to take him back to his room, make it look like an accident," he said, getting up from the couch. "Get dressed. We need to do what we came for and get out of here."

I nodded, standing as well. I must have stood too quickly, though, for the room swam in my vision, and my knees buckled.

"Fuck!" Kade moved fast, catching me before I could hit the floor.

My hands shook slightly as I clung to him, waiting for the room to stop spinning.

"What's wrong?" he demanded anxiously. "Did you hit your head? Did he hit you?" I shook my head.

"No, no. I just . . . was dizzy for a moment, that's all," I said weakly.

Kade seemed to process this. "When was the last time you ate?" he asked.

I shrugged. "This morning, maybe?" It seemed so long ago.

"You're a shitload of trouble," he grunted, helping me to my feet and steadying me. "Can you get dressed by yourself?"

I nodded, my cheeks flaming at the thought of him having to help me dress.

Wrapping the blanket around me like a toga, I shuffled back to the bedroom, Kade close on my heels. I stopped short when I walked through the French doors. Stephen's body was on the ground, his head bent at such an angle that I knew his neck was broken. His eyes stared ahead sightlessly. My stomach rolled, but I took a deep breath and gritted my teeth. I absolutely would not throw up in front of Kade again.

Hooking his hands under Stephen's armpits, Kade dragged him to the door. After checking to make sure the hallway was clear, I unlocked Stephen's room and Kade dragged him inside. Grabbing Stephen's security badge off his pants, I retreated back to my room, letting Kade do whatever he was going to do to stage Stephen's untimely demise.

Filling a glass with water from the tap, I drank it down, hoping it would help clear my head. Water was all over the floor, so I grabbed some towels and sopped it up.

Pulling clothes from my suitcase, I hurriedly pulled on a pair of jeans and a black turtleneck, pulling my hair back into a tight ponytail. I had forgotten to bring tennis shoes, so I slipped my feet into a pair of black flats.

By the time Kade came back, I felt I'd regained some of my armor, though the memory of what I'd been enduring and what Kade had seen in this hotel room made it difficult for me to look him in the eye. A mixture of rage and shame filled me and I would have given anything for someone else, anyone else, to have saved me. I knew Kade thought I was useless trash, and somehow having him see someone treating me that way made it feel more like it was true.

"You ready?" he asked and I nodded. I grabbed my purse and we left the room. We didn't speak until we were on the street.

"Let's get some food in you," Kade said, his hand moving to lightly grasp my elbow. It was cold outside, the wind gusting in our faces, and I was glad I'd pulled my hair out of the way.

"I'm fine," I said. "Let's just get to the data center."

"Forget it," Kade said firmly, pulling me down the sidewalk. "I'm not having you pass out on me because you're too stubborn to eat."

"I won't pass out," I said through gritted teeth. "I just want to get this over with."

"All in good time," he said. "It's better anyway if we go later. Fewer people will be in the building. Now, let's eat." He started to pull me into a small, dimly lit pub.

"No!" I said, trying to pull away, my voice near panic.

Kade stopped and looked down at me, his eyes narrowing. "What's the problem?" he said, and I inwardly cringed at the irritation in his voice.

I couldn't explain it, but the thought of sitting across from him and eating, pretending nothing had happened, was enough to make me want to do anything to avoid it. I wasn't able to be detached, like he was, and knew I would wonder the entire time if all he could see when he looked at me was the humiliation I'd endured. If, in his mind's eye, he saw me naked on the bed, face shoved into the covers, about to be raped. Of course, I could tell him none of this.

"I just . . . can't," I said weakly, avoiding his eyes.

I felt him studying me. Then his hand was under my chin, lifting it toward him. I looked down, refusing his implied request.

"Look at me," he said softly.

I shook my head, biting my lip to keep from crying. Two tears slid down my cheek anyway. I felt his thumbs brush them away.

"Keep it together, Kathleen," he said quietly. "Any other woman would have needed a sedative after what that bastard did tonight. You're stronger than that."

More tears fell and he brushed those away too, his thumbs lingering on my cheekbones.

"It wasn't your fault, Kathleen," he said earnestly. "Don't blame yourself for what he did."

I did raise my eyes then and I don't know what he saw in them, but he cursed under his breath. Then his lips settled on mine with a sweetness I would never have thought he possessed. He didn't try to deepen the kiss; it was more like a benediction. I savored the touch, feeling like it could heal the part of me that Stephen had broken back in that hotel room.

Kade touched his forehead to mine, our breath mingling in the cold night air. We stood like that for several minutes, his hands wrapped gently around the back of my neck, his thumbs caressing my face, while my hands rested on his arms. When he finally did pull back, I was able to look at him without wanting to bury my face in shame.

"Please," I whispered, "don't tell . . . anyone . . . about what happened."

Both of us knew who I was talking about; I didn't think I could bear it if Blane ever found out. Kade's jaw tightened, but he gave me a curt nod and somehow I knew he wouldn't break his word to me.

"I'm hungry," I said, and Kade's lips tipped up a little at the corners.

"It's about fucking time," he said, grabbing my hand and pulling me into the pub. This time, I went willingly.

CHAPTER FIFTEEN

K ade and I were seated in a corner booth of the pub. He sat across from me with his back to the wall. A tired-looking waitress came up to us for our order.

"Water for me, Coke for her," Kade answered.

"Diet Coke," I interjected, but Kade cut me off.

"No, regular," he told the waitress, who nodded and left.

"You need the sugar," he said once she'd gone. This seemed high-handed to me, but I didn't want to argue over something petty.

Glancing through the menu, I tried to find something appealing. I settled on a turkey sandwich with a baked potato instead of fries.

"Does the potato come with sour cream and cheese?" I asked.

The waitress nodded. "Bacon, too, if you want it," she said.

"That would be great." Bacon should have its own food group.

Kade ordered a sandwich as well and the waitress left us alone.

I sipped at my Coke and grudgingly admitted that the sugar was making me feel better. Even if it was transient energy, I no longer felt like I could lay my head down on the table and fall asleep. We sat in silence for a few minutes before I asked a question that had been hovering in the back of my mind.

"How did you and Blane . . . find each other?" I asked.

Kade's eyes narrowed and I thought he wasn't going to answer me.

"My mother died and Blane's father's name was listed on my birth certificate," he said flatly. "They wanted to pass guardianship to him."

"When did she die?"

"My mother died of cancer when I was six. I was shuffled around the system for a few years. I was on my twelfth foster home when Blane found me."

My eyes widened in surprise and sympathy. Twelve foster homes. I couldn't begin to imagine how horrible that would be for a child, especially one so young.

"Blane's father didn't take care of you when your mother died?" I asked incredulously, my opinion of the man sinking lower every minute.

Kade's lips curved in a humorless smile. "He had a reputation to consider," he said bitterly. "It wouldn't have looked good, taking his orphaned bastard in, now would it?"

"But Blane took you in," I said, and it wasn't a question.

I could tell by the look in Kade's eyes that I was right, and he slowly nodded.

"Blane did," he affirmed. Our eyes met and held and I saw again in them the same steadfast loyalty to Blane that I'd seen that morning when he was in my bedroom.

"Blane said he and his father had parted ways before he went into the Navy," I said. "Was that because of you?"

Kade nodded. "And because Blane wouldn't toe the party line. The old man was a lifelong Democrat who came from a long line of lifelong Democrats. Blane thought differently and the old man never forgave him for it. Blane was fourteen when he found out about me. He tried to get the old man to take me in, but he wouldn't."

"When did he die?" I asked.

"When Blane was eighteen."

"Did his mother know?"

"I'm not sure," Kade answered. "Does a wife ever really not know when her husband is cheating on her? Whether or not she knew about me, I couldn't say. Probably not."

"Did Blane tell her?" I didn't know why he was answering my questions, but so long as he did, I wasn't going to stop asking.

Kade shook his head. "She was a gentle woman. Fragile. And she loved his father, even if he was a cheating asshole. His death seemed to weaken her. She died not very long after him."

That was sad, being so in love with someone who wouldn't be faithful. I couldn't imagine a scenario where it wouldn't matter to me—that I would love someone to the point of looking the other way. It seemed so . . . weak somehow. I tried not to make judgments on Blane's mother, but I couldn't imagine giving up on life when I had a son who needed me.

"You're quite a bit younger than Blane," I said, then paused as the waitress set our food in front of us.

The food distracted me for a few minutes, the smell making me realize how famished I actually was. I dug into my potato, closing my eyes in pleasure when the coolness of the sour cream combined with the heat of the vegetable hit my tongue.

When I opened my eyes, Kade was watching me, the corner of his mouth twitching upward. "Good?" he asked simply.

I mumbled an affirmative response around the next bite.

When I'd taken the edge off my hunger, I returned my attention to Kade, eyeing him speculatively. His brow arched in an unspoken question.

"You're, what, ten years younger than Blane?" I asked.

"Eight."

"Did he come find you when his father died?"

Kade nodded, finishing off his sandwich.

We were interrupted by a woman sliding into the seat next to Kade. My eyebrows flew upward as she grasped his jaw lightly before placing her mouth on his. I watched, dumbfounded for a moment as they kissed, my stomach tightening into a knot. Then I jumped and let out a squeak when a large black man sat down next to me, his arm resting on the back of the booth behind me.

The woman finally broke the kiss and snagged a fry off Kade's plate.

"About time you guys showed up," Kade said, unfazed.

The woman cracked a smile at him. She was petite and lovely with nearly black hair and bright-green eyes.

"Wouldn't want you to take us for granted, Kade," the woman said lightly, and I was surprised to hear her speak with an accent. Irish, maybe?

"Who's your fine friend, Kade?" the black man asked.

I turned toward him and looked up, and up some more. He was huge, and although he was smiling, his eyes were

TIFFANY SNOW

calculatingly assessing me. I decided right then and there that I would never want to be on his bad side. His chest and arms were massive and I bet he could squash me like a bug.

"Ah yes, I should introduce you," Kade said smoothly. "Kathleen, this is Terrance and Branna."

"Nice to meet you," I said automatically, watching as Branna ate another fry. She sat very close to Kade, who didn't seem to mind.

"Terrance and Branna are going to help us out tonight," Kade explained. Turning to Branna he asked, "Were you able to tie in to the cameras?"

Branna nodded, smiling slightly. "Of course. I'm now able to control them remotely. They'll only see what I want them to see."

"You never disappoint," Kade murmured, and Branna seemed pleased with his praise.

"How are you getting in?" Terrance asked, and Kade swung his gaze to him.

"It's not the getting in I'm worried about," he said wryly. "Where's Rusty? Didn't he come with you guys?"

Branna rolled her eyes. "He's outside with the van. Said he didn't want to leave it alone in a bad neighborhood."

"Bad neighborhood?" I asked, confused. We were actually in a nice part of town.

Kade sighed. "Same old paranoid Rusty, I see."

"You got that right," agreed Terrance with a huff.

Kade signaled for the check and tucked some money into the small leather folder when it came. We climbed out of the booth and surreptitiously I looked over Branna. She had a figure any woman would envy—a tiny waist and rounded hips—encased in skintight black jeans and heeled leather boots that went to her knees. Her hair was thick and wavy and she wore it unbound. A green shirt the same color as her eyes was molded to her chest and she wore a black vest over the top. As she walked away from me, I saw a telltale bulge in the small of her back that told me she had a gun.

Outside, Terrance and Branna led us around the corner to a van parked on the side of the street. Terrance knocked on the side door sharply. When nothing happened, he rapped again, calling out in an irritated voice, "Open the fucking door, Rusty."

The door cautiously slid open to reveal a slight figure wearing glasses and a ball cap as he leaned out the opening. "You're supposed to use the code knock, Terrance," he argued in a petulant voice. "Three short, two long, two short. Then I know it's you." He pushed the glasses farther up his nose.

"Fuck that stupid code," Terrance groused. "I ain't doin' that."

I watched Branna and Kade exchange a look of mutual understanding as Terrance and Rusty continued to bicker. They were obviously familiar with this scene. Feeling uncomfortably like an outsider, I shifted nervously from one foot to another. This drew Kade's attention to me and his amused smirk faded.

"If you two are done," he interjected, effectively silencing Terrance and Rusty, "let's get on with it."

With a final huff of disdain, Terrance moved around and got in the driver's seat while Branna climbed in the passenger side. Kade motioned for me to climb in the van as well.

"Who's she?" Rusty asked, staring at me as I settled myself inside and Kade slid the side door shut.

"She's our ticket inside," Kade answered.

"You got a key card?" Rusty said in disbelief.

"Give it to him," Kade ordered me and I did as he said. "Rusty, we need this to be someone other than Stephen Avery."

Rusty took the card eagerly, turning it over in his hands. "Why?"

"Because Avery's dead," Kade replied.

Rusty didn't seem surprised by this. "Then he can't very well go running about the data center, can he," Rusty asked rhetorically, taking the card and disappearing into the back of the van.

Twisting around in my seat, I saw that the back had been torn out and replaced with a shelf bolted to the side that held computer equipment. A folding chair sat in front of it. I watched as Rusty sat down and put the card into some type of device.

"What's he doing?" I asked Kade in an undertone.

"Changing the base code so it will still open the doors, but not as Stephen Avery," he answered.

Turning back around, I saw Branna watching me. I met her stare.

"You're not taking her inside with you?" she asked Kade disapprovingly.

"Was planning on it," he answered shortly.

"That's foolish, Kade," she said with a snort. "She'll get herself killed and maybe you along with her." I decided I didn't like being talked about as if I weren't there.

"'She,'" I interjected forcefully, "won't be getting anyone killed."

Branna's eyes narrowed at me. "So why are you here, sweetie?" The way she said "sweetie," dripping with condescension, made me want to grind my teeth.

"She's my backup," Kade answered evenly, surprising me. "And she knows which server we need to target. Something we haven't been able to figure out."

Branna's face flushed with anger before she quickly turned away.

When we were no longer being watched, Kade leaned over toward me. "You do know which server it is, right?" he whispered in my ear, his warm breath tickling my skin.

I smiled and nodded.

"Good."

He settled back in his seat. I wondered what he would have done if I'd said I hadn't the faintest clue which server it was.

A few minutes later, we pulled up to a large, squat building. The lights outside shining on the sign proclaimed it to be TecSol—DataCenter Midwest. I took a deep breath.

Climbing back across the van toward us, Rusty held out the security badge.

"It should still get you where you need to go," he said as Kade pocketed it. He handed him a small earpiece. "I'll guide you through the building with this for as long as I can. The shielding might be too great to receive a signal once you're underground."

"Understood," Kade said, fitting it to his ear.

"I can get you into the perimeter of the building through a side door," Rusty continued, "but you'll need to use the key card from there." Kade checked his gun and ammunition while Rusty talked, then tucked it in the small of his back.

"Give me an extra gun, Rusty," Kade said, and Rusty obediently handed him one. Kade held it out, grip first, to me. "You know how to fire a gun?"

Before I could answer, Branna burst out. "What the hell are you doing? She's a child! Don't give her a gun! She'll likely shoot herself or you."

Well, thanks for the vote of confidence, I thought grimly.

I took the gun from Kade, sliding the magazine out to make sure it was loaded before locking it back into place. I checked to make sure the safety was on and shoved it in the back of my pants. I silently thanked my dad for teaching me how to use a gun.

"Yeah, I know how to fire a gun," I said, ignoring Branna.

No one said anything, but I thought I saw a flicker of appreciation in Kade's eyes.

"Branna," Kade said, turning toward her, and I noticed she looked furious, "keep the cameras covered. And Terrance, be ready to split should it go bad. Cover your own asses."

All three nodded, their expressions serious.

Kade and I exited the van and I watched as Branna climbed into the back with Rusty. Rusty checked to make sure Kade could hear him on the earpiece.

"Good luck, Kade," Branna said, her eyes glued to him. He didn't speak, merely acknowledging her with a curt nod. She completely ignored me.

I knew then, by the look in her eyes, that she was in love with him. I couldn't tell if he knew or felt the same. I would have almost felt sorry for her if she hadn't been such a bitch to me. The van door slid shut and it slowly rolled away.

"They'll just go a few streets over and set up," Kade assured me. "Let's go."

The street was deserted and quiet. Kade took my hand in his and led me behind the building into the shadows. I stayed quiet, assuming he was listening to Rusty direct him in his ear. We reached a door and, with a quiet click, it unlocked and we slipped inside. The door shut behind us, the lock clicking back on, and I tried not to think of how ominous that sounded.

We were at the end of a hallway, a door to our right proclaiming an entrance to a stairwell. The building was well lit and quiet. There was a constant thrumming of sound just below my range of hearing, which I could feel nonetheless. My blood was racing and fear lapped at me. I tried to concentrate on breathing. I was Kade's backup. I couldn't, wouldn't, let anything happen to him, not least of all because he was Blane's little brother.

Dropping my hand, Kade pulled out his gun and I copied him, thumbing the safety off. Target practice was one thing, but I didn't know if I'd be able to actually shoot someone, should the need arise. I hoped it wouldn't come to that.

Going into the stairwell, we quietly made our way down three flights. When we reached the bottom, Kade flashed the key card and the lock clicked. Easing the door open slowly, Kade made sure the hallway was deserted before entering. I hurried after him.

"Just lost the signal," Kade muttered. "The shielding down here is thick enough to withstand bombs," he explained. "We're on our own now."

I swallowed nervously. Kade's eyes were bright with excitement.

I followed him down the hallway, bypassing several locked doors on the way. Nervously, I glanced at the numerous cameras in the ceiling.

"Are you sure Branna's going to be able to work the cameras?" I asked.

"Absolutely," he answered. "She's the best."

I wondered, a little snidely, what else she was "the best" at.

"So what's the name of the server?" he asked quietly as we walked.

"EVE0928," I answered. "What are you going to do when you find it?"

"Find out who's really running this operation," he said curtly, offering nothing further.

We reached the end of the hall, and a large double door barred our path. Kade looked at me.

"Beyond this is the main data center," he said. "There are going to be guards and workers we'll need to neutralize."

"By neutralize, I hope you don't mean what I think you mean," I said warningly. "These people aren't the ones responsible for all this. They don't deserve to die."

Kade just looked at me for a moment, his expression unreadable.

"At least *try* to remember I'm on your side," he said finally.

I flushed and nodded.

Flashing the key card in front of the lock, the door clicked open and Kade pushed through it quickly, with me hot on his heels.

Surprisingly, only one man was there, sitting behind a counter in front of a bank of computer monitors. He turned to see who had entered the room. When he saw Kade pointing a gun at him, he jumped to his feet, lunging for something behind the counter.

A gunshot rang out and the man yelled in pain, clutching his arm where Kade's bullet had hit him.

"I wouldn't do that, if I were you," Kade said calmly.

I watched as the man eased backward, away from what I now saw was a button on the wall. His hand was now crimson with blood.

"Back away, against the wall, and toss your cell phone on the floor," Kade ordered. The man did as he was told. Kade looked at me pointedly and I scooped up the phone, my hands shaking. Glancing around, I saw a door to a restroom and hurried inside, dropping it into a toilet. When I came back out, Kade motioned me over to him.

"Keep your gun on him," he said.

I obeyed, trying to steady my hand as I lifted my gun.

"What are you going to do?" I asked, watching him as he rounded to the other side of the counter and bent over a computer monitor and keyboard.

"I'm finding our server," he said, his eyes on the screen. Beyond him was a labyrinth of row upon row of server racks.

Suddenly, I was really glad he was here. There was no way I could have found the server on my own.

"Got it," he said. I expected him to head toward the server racks, but he didn't.

"Well, where is it?" I asked impatiently. I didn't know what Kade was doing, but I still knew what I had to do. The thumb drive was burning a hole in my pocket. I debated whether or not I should tell Kade about it, but opted to keep quiet.

"Rack 518," he answered distractedly. I watched as his fingers flew over the keyboard.

A click behind me made me turn, then I watched in horror as the door flew open. I dove in front of the counter just as gunshots rang out, the tile where I'd just been standing chipping from the bullets.

A hand clamped around my arm and I looked up. It was the guy Kade had shot and he was wrestling the gun out of my fingers. I panicked when I lost my grip on it, sure he was going to shoot me, and raised my knee with all my strength. It connected with his crotch and he doubled over in pain.

Scrambling to my feet, I crouched low, running in front of the counter toward the server racks. Behind me, I heard voices shouting and more gunshots. I couldn't see Kade anywhere and I was terrified he'd been hit.

I made it into a row just as I heard gunshots hitting metal. Then the sound abruptly stopped.

"Don't shoot at the servers, you moron!" a man shouted.

I kept running and now I heard footsteps following me.

Running down the row, I saw it was an even larger room than I'd thought. The racks were over six feet tall and, for once, I was glad of my short stature. Seeing an aisle to my right, I turned, running a short distance before turning down another row. I did that a few more times, then stopped to listen, my chest heaving.

I could hear running footsteps, but I couldn't tell exactly how far away they were or from which direction they were coming. My heart was racing and blood thundered in my ears. Looking across the row, I saw a number on the rack: 407. With a start, I remembered the number Kade had told me. If I was lucky, I might be able to find it. I covered my mouth with my hands, trying to quiet my breathing.

I pulled off the flats I was wearing; their hard soles made noise with each step. I considered carrying them with me but knew I'd need my hands free. Cursing the fact that I'd lost my gun, I made my way down the row, the tile floor cold under my bare feet.

It had gone completely quiet. Goose bumps appeared on my arms and I knew what it felt like to be hunted. Coming to a break in the racks, I pressed my back up against the cold metal, taking a deep breath before I took a quick peek around the corner. Seeing no one, I quickly skittered across the open space into the safety of another row, breathing a sigh of relief when no shots rang out.

I was in the high four hundreds now, my eyes skimming the labels on the racks as I hurried past. Not much farther. Another break in the seemingly endless maze of racks made me repeat my hesitant peek-and-skitter. I was a step away from the safety of another row when I heard someone shout. A quick glance to my left and I saw a man barreling toward me. Throwing caution and quiet to the wind, I took off.

Fifty feet later, I was skidding to a stop in front of rack 518. I wasted precious seconds trying to get the door to the rack open, the man rapidly running down the aisle toward me. Finally, the door opened and I quickly scanned the servers stacked inside, stopping when I saw EVE0928. I inwardly cursed when I saw that it had some sort of metal cover over the front.

Fear gave me strength and I forcefully yanked it off. Groping in my pocket, I pulled out the thumb drive, sticking it in a slot on the front just as the man reached me.

He clamped down on my shoulder and spun me around. I used the momentum to bring up my hands, which were still grasping the long rectangular metal cover. With a sickening crunch, it hit him on the side of the head and he staggered back. I pressed my advantage, adrenaline and fear spiking in my blood. I swung again and connected with his elbow, causing him to drop the gun he'd been holding.

Dropping the metal cover, I dove for the gun, my fingers closing around it as the man landed on me. We wrestled over the gun in near silence; only our heavy breathing and grunts of exertion could be heard. I was determined that I was not going to let go, but his hands were like vises on my arms and hands.

I was startled when the gun went off, and so was he. Our eyes met for a moment and I had just a split second of realization that *I* hadn't been hit before the man collapsed on top of me.

Struggling under his weight, I shoved him far enough off of me to be able to crawl out the rest of the way. Blood coated my hands and I hastily wiped them off on my jeans. Tears stung my eyes, but I blinked them away. No time to fall apart right now.

A touch on my back had me spinning around and I gasped when I saw it was Kade.

"Oh my God," I stammered, shaken. "Kade, I could have killed you!"

He just smirked at me. "Not a chance, princess," he said.

Glancing over my shoulder, he took in the scene. There was a pool of blood slowly spreading beneath the dead guy, and the door on rack 518 stood open. When his eyes met mine again, they examined me shrewdly.

"What did you do?" he asked, his voice hard.

"I didn't mean to kill him," I hastily explained. "We were fighting and—"

"Not that," he interrupted impatiently. "Like I care if you killed him. I meant, what did you do to the server?" His hand was tightly grasping my arm now and I winced.

"I . . . I thought it would be best to compromise it," I said weakly.

"Did you suddenly grow more brain cells overnight?" he snapped at me. "How the hell do you think you compromised it?"

My temper flared at that. "A friend helped," I explained curtly. "She's a computer programmer. Works for some company in Japan. She wrote a worm that uploaded into the system from the thumb drive." I didn't see any harm in telling him now that the deed was done.

"And you're just telling me this now?" he said in disbelief. I looked at him for a moment, not speaking, until realization followed by bitterness crossed his face. "You didn't trust me," he said.

I felt a pang of regret, but it was too late now. And the look on his face said so even if I hadn't already known.

"I'm sorry," I whispered.

The hardness in his eyes didn't change, though I was sure he'd heard me. He glanced down at his watch then back up at me.

"That was a bad decision."

The way he said it made my blood run cold. Then everything went dark.

I gasped in surprise. It was so black, I couldn't see anything. My eyes blinked rapidly, but there was no light for them to absorb. It didn't matter if they were open or closed—it looked the same. Panic clawed at my throat and I reached out blindly toward Kade, praying he hadn't left me alone. My fingers touched nothing but air.

"Please, don't leave me," I said, my voice sounding strangled.

"I'm not going to leave you."

My knees nearly gave out in relief when I heard his voice.

"Though I probably should." He grabbed my arm and pulled me toward him. I stumbled, coming up hard against his chest. I felt hands on my head and suddenly I could see again. He'd put night-vision goggles on me and I saw he wore an identical pair.

"You planned this?" I breathed, still shaken.

"How did you think we were going to get out of here?"

Not giving me a chance to answer, he pulled me forward and we were jogging back down the rows, headed toward the exit, I hoped.

I saw a couple of men fumbling in vain in the darkness and I gave them a wide berth. We finally reached the exit and were through, moving quickly down the hall and up the stairs. I didn't breathe properly until we were outside and I was ripping the goggles off my face.

Kade had a hold of my hand and didn't release it as we ran through the adjacent parking lot to the next street over. The concrete was rough on my feet as rocks and debris cut into my skin, but I bit my lip and kept my silence.

We stopped when we reached the van, silently parked on the street. The side door slid open as we jogged up and climbed inside. Terrance turned from the driver's seat, a broad smile showing the vivid white of his teeth in his dark face.

"Nice work, Terrance," Kade said, and I was annoyed to realize he was barely breathing hard. I was huffing and wheezing like a water buffalo scaling Mount Everest. Kade handed Rusty the night-vision goggles and I saw Branna looking Kade over as if searching for injuries.

"Yo, no problem, my man," Terrance said. "One city block power outage requested and that's what you got." He looked over at me. "And I see the girl's still alive."

"She held her own," Kade replied evenly.

Terrance grinned at me and I tentatively smiled back. He was still scary, even smiling.

Kade looked over at me as I struggled to catch my breath.

"You really need to get in better shape," he mused. I just glared at him, not wanting to waste any of my precious air on a retort.

"The money will be in your accounts by tomorrow," Kade said to them and Terrance nodded.

"Where to?" Terrance asked. Kade gave him an address. A few minutes later, we pulled up to a small, shabby motel on the outskirts of the city.

Kade reached out and grasped Terrance's hand in a firm grip. "A pleasure working with you," he said, "as always."

Terrance's grin widened. "Need transport tomorrow?" he asked.

Kade shook his head. "Got it covered," he answered. "Until next time . . ."

Terrance grinned, giving him a two-fingered salute, and Branna blew him a kiss. Rusty handed me my purse, which I'd left in the van, then the door slid shut and the van rolled away into the night.

Kade started across the gravel lot toward the flashing neon sign proclaiming Office. I hesitated, eyeing the gravel with trepidation. My feet were burning and each step was agony. The long stretch of gravel made me want to stomp my foot in frustration, except I knew it would hurt like hell.

After a few feet, Kade seemed to realize I wasn't with him and he turned around.

"Are you waiting for an engraved invitation?" he asked, sarcasm thick in his voice.

I despised the fact that I'd have to betray my weakness to him and resolved that I'd cross the gravel lot come hell or high water. That resolve lasted two steps before I was immobilized, unable to take another step. My face was contorted in a grimace of pain.

"What's wrong?" Kade asked, walking quickly back to me. Glancing down, he noticed my feet. "Damn it, Kathleen!" he exclaimed. "Why the hell didn't you tell me you were barefoot? What happened to your shoes?"

I was trying to ignore the pain, so it took me a second to answer. "They made noise," I explained through gritted teeth. "I took them off and left them. I'm all right."

I shrugged off his concern. Nothing could be done about it now. I'd worry about it later. Right now I just wanted to get across this damn lot, find a bed, and sleep for a few days, at least.

"Have I mentioned what a pain in the ass you are?" Kade said, which made me want to cross my arms and stick my tongue out at him like I was twelve. "Next time, pack sensible shoes."

"I'll make sure to remember that the next time I plan on breaking and entering," I retorted sarcastically. He ignored me. I yelped in surprise as he abruptly bent over and hoisted me in his arms.

"What are you doing?" I screeched. There was no way I was going to let him carry me like I was some helpless damsel in distress. "Put me down!"

The look he gave me made me hastily shut my mouth, but I still glared at him mutinously.

Kade swiftly crossed the lot and deposited me in a decrepit plastic chair outside the office door. He leaned down so his face was inches away, his eyes intent on mine.

"Stay here," he ordered. I pressed my lips together and raised my chin haughtily. For some reason, he seemed to bring out the rebellious side of me. I wasn't stupid enough to disobey him, however. The mere thought of walking made me cringe. Kade disappeared inside and came back a few minutes later.

"Not the Ritz, but it'll do for tonight," he said. I shrugged, not caring where we stayed so long as I could get some sleep soon. With a sigh, I heaved myself up but I had to grab on to the chair again as pain shot through me.

Kade handed me a metal key with a plastic tag attached. I took it, looking questioningly at him, before he again lifted me in his arms. My face flushed and I resolutely kept my face averted from his.

He carried me down the motel walkway, finally stopping in front of a door marked 119—or rather, it would have said 119 if the nine hadn't been hanging loosely upside down. Kade cleared his throat pointedly and I hurriedly stuck the key in the knob and unlocked the door, pushing it inward as Kade carried me inside the darkened motel room.

I grimaced, realizing what a parody this was of my childhood dream of an adoring husband carrying me across the threshold of a beautiful hotel room on our wedding night.

Instead, I was being carried by a man who barely tolerated me into a motel that, I was sure, rented rooms by the hour.

He placed me on the bed, the springs complaining loudly, then flipped on the lamp by the bed before closing and bolting the door. I glanced around the room, noting the stark difference between it and the posh suite I'd been in just hours ago. Yeah, this was the type of motel suited to my sad budget. Faded carpet, cheap bedspread, cardboard-like pillows. I sighed. I understood that we needed to lie low, but maybe I could suggest a Holiday Inn next time as opposed to a No-Tell Motel?

Kade pulled out his cell phone and turned away as he punched in a few numbers and held it to his ear. I strained to hear.

"Agent Donovan," he said, "it's good to talk to you again."

A pause as he listened before continuing.

"Yes, it's done. I'd be interested to know what you found."

He listened again, and then his gaze swung to me. I couldn't read what was in his eyes as the other man talked for a long time.

Finally, Kade spoke again. "No, that wasn't what I was expecting either," he said carefully. "But enough to shut it down, correct?" The other person must have answered in the affirmative, because Kade's lips quirked upward in a smirk.

"Excellent. Good talking to you, Donovan. Give my regards to your wife." He snapped the phone shut.

"What was that all about?" I asked.

"Sometimes the FBI needs people to do their dirty work for them," he said.

I looked at him questioningly for a moment before it clicked into place. "You mean, you?" I asked. "The FBI wanted you to break into TecSol?"

"Must you act so surprised?" he asked, pretending to be hurt. Then he abruptly turned serious. "They needed someone to send a trace to them for the network traffic," he said. "But the FBI deliberately monitoring the servers of the company handling online election votes?" He shook his head. "Not good for publicity if they got caught."

"So they had you do it because you're off the books," I said, my tired brain trying to piece it all together. "They could trust you because you used to be one of them."

Kade shrugged with false modesty. "Blane was the one who caught on to the whole thing and brought me in," he said. "I just helped pull in the big guns to take them down." His self-satisfied smirk faltered a bit.

"What?" I asked. "What's wrong?"

"Your friend, the girl programmer," he said carefully, his brows drawing together in a frown. "The code she gave you. She told you it would compromise the system?"

I nodded. "Didn't it?" I asked, suddenly afraid of what he might say.

"It did," he said slowly, watching me. "Just not in the way you probably expected."

"What do you mean?" I asked, a sense of foreboding filling me. "Just tell me."

Kade's expression turned grim. "She lied to you, Kathleen. The code you installed didn't disable the system, it just installed a secondary path for the traffic."

"A secondary path? To where?" I was struggling to understand the technospeak.

"The data was being copied to China."

"What?" I reeled in shock. "Why China?"

"Probably so they could get their hands on the encryption algorithm," Kade answered. "It would be useful for espionage purposes, especially if it was used in future elections."

I ran a tired hand over my face, trying to understand. CJ had lied to me. Used me. I remembered her just this morning telling me no one would blame me if I just left TecSol and forgot the whole thing. How could I have been so stupid? I'd just blindly done exactly what she'd wanted me to do.

"Kathleen."

I didn't hear him, so lost was I in my own dismay and confusion. She'd been the one to save me from James.

"Kathleen!"

I looked up then, the urgency in his voice breaking through my haze. His eyes were narrowed as he crouched in front of me, his hand gripping mine.

"It still worked," he said, his face moving closer to mine, as if to emphasize his words. "The fact that the data was being sent outside the country will bring TecSol to its knees."

"But you still don't know who was behind it here, do you?" I asked shrewdly. He didn't have to sugarcoat this for me.

His jaw clenched as if he didn't want to answer. "No," he finally said. "But we will. They'll try again, some other way, and we'll get them."

My eyes searched his, wanting to believe he was telling me the truth, that I hadn't completely and irrevocably screwed everything up with my blind faith and naive trust in a complete stranger.

"What about the Santini brothers?" I persisted. "They still want me dead." I remembered what he'd said this morning. "Aren't they going to come after you when they find out I'm still alive? You took their money."

His face closed off then and I wondered if he'd told me everything.

"Blane has enough on the Santini brothers to make sure they'll go away for a long time," he said. "Don't worry about them." He smirked. "And I was able to relieve them of twenty thousand of their dollars."

That coaxed a smile out of me. He sounded like a little boy who had managed to steal candy without getting caught, not a hired assassin who had been paid for a hit he hadn't delivered.

"Don't spend it all in one place," I teased lightly before glancing at the clock next to the bed. The glowing numbers proclaimed it to be after three in the morning.

I was bone-tired, the aftereffect of the adrenaline wearing off, and my eyes slipped shut. I shoved a weary hand through my hair, stopping when I realized it was still in a ponytail, and roughly tugged it out. I sighed in pleasure when my hair was no longer encumbered and finger combed it back over my shoulders. My eyes flew open when Kade stood abruptly, turning his back to me.

"Let's get your feet taken care of," he muttered before disappearing into the bathroom. I heard the sound of water running into the tub.

A while later, and I don't know how long because I'd slumped over sideways on the bed and fallen asleep, I felt hands working at the fastening of my jeans.

With a start, I jerked my eyes open to see Kade tugging my jeans down over my hips.

"What the hell are you doing?" I asked in shock, disbelief edging my voice. I couldn't believe he was undressing me. I scrambled for my jeans even as he dragged them down and off my legs.

"I didn't think you'd want to get your clothes wet while your feet soaked," he said evenly, ignoring my protests as he lifted me in his arms again. I blushed furiously even though he'd seen much more of me earlier tonight.

His face was mere inches away and our gazes caught, his blue eyes staring intently into mine. My breathing hitched anew as I looked at him. Dark brows and long lashes accentuated his eyes, and his face was framed by thick hair that lay in careless waves. A hard, square jaw roughened with a five-o'clock shadow framed his lips.

"Don't look at me like that," he murmured, and my eyes jerked guiltily back up to his.

He sat me down on the closed toilet, swinging my legs over the side of the tub into the hot water. My breath hissed between my teeth as the water touched my battered skin, and my hands balled into fists. Crouching down, Kade took a foot and gently washed it with a cloth. I bit my lip, refusing to make a sound even as my nails dug into my palms.

When he finished one, he moved on to the other, taking particular care with my damaged skin. The silence was thick between us, but not uncomfortable. The water felt good and soothing now, the burning greatly lessened. I wiggled my toes experimentally and was relieved when it produced only a twinge of discomfort.

No longer distracted by pain, I watched Kade's hands move under the water, his fingers long and graceful. He'd pushed his sleeves up and I was entranced by the fine, dark hairs sprinkled across his forearms. His nearness seemed to make the tiny bathroom even smaller, his chest pressing against my legs as he worked.

Kade reached across me farther to pull the plug, and the water began to drain. Grabbing a towel, he swung my legs back out of the tub as he sat back on his heels facing me. Studiously avoiding my eyes, he carefully dried my feet and calves.

I tried to think of something else, anything else. He was just helping me. It wasn't sexual. He was Blane's brother, for crying out loud. And so what if he'd kissed me once before? I hadn't known then who he was.

The towel moved up my calves to my knees and I watched as Kade's eyes followed. His gaze settle between my parted thighs and his movements stilled. Time seemed to halt as I watched him, my breath seizing in my chest.

Jerking his hands away, he stood before picking me up again, one arm under my knees and the other behind my back. I thought of protesting that I could walk by myself, but I couldn't get the words out.

Sitting me down on the bed, he crouched down again to inspect my feet. They were much better now and I felt the need to acknowledge his taking care of me.

"Thank you," I said quietly. "For helping me," I clarified. He looked up at me, his gaze intent through his dark lashes.

"And for not leaving me there." This last was said in a much smaller voice.

To my surprise, he leaned forward, turned, and rested his head in my lap with a sigh. The stubble of his jaw scraped the skin of my thighs. Hesitantly, I laid my hand on his head, uncertain what to do. His arms loosely circled my hips.

He said nothing, seeming content to just rest there, though I thought for sure the hard floor must be hurting his knees. I moved my fingers slowly through his hair, neither of us speaking. Kade seemed tired. Not just physically, but mentally as well. I wondered if he ever got to let down the guard he kept so carefully in place. Or if there was still the little boy inside whose mother had died and left him alone and whose father hadn't wanted him. In spite of everything, my heart ached for him.

His voice broke the silence. "Do you trust me now?" he asked quietly, the warmth of his breath brushing my thigh.

"Yes," I whispered without hesitation. How could I not? He'd saved my life tonight.

We sat like that for a long time, his dark hair a stark contrast to the whiteness of my skin, my fingers running absently through the silken locks. Then he turned his head slightly, his lips brushing the skin of my thigh, and the air seemed suddenly charged with heightened awareness.

The shrill ringing of his cell phone made me start and he reluctantly pulled back, pressing his lips to the inside of my knee before he rose to his feet.

"Yeah," he answered the phone, his gaze lingering on me. I watched as he listened to whomever was on the other end. To my disappointment, Kade's face seemed to gradually shutter as the conversation dragged on, his familiar mask dropping into place.

"Yeah, give me a minute," he said into the phone. He held the phone to his chest as he leaned over me.

"I'll be right back," he said, brushing the back of his fingers against my cheek.

"Okay," I said uncertainly.

He pressed his lips briefly to my forehead. He grabbed the key and stepped out of the motel room, the door swinging shut behind him.

I waited for a while, struggling to keep my eyes open. Eventually, I got chilly so climbed under the covers. Fighting a losing battle and wondering what was keeping him so long, I finally slipped into an exhausted slumber.

When I woke, hours later, Kade was gone.

CHAPTER SIXTEEN

I couldn't say I blamed Kade for leaving. What had happened last night, what might have happened if he'd returned, would have been a mistake. The Kade I'd seen last night had exerted a powerful pull on me. It was best he had gone.

My thoughts turned to Blane and I wondered how he was doing, if the gunshot wound was as superficial as he'd claimed. My face heated when I thought of the kiss Kade had placed on my thigh. They were brothers, for crying out loud. I remembered how Kade had said he wouldn't let a woman come between them. That was the last thing I wanted to do, especially after hearing more of Kade's story and how much Blane meant to him. Kade would hate me and as for Blane . . . well, no doubt, he would as well.

Blane and I weren't officially together, had never been actually, and my feelings for him were complicated. I was afraid I was already half in love with him. I dared not hope he felt something for me, though he'd certainly seemed upset when he'd thought I was dead.

Something caught my eye and I realized my suitcase was sitting in the corner of the room. Kade must have retrieved it from the hotel for me. He reminded me of a porcupine, all prickly and sharp on the outside to keep people away.

But underneath, he was a good man whose loyalty to his brother was to be admired. And if there was a tiny bit of truth to the "us" Kade had referred to yesterday, that didn't mean I had to think about it.

I rummaged in my suitcase, grabbing some toiletries. A shower would do me a world of good. My feet felt much better and my body was only slightly sore from the abuse I'd taken at Stephen's hands.

Memories of Kade in this bathroom last night assaulted me as I turned on the water and climbed under the shower spray. The care he had taken with me, the way he'd trusted me enough to reveal a hint of his vulnerability, it didn't fit with the image of him I had in my head. It was definitely for the best that Kade had gotten that phone call.

A few minutes later, I was feeling much better. I wrapped a towel around myself and opened the bathroom door, and I nearly fainted on the spot.

Blane sat in a chair by the window, his arms braced on his spread knees as he leaned forward, his hands clasped loosely together. His head came up when I opened the door and our eyes met. My vision immediately blurred as tears filled my eyes.

"Blane," I managed, but I could get nothing else past the lump in my throat. I felt like the knots inside me had finally loosened and relaxed. Blane was here.

In a flash, he was in front of me, his arms wrapping around my waist as he hauled me against him. My arms wound around his neck as his mouth found mine, kissing me hungrily. It was many minutes later before we finally came up for air.

"How did you get here?" I asked breathlessly. "How did you know where I was?"

It seemed like something out of a dream that he could suddenly be here with me. I remembered with a shudder how I'd last seen him, bleeding and passed out in Kade's car.

He brushed my wet hair back from my face as he answered. "I called Kade last night. He told me what had happened, where you guys were. I got here a couple of hours ago."

I realized with a start that Blane must have been the call Kade had gotten. The very timely call when he'd kissed my skin and I'd held his head and let him. I hurriedly pushed those thoughts to the back of my mind.

"Where were you earlier?" I asked, confused. "And where's Kade?"

He nodded toward the table by the door, where I'd completely missed seeing a white paper bag and two steaming cups.

"Kade left when I got here," he said. "And I thought you might be hungry when you woke up."

Well, at least I knew Kade hadn't left me alone all night.

"Is that coffee?" I said wonderingly. The only thing that could tear me out of Blane's arms right now was the promising aroma of hot coffee. He smiled a little at me.

"And donuts," he said. I wriggled and he put me down. Eagerly, I opened the bag, grinning in delight when I saw glazed donuts inside. Grabbing one, I folded my legs under myself and sat in the chair. The sugary glaze melted on my tongue and my eyes drifted shut.

"They're amazing," I said, mouth full of donut, as Blane approached to sit on the edge of the bed in front of me. I held my donut out and fed him a bite. I removed the lid from one of the cups and took a careful sip. The coffee was strong, but I wasn't complaining. I finished off the donut, licking the remaining icing from my fingers.

"How's your shoulder?" I asked.

"It'll be fine," he said. "They patched me up pretty quick. A few stitches and some antibiotics. A couple of weeks and it'll be healed."

"Thank God," I said, relief evident in my voice.

"Kade told me about last night," he said carefully, and I nearly choked on my coffee.

Kade had told him about Stephen? My mouth opened and shut, but nothing came out as Blane watched me.

"I wish you hadn't gone into the data center with him," he said, and I blew out the breath I'd been holding. He hadn't been talking about Stephen. Of course he'd meant the data center.

"As a matter of fact," he continued, his eyes narrowing, "I distinctly remember telling him to not let you go."

I took another nervous sip of my coffee before I answered, scalding my tongue in the process.

"It's not his fault," I said. "I needed to come here. Needed to try and do the right thing." I met his eyes, pleading for him to understand. "Please try to understand."

He seemed to consider this for a moment before finally sighing. "You could have been killed," he said roughly, leaning forward and placing his hands on my thighs.

"But I wasn't," I replied, smiling brightly. I pushed the scene with Stephen to the back of my mind.

"How did you end up captured at TecSol anyway?" I asked, anxious to turn his attention away from me. "Kade showed me the photographs they'd taken of us. How did you get them?"

Blane's jaw clenched and his grip on my legs tightened. "I could throttle him for showing you those," he said. "Frank Santini showed up at my house that night. He wanted to blackmail me. The Santinis specialize in politicians. It's how they manage to stay just beyond the reach of law enforcement. I refused to be blackmailed, so he tried a different tactic." His expression hardened even further.

"What?" I prompted when he didn't continue.

"They said they had you," he said simply, as if it were obvious that was the only method of persuasion they'd needed.

My breath caught in my throat, and my eyes widened in shock. I had no idea what to say to that.

Reaching for my waist, he pulled me forward and I stood, moving between his spread legs. He kept pulling me until I settled on my knees, straddling his lap. His hand slid under my towel, tugging until it loosened and fell to the floor. I felt my face heat. Blane smiled, trailing his hand down the side of my face.

"There's that blush," he murmured, almost to himself, before curving his hand around the back of my neck and kissing me. Our tongues entwined as he deepened the kiss, his hand slowly stroking up and down my back.

I pressed closer, needing to feel his body against mine. His erection was hard between my legs and I ground myself against him. He groaned, his hands biting into my hips. One lifted to cup my breast and I arched my back, offering myself to him as his lips trailed down my neck.

"Not here," he whispered against my skin before reluctantly leaning back. "I want you, but let's get out of here. I can't believe he brought you to this place."

I bit my tongue to silence the immediate defense of Kade that sprang to my lips. I really, really didn't want to talk about Kade with Blane.

I moved off Blane's lap, grabbing the towel and wrapping it around myself. I hurried to the suitcase, pulling out a pair of gray slacks and a black sweater, then I brushed my hair and dressed in the bathroom. After a few minutes, I was ready to go. I grabbed my purse and my coffee while Blane carried the suitcase outside to his car.

We drove for a while in comfortable silence, my hand clasped in Blane's as the miles flew past. Some things were still bothering me, though, and while I didn't want to ruin the moment, I needed closure.

"Kade said you were going to put the Santini brothers away for a long time," I said, breaking the quiet.

Blane nodded. "That's right."

"How?"

"I taped Frank," he said. "I knew they would try to use my being at that party to blackmail me, so I set him up, waited for him to approach me. Which, of course, he did. He couldn't resist. The police brought him and his brother in for questioning and they ratted out Gage and his part in the murder of your neighbor and Mark, in return for a deal with the prosecutor."

I breathed a sigh of relief. It was over. Finally. I could relax. No one would be coming after me.

"Are you going to tell me why you were even there in the first place?" I asked.

"I could ask you the same question," Blane said wryly. "That was certainly the last place I expected to see you."

"I had a lead on who killed Sheila," I protested. "I had to go. But you and Kade seemed to know everyone there."

"Kade and I spent the last several months infiltrating that operation because that's where we suspected the money was coming from to fund TecSol. The Santini brothers ran the prostitution ring and Gage helped launder the money before funneling it to TecSol. Frank Santini invited me there for the very purpose of trying to blackmail me." Blane glanced my way again before his eyes swung back to the road.

"Until the other night, I hadn't given them an opportunity to do so."

I digested this. So Blane hadn't lied to me about not being a customer. The other times he'd gone to one of those parties, he hadn't been with another woman while he was there.

"What about James?" I asked. It took a little longer for Blane to answer me and I glanced over at him curiously. His hands had tightened on the steering wheel.

"Nothing happened to James," he answered flatly, and my mouth fell open in shock.

"What do you mean?" I said, aghast. "It was because of him that Sheila was murdered and he nearly got me killed as well!"

"I know," Blane said grimly, "but his father took all the blame for those things, exonerating James entirely. He's free to do as he pleases."

I blew out a sigh, trying not to feel dejected. I remembered how my dad would come home some nights after having seen a criminal freed on a technicality or some such thing. He'd told me then that the guilty invariably would be caught again—that their good fortune made them careless—and they would eventually pay for their crimes. At some point James would do something stupid and then there would be no easy out for him.

The afternoon sun shone through my window, and before long I found myself drifting off. I was awakened by Blane pressing light kisses to my jaw and cheek. I smiled sleepily.

"We're back," he said softly. "I would have taken you to my house, but I thought you might prefer to be at your own place." His words seemed to hold an unspoken question, but I wasn't positive. It could have been wishful thinking on my part.

"Thank you," I said, rousing myself and running a hand through my hair.

He got out and carried my bag as we walked up the stairs. I looked over at CJ's apartment. With a pang, I realized it was empty. I guess I'd hoped, even though Kade had said otherwise, that he'd been wrong.

I went to unlock my door but paused when I saw a scrap of paper taped to it. Peeling it off, I unfolded and read it as Blane looked over my shoulder.

Kathleen—
I'm sorry.
—CJ

I felt like the wind had been knocked out of me. What did this mean? She was sorry she'd set me up? I crumpled the note in my hand, shoving it into my pocket.

Blane unlocked the door and guided me inside, setting my suitcase down before closing the door behind us.

"You okay?" he asked, tucking a lock of my hair behind my ear.

"I'll be fine," I answered. I didn't want to think about CJ right now.

A meowing caught my attention and I turned away, surprised.

"Tigger!" I cried out happily as an orange ball of fluff launched itself at me. I caught him up in my arms, his purring a most welcome sound.

"I had Mona bring him over today," Blane explained. "I thought you'd be wanting him back home."

Too overwhelmed with emotion to speak, I just nodded. I felt like I'd come a long way in a short amount of time, remembering the first night Blane had been in my apartment while I comforted Tigger in my arms.

Blane placed his fingers under my chin, lifting my face toward his. His lips settled on mine with a gentleness and reverence that made my heart ache. Tigger squirmed in my arms and I let him jump to the ground, moving forward so I could twine my arms around Blane's neck. He broke off the kiss and pulled back slightly to look at me, his hands cupping my face. His eyes were the same stormy gray I remembered and it seemed like I would drown in them.

"I spent twenty-four hours not knowing if you were dead or alive," he said, his thumbs brushing my cheeks.

Then he was kissing me again and the tenderness had been replaced by hunger. His mouth moved along my jaw to my neck and heat curled low in my belly. I clutched at his shirt to keep my knees from buckling. I felt him tugging at my shirt and helped him pull it over my head. I cradled his head to my chest as his tongue traced the top edges of the black lace bra I wore.

Scooping me up in his arms, he carried me to the bedroom. I kicked off my shoes and distantly heard them thud to the floor. Laying me down on top of my bed, he stood and quickly removed his clothes. The sun hadn't yet set so there was enough light in the room for me to see him, and my heart started pounding.

His body was the epitome of male perfection. The muscles in his arms and chest rippled with every movement he made. Even the bandage by his shoulder only served to accentuate his maleness. His abdomen was hard and begged to be touched. My eyes drifted downward and I felt my cheeks burn.

Blane laughed softly as he bent over me, tugging open the fastening on my pants and sliding them and my underwear down my legs, leaving me clad in just my bra.

"I love it when you blush," he said, which caused me to turn even redder.

Pulling me into his arms, he kissed me again and I forgot about my shyness. He turned so that I was lying on top of him, straddling his hips. His fingers made quick work of the fastening on my bra and then I was gasping for air, my head falling back as his hands found my breasts.

Forcing my eyes open, I looked down at him. His eyes smoldered as he watched me. My hands were splayed on his chest. They looked very small and white against his skin. Tentatively, I traced the line of his jaw down his neck. He grew still under my touch. I hesitated, uncertain if I should continue.

"Do whatever you want, Kat," he said softly.

Taking the opportunity, and screwing up my courage, I scooted down so I could press my mouth to his chest. His skin was warm, the muscles beneath hard, as I traced the contours of his chest down his abdomen, my lips and tongue marking him. I could feel his heart beating faster and I smiled against his skin. It was nice to know I had the same effect on him as he had on me.

My hair was getting in my way, so I flipped it over to the side. Blane buried his fingers in the strands as they trailed across his chest.

I had reached his waist now, and my tongue traced a long scar I found near his hip. His erection jerked in response. I was nervous but wanted to touch him. My fingers tentatively wrapped around his length and he groaned. Encouraged, I leaned forward, taking him in my mouth. He grunted a curse, his hips jerking upward as I moved to take him deeper. My arousal throbbed between my legs and I moaned around him. Then he was tugging me upward and away from him and I mewled in disappointment.

"It's going to be over way too quick if you keep doing that," he breathed against my lips before kissing me, his tongue stroking mine. His hands moved down my back to my rear before pressing me closer. I yelped in pain, jerking away instinctively. He'd inadvertently found the marks from the belt Avery had hit me with.

"What is it? Did I hurt you?" he asked anxiously and I quickly shook my head in denial. The last thing I wanted was for him to get a good look at the welts.

"I'm fine," I said, moving to kiss him again. He evaded me, his hands now skimming my skin, searching. Blane was no fool and I knew he'd find out my little secret in about two seconds if I didn't do something. Then this wonderful reunion would be over before it even got started.

Rising up, I grasped his erection in my hand and lowered myself onto him. My breath caught at the twinge of pain, my body still unaccustomed to his size, but it quickly faded. Blane's breath hissed between his teeth, his hands biting into my hips as I settled myself with him deep inside me.

My hair was in the way again, so I raised my arms, brushing it back from my face and tossing it behind me with a flip of my head.

"God, you're amazing," Blane rasped, his hands now sliding up my ribs to cup my breasts. I felt a smile curve my lips at his praise.

I raised myself up before slowly sliding back down onto him and was rewarded with another hiss from Blane. My legs trembled slightly when I rose up again and a cry was startled from me when his hips lifted to drive into me. Then he sat up and turned us, flipping me onto my back.

My legs lifted to curve around him as he thrust inside me. His arms were wrapped around me and he pressed kisses to my cheeks, my forehead, and my lips as he moved slow and deep. Each stroke brushed against the tight bundle of nerves at the apex of my thighs until my entire body was trembling and slick with sweat. I clutched at his shoulders, my breath coming in pants.

"You're mine now, Kat," he whispered, his lips at my ear.

Then he was moving faster, harder, and I was crying out his name, tears leaking from my eyes as I came apart beneath him. He drove into me even harder before a wordless shout erupted from him, his body shuddering in my arms.

Blane's weight settled heavily on me, but I didn't mind. His lips found mine again, the kiss tender and deep, our bodies still locked together.

Moving to the side, he turned me so I was cuddled against him, his shoulder pillowing my head as his hand absently stroked my hair. I sighed deeply, a satisfied smile curving my lips.

"That was so much better than Donny Lester," I said smugly.

Blane's hand paused in my hair before he burst into laughter. I loved hearing him laugh. He pulled me on top of him and I rested my chin on my folded arms, drinking in the sight of him. This time when he smiled, it reached all the way to his eyes.

"I would hope so," he finally said when his laughter subsided. "Though with a name like that, the poor guy didn't stand a chance."

I giggled at that and had to agree. "Donny Lester" and "amazing sex" just didn't belong in the same sentence.

My stomach growled then and I flushed. Blane chuckled and made me stay in bed while he went to the refrigerator, coming back with some fruit and cheese. We took turns feeding each other, laughing and talking, and I couldn't remember the last time I'd felt as happy as I was at that moment.

He made love to me again, and afterward, we lay in the dark, talking quietly. It seemed he wanted to know everything about me, and I told him of my childhood and my parents. He listened patiently as I spoke about my aborted attempt at college, caring for my mother during her illness, and selling our family home before coming to Indianapolis. When we finally fell asleep, I was spooned in Blane's arms, his warm breath caressing my bare shoulder.

I woke hours later in the night, the bottoms of my feet throbbing. Carefully detangling my limbs from Blane's and leaving him asleep in the bed, I grabbed his shirt from the floor and pulled it on over my head. His cologne wafted up from the fabric and I smiled.

Padding barefoot into the bathroom, I quietly pulled the door closed behind me. I found some salve and Band-Aids and applied them to the worst of the scrapes and cuts marring the soles of my feet.

My thoughts unwittingly drifted to Kade. A part of me worried about him, though I knew it was ridiculous. He was quite capable of taking care of himself. I wondered where he'd gone, if he'd come back to Indy or went wherever he'd been before Blane had called for him to come here. The thought crossed my mind that he might have gone back to Chicago to see Branna. Something twisted inside at that thought and uncomfortably I pushed it away.

Leaving the bathroom, I headed to the kitchen for a drink of water. After filling up a glass, I turned my back and leaned against the cool kitchen counter as I drank. I glanced toward my living room. Something sitting on the coffee table caught my eye.

Frowning, I set my glass down and hesitantly walked into the room. I switched on a lamp and saw a large manila envelope on the table. I was quite certain it hadn't been there earlier.

With some trepidation, I picked it up and opened it, peeking inside. I gasped in surprise at the contents before turning it upside down. A thick sheaf of crisp bills cascaded out onto the table.

My knees gave way and I sat heavily on the couch, unable to take my eyes off the money. Slowly, I reached out and started gathering the bills, a suspicion forming in my mind as I counted. Ten minutes later, I had my answer as I sat staring at exactly twenty thousand dollars, which now sat in a neat and tidy pile in front of me. The price for my life.

Grasping the manila envelope, I turned it over in my hand, only now seeing the short line of handwriting on one side. I held it closer so I could read it.

Buy some decent shoes.

ABOUT THE AUTHOR

Tiffany Snow has been reading romance novels since she was too young to read romance novels. After fifteen years working in the Information Technology field, Tiffany now works her dream job of writing full time.

Tiffany makes her home in the Midwest with her husband and two daughters. She can be reached at tiffany@tiffanyasnow. com. Visit her on her website, www.TiffanyASnow.com, to keep up with the latest in *The Kathleen Turner Series*.

Turn the page for a sneak peek at the second book in *The Kathleen Turner Series, Turn to Me.*

Turn to Me

CHAPTER ONE

Hey, pretty girl, give me your cash and I won't mess up your fancy dress."

I started, my pulse picking up as my brain processed the words. I was cold. Freezing, actually, and my feet were killing me. December in Indianapolis was bad enough—add to it walking the streets alone at night wearing nothing but an evening gown and four-inch heels, and you had the ingredients for a truly wretched experience. Well, at least I'd thought that was the worst it could get. Apparently, I'd been wrong.

Turning, I watched as a man stepped out of the shadows. He was a hulking brute, big enough to easily outweigh me by a hundred pounds or more. The scattered light from a nearby streetlamp glinted off the knife he was holding and I swallowed heavily. I hated knives. Knives meant pain, whereas guns meant death. Maybe I was in the minority, but death was the preferred of the two to my way of thinking. I wasn't a big fan of pain.

"I don't have any money," I said, trying to stay calm. I glanced around, keeping an eye on him as he advanced toward me. Unfortunately, no one was around. I backed away as he got closer but knew I didn't stand a chance if I tried to run, not with these shoes.

"Then I'll take the pretty necklace," he sneered, leaping forward and grabbing my arm. I shrieked in surprise but was silenced when he pressed the cold steel of the blade to my neck.

"Shut up, bitch," he snarled.

I was breathing hard, fear and adrenaline pumping through my veins. He towered over me, pushing against me until my back was against the cold brick wall. The rough stones abraded the exposed skin of my back.

"Give me the necklace or you'll regret it." His breath was hot and fetid against my face.

"No," I said, helpless anger rising in me. I'd been given the necklace mere hours ago, Blane fastening it around my neck as I'd gotten dressed for this evening.

It suddenly seemed terribly ironic that a night that had started with such promise was ending in terror.

~

The day had begun well enough. I'd had the day shift at The Drop, a local place where I tended bar. I know the current in-vogue term was *mixologist,* but neither I nor the patrons had any illusions about what I did—which was pour drinks. On Saturdays I usually worked the night shift, but today I'd traded with Lucy so I could have tonight off to be with Blane.

Blane Kirk was my boyfriend, although the term was at once both too adolescent and too committed to actually describe him and our relationship. Blane was a high-profile lawyer in Indianapolis, with aspirations for public office. A former Navy SEAL, he was over six feet of male perfection, complete with dirty blond hair, a square jaw, and eyes a tantalizing mix of gray and green, the color drifting more one way or the other depending on what he was wearing. Women had been an interchangeable accessory to Blane, and I wasn't sure that wouldn't be the case with me. Blane and I had started dating about six weeks ago, right after Halloween. I know that doesn't sound like very long, but considering how often Blane usually changed girlfriends, I was cautiously optimistic. Optimistic about what? Well I wasn't sure of that either.

Considering the differences between us, it was difficult most days to believe that Blane would choose to be with me. As the daughter of a housewife and a police officer from Rushville, Indiana, Kathleen Turner—yeah, that's me—wasn't a name people knew. I take that back. People knew the name, but I wasn't *that* Kathleen Turner. Turner was the family name, and choosing a celebrity to be named after was the tradition. Just ask my dad, Ted Turner, or my grandma, Tina Turner. Except neither one was with me any longer, so I alone was left to carry on the Turner tradition or curse, depending on your point of view.

I'd moved to Indianapolis eight months ago and had taken a job working as a runner for Blane's law firm. It took both gigs to make ends meet and I hadn't given up the day job, even though I was sleeping with the boss. Incredibly tacky of me, but I needed the job. We kept it discreet because while Blane didn't care at all what people said, I did.

Blane had asked me to go with him to a victory dinner/ fund-raiser tonight for someone he knew that had been reelected to Congress in the last election. I'd seen in the paper that plates were seven thousand dollars each. I'd swallowed hard and hoped the food would be really good for that kind of price tag.

After my Saturday shift, I had dashed home, hopping into the shower to quickly wash my hair and shave my legs. I had time to blow my long, strawberry blonde hair dry, pin it up, and throw on some makeup before I heard his knock on my door.

I'd learned a hard lesson a few weeks ago about checking the peephole in my door, and I remembered that tonight. I checked first before opening the door, and my breath caught, as it nearly always did, when I saw Blane.

My doorway was filled with wide shoulders encased in a charcoal-gray suit jacket that tapered to lean hips. A white shirt peeked from beneath his jacket and tie. Currently, a hand was braced high against the jamb of my door, opening his jacket enough for me to see the gun tucked into the holster against his side. Indiana was a conceal state, and Blane had a permit to carry, which he always did. That habit had saved my life once.

"You're early," I said, smiling and opening the door wider to let him in. He unfolded his tall frame from where he'd been leaning and came inside, closing the door behind him and stepping into my personal space. The whole apartment seemed smaller with him in it, not that it was very big to begin with. He took in my appearance—I was still wrapped in a towel from my shower—and the gleam that came into his eyes made my heart beat faster.

"How early?" he asked, his voice a low rasp as he moved even closer, his hand coming up to trace the top edge of my towel. Words failed me when his lips and tongue touched the bare skin of my shoulder. I tipped my head to the side, my eyes fluttering shut. He sucked lightly at the juncture of my neck and shoulder and I inhaled deeply, the scent of his cologne enveloping and enticing me. When I felt him loosen the towel and it dropped to the floor, I found my voice.

"You'll mess up my hair," I managed breathlessly as his hand slipped between my thighs. I clutched at his shoulders for support, his fingers moving with practiced ease and causing my legs to tremble.

"There are ways to avoid that," he whispered in my ear, sending a delicious shiver through me. And indeed, there were, as he proceeded to show me.

Half an hour later, I was slipping on my dress and repairing the damage done to my lip gloss. True to his word, not a hair of mine was out of place, though my skin now had a telltale flush.

My dress was a deep midnight blue, and I thought it brought out my eyes, since they were nearly the same shade. It was a long, satin sheath with a sweetheart neckline, the straps reaching over the outer curve of my shoulders. The cut emphasized my cleavage, something I'd been blessed with plenty of. A long slit ran up the side, shifting and revealing my legs as I walked. I stepped into a pair of silver heels that helped make up for my sad lack of stature and surveyed myself with a critical eye in the mirror. The dress demanded a necklace, but jewelry—even the costume sort—was an unnecessary expense when I worked two jobs just to pay the bills. I'd found a pair of rhinestone earrings that now dangled from my ears and sparkled when I turned my head.

"You forgot something," Blane said, surprising me as he stepped into the mirror's reflection. I looked at the couple we made and was gratified by the sight. We looked good together, I thought.

My eyes widened as I watched his hands come up to place a necklace on me. As he did the catch, my jaw dropped at the sight of the large, oval sapphire pendant now nestled between my breasts. Surrounded in diamonds, it glittered brightly as it hung from a long double chain.

"I'll let you put on these," he said, his arm reaching around in front of me.

I glanced down to see he was holding a velvet jewelry box, opened to display a set of matching diamond-and-sapphire earrings. I reached out cautiously to touch them, the movement causing them to sparkle in the light.
"Blane," I began, "I . . . I don't know what to say. It's too much." I was stunned. I had never been given something like this. Tears pricked my eyes and the earrings swam in my vision. I blinked them back. It would totally ruin the moment if my mascara ran.

"Say you'll wear them," he cajoled, his lips at my ear as his other arm slid around my waist to pull me back against his chest. "The stone reminded me of the color of your eyes. I want you to have them."

I put on the earrings as he watched me and left the rhinestones on my bureau. A thought occurred to me and my eyes flew to his in the mirror. Was this my "going away" present? Blane always gave a gift to his girlfriends when he broke up with them, though usually they were chosen by his secretary, Clarice.

"You're beautiful," he complimented me, the warmth in his eyes easing my worry. The heat from his hands seeped through the thin satin, and I berated myself for thinking he had other motives for the gift.

He glanced at his watch. "We'd better go."

I grabbed the silver clutch bag I'd gotten to go with the dress and headed for my apartment door.

"Wait," Blane said. "Where's your coat?"

I grimaced. I hated wearing coats and usually only did so when Mother Nature forced the issue by spreading snow on the ground.

"You have to wear a coat," Blane insisted, going to my tiny coat closet and pulling out the long black trench coat he'd given me a few weeks ago. "It's freezing outside."

I reluctantly let him put it on me, though I didn't think it went with my dress at all, and locked my apartment door on the way out. I lived on the top floor of a two-story building in an area of downtown Indy where you made sure to lock your car at night.

Blane took my hand as we went down the stairs, and I was grateful for his solid presence next to me, unpracticed as I was in walking in heels this high. It's not like I went many places where I had cause to dress up—except church occasionally, but somehow I didn't think silver strappy sandals with a four-inch heel were Sunday morning Baptist attire.

He helped me into his black Jaguar, which, let me say, was difficult to get into in the getup I was wearing. As he watched me carefully swing my legs into the car, Blane let out a chuckle.

"What?" I said, my voice testy.

"I was just wondering if you were going to emulate Britney again," he said, propping his arms against the door as he leaned toward me. My cheeks grew warm as I realized he was referring to my beloved pop princess, Britney Spears. I was a huge fan and could do a dead-on impression of her singing, which I'd had cause to do this past Halloween when all the girls at The Drop dressed up as pop divas for the holiday bash. In this instance, I didn't think Blane was referring to Britney's singing so much as her inadvertent flashing of some very private areas when climbing into and out of cars.

"You're assuming I'm not wearing anything under my dress," I said breezily, deciding to give as good as I got.

"Are you?" I noticed the gleam was back in his eyes as they dropped to where the cut of my dress had opened to expose the length of my thigh.

"If you're lucky, you might find out later," I teased. His lips curved in a wicked grin and he stepped back, shutting the car door.

A few minutes later, we arrived at the hotel. The fundraiser was taking place in one of the large ballrooms of the nicest and most expensive hotel in Indy. A valet took the keys and Blane helped me out of the low-slung car. I emerged as gracefully as I could without exposing anything I shouldn't. Offering me his arm, we went inside, where Blane checked our coats, pocketing the small ticket for retrieving them.

I was really nervous. This was the first public function I'd been to with Blane. He'd taken me to dinner and on other casual dates, but this was the first time I was his "plus one" at something relating to his job. I knew Blane was ambitious; his career was on the fast track to public office, though he hadn't said which one. He came from a family of lawyers and politicians, with a grandfather who had been a senator and a great-grandfather who had been on the Massachusetts Supreme Court. Blane was only fourteen when he had a falling out with his father, then cemented the divide when he joined the Navy, but politics was still in his blood.

There would be a lot of people here tonight he'd want to connect with to increase his network of contacts, people who could help or hinder his future plans, whatever those might be. I didn't want to embarrass him in any way, though I felt far out of my element as I observed the ballroom and foyer full of people. They milled around chatting in groups, most with a cocktail or glass of wine in their hands. I swallowed hard, my palms clammy from nerves.

"Don't worry," Blane whispered, settling his hand on the small of my back. "You'll be fine. I promise, I'm the only one who'll bite you."

I smiled, my eyes catching his, and breathed easier. His attempt to tease me, make me smile, had bolstered my courage. I nodded, took a deep breath, and didn't resist when he led us to a group of people nearby.

"Kirk! There you are! We wondered when you'd be arriving." The greeting came from a man who looked to be about Blane's age and height but was much slighter of build. He had dark hair and eyes, and was holding a highball glass with a clear liquid inside. A woman stood next to him, as tall as he, wearing a black-velvet gown that wrapped around her torso and legs before flaring at mid-calf. I wondered how she was able to walk in it. Her dark hair was piled in loose curls on top of her head, a few escaped coils trailing down her ears and neck. The darkness of her dress and hair accentuated the fairness of her skin. She held a glass of champagne in one manicured hand.

"George, good to see you," Blane replied, shaking the man's hand. "And I see your wife, Sarah, is looking as lovely as ever." Sarah smiled back at him, giving him a quick once-over. Blane had his politician's smile firmly in place. I called it that because it was wide and friendly but never really reached his eyes. "Congratulations on your win," Blane continued, returning his attention to George. "But that was never in doubt, was it?"

George laughed, clapping Blane on the shoulder. "I never lose, my friend. Something you should keep in mind when you decide to stop keeping secrets and tell me what office you want." George's gaze flicked to me and I pasted on a bright smile.

"I'd like to introduce Kathleen Turner," Blane said, his hand moving again to my back. "Kathleen, this is George Bradshaw. He is the campaign manager for the senator. This is his wife, Sarah."

"Pleased to meet you," I said, politely grasping hands with first George, then Sarah. Sarah's fingers barely brushed mine before she dismissed me, turning back to Blane.

"Likewise," George said. I noticed he took in my appearance with a calculated gaze, his eyes lingering on the pendant Blane had given me. At least, I hoped it was the pendant though it could have just been my cleavage. "And what do you do, Kathleen?"

My smile grew forced. I hadn't thought about this part. I should have known someone was bound to ask that question. I flushed as I realized I had only two answers to give, neither of which I wanted to say.

"She works at the firm," Blane smoothly interjected.

"A fellow lawyer," George said, assuming what my job was. "Always knew Blane would find a like-minded woman." He lifted his glass as if to toast me.

"Not . . . exactly," I stammered, not wanting to lie. Lies always came back to bite you in the ass.

We were interrupted by another man stepping into our small circle. He was an older man with silver hair who carried his age well though he had to be in his sixties. About Blane's height, he stood straight and tall in a dark suit and tie. He vaguely reminded me of Blane, exuding a palpable presence and energy that made him the center of attention. George and Sarah stepped back in deference as the man clapped Blane on the shoulder and grasped his hand firmly.

"Knew you wouldn't let me down, Blane," he said, smiling warmly. I watched as Blane responded in a much more natural way, grinning broadly and giving the man's hand a firm shake.

"I know better than to do that, sir," Blane replied with a twinkle in his eye. "Let me introduce you." And just like that, my nerves were back. I could tell this was someone Blane genuinely liked. I just hoped he wouldn't ask me what I did for a living.

"This is Kathleen Turner," Blane said. "Kathleen, this is Senator Robert Keaston."

My eyes widened in surprise. I had known this evening was for a senator, but I hadn't realized it was this particular one. Even I, who followed politics not at all, knew the name, as often as it was in the news. Robert Keaston was a powerful senator who had been elected and reelected so many times, I wondered why he was still subjected to the formality.

"Pleased to meet you," I managed to squeak out through lips frozen into a smile.

"Likewise, my dear," the senator said, giving me a quick look-over.

"Where's Vivian?" Blane asked, diverting the senator's attention from me before he could ask any questions.

"Oh, she's over there with some other hens wanting to talk her ear off about some charity or another," answered Keaston with a wave of his hand. "You're sitting with me tonight, aren't you, Blane?"

"I don't think so, sir," Blane said regretfully. "I'm sure they have me seated elsewhere."

"Well, we'll fix that," Keaston replied, gesturing to a woman hovering nearby. She quickly came forward and he said something to her too low for me to overhear. With a nod, she left to do his bidding.

"That's not necessary, sir," Blane protested, but Keaston waved his hand dismissively.

"You may not be of the right party," Keaston said with a mock glare of disapproval, then he smiled, "but you're family."

Shock went through me and I couldn't stop a quick look at Blane. He glanced uncomfortably at me before returning his attention to Keaston.

Family? Blane was related to one of the most powerful men in the US Senate? That would have been helpful to know. If I'd felt out of place before, now I felt like a downright intruder.

"I have to do the rounds, Blane," the senator said, "I'm sure you understand."

Blane nodded. "Of course."

"But I'll see you at dinner." Keaston looked my way and gave a short nod of dismissal. "My dear."

I automatically smiled and watched as Keaston ambled toward another knot of people, all of whom turned his way with fawning smiles. George and Sarah had drifted off as well, leaving Blane and me with a blessed moment alone in the midst of the crowd. I looked up at Blane.

"Family?" I asked, hoping that perhaps the senator hadn't meant it in the blood-relation sense.

"Great-uncle," he answered shortly, dashing that hope.

"Why didn't you tell me?" I asked, trying to keep the dismay from my voice.

"I didn't think it mattered," he replied quietly, taking my hand. "Does it?"

I didn't know what to say. I felt like the proverbial fish out of water and my mouth moved soundlessly, as if I were gasping for air. How was I to explain to Blane, who no doubt had never felt out of place in his life, how this news had impacted me? I was saved from replying as yet another couple came by to greet Blane.

I had underestimated the number of people who knew Blane and wanted to ingratiate themselves with him. I lost track of the names almost immediately after I was introduced, but I marveled at how Blane was never at a loss for a name or a smile. I watched with admiration as he wove his magic around those with whom he spoke, seeing in their eyes how he captivated them as he made each person feel special, sending them on their way with the certainty that they were important to him. It was amazing and I was proud of his skills, which seemed to come very naturally indeed. My smile grew less forced as it became clear that no one had any interest in me. They barely paid me any attention at all. I was glad to melt into the background at Blane's side.

Blane and I made our way around the room, and I was feeling more relaxed since it seemed nothing was really expected of me except to smile and nod. Blane's hand was reassuring on the small of my back as we turned toward another couple. I stiffened immediately.

It was Kandi-with-an-*i*, the woman Blane had dated just before me. She'd been none too happy about losing Blane and had expressed her contempt for me on Halloween, showing up at The Drop dressed in a fairy costume that I'm sure cost more than I had made that night. She was beautiful and had made no bones about the fact that she felt Blane was slumming it by being with me. Tall with long, straight blonde hair, tonight she wore a red dress that hugged her body. She was absolutely stunning and I hated her.

"Nice to see you again, Blane," she greeted him, ignoring me completely.

"Kandi," Blane replied evenly, "I didn't realize you'd be here this evening."

"I'm here with my father," she said with a smug smile, tipping her head toward a knot of people standing a short ways away. "You know what good friends he and the senator are."

Blane gave a curt nod. "Of course," he said. "How are you?"

She moved closer to him, insinuating herself between us so Blane's hand was forced to release mine.

"I'm very good, as I'm sure you remember," I heard her say huskily. Her breasts brushed suggestively against his arm as she leaned into him.

My eyes narrowed. The tramp. I may not have grown up with her wealth and privilege, but at least I had manners, though I was having a hard time remembering them at the moment. I very much wanted to grab a hunk of her pretty blonde hair and yank. Hard.

"Call me," I heard her whisper in his ear before she walked away, her hand trailing lightly across his chest.

"Sorry about that," Blane said quietly, a grimace passing quickly over his face when he looked at me. I made my lips stretch into a tight smile.

"She's very pretty," I said diplomatically. I struggled not to sound jealous or bitchy. I didn't think I'd succeeded.

"Most people would say so," he replied. He slid his arm around my back and tugged my stiff body closer to him, overcoming my resistance with ease. "But she's not my type. Not anymore."

"Oh, really?" I said sarcastically, trying to ignore the effect of the heat from his body as it warmed me through the thin material of my dress. "What's your type?"

Blane bent and leaned close to me. "I prefer a woman with long hair the color of the sunset and eyes as clear blue as a twilight sky. She's got an Irish temper and likes her bourbon. Her guilty pleasure is a certain well-known pop princess and she has a passion for rocky road ice cream. Her skin is the color of peaches bathed in cream and is as smooth as silk."

His lips brushed against my ear as he spoke, sending a thrill of heat through me. I looked up at him and couldn't hold on to my irritation at Kandi. I melted into him, as he had no doubt known I would. The corners of his lips were tipped up ever so slightly, as if he were thinking about smiling. I was mesmerized by the stormy gray of his eyes, flecks of green sparkling from their depths.

"And if I were to tell her about the perfection of her breasts," he continued, the huskiness of his voice making me shiver, "that her body was made to fit mine—or how the noises she makes when I make love to her drive me crazy— she'd blush nearly to her toes."

My mouth dropped open at his audacity and I blushed, as he'd predicted. Regardless, I couldn't help smiling and as he let out a small huff of laughter, the tension Kandi had created began to dissipate.

"Let's find our seats," he said, his eyes twinkling. "I'm starving."

Blane took my hand and led me to a table near the front. It seemed Senator Keaston was as good as his word, because our seats were with him and a woman I assumed was his wife. She looked to be only in her fifties, though I thought looks might be deceiving. To my dismay, I saw that Kandi and a man who was obviously her father were also seated at the table. George and Sarah Bradshaw were there, too. One other couple we'd met that evening rounded out the seats, the man a member of the senator's staff, though I couldn't remember either of their names.

"Blane!" the older woman happily exclaimed. She went to rise from her chair but Blane quickly stepped to her side, forestalling her and pressing a chaste kiss to her cheek.

"Good evening, Vivian," Blane said warmly. "Don't get up."

"Robert said you were here tonight," she said as Blane held out my chair for me to sit down. "Thank you for coming to support him."

"I wouldn't have missed it," Blane replied, sliding into the seat on my left. He'd seated me beside Vivian. I wanted to grumble about Kandi's place at his left side, but that would have been catty.

Blane introduced me to the very kind and gracious Vivian. I liked her immediately. I could tell that Blane was very fond of her as well. Tall but slight, she had a powerful presence about her.

Dinner was served and I kept quiet as I ate, listening to the small talk at the table and trying to make sure I didn't drip anything on my dress. Kandi chatted easily with the senator and Vivian as well as the others. I tried not to feel like a kid at the grown-ups' table.

I observed with growing dismay as Kandi drew Blane into conversation with George and Sarah, frequently laying her hand possessively on his arm. Blane couldn't very well be rude to her in front of everyone, but I was disgruntled to see how friendly he was with her as they joined in the laughter around the table.

I ate a tiny bite of some kind of fish they'd served, my appetite now gone, and pushed my food around on my plate in glum silence.

I think Vivian must have felt sorry for me being left out of the conversation, because she turned to me and asked, "Kathleen, isn't it?"

I swallowed the lump of fish, quickly passing my napkin over my mouth as I nodded. "Yes, ma'am."

"Please, call me Vivian," she said with a smile. "And what do you do for a living, Kathleen?"

I shifted uneasily, but knew I couldn't lie to her. Fortunately, everyone else was still involved in their own conversations, so no one was really paying attention to us. "I work for Blane as a runner," I said, "and I tend bar at night."

Vivian's eyes widened a fraction in surprise before she masked it. "I see," she said kindly. "And are you from Indianapolis?" Beyond her, I saw the senator's eyes flick in our direction, and I knew that while he was talking to his staff person next to him, he was also listening to us.

"No, ma'am," I answered, unable to shake my mother's lessons in manners enough to call Vivian by her given name—respect for my elders had been drilled into me. "I'm from Rushville, Indiana. My parents grew up there."

"And what do they do?"

"My dad was a policeman," I said. "My mother stayed home. They both passed some years ago."

"I'm so sorry," Vivian said sympathetically, and to my surprise, her hand reached out to grasp mine. "Do you have other family? A brother or sister, perhaps?"

I shook my head. "I have an uncle and cousin, but we don't keep in touch." Truthfully, I couldn't even say where my dad's brother and son lived anymore. It had been years since I'd heard from them, since Mom's funeral, actually.

Vivian's grip on my hand tightened, her face creasing in a frown. "You're awfully young to be on your own," she remarked thoughtfully.

My smile was tense. I was unsure how to respond. I didn't want her pity, but neither did I want to appear rude. "I do all right," I said, slipping my hand from hers.

"So, Blane," the senator said, bringing everyone's attention to him, "are you going to tell us how the Waters trial is going? A lot of important people in Washington are watching to see how this turns out. You win this case, it'll be the biggest moment of your career. So far."

Everyone's eyes turned to Blane. All were waiting for his answer, their interest in this topic obvious.

I looked at Blane in confusion. What Waters trial? Biggest moment of his career? What was Keaston talking about?

Blane didn't usually say much about his work. I didn't know why—if he just didn't want to talk work after hours, or if he didn't think I was interested. While you might think I'd know everything going on at the firm since I worked there, regardless of what Blane did or didn't tell me, I was frequently out of the office making runs. Even when I wasn't in the office, I was still separated from Blane by four floors.

"It's going well," Blane replied, his face a mask of polite indifference.

Senator Keaston chuckled. "From what I hear, it's going better than that, son," he said. "You win this case, your name will be on everyone's short list."

Short list? Short list for what? My confusion increased. I tried to catch Blane's eye but he just shook his head, not looking at me.

"I don't know about that," he said. "The prosecution is pretty tough. We'll just have to see how it turns out. It'll be in the jury's hands."

"You'll beat James," Kandi said confidently. "He's no match for you in front of a jury and everyone knows it."

"James?" I interrupted incredulously. "James Gage?" This time Blane did turn to look at me, his expression unreadable.

"Yes, dear." Kandi was the one to answer my question. Her voice dripped condescension. "You do know the name of the district attorney, don't you?"

My face heated at her disdain but I refused to look at her, my gaze still locked with Blane's. I couldn't believe he hadn't told me.

James Gage was the son of the former senior partner at Blane's firm of Gage, Kirk, and Trent, now just Kirk and Trent. His father, William Gage, had been indicted for fraud and accessory to murder. William had been behind the recent scandal that involved a local computer company, TecSol, rigging online election voting. He'd also been responsible for the death of my friend Sheila and her boyfriend, Mark, who had worked for TecSol. James had been involved as well but had gotten off scot-free, even winning the election for Indianapolis District Attorney.

James and I had gone on one date—a date he felt gave him license to be jealous of Blane's attention to me. Remember I said I'd learned the hard way about checking the peephole in my door before opening it? That was because of James, who had hit me and tried to choke me when he found out Blane and I were together. Only the quick actions of CJ, my neighbor at the time and someone I'd thought of as a friend, had saved me from even graver injury.

James had always been jealous of Blane, waging a competition to which Blane had been oblivious. I was alarmed that they were going up against each other in what was apparently a very important trial, and hurt that Blane had said nothing about this to me. James was dangerous and volatile, not to be trusted. Would he do something stupid if he lost a big case to Blane?

My dismay must have shown on my face, because Blane's jaw clenched tightly before he looked away. I realized everyone was watching us now, and I focused on my plate to keep from meeting all those eyes. I was embarrassed—everyone had known about something quite vital in Blane's life except me, his girlfriend.

"We missed you and Kade at Thanksgiving," Vivian said to Blane, changing the topic of conversation and taking the attention away from me. It was the kind of comment my mother would have made. It demanded an explanation, even if she hadn't asked for one.

"We celebrated here," Blane replied.

I was surprised Vivian knew about Kade. Kade was Blane's illegitimate half brother. Their father had been unfaithful to Blane's mother, though he'd refused to claim Kade as his when Kade's mother died.

Kade went by Kade Dennon and, as far as I knew, very few people knew of the relation. Kade was a former FBI agent, specializing in cyber crimes. I hadn't known any of that when I'd first met him, though, and had known only that he was an assassin for hire. Kade had quit the FBI a few years ago and gone freelance, something Blane abided but didn't necessarily condone. Kade was as dark as Blane was light, with black hair and piercing blue eyes, though he had the same charisma and aura of danger as his older brother.

Blane wasn't quite being truthful with Vivian—we had celebrated here in Indy, but Kade had not joined us for the festivities. He'd disappeared several weeks ago, right after the election. Blane said Kade stayed in touch with him, but I hadn't asked where he was and Blane hadn't offered the information.

Kade was an enigma to me—we'd begun by hating each other, but he'd saved my life when I'd been moments away from being raped and killed. I'd never breathed a word about it to Blane and to my knowledge, Kade hadn't either. The shame and humiliation of the incident still sometimes haunted my nightmares, and the last thing I wanted was to see pity in Blane's eyes when he looked at me.

Kade had also been paid twenty thousand dollars to kill me, then had turned around and given that money to me. It seemed Kade and I had called an uneasy truce, though I'd wondered if my being around was what had kept him from Blane at Thanksgiving. Kade was utterly loyal and devoted to Blane, and I felt a pang of remorse that his dislike of me might have been the reason he'd stayed away from his brother for the holiday.

Blane deftly turned the conversation to other topics and I kept my mouth shut, regretting my earlier outburst that displayed my woeful lack of knowledge about his life. Thankfully, dinner was over soon and people began drifting to the dance floor, the strains of a slow jazz number coming from the five-person band. The smoky sound of the saxophone drifted through the room as I contemplated what Senator Keaston had said.

"Dance with me," Blane said quietly, resting his arm on the back of my chair and leaning over me. He caught a loose tendril of my hair and gently wrapped it around his finger. Our eyes met. I nodded and he rose, helping me from my chair and taking my elbow to lead me to the dance floor. I could sense Kandi's glare burning a hole in my back as we walked away.

Blane took me in his arms and I felt my body stiffen, holding myself slightly apart from him; I was angry after all. I stared eye level at his shirt, crisp and white as it peeked out from beneath his jacket, and said nothing, still reeling from the realization of what he'd kept from me.

After a few minutes of dancing in tense silence, I finally spoke. "Why didn't you tell me?" I asked, unable to hold the question in any longer.

He sighed. "I know how you feel about James," he answered, "and this doesn't involve you. He's my problem now."

My temper flared and I glared up at him. "So my role in this relationship is to look pretty, keep quiet, and warm your bed, but not really be a part of your life?"

His hands dug into my hips. "I never said that," he replied, his eyes narrowing. That usually signified a warning that his anger was close to the surface, but I ignored it.

"It's what you don't say that speaks volumes, Blane," I bit out, my heart hurting at the truth of it. "What did Keaston mean by 'short list'? What short list will you be on if you win this case?"

I didn't think he was going to answer me, his jaw locked tight, but finally he spoke.

"Governor. He was talking about the short list for governor."

My jaw dropped open in shock and my feet stumbled. Only Blane's tight grip kept me from falling.

"Of Indiana?" I squeaked, then wanted to kick myself for the stupid question. Blane gave a curt nod, watching me.

"Excuse me," I said, stepping out of his grip. I had to get away for a few minutes, regain my control and equilibrium.

I didn't want to break down into tears in the middle of the dance floor. He let me go, watching as I walked away.

I found a ladies' room and hid in a stall, taking deep breaths.

I had hoped Blane felt more for me. I wanted to be more than another transient woman in his life and his bed. I'd known Blane was a player, had seen him discard women without a backward glance. Why I thought I'd be different, I had no idea. My naiveté was my own undoing. I wanted to be a real part of his life, but the fact that he hadn't told me about the case, that he had thoughts of running for governor, made my wants seem laughable. Sometimes my outlook on life was too hopeful for my own good.

I realized I couldn't hide in the bathroom all night and surveyed myself in the mirror, tucking a few strands of hair that had gotten loose back up into some pins. The light caught on my necklace and I touched it, remembering the look in Blane's eyes when he'd given it to me mere hours ago. A hint of doubt crept into my mind. Maybe I was wrong; maybe Blane had a good reason for not telling me about all this. It wasn't like I'd given him a chance to talk before rushing off.

I resolved to give him a chance to explain, to tell me why he'd kept this news from me, and that resolve lasted until I walked into the ballroom and saw him dancing with Kandi in his arms.

Well.

Turning on my heel, I walked out and didn't stop walking until I hit the street. It was cold and I shivered, belatedly realizing I'd left my coat inside. I couldn't have retrieved it anyway; Blane still had the ticket.

It was late and the streets were nearly empty, the sidewalk even more so. I had my purse with me but only had a few dollars, not enough for a cab. There was a bus stop a few blocks away, so I trudged onward. I'd catch the bus toward my apartment and walk the last few blocks from where it dropped me off. It was nearly ten and I knew it picked up every hour.

I walked morosely, watching the sidewalk so I didn't trip. I was regretting the shoes now, but it wasn't as if I'd known I'd be hiking in them by the end of the evening. I sniffed, telling myself it was the cold making my nose run. My toes were numb and I was freezing. I wrapped my arms around myself to try to stay warm. The wind went right through the satin fabric of my dress and before long I was shivering. I cursed the cold, my choice of attire tonight, the fact that I'd agreed to come with Blane in the first place, and Kandi-with-an-*i* on general principle. It was quite clear she had more of a history with Blane than I'd realized or that he'd bothered to tell me.

I turned down a side street and saw the bus stop a block away. Finally. I picked up the pace a little but was brought to a jarring halt by the voice echoing out of the darkness.

"Hey, pretty girl, give me your cash and I won't mess up your fancy dress."

~

"Give me the necklace or you'll regret it," the mugger said, jerking me back to the imminently dangerous here and now.

"My husband is on his way," I lied, grasping for straws.

He laughed cruelly. "You're a shitty liar," he scoffed. His hand closed around the pendant and yanked, the chain of the necklace biting painfully into my skin before it broke. He stepped back, admiring his prize.

"No!" I leapt forward and grabbed his fist, clenched tightly around the pendant. I had to get it back. Surprised, he turned sharply to avoid my lunge, the movement causing the knife to bite into the skin of my arm. I ignored the sharp burn. "Give that back!"

"Get off me," he growled, shoving me away. Furious, I came back at him again, grabbing the hand holding my necklace and sinking my teeth into it. He yelled in pain. Unable to get any leverage between us, his arm came down hard and he slammed a fist into my back. I was forced to release him, the painful blow knocking the wind from my lungs and leaving me unprepared for his punch to my stomach. I doubled over, the pain excruciating.

His hand closed around my neck and he pulled me upright before carelessly tossing me away. I hit the concrete hard, my hands taking the brunt of it, but still smacked the side of my face on the ground. I couldn't move. My face ached and my thigh burned from where it had scraped the asphalt, and I struggled to breathe through the pain in my back and stomach.

"Fucking bitch," he muttered angrily. His shoe scraped behind me and I made myself turn over, not wanting to have my back to him. I saw the kick coming too late to protect myself, and I cried out when it connected. I curled into myself, trying to become as small a target as possible. He hauled back to kick me again.

A shape came hurtling out of the darkness, tackling the mugger to the ground. I watched them grapple. The knife glinted briefly in the light before it was kicked out of the thug's hand. The sound of grunts and flesh hitting bone filled the alley.

I struggled to sit up, gasping at the aches and pains, and saw my rescuer had gotten the upper hand as he straddled the attacker. His fists continued to pummel the man, though I thought for sure the mugger was unconscious by now, as still as he was.

I stumbled to my feet, tottering forward carefully on my ill-used heels. He still wasn't stopping, his blows landing punishingly hard as I winced, afraid he was going to kill him. I moved as close as I dared.

"Stop," I implored, grabbing onto one of the man's arms with both of my hands. "You're going to kill him!"

The man easily jerked his arm out of my grip, turning his head sharply to face me—and I froze in shock.

It was Blane. I didn't know where he'd come from or how he'd found me, but he had. His face was a mask of rage as he took in my appearance and I took a shaky step back, afraid of what he might do. I watched as the anger drained away from his face. He spared one last glance for the unconscious mugger and I heard him snarl, "Fucking piece of shit," then he stood and was at my side in an instant.

"Are you all right?" he asked, turning me toward the light. He sucked in a breath and I knew I must look awful, blood trailing in a thin stream down my arm from the shallow cut the knife had made. I could feel my cheek swelling from where I'd hit the concrete. Blane's finger gently brushed my cheekbone, coming away with blood. Quickly removing his jacket, he placed it around my shoulders, pulling it tightly closed. Shock started to set in and I began to shake.

"Shh, Kat," he whispered, pulling me into his arms. "You're safe now. I've got you."

Tears spilled over my eyes as I leaned into him and basked in the comfort he offered, deeply breathing in cologne mixed with the musky scent of his sweat.

"Thank you," I mumbled against his shirt. In response, he pressed his lips lightly to my forehead.

"Let's get you someplace warm," he said, turning us toward the mouth of the alley.

"Wait!" I scrambled out of Blane's arms and ran back to the mugger. Prying open his fist, I grabbed my necklace. The man groaned but didn't open his eyes. I was glad Blane hadn't killed him, though I wondered briefly what would have happened if I hadn't stopped him.

As I returned back to Blane, he looked questioningly at me. I shrugged. "He took the necklace you gave me."

Blane didn't move. "You fought him over the necklace?" he asked, his tone chilling.

Grimacing, I muttered, "You gave it to me. I didn't want him to have it."

"Christ, Kat!" Blane exploded. "I would have bought you another one! It wasn't worth your life! He could have killed you!"

I bit my lip, knowing he was right but not wanting to admit it. I had acted irrationally, but hadn't been able to stop myself. I'd just been overcome with anger that he would dare to take something precious to me. It wasn't even that it was an expensive necklace—it was just that Blane had given it to me. I said none of this, just looked up at Blane and hoped he would drop it. Huffing with exasperation, he pulled me to him, wrapping me tightly in his arms and resting his chin on top of my head.

"Never a dull moment, Kat," he said with a sigh.

We emerged from the mouth of the alley to find two police cars pulling up, sirens blaring. A blinding light flashed at me and I realized there were a few photographers there, too. A quick glance at Blane made it obvious that he'd been in a fight. His hair was tousled and a bit of blood marred the corner of his mouth. His once-white shirt was stained and torn, the cuffs open from where the buttons had come off. I saw his knuckles were raw, scraped and bloody from the fight. The veneer of gentility he'd worn earlier was gone. He looked altogether masculine and dangerous.

A cop stepped up to us, blocking the photographers. "Mr. Kirk, is that you?" he asked. At Blane's nod, he turned his attention to me. "You must be the victim. Someone heard you scream and called 911. You all right, miss?"

"I'm fine," I said, my voice too weak for my liking. The cop nodded and stepped past us toward the prone and now groaning mugger lying on the ground.

"Hey! That's Blane Kirk!" The words came from one of the photographers and seemed to ignite a frenzy of flashbulbs.

Turning me gently toward his chest, Blane hid my face from the cameras as we moved forward through the photographers and a small crowd of onlookers that had gathered. Flashes continued to go off, and I didn't know how Blane wasn't blinded by them. When we reached the street, he let out a piercing whistle and a passing taxi pulled to a stop.

Blane opened the door, eased me inside, and carefully shut it. Leaning into the open driver's window, he spoke to the cabbie. "Take her home and help her inside."

I saw him give the driver several bills before he turned to speak to me. "I'll handle the cops and press," he said. "I'll come by when I'm through."

I nodded silently, grateful to be going home. The adrenaline was wearing off and my body was forcefully reminding me of the abuse I'd just endured.

With one last searching gaze, Blane backed away. The driver pulled into the street and I turned in my seat to look out the back window. Blane stood watching until I was out of sight. Flashbulbs brightly illuminated his torn white shirt and body every few seconds, the silence of the scene from the confines of the cab making it appear eerie as the flashes bathed Blane with their cold glare.

Here ends the first chapter of
Turn to Me.

Check Tiffany's website—www.TiffanyASnow.com—for more information on *The Kathleen Turner Series.*

ACKNOWLEDGMENTS

Thank you to Nikki for her encouragement and tireless editing, suggestions, and feedback. Her work helped make this a better book in many, many ways. Thanks for sticking with me.

Thank you to Zoi Juvris for her willingness to lend her expertise to help a novice and near stranger. Her kindness was much appreciated.

And lastly, thank you to Rush, who taught me that my only limitations were my own talent and those limits that I placed on myself.